Dream of a Vast Blue Cavern

Dreams of QaiMaj: Book I
By Selah J Tay-Song

Cover illustration by Benjamin P. Roque
Cover design by Benjamin P. Roque
Interior illustrations by Selah J Tay-Song

To order copies of this book, please visit:
www.dreamsofqaimaj.com

To contact the author, please visit:
www.selahjtaysong.com

Printed in the USA

First Printing: December 2012
Second Printing: April 2014
Staff Chronicles

ISBN: 978-0615737263

For my mother, Anna
Thank you for encouraging me
To follow my dreams
Even the crazy one about writing books

Acknowledgements

There are so many people without whom this book would not exist. Teresa Edgerton, who applied the critical eye of a developmental editor, and came up with the idea behind "websilk." Laurel Leigh, who patiently spent several years teaching me how to write a scene. All the members of TPWG writing group, whose iron-hard criticism, and unfailing support, kept me on track. Any faults that remain in this work are entirely mine; the people mentioned here did what they could.

Thanks are due to all the teachers and mentors who have helped me along the way; there are too many to name here.

Most of all, thanks to my family and friends who have been encouraging me for years; especially Elanos Mansker for buying me a laptop to write my first book on, and Mandala Cascade for being my biggest fan from the very beginning. Thanks to all of you who have taken the time to visit my website and read the short stories there; your support is what encourages me to keep writing on the really tough days.

Finally, a special thank you to my sweetheart, Hans. Thanks for helping me through the worst moments and celebrating with me in the best. Thanks for believing in me every moment of every day for the last ten years, even on those days when I could not believe in myself.

Table of Contents

Part 1: War

    Chapter 1: Whispers of War

    Interlude

    Chapter 2: Council Interrupted

    Chapter 3: Sealed for Siege

    Chapter 4: Holding Grimshore

Part 2: Exile

    Interlude

    Chapter 5: Whispers of Treason

    Chapter 6: Council of Exiles

    Chapter 7: Dreams of V'lturhst

    Interlude

    Chapter 8: The Heroes Return

    Chapter 9: Iskalon Stands

    Chapter 10: Iskalon's Sacrifice

Part 3: Captive

    Interlude

    Chapter 11: Marked by Fire

    Chapter 12: A Dangerous Decision

    Interlude

    Chapter 13: Rockfall

    Chapter 14: A New Crown

    Interlude

    Chapter 15: Into the Ice

    Chapter 16: A Slow Death

Part 4: Burial

    Interlude

    Chapter 17: In the Heart of Chraun

    Chapter 18: A Vast Blue Cavern

    Epilogue: Resignation

    Glossary

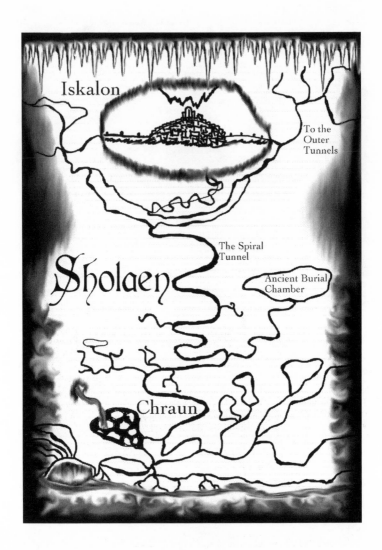

Khell

Stormbirth Waters

Nuambe Khell
Summer Camp

Pebble
Beach

Liathua Khell
Summer Camp

Doaltooth
Mountains

Liathua Khell
Winter Camp

Desolation
Mountains

Iskalon

Bridge of
Ancestors

Sparkling
Beach

Cataya's Shore

Bridge of
Prosperity

King's
Bridge

Council
Hall

Grimshore

Common Beach

Fire Bridge

Part I ~ War

Under the brown fog of a winter dawn,
A crowd flowed over London Bridge, so many,
I had not thought death had undone so many.

The Waste Land, T. S. Eliot

Chapter I

Whispers of War

Stasia

Stasia leaned against rough rock and Dreamed. Cool water from a ceiling spring slid down her back, but she barely noticed. She drew T'Jas from the cold, filling her reservoir of power. The water matted her long hair, and soaked through her websilk dress, chilling her skin. She saw the span of the tunnel, every crack and crevice, as if she held aloft the brightest icelight she could make. Everything she saw was a clear reflection of the Dream she'd woken from, roughly an hour past, overlaid on the reality of the tunnel, which was in truth pitch dark. Sometimes, she could trust this second sight. But if anything had changed, a rock shifting here, a wide-winged flat crawling over the walls, the Dream would be useless.

And now, entering the territory where the enemy Flames patrolled, it would be worse than useless. There had been no Flames in her Dream, and if one came down the tunnel now, she wouldn't see him. Stasia held her T'Jas close and ready, but let go of the Dream-sight. The imposing darkness of the tunnel snapped in front of her eyes. The faint blue vaerce covering her skin glowed brighter, but one of them, on the back of her hand by her littlest knuckle, winked out altogether as T'Jas use shortened her life by another instant.

She did not dare make an icelight; it would announce her presence like the scream of a cave howler. The tunnel was so dark that she saw no difference when she squeezed her eyes closed. Her hands brushed along stone on either side, feeling the tiny trails left by rockworms, the twists and turns, the alcoves peppering the walls.

The tunnel linking Iskalon, the upper region of Sholaen, to Chraun, the lower region, spiraled like a staircase, sometimes oppressively narrow, sometimes so wide she became disoriented. Stasia could feel a faint gradient of heat wafting upwards. The distance to Chraun was not quite two hours by foot, and if she had truly been walking for over an hour, as she felt she had, then she was closer to the enemy realm than she was to her home. The time had passed more quickly in the Dream, so she had not worn ice armor, thinking that she would reach her destination much closer to Iskalon. She did not want to admit fear, even to herself, but the heat terrified her. It would drain her T'Jas, leave her sick, even unconscious, if it intensified. Only the strength of the Dream urged her on against fear, compelling her further down into Flame territory.

The heat did grow, and Stasia's stomach protested with a churn of acid. She took a deep breath, and smelled the sulfur of the realm of Chraun. Then she saw what she had been dreading: torchlight, in the distance. The echoes of footsteps, a soft chime of metal against metal, growing nearer. A Flame approached her. How long since she had passed a spur where she might hide? But the Flames often entered the spurs, looking for slink to hunt. She should turn now and run all the way back to Iskalon.

Instead of doing what was smart and safe, she Dreamed; the approaching light snapped off, and the Dream-sight revealed the tunnel walls again. High up the sheer rock face was a little alcove, large enough for her to curl into. She placed her hands on the rock; there were enough cracks in it to get purchase. That was good. Bad enough that Dreaming her way down this tunnel had cost her a vaerce; using T'Jas to float to the top of the alcove would likely cost another. Each vaerce was negligible alone, but as older Icers often admonished, together they added up to years. Those who ignored their vaerce died young of T'Jas exhaustion, examples to other young Icers who thought to cheat their fate.

As she scaled the wall, Stasia felt the air grow warmer. The cold air settled on the tunnel floor, and the air in the middle of the tunnel was a blend, neither hot nor cold, but at the ceiling warm air had risen and filled the alcove. The heat fascinated and repulsed her. Sometimes in the Dream, the heat did not hurt, but it was agony now. Another wave of nausea rolled over her, stronger, making her gag. She clenched her teeth and grasped the edge, pulling herself into the little cave, so that her whole body was surrounded by warm air. Her cold T'Jas began to trickle away. There was T'Jas in the heat just as there was in the cold, and she could have pulled it inside of her, but to do so would mean death. Pressure pounded in her head, and her heart was weak. *I should have run,* she chided herself. *Now I will be trapped and helpless. Father is right. I need to think before I go recklessly following the Dream.*

The Dream dissipated as her cold T'Jas ebbed to a memory. Torchlight blossomed in her view again, brightening as it rounded the bend. It hurt her eyes, and she squeezed them shut, relying on sound. The footfalls were swift and solitary. Something dragged over the ground behind them with the slightest scraping noise, like a soft and supple hide. The Flame would be large, at least twice Stasia's size; all Flames were much larger than Icers. He—or perhaps she, there was no way to know—moved lithely over the rough tunnel floor, his footfalls surprisingly quiet. Stasia didn't breathe, didn't move.

The red glow on her eyelids faded along with the echo

of footsteps. When both were gone completely, she opened her eyes, blinking, and forced herself out of the alcove. She let herself fall to the floor where cool air settled, and she lay there for several moments, drawing T'Jas from the cold rocks. The effects of the heat faded from her body; her stomach settled and her breathing became more even. The sensible thing to do would be to turn back. Another Flame, or a whole troop of them, could come around the corner any moment. The Spiral Tunnel was supposed to be neutral ground, but Stasia did not trust the Flames not to break that neutrality. After all, they raided the outer caves of Iskalon from time to time, taking human prisoners; what would stop them from taking a lone Icer captive? At best, if she met a Flame, they would fight, and while she did not fear a battle further up the tunnel, T'Jas was so precious here, and she without armor—she was sure to lose.

And yet, the Dream compelled her onward, almost as if it had a will separate of hers. She had not yet reached its destination. Just a little farther, she decided. She stood and continued down the tunnel, toward the heat, stopping to explore every cave she passed.

When the cool air on her ankles sank completely into the rock and the air around her head became oppressively hot, she found what she sought. The opening was tiny, little more than a crack in the back of another tiny cave, the sort of place where deadly pitvipers lurked. Flats skittered and made squeaks of protest as her hands disturbed them in her exploration. Sticky webs of giant spele spiders came away on her fingers. She pulled her body into the tight crevice.

The rocks were rough where her skin was bare, and her websilk dress caught on tiny outcroppings, which tore gaping holes in the delicate fabric. She tried to breathe through her nose, but couldn't get enough air; when she opened her mouth she inhaled debris, chewing grit between her teeth. The tunnel sloped upward, and the warm air settled behind, to her relief. The cold grew and she drew T'Jas from it. The tunnel narrowed even further, and she pushed against the walls with her hands and feet, propelling herself forward.

Again, a light appeared in the distance, but this was a soft purple glow. It grew brighter, until she could see it gleaming on the walls, and as though being birthed by the tunnel, she squeezed out into an immense cavern. She did not get to her feet, but lay on the floor on her back, catching her breath. Icy cold air settled over her, calming her stomach and giving her strength. She drew T'Jas; the Dream-sight covered the cavern like a veil.

The Dream showed a vast blue ceiling spread out above her head, bluer than the purest lapis. At its apex shone a brilliant yellow light. Stasia lay on a floor soft like fur and the color of emeralds. More bits of color rose from the floor around her, ruby and opal and sapphire, fluttering as though blown by a giant, gentle breath. The warmth bled down onto her face, but it did not burn, it invigorated and gave her strength. The ground held her in a way no cavern floor ever had. The ceiling above seemed limitless, like she could float toward it forever and never touch it.

V'lturhst. That was what the Heritage called this place, and it was a legend; according to them, it did not exist. To speak of it was blasphemy. Cataya herself had condemned it. But Stasia Dreamed of it nearly every time she slept, and she did not see how something so wonderful could be forbidden. Her father and sisters called it a foolish fancy, but Stasia knew better. Her Dreams were prophetic; in them she could see real occurrences, present and future, that she would not have known otherwise, so why would her Dream of V'lturhst be any different? She knew it was real, and she followed the Dream, searching for the real V'lturhst.

Stasia let the Dream-sight go, daring to believe that perhaps this time she had found it. But she saw only frosty rock walls, lit by a ceiling of glowing amethyst-colored ice in a shaft that went on to infinity. It glowed brighter than a normal icelight, infused with T'Jas left by the Ancestors thousands of years prior. Glinting metal specks peppered the purple-blue depths. It was just another Burial Shaft.

At least it was one she had never seen. There were many Burial Shafts closer to Iskalon, most of them above Lake Lentok, but she had never heard of one so close to Chraun. It must be very ancient indeed. Stasia was here; she might as well look at what she had found. She drew T'Jas deeply from the ice on the walls, weighed curiosity against a few distant moments of old age, and drifted upward until her nose pressed against the icy ceiling.

As she rose, what had appeared from a distance to be specks crystalized into people, corpses frozen in time, clothed in copper-scale garments. Iskalon had run out of copper centuries ago. There were a few antiques still made of the precious metal, but the people of Iskalon scarcely wore metal garments any more. This was an old burial chamber, abandoned hundreds, perhaps thousands of years prior, perhaps even before the first King of Chraun had left Iskalon and forged his kingdom. Curious in spite of her disappointment, Stasia peered forward, inspecting the closest figure. It was a woman, her pale skin so thin that dark veins showed through. Gleaming red hair framed closed eyes and a serene smile. The copper scales, each the size of Stasia's thumb, dangled over her voluptuous body, gathering in a cascade of smaller scales under her chin and flaring at her wrists and ankles.

A loud pounding sound came up the tunnel, followed by a yell. Stasia whipped around to face the entrance of the cave. Someone was coming. She drew more T'Jas from the cold air. She could not manipulate burial ice; only a corpse could penetrate it, so she dropped down to where ordinary ice coated the walls of the great cavern, and she drew it to her body and her websilk dress, coating herself in it. If a Flame attacked, she would be protected from the first blow. She descended further, determined to face what came bravely, and hovered above the entrance, waiting.

A four-legged creature nearly the same size as Stasia burst out of the tunnel and paced the cavern, sniffing the ground where she had lain. She relaxed and dropped down beside the slink, letting her ice coating disintegrate to powder ice and fall with her. The feline raised its head, looking at her with huge, dark, contemptuous eyes. Then it sat and began calmly washing its ears. Its dark fur blended into the rock, and shone blue-black in the light of the burial ice. It was covered with cavewebs, dust, and debris. No amount of bathing would ever rid the creature of its powerful musky smell. Stasia stared at the slink, anger and creeping sympathy battling within her.

"He's stuck, isn't he, Musche?"

The slink ignored her and began working vigorously on its tail, erasing all traces of the journey down the tunnel. Another yell came echoing up.

"Curse him, he'll draw the Flames with that racket," Stasia muttered.

The slink released his tail and gave her a look that said she might want to do something about that. Stasia bared her teeth, then turned and placed her hands on either side of the tunnel. How much time would this take from her life? A month? More? It couldn't be helped. She imagined herself trapped in the tight tunnel, unable to move back or forward. Even for someone accustomed to navigating dark tunnels, it was a horrid feeling. Besides, he *would* draw the Flames if he kept yelling.

She took a deep breath and released T'Jas into the rock. The tunnel shuddered, and the walls pressed apart, widening the passage. She managed the structure of the rock so that the tunnel walls became dense, rather than putting pressure on the rock beyond it. Stasia strained, sending T'Jas all the way down the tunnel. In spite of all the cold in the cave, she was pushing her power to its limit. Flesh, ice, and air were easy to manipulate; stone was stubborn, complex, and nearly impossible to budge. "Melt

ou're supposed to save my life, not shorten it," she
ed, but then she went silent, saving her breath.

hen it was done, she stood back, gasping for air, and
nishing her cold. She glanced down and realized for
first time that she was as covered with debris as the
k, and gaping holes in her websilk dress exposed
tches of pale skin beneath. Three vaerce had faded from
e back of her hand, but she was too elated with
drenaline and T'Jas to care, and she had millions more.
She was dripping cold sweat, and it mixed with the dust
and muddied her dress and her skin. She started to tidy
herself, then stopped, annoyed. If he saw her looking like
one of the guildless, it was his own fault for following her.
She stood still at the entrance, eyes blazing like a Flame's
torch. Footsteps approached, echoing into the cave. Steel
scraped against stone; the tunnel was wider, but still
narrow enough for him to touch the sides.

Glace hunched in the entrance, his dark leather armor
fading into the blackness of the tunnel, his face and
weapons glowing purple in the burial ice. The mace at his
side clinked against the battle-axe in his belt as he climbed
down into the cave. No longer stooped, he towered over
her, nearly seven feet tall. His sandy blonde hair was dull
from dust and cavewebs. His blue eyes met hers for a
second; then he looked at the ground, as if he was a
nameless Palace Guard and she was any Icer, just another
task on his duty roster. His deference made her even
angrier.

As he stood silently looking at the cavern floor, Stasia
studied him, letting the silence compound. He was not just
another Palace Guard. He was Captain of her ten guards, a
human Warrior of great renown. Young Ladies flocked to
the training square when he was practicing. Not Stasia.
Well, not unless her friends dragged her along. His face,
covered in battle scars, ruined the perfect beauty. He could
have them healed; even Stasia would do it for him, but he
refused. Something about mistakes, he'd mumbled when

she asked him. He carried all of his weapons, all of the time, from the daggers in his boots to the two long-swords strapped across his back.

He was also the bane of Stasia's existence. She pursed her lips tightly, letting the anger she felt spark from her eyes. With his eyes glued to the floor, the effect was lost. Unable to bear his silent deference, she said, "Well. My jailer has arrived at last."

That brought his gaze up, and the anger in his blue eyes matched hers. "Your father—"

"Has commanded this that and the other, and you are here to carry out his orders to the letter." Stasia, satisfied at getting a reaction out of him, pushed further. "Do you intend to carry me back? Perhaps over your shoulder, like a sack of fungal fodder?"

Glace fingered his mace. Stasia wondered what went on in that big head of his. What kinds of thoughts did a man like Glace think? She had known, once. She had known him since she was six years old. They had been best of friends, co-conspirators, driving Stasia's tutors mad with their antics. When Stasia was fourteen, she had begun to notice what drew the other Ladies to watch him at practice, but at that same time, Glace had been conscripted, sent away from her for more experience in the field, Father said. After four years, he had been returned to her side, but he was a different person. Distant and cold. Professional. He refused to call her by her name, and would not laugh and conspire with her as he once had.

"Your father sent me to summon you to council, Princess. There is an important meeting. Your presence is required."

Stasia let her hands drop to her hips, satisfaction melting into anger again. Why did her father continue to demand that she attend the meetings? She had tried to participate, last year when she came of age and became an official citizen. But the meetings were all the same: long-winded old councilors droning on about taxes and rights to this or that cavern. It bored her right to sleep on more than one occasion. When the time came for the citizens to speak from the benches, her twelve sisters had plenty to say. Even if she'd wanted to speak, her voice would not be heard. Issues she cared about, like the treatment of the guildless, did not even come up. No, there was no reason for her to attend another Council. She puffed up her chest like a pitviper getting ready for a fight.

"Mother of a molebear! Important? As if anything those duffers have to say could be more important than this. Look what I've found, Glace!" She gestured at the ceiling, then drew T'Jas from the cold and lifted him gently in the air. Though he had been born into the Warrior Guild, Glace had a passion for history, and in his free time he spent hours in the older burial chambers near Iskalon, peering up the shafts through the thick glass lens of his shiny brass iceospectacle.

As she guessed, Glace was fascinated. "Copper," he said, his fingers tracing the outline of the nearest corpse through the ice. "Icers have not used copper like this since the reign of Queen Cataya! Look at the way the plates overlap, the elegant simplicity, the lack of gems. A perfect example of the post-Catayan styles. This cave must be several thousand years old, Princess. Look at the dagger on her belt. They hadn't yet found the iron ore for steel, so they used stone. That's obsidian, I'm guessing. The records say . . ."

Stasia floated on a raft of cold air beside him. Another vaerce was fading from her hand, but the look of pure joy on Glace's face was worth it. She could scarcely remember when she had seen him so happy. Below them, Musche had finished his bath and paced around the cave, sniffing the walls, rubbing his face against them. Best of all, the council might be over by the time Glace remembered his mission and forced her to return.

Of course, the Captain of her Guard was just trying to do his job. Stasia felt a twinge of guilt as she listened to him ramble. It wasn't his fault that Father was overprotective. If she missed the Council because Glace was distracted and neglected his duty, he would get in trouble. His sense of honor wouldn't allow him to let her take the blame; he would surely be reprimanded.

"Glace? Let's go." She leaned in closer, trying to catch his attention.

"Look up there, the fifth body in. See how the costume changes? That is pre-Catayan, extremely rare. Wish I had my iceospectacle. Are you sure you can't tunnel through burial ice?"

"Of course not. Even if I could, I wouldn't. Princess or not, the Heritage would hang me, Glace. You know that. Come on, we need to get back to Iskalon."

He looked her in the eyes, and she saw a wave of shame wash over him. He had forgotten his mission; had, in a way, disobeyed his orders. Frustrated as she was, her heart went out to him. "It was my fault, Glace. I distracted you on purpose."

"We're nearly two hours from the Council Hall, Princess. It will be half over by the time we arrive."

"We'll run all the way back," Stasia promised, dropping them both to the floor. His disappointment as he eyed the infinite shaft of ice one last time was a shadow of her own. Years of searching the tunnels like this, and still she had not found the Dream. Closing her eyes, since it was pointless to leave them open, she grasped Glace's hand and raced down the tunnel, back toward the edge of Flame territory.

Glace

Glace squeezed through the cramped spur tunnel as quickly as he could, praying that Stasia would not reach the Spiral very far ahead of him. The Scouts reported Chraun had been active recently, increasing raids, patrolling the neutral territory, perhaps even breaking old treaties and mining something up here. Bad enough that he had been distracted by the burial chamber—what a find!—and Stasia would be late for Council; the last thing he needed was to run into a patrol. Even one Flame would be a danger in these tunnels.

When he popped out of the spur into the spacious Spiral, Stasia was waiting in the dark, by the entrance. "Walk," he said, using his command voice, hoping she wouldn't argue. "Better to be late than run headlong into a Flame patrol."

Thankfully, she complied without protest. She probably preferred the delay, though it grated at his nerves. Walking, her strides were half his, and what had taken him a mere half-hour took more than an hour. *Perhaps I should carry her,* he thought, grinning in the dark, *like a sack of fungal fodder.*

As the tunnel flattened, widened and straightened, the air changed from the strange gradients of warm and cool to being solidly, deliciously cold. The heat did not make Glace ill as it did an Icer, but he did not like it. He was more comfortable in the cold, and he breathed in deep, sulfur-free breaths, glad to be home. The strange dreams and notions that possessed his little mistress to wander so far away baffled him, and he feared for her every time she ran off.

As soon as he saw blue icelights glowing in the distance, Glace grabbed Stasia's hand and pulled her down the tunnel as if they were children again. She did not resist, and for a moment he was able to forget the tension that had grown between them, and pretend they were children, playing hideme in the fungal caverns. The tunnel widened further, and branched into a labyrinth of different passages. They all led to Iskalon, but Glace picked the most direct. It would take them through the guildless tunnel, but it could not be helped. They had to make the Council.

When the new tunnel widened to a huge cavern, they

startled two Guildsmen who were harvesting lacy morchella fungi from densely spaced columns. The ceiling was coated with a thin covering of burial ice, left in these caverns by the Ancestors. At the base of the columns, sour vase fungi grew in large brown funnels. Giant mounds of bolete mushrooms, broad, table-like bellinis, and slender piota caps teetering on thin stalks carpeted the vast cavern floor. In open spaces between the columns, stone vats of sweet, refreshing fineslime in its pre-spore stage awaited processing into sorbets. Vines of bulbous bliss fungi hung from the low ceiling. Not pausing in his stride, Glace reached up and grabbed a handful. Stasia giggled beside him like she had when they were children. He tossed the sweet, juicy harvest to her, and she caught it in midair, munching as she ran. She was beautiful, her pale skin shining blue with millions of tiny dots, her silver hair wild behind her, her yellow-green eyes glinting like gems. The skin on her hand was soft and cool and he could feel her pulse beating against his.

He would die someday protecting her. He had known that since he was twelve, and found her wandering alone in the wild Outer Tunnels. When he brought her back to the Palace, King Krevas had charged Glace with her safety. "If necessary, you will lay down your life to keep her safe," Krevas ordered. Glace agreed. The little silver-haired cherub, playing with a power she didn't understand yet, would need protection.

But when Glace was twenty, he had been sent away from her for four whole years, relieved of duty by the King to train in the army and gain real battle experience. "You won't learn how to protect her in the halls of the Palace," Glace's father had said, in agreement with the King's decision. Glace did not regret his training, protecting Iskalon from raids and fighting real Flames and their well-armed Semija Warriors. He had made mistakes in battle and learned from them. Each scar on his face was a reminder of a particular mistake.

He had returned to his position as Captain of her Guard to find a different Stasia, no longer a little girl, but a beautiful, confident woman, a true princess. She was distracted by strange dreams that led her on strange quests. She disagreed with her father about where her boundaries should lie. And while Glace had learned duty, discipline and deference in the army, Stasia seemed to think that he was still her equal. Glace knew better. She was a princess, and he could not be familiar with her, could not meet her eyes or laugh with her. And he must somehow keep her from roaming into dangerous places. As a child, she had been easy to distract from her whims; now she was single-minded and sly, able to evade Glace and her other Guards with ease.

They passed through the fungal fields and into a long tunnel bordered with livestock dens, thick with the smell of manure. The stout, meaty cababar snarled and huffed as they passed. Small, sleek raihan raised their sharp horns and stomped their feet. Stasia paused to stroke the silky fur of the smaller chirat in their crowded pen, from which fine chirsh was woven for ice-armor and clothes. Glace tugged her along, stepping over shaggy baby molebear milling around on the tunnel floor. Musche hissed at their lumbering, protective mother, and Glace snapped the fingers of his free hand. The slink backed off and pushed past Stasia's legs, eager to be out of that passage. They took another turn, and then the tunnel of the guildless loomed before them. The guildless always made Glace uneasy.

Dressed in scavenged lakehide and chirsh rags, they milled in the wide tunnel, reaching out for alms. The stench here was worse than in the stock dens. Dirty faces crowded close, and quiet voices begged for food. Stasia stopped suddenly, and Glace almost crashed into her back. He tugged at her hand, urging her on, but she shook it free and looked down at her dress.

"It is ruined already," she said. "The Palace servants

will throw it on the midden."

She began plucking off the sapphires and diamonds that were sewn on the collar and wrists, placing them into outstretched hands. Glace growled in frustration. True, the expensive websilk was torn to shreds by her wild trek, but the servants would have salvaged the gems. And if she really intended to pluck off every stone, it would eat up the time they had gained by coming this route. But he could not stop her short of picking her up and carrying her away, and he must not do that. Duty, discipline and deference, he reminded himself. He pulled a dagger from his belt and helped her by cutting away the gems. They were tiny and scattered from his fingers to the ground, where the guildless groveled for them. Stasia gave him a glare and knelt on the dirty floor to help the people pick them up. More and more of the guildless crowded near, and Glace began to push them back, saying "That's enough, now. Make way. The Princess is late to an important meeting." He took her hand and pulled her to her feet, guiding her through the crowded tunnel. It was only when the guildless dwindled behind them that Glace relaxed and eased his grip on Stasia's hand.

Ten minutes more down a narrow, empty tunnel brought them to an entrance to Iskalon. Glace led Stasia into the grand, vast cavern. It was the biggest cavern in all of Sholaen, and it was Glace's home. To walk from where they stood at the foot of the Fire Bridge, across the island and to the other side of the King's bridge, would take an entire hour, the cavern was so vast. They were still about a half hour from the Council Hall, and Glace chafed at any delay, but he stopped Stasia and stood with her for a moment, looking out across Lake Lentok.

The lake's dark waters glittered with the reflection of the icelights of the Palace, which hung from the ceiling like giant, sparkling stalam, illuminating the whole vast cavern. The entire construction was ice, and grand balconies hung off the lowest levels, where Icers and Royalty could sit and view the city. The city stood on the island. It looked dim and dull under the Palace, rising from the lake to its pinnacle, the Council Hall, in the very center of the city, and reaching across the lake with four bridges. The Bridge of Ancestors rose far on the other side, and Glace could see the distant purple glow of the entrance to the burial chambers beyond it.

At the foot of the Fire Bridge, Glace could hear the lapping of Lentok's shore, disturbed by Fishing Guild skiffs, and the trickle of a nearby stream, running off the lake and disappearing into a low tunnel in the cavern wall behind where he stood.

Stasia turned to face him. She was breathless, dirty sweat running down her skin, a wild look in her eyes. The holes in her dress, made worse by pulling the gems off, left little to the imagination. Her vaerce glowed faintly in the bright light of the Palace. She was framed by the tall abutments of the Fire Bridge. Beyond her, a Guard whom Glace did not recognize paced before the small gear-house atop the left abutment.

"Shall I escort you to your quarters before we attend the Council, for fresh garments?"

The wild look spread from her eyes to her mouth when she smiled. "Let Father and the rest see me as I am. It will serve him right, for dragging me to another meeting."

Glace shrugged. That was between her and the King. And the entire Council, apparently. His duty was to protect her from physical harm, not from ridicule or paternal punishment. He stared for a moment at the sway of her behind, and the tantalizing holes in her dress, as she marched across the bridge in front of him. Then he shook himself. He was pretty sure ogling the princess was not included in duty, discipline, and deference. He cast his eyes down again.

Glace followed Stasia across the long bridge. A few carts wheeled creakily in the opposite direction, bearing supplies for the stock tunnels, and Glace saluted a Scout riding out on a raihan. At the end of the bridge, the fishy stench of Grimshore wafted up, and Glace hurried his charge through the narrow stone streets, uphill to the crest of the island. They passed the small hide-and-bone huts of labor Guildsmen, the fishers, miners and fungal workers. Here and there a grosbox fungus grew, a giant, hard mushroom from which a house would be hollowed. Little fungal gardens surrounded the houses and bordered the lanes, tended by a wife or son here, an elderly man there; they were cultivating and harvesting a few morchellas as well as medicinal mushrooms like bittercap and the dark, earthy truffide. Colorcaps blazed like gems, their variety of colors and lacy caps vivid under the bright blue glow of the Palace. Another time, Glace would have picked one and tucked it behind Stasia's ear, and been rewarded with a smile, but he felt no desire to add to her brazen appearance today.

Beyond the small houses by the shores of the lake, the roads grew steeper, and the houses grew larger, several-story stone constructions housing the higher Guildsmen and their families; cooks, scribes, neithild handlers who produced websilk, gem cutters and tanners and healers. These houses stood quiet and empty; their inhabitants were in the Guild-houses working, in the Council Meeting, or in the Market.

Market Avenue, the wide lane surrounding the Council Hall, was a buzz of activity compared to the quiet streets. Smooth paving stones between the stalls were covered with carts pulled by big, shaggy molebear, laden with fish, gems, metals, fungi, rocksalt, and ice. At each stall, Guildsmen inscribed trades and purchases on gold plate, weighed out goods, and wrapped up packages. The smell of salted fish, pickled cababar, and bliss fungi pastries filled the air. A flag of chirsh interwoven with bright silver threads announced the cart of the royal tax collectors, who shopped the stalls and carried goods back to the Palace for the members of the Royal family, the Icers, and the

Warrior Guild. Molebear hides piled on the cart would be made into boiled leather armor for new recruits; the King was expanding the army in response to the Scouts' reports.

Stasia nodded to the wave of bows and curtseys that rippled around her, but Glace saw people whispering to each other after she had passed. Those whispers would reach Krevas' ears, and he would be angry with his wayward daughter. Of course, it would be nothing compared to his anger when he saw her enter the Council. Glace reminded himself again that her decorum was not part of his duty.

The Hall of the Council sat in the very center of Iskalon, surrounded in a great circle by Market Ave. The building had been shaped with T'Jas out of strong basalt, made to look like a fountain of frozen water spouting from the center of the lake surrounding the city. The rock was tiled in differing shades of blue gemstones, accentuating the dimensions of the water-jet. It towered above elaborate Guild-houses and the smaller family homes radiating from the center of the island to the shores of Lake Lentok.

In front of the main entrance to the Council Hall, a giant stone likeness of Queen Cataya stood watching the Market, over forty feet tall. Her dress was pure white, shaped from the finest limestone, and her eyes sparkled dark with onyx. An Ancestor, the first Queen and Founder of Iskalon, patron of the Heritage, and the only Dreamer known to history, before Stasia's talent had been discovered. An acolyte of the Heritage stood watch by the stone folds of her skirt, chanting Her goodness. Glace removed the sword at his hip and knelt on it among offerings of colorcap, choice meats and fine gems. Even Stasia bowed before the greatest Queen Iskalon had ever seen.

But her bow was brief. Before Glace had sheathed his sword, she had marched right up the sapphire-inlaid steps and announced herself to the two warriors guarding the giant stone entryway. The Warriors struggled to keep smirks off their faces as they admitted her, but a hard look from Glace reminded them of their duty, and they straightened and resumed menacing postures. Glace snapped his fingers and pointed at an out-of-the-way spot by the steps; Musche wandered over to it nonchalantly and sniffed, then paced as if considering lying down. Glace grinned as he headed through the door his mistress had taken into the Hall. The slink liked to pretend it had a choice. Perhaps he should take that tactic with Stasia.

The little princess must have run all the way to the council room, because she was gone when Glace entered the building. He hurried through the maze of ornately tiled corridors until he reached the center of the Hall. The double door of the council room was wide open, the icelights within dim. Stasia stared into the room, so still that he could hear her short breaths. Glace stopped just behind her, peering over her head. The grand, circular room was empty.

Stasia chewed at her lip pensively. Glace was ashamed at having failed in his duty to get her to the council, but also relieved for Stasia's sake. She had missed the council, but at least she could change before facing her father's wrath.

Footsteps echoed behind Glace, and he spun, one hand on his mace, the other on his axe. There was little danger here in the heart of Iskalon, but he was still on edge from the trek into the neutral territory. Stasia turned as well, and Glace felt the air warm almost imperceptibly. She had pulled T'Jas into herself, preparing to fight.

The footsteps grew louder, and Glace relaxed when he saw that it was Prince Casser, King Krevas' brother and Stasia's uncle. Glace gave him a Warrior's salute, fist to heart, and the Prince returned it curtly. Anger glinted in his dark eyes, and he ran his hand through salt and pepper hair before speaking. Unlike Stasia, his skin was bare of the glowing blue dots; whatever vitality remained in him, it was hidden under his glistening, wooly ice-armor.

"You go too far, Stasia. You will push your father too hard one day."

"I didn't know the Council was meeting. Besides, normally the discussion lasts through second chime." Stasia paced into the center of the room. Glace followed her, leaning against a column. Now that she was safe, he would have liked to put his second, Warrior Glint, in charge of guarding Stasia, and take a shower and get a snack in the mess. But he could not walk away from Prince Casser without being dismissed.

"You are lucky that this one didn't last. If your father saw you come in looking like one of the guildless, he might give you to them."

"Ah, well. I can't have missed much. Father won't be happy, but then, he never is. To be honest I'm a bit relieved. I didn't really want to spend my time listening to the old duffers snap at each other like eels." She fingered the blue tiles on a nearby column. Glace pulled a dagger from his boot and polished it silently against the oil-rich chirsh of his doublet, where it hung over the skirt of his armor. The blade could use a sharpening, but the noise would be intrusive.

"You should have been here, Stasia. The Council deadlocked, and they will meet again at first chime to resolve it. We don't have much time, and they are stalling all they can. Your presence is required at that meeting, do you understand?"

Stasia began pacing again, ranging farther into the room with each pass. "Yes, Uncle Casser. I'll be here." She still sounded flippant. Glace had heard her promise that to the King himself, and still miss the Council. "What's the big deal, anyway? Don't we get enough in taxes from the Guilds already?"

"Chraun is planning to attack Iskalon."

Stasia stopped mid-step and stared at her uncle. Glace's thumb slipped over the edge of the dagger and he cursed quietly, then stuck his thumb in his mouth, sucking at the blood welling out of the cut. War. Iskalon had not seen war in nearly a hundred years, certainly not in his lifetime. Glace was not afraid to fight. What terrified him was the thought of trying to keep Stasia from running straight for the front lines.

"Captain Glace?"

"Yes, Majesty." He sheathed the dagger and saluted again, standing at attention.

"Glace, take her to her room and see that she gets changed. Krevas has enough to worry about without rumors flying around that his daughter is a guildless harlot. And watch her carefully until tomorrow's meeting. Sleep outside her chambers, eat when she eats. You are relieved of all other duties."

"Yes, Majesty." Stasia glared at Glace, and his heart sank. She was going to make it difficult, and this new restriction would only make the tension between them worse.

"I'm not a child, Uncle."

"Then act your age, Stas." Prince Casser's tone was sharp, and Glace saw Stasia grip the skirt of her dress; in anger or fear, he could not say. "If you were young enough, I'd spank you and put you on rations. You are certainly not a child. Nineteen makes you old enough to sit in Council like any other citizen. Krevas must have the support he needs to pass martial law. Iskalon must respond to this attack with unity."

Prince Casser turned on his heels and marched out of the room. Stasia rounded on Glace and gave him a solid, silent glare. Glace looked at the floor, waiting for her anger. When she did not speak, he looked up again. Her glare had dissolved and she looked vulnerable, a little afraid. "To think!" she said. "We were just in the Spiral Tunnel! We might have been killed, or captured."

Glace nodded. At least she realized that. "Princess, I must escort you to your quarters now."

The vulnerability faded as if it had never existed,

dissolving into another glare. "Don't you ever think of anything but duty, Glace?"

Glace met her eyes. He knew that his duty was to quietly obey orders, to be stoic and deferential to his charge. He knew that he risked a reprimand. But Stasia would try a molebear's patience. He reached out and scooped her up in his arms. She let out a cry of surprise, but did not resist, and the protest turned into an amused giggle. He cradled her to his chest like a child and carried her from the council room, down the hall, down back streets to the King's bridge, and up into the Palace. She laughed like a child the whole way, and when he deposited her safely at her door, they were both breathless and laughing together.

Dynat

King Dynat Sikur Antah, Defender of Chraun, Prince of Flames, Keeper of the Lava River, True Ruler of all Sholaen, Chosen of the Fire Spirit, sat on his throne, basking in heat and glory.

The hard stone seat dug into his bones, but Dynat scarcely felt the pain. His lava mesh pulsed just beneath his skin like a second set of veins, holding his T'Jas close. His hands rested on the rough, dark basalt of the arms. The mighty throne that held him was suspended above the rocky cavern floor by a jumbled mass of stalas, dangled from the high ceiling by thin columns of stalam. When he closed his eyes, Dynat could feel the heat seeping toward him from the great Lava River, hear the roar as it traversed the back of the vast cavern. Above the constant white noise of the river, the Fire Spirit whispered to him, its face, as always, consumed by flames, hovering in Dynat's mind, looking through his eyes.

Attaaack . . . The voice whispered. It whispered other things, as well. Instructions, threats, praise; the voice was a constant burble, difficult to pull meaning from. But in this moment, one word stood out above all. *Attaaaack . . .*

Dynat opened his eyes and saw the river's dim red glow cast onto the two Flames standing before him. General Medoc, a tall man with a few white streaks in his dark hair, stood straight and stiff, speaking. He was old for a Flame; life in Chraun was short but, for Noble Flames, sweet. His lava mesh ran in neat hexagonal patterns. His small mustache was trim. Every scale of his steel armor was in place. If Dynat's Kinyara, standing beside him in her chaotic, feathery lava mesh, reached out and pushed against his arm with one of her long nails, he imagined Medoc might topple over.

Kinyara Bolv was the opposite of Medoc in every way. Her features were plain, almost masculine, and she tried to distract attention from them by wearing a scalecloth skirt of gold that showed off her long legs, complemented by a bright bustier of firedrop gemcloth, the tiny gems bound so tightly between woven gold threads that no skin showed between warp and weft, though plenty of skin showed around the garment. The outfit was finished with gold plated spike heels with gold laces running all the way to her knees. Though another man might have preferred a greater beauty, Dynat did not care. She was a Lady of surprising talents, both personal and governmental. As a Kinyara should be. Cousin and lover to Dynat, she kept the political wheels of Chraun greased in his favor.

" . . . might bankrupt the Royal treasury. We stand to lose at least one third of our Flame Warriors—three thousand good men, dead. The Semija losses will be much greater, possibly as many as forty thousand." Medoc always had a logical argument with numbers and facts ready. It made Dynat's head hurt even more than the Fire Spirit's commands.

Bolv spoke up in her throaty voice. "But by your own figures in your last report, General, we stand to capture more than half of Iskalon's untrained Semija. That's twenty thousand more than what we'll lose, for a net gain."

"I do not consider sixty thousand untrained Semija a gain over forty thousand well-trained ones. Feeding and housing sixty thousand useless bodies is not my idea of gains. Even so, my main concern is losing a third of my Flames. Recruiting to fill the gaps will take time, and bribes to the Nobles to encourage their sons to enlist will be costly, Majesty."

"So you advise that we do not attack?"

"A raid might be in order, perhaps an extensive raid. I suggest that the gains from annihilating the Icers do not merit the costs."

As the quiet roar of the river retook the cavern during the pause in conversation, the Fire Spirit's guttural command to attack softened into a hissing noise, which finally coalesced into a word. *Princessssss . . .*

The day Dynat had taken the throne from his slain father, twelve years past, the Fire Spirit had ordered him to capture the princesses of Iskalon. Dynat had commanded raids on the frozen tunnels, tried sending Semija disguised as escapees, even sent Flame envoys under a false banner of peace. None had come close to a princess. The royal Icers were too well guarded. His patience, and more importantly, the Fire Spirit's, was at an end. Iskalon must be razed, leaving the princesses nowhere to hide.

Dynat turned to Bolv. She was full of glory, and her thoughts would be happier than Medoc's stiff numbers. "Kinyara? What do you advise?"

Bolv's dark eyes shone with red glee. "There is no better time than now, Majesty. The frozen ones are unprepared for an attack of this scale. In our army, it will boost morale and let off steam. The Officers are restless. It has been a long time since the last war. Fights break out every day, and reports of abuse among the Semija are high. The Iskalon Semija can be trained. They can grow food to feed themselves."

Medoc's face pinched and his mustache rose into an upside-down V as he spoke. "In what tunnels will they grow this food, Kinyara? The glowmold needed to light the fungal caverns is scarce as it is. In the time it takes to raise more cababar, the new Semija will have starved to death. And what of our losses? Such a blow to our army will lower morale, not boost it. The Warriors who come back with only days to live, they will be full of fire and desperate to live out their last days to the fullest. Do you think abuses of Semija will decrease? Do you think they will stop at abusing Semija? A few hotheads we can handle, but thousands? We may have to execute our own heroes."

Dynat nodded, thinking. There was truth to what both of his advisors said. None of it mattered. He would attack Iskalon, because the Fire Spirit willed it. Even now, a face of flames whispered strange commands. *Take all the princesses alive*, it said. *Destroy everything else. Raze Iskalon with fire.*

If the Fire Spirit wanted the princesses, they would have to bring down the whole Kingdom and snatch them up in the resulting chaos. They would have to patrol the lake and tunnels between Chraun and Iskalon, leaving the princesses nowhere to hide.

He would do it, because the Fire Spirit willed it. The question was, how? The firesticks would only last so long in the freezing lake cavern, only give them so much advantage. And how was he to keep the troops from killing the princesses in the battle? According to Medoc's spies, there were thirteen of them. They might easily be disguised as civilians. And why—

No. It was not for him to question the Fire Spirit.

Medoc and Bolv were eyeing each other tensely. Medoc looked pensive, Bolv eager. Dynat recalled that her father had been killed in a raid on Iskalon, by one of their humans. A shameful death.

"Begin drawing up the battle plans, Medoc." He stood and stretched, then removed the heavy golden circlet from his head, fingering the crouching golden slink adorning the metal ring. King Bretle's emblem had been a simple, glowing ember, but Dynat had replaced it with the slink at his own coronation. As he always did when he left the throne room, he set the crown on the seat behind him, and used T'Jas to fuse the metal to the rock. "Prepare the troops. I will think on how to minimize our losses."

"Yes, Majesty." They knelt as he left the room.

The Fire Spirit was a dull hum in the very back of his mind; the voice usually receded after Dynat acted on a command. Those commands had saved his life when he was thirteen years old, the first time the Fire Spirit had come to him, and led him from a pitiful life in the Orphan Tunnels to his position on the throne of Chraun. The instructions were often vague and confusing, but they had never yet failed Dynat.

Dynat's quarters were adjacent to the throne room, up a short sloping passage, the bedrooms overlooking the Lava River. Bolv's pet flat skittered over the wall toward him when he entered, and he picked it up, stroked its furry back, then set it back where it was crawling. "Detestable thing," he said fondly. "I'll throw you out one of these days."

Bolv's furnishings were elegant yet simple; she had expensive tastes, yet she did not fill his caves with the gaudy gems and flashy lava paintings that many wealthy Flames enjoyed. The walls were shaped into flat, sharp angles, coated with limestone to lighten the dark basalt beneath. One painting graced the wall of the parlor, an ascetic single-line piece by Lord Roughert. Simple, light, limestone chairs lined the walls, and an expensive rug, woven from hundreds of jewelsnake skins, graced the middle of the floor.

On the wall opposite the painting, Dynat could see himself in the polished obsidian mirror, towering in the small parlor, his dark hair pulled back from his round face, his light-weight, gold plate armor gleaming in the torchlight. Even without the crown, he looked and felt like a King, tall and imposing, in command of himself and the realm. Flames danced in his eyes, and at first glance they could be mistaken for the reflection of the firestone torch behind him, but a closer look showed the flames were smaller and brighter. The Fire Spirit himself shone in Dynat's eyes. He smiled.

Turning from the mirror, Dynat went to his bedroom. It had three stone walls, the fourth an open balcony above the Lava River. The heat here was even more intense than in the throne room. Dynat closed the door behind him, sat down on a cushioned chair by the railing, and took a crucible from the table nearby. Closing his eyes, he drew T'Jas and concentrated. His lava mesh rippled and buckled under his skin. He used T'Jas to make a small opening by his collarbone, and let the lava pour from his skin into the crucible. After a few moments, it was gone completely, leaving only ghost tunnels next to his veins. He set the crucible on the table, where the heat from the river would keep the lava soft. The lava would be a hindrance in his skin, in the cold places he was going, but he would pour it back in to fill his mesh later.

Returning to the parlor, he called for his hunting cloak and patted the head of the Semija who brought it. She was a pretty one, with smooth olive skin and long lashes, the hippole hide dress she wore simple and elegant as the furniture, thin-tanned for the hot caverns and embroidered sparsely with fine gems. Bolv kept her Semija as elegantly as she did their apartments.

For a moment, Dynat considered skipping the hunt, and instead visiting the baths, eating fried noodlesnake and listening to the drums, letting the Nobles surround him and congratulate him on his decision to attack Iskalon. He decided to hunt, instead. An active pastime suited his mood better, and he was tired of courtiers and flattery.

The cloak clung to his shoulders, holding in his heat, deliciously warm and soft. It was made from slink that he himself had killed, five hides in total. The folds hung to his ankles, barely trailing on the ground, wide enough to wrap around himself thrice. The dark fur was soft against the bare skin on his calves and arms. It muffled the clink of his armor as he moved.

Dynat left his quarters and marched through Chraun, heading for colder tunnels. His Honor Guard surrounded him at a distance, five Flame Warriors scouting ahead and five following behind.

In the tunnels of the Noble Flames near his quarters, Lords and Ladies bedecked in gems and precious metals bowed deeply and murmured obsequious greetings. Dynat acknowledged them with the slightest inclination of his own head. The Semija trailing their masters prostrated themselves on the smooth tunnel floors. Dynat did not acknowledge them at all. He walked away from the Noble halls, up gently sloping tunnels toward the common Flame quarters. His path brought him through the broad Market Tunnel, its walls pocked with little alcoves where the merchants called out their goods—cababar pies, jewelry, scalecloth, tamed flats and rootingshrew, hippole milk, slink furs, furniture, and trained Semija. The merchants were all commoners, renting caves from the nobles who owned them and buying rights to livestock, metals, fungi and other commodities from which their wares were made. Their customers were other commoners and Semija making purchases for their owners. A ripple of quiet reverence passed through the Market Tunnel after Dynat. He did not acknowledge the shuffle of bows and kneeling that surrounded him, but he walked a little slower, allowing the people the honor of his presence.

When he left the Market and passed the bathing caverns, he heard the echoing beat of the drums and the shouts of Nobles at play, smelled the heady sulfur aroma. He could hand his cloak off to a passing Semija and step into the pools. His private pool waited, empty. He could even order the courtiers away, and simply lie in relaxation. He walked on.

A short way beyond the last bathing cavern the Spiral

Tunnel rose, the gateway to the icy tunnels above. There were smaller, more gradual ways to infiltrate Iskalon, but the Spiral Tunnel was the steepest, and the safest. Centuries past, it had been deemed "neutral." Chraun honored the Treaties, but Dynat did not trust the treacherous Icers to hold to them. There was likely a wealth of metal and gems to be had in the rock between Iskalon and Chraun, but Chraun did not mine these tunnels. Only slink hunting was allowed, and only because it had been provisioned in the Treaties. The tunnel had many pockets in its walls where warm air, rising from the tunnels of Chraun, gathered, giving a Flame something to draw on. Of course, there were also icy pockets, wells of cold in the tunnel floor.

Drawing the cloak close around his shoulders, Dynat pulled heat into his core and ordered the guards to wait. They did not like it, but they obeyed. He started up the tunnel, completely alone at last. When the lights from the Flame torches lining the walls of Chraun faded, Dynat pulled a stick of firestone from his belt, and used T'Jas to light it. The flame that sprang from the end was vigorous, illuminating the uneven walls of the tunnel. The way was steep, and soon he was panting from exertion. The rocks were loose and rough, not neatly shaped and swept as they were in Chraun, and he could feel each sharp angle through the soft leather soles of his boots. Thicker soles would have provided greater protection, but they would also make more noise.

Dynat didn't mind the sharp rocks. He was exhilarated, free in a way he could not feel on the throne, in the baths, or even in his quarters with only Bolv and the Semija. The Fire Spirit was quiet altogether, though Dynat could sense its presence in the back of his mind. The quiet was welcome, a brief reprieve from a constant babble, but at the same time disturbing, as if he had lost one of his senses, his sight or hearing or sense of direction.

Dynat could not feel the vibrations that traveled from

the gong cave through all of Chraun and marked off time, but he guessed that an entire hour had passed before the heat started to fade and cold crept in around his ankles. The cold made his stomach churn and unnerved him, but it also lit a passionate eagerness within him. Slink were creatures of the ice, but their young needed warmth, so the adults came down to the warm alcoves to bear. The Spiral Tunnel was the only place where slink could breed.

The gaping mouths of offshoot tunnels began to appear in his torchlight, most of them dead ends. He dimmed the flame, without completely letting it go out. He did not want its light to warn his quarry. He kept climbing. The cold air rose above his knees. His T'Jas weakened as he tried to keep his body warm. Fear shot through his belly, followed by adrenaline, pounding through his veins, giving his body strength. It was time to choose a tunnel.

Prompted by the thrill of danger, Dynat let his flame extinguish completely and tucked the firestone back into his waistband. The darkness was absolute and terrifying. He rested, catching his breath, caressing the rock of the tunnel walls under his fingers, listening to the skittering and squeaking of flats. The pain of the cold bit into his skin where the cloak did not cover it, and his stomach rolled with nausea. It was a necessary pain. To kill a slink with T'Jas held no honor, no challenge.

Once he had grown more accustomed to the cold and pain; once he was able to quiet the churning in his stomach and the dizziness in his head, Dynat moved forward into the tunnel. Blind, he used a hand on one wall to orient, and listened carefully. Water dripped in the distance, and beyond it came the sound he was seeking—the soft, nearly silent mewling of slink kits. He smiled in the dark.

He moved toward the sound, stepping carefully over the rubble of rocks eroding from the walls of the long abandoned tunnel, moving his hand softly along the wall, trying not to disturb the flats; an alteration in their normal sounds might warn the slink. When the flats became too thick to avoid, Dynat crouched down and moved low, stalking along the tunnel floor. The mewling grew louder, and soon he could hear the soft breathing of the adult slink, the rasping of her tongue over the kits, and the low hum of her purr. He was directly below her alcove.

Dynat stood up straight. From the sounds, he guessed the alcove was six or seven feet above his head. He could sense the heat emanating from the bodies and pooling against the ceiling. He threw back his head and let out a loud, primal snarl, a passing imitation of a slink's challenge.

The purring ceased, and the washing. The breathing quieted to near silence. Even the mewling stopped. The sounds of flats invaded the silence as they crawled away in alarm. Then there was a scrambling noise, scraping of claws against rock, and a tiny rockfall of bones, dust, and feces tumbled down the wall toward him. He dodged it and waited for the slink to respond to his challenge. Instinct would drive her to protect her kits from his intrusion.

The scrambling sound became frantic, then faded slowly into the distance. The mewling started again, loud and desperate. He growled under his breath. Had the slink fled, leaving her kits unprotected? Moving slowly, listening, he scaled the side of the tunnel, searching for tiny outcroppings on which to place his hands and feet. The rough wall abraded his skin, tearing at the ghost veins where his lava mesh had been. Within moments he placed his hands on the shelf of the alcove, and felt the welcome warmth from the ceiling. The rock, washed with heat rising from Chraun for many eons, offered a tiny source of T'Jas. Not enough to be of much use, but soothing all the same.

Dynat had no wish to be soothed. He wanted an enraged, protective mother slink to battle, hand to claw. He wanted to feel a mass of muscles under his palms, writhing and struggling. He wanted to feel the real danger of death, to feel that the slink might rip his flesh and destroy him forever. He wanted to defeat death, and return to life with a new appreciation. He reached into the alcove, feeling for the nest. His hands found the terrified mewling kits. There were two of them, softer than soft, long tickle-y whiskers, moist tiny noses. They cringed away from his hands. It seemed the mother had abandoned them.

Dynat heaved himself all the way onto the ledge, crouching with his legs dangling over the edge. He drew out his firestone again, and lit it using T'Jas from the heat in the alcove. It was a tiny, sickly flame, just enough to reveal the two squirming, helpless kits. Their fur was beginning to grow, casting a dark shadow over the pale skin visible beneath. He did not even consider killing them—it would be like squashing a rockworm, easy and honor-less. He was about to twist back around to let himself down, to look for more satisfying quarry, when he saw a glint in the back of the alcove, lit by his meager torch. It disappeared, then reappeared, then disappeared. Dynat strained to listen past the mewling kits.

Keeping the torch, driven now by curiosity more than the hunt, Dynat pulled himself fully into the alcove, crouched nearly in a squat, and wriggled past the kits toward the back. To his surprise, the tiny cave did not terminate in a rough stone wall, but continued in a very narrow tunnel whose end he could not see. So. The mother was a coward with a back-door escape. Dynat held the firestone in his mouth, and squeezed through the passage. He went like this for a long time, listening to the near silent footpads ahead. The mewling faded away behind him.

At last the tunnel ended. Dynat saw the slink clearly in the torchlight, backed against the wall, her huge eyes full of fear. Behind her, a third kit mewled. Blood dripped from a wound on her foreleg, and when she curled back her lips in a warning snarl, he saw that several teeth were missing. Her huge ears were battered and torn. She was clinging to life, hardly a worthy opponent. The situation became clear, and Dynat's fury subsided, replaced by disappointment.

She had been attacked recently, probably by a roaming male slink. She had won that battle, but at great cost. She knew she would not win another challenge, so she had cut her losses, sacrificed two of her kits and tried to save the one she could carry. Dynat had wasted his time here. Killing her might get him a decent pelt, but there would be no honor, no glory, no joy. He would not have conquered death; merely bestowed it. He might as well go down to the cababar caves and slaughter a breeding fem. He would back out of the tunnel, find another spur and start the hunt again. Or he could forget hunting and bathe. Or he could forget bathing and pull Bolv from her duties, let his passion out in her arms.

A strange scent wafted up from the back of the tunnel. Sweet, hot and acrid, it burned in his nostrils and his throat. It was different from anything he had ever smelled before. Pushing the torch further, ignoring the frantic snarls from the slink, he strained to see past her. The tunnel did not end behind her; there was merely a small boulder that covered half the passage. The smell was coming from beyond that barrier. The slink's whisker caught fire from his torch, sizzled and smoked. Desperate, the creature turned away from the torchlight and picked up her kit, then squeezed over the boulder, pushed herself through with hind legs, and disappeared into the dark. Dynat heard a splashing sound like she was walking through water.

Curiosity drew Dynat forward. He could not pull his whole body past the barrier, but he was able to lean over it, pushing his arms and face a little further down the tunnel. He did not have enough heat to simply shape it away with T'Jas. He reached out with the torch, straining to see what was down there. Just beyond the barrier, the tunnel widened into a large cavern with a low ceiling. Gleaming on its floor was a pool of black liquid, large as the communal bath in Chraun where common Flames swam laps. The slink's eyes glinted, the only sign of her as she splashed through the shallows. Fascinated, Dynat inhaled deeply, tasting the smell in his mouth.

Without warning, the Fire Spirit burned bright in his mind. It did not speak, merely burned, a face of flames, consuming everything else, threatening to destroy Dynat. The sudden change charged Dynat's T'Jas, and the flame on his torch sprang to life, reaching for the black pool. When it touched the surface of the liquid, the entire cavern exploded into flame. The surface of the pool burned like firestone, emitting a choking black smoke. As quickly as it had arrived, the Fire Spirit receded, leaving Dynat empty again. The pool continued to burn.

Dynat drank deeply from the fire. T'Jas filled him, and heat blazed down the tunnel. He dissolved the boulder and widened the walls, crawling forward. The cave was an oven, and Dynat basked in it. He pulled off his cloak to keep it from burning and left it behind in the tunnel. How could water burn like that? He dipped his fingers into the pool, and pulled out a handful of flames. The liquid was thick and dark, opaque, slick like blood. It held fire more strongly than the highest quality firestone could. Coated in this stuff, carrying it in buckets, Dynat's Flames could go to battle armed with fire. He did not think it would harden in the cold like lava.

It must not be wasted. Dynat used T'Jas to pull the oxygen from the air. He choked, feeling lightheaded, but kept the air empty, counting off seconds until the flames subsided, then died down altogether. Releasing T'Jas, he breathed deeply, then carefully re-lit his torch, keeping it far from the liquid. The cavern's low ceiling was blackened by the smoke, and the slink's dark bones lurked in the shallows. Dynat scarcely saw them. He could only see glory and success. Once again, the Fire Spirit had shown him the way.

Firebloooood, the voice whispered in his mind, and then was silent again. Dynat grinned.

With Fireblood, he would make Iskalon burn forever.

Interlude

Khell, Seventeen Summers Prior

Maia

Maia crouched in her mother's egla. The dwelling was dome-shaped, constructed out of thick blocks of ice, and the view through the smoke hole at the top flickered from the dark underbelly of giant birds to bare blue sky in a regular pattern. Black, blue, black, blue. It was pretty, like watching the clouds roll in off the Stormbirth Waters and scatter over the ice plains toward the mountains. Grandmother held her close beside the cold fire pit, pressing a warm, wrinkled hand against Maia's mouth. "Don't make a sound," Grandmother whispered, her voice so faint it sounded like falling snow.

Maia stood frozen beneath her grandmother's furs. Mother and Father were outside, talking to the Dhuciri who rode the birds, giving them what they wanted so they would go away and not come back for a long time. Eight winters old, a big girl Mother said, she knew better than to make a noise. The egla protected them only if the Dhuciri did not know they hid inside. Grandmother's hand pressed so hard that Maia's teeth hurt.

A shout rang out, from somewhere in camp, followed by sharp cries from the birds and the loud rustle of flapping wings.

"No." The word was barely audible on Grandmother's lips. Maia felt her face released, her small body pushed forward so that she

stumbled over the charred seaweed in the fire pit. Grandmother held her at arm's length and looked into her face. "They have discovered the people in the egla. They will be here soon."

Maia said nothing. There was nothing to say. But Grandmother kept talking, as if by doing so she could reverse the will of fate. She pulled a small leather pouch from her belt, snapping the sinew ties that held it there, thrust it at the girl's chest. "Take this," she said. "There will be two missing. But yours will rest there, someday."

Maia stared at the pouch, astounded. She knew what Grandmother offered her. She took it with fingers numb from the dropping temperature in the egla.

"Now go," Grandmother breathed. "Run as far and fast as your little legs will carry you."

The egla began to disintegrate; its ice walls turned to powdery snow and fell on them, drifting down from the ceiling, blowing in from the sides. In a moment the egla was gone, and through the whirlwind of snow Maia could see patches of sky and tall, dark figures approaching with hungry eyes.

"Run," Grandmother commanded, and Maia ran, her flight obscured by the drifting snow and covered by Grandmother's angry chants at the Dhuciri.

She did not stop or look back until she crested the ridge that stood between the summer village of her people, at the shore of the Stormbirth Waters, and the vast plain of ice stretching across the whole continent of Khell. The egla were all gone, the belongings of the tribe scattered, and a black dust finer and darker than snow blew across the ice. The smell of death and decay that always followed Dhuciri traveled on the wind. A line of chained people marched to the cliffs where huge, dark birds waited.

Maia turned and ran down the back of the ridge, out onto the endless icy plain.

Chapter 2

Council Interrupted

Stasia

Stasia floated in the air just beneath the purple Burial Shaft, staring up into its depths. Distance made the furthest corpses appear as glittery dots, suspended in ice and time, drifting glacially along. She watched the closest figure, her shining red locks, the overlapping copper scales, her near-translucent skin. She stared so intently that she didn't even notice when her nose bumped against the surface of the burial ice.

The copper-clad woman looked peaceful, her jaw relaxed, her eyelashes making gentle semi-circles above her cheeks. Her lips rested in a serene pink line. Stasia could see tiny freckles on her cheeks that she hadn't noticed before.

Stasia blinked, and when her eyes opened again they were staring into wide green ones. The coppery woman had opened her eyes and was staring at Stasia like a living person. At the same time, Stasia's nose broke the surface of the burial ice. She was pulled upward into the ice. She struggled. "I'm not dead!" she tried to scream, but it came out muffled.

The copper woman's mouth was open in a welcoming smile. She reached an arm out toward Stasia, and Stasia renewed her struggle. She dreaded those dead fingers closing on her skin. But the woman didn't touch her. Instead, she beckoned.

"Come, Stasia." The woman raised her other arm and pointed upward, into the infinite shaft of ice. "Join us in our journey to V'lturhst."

The burial ice surrounded her completely. "No! I'm not dead!" But she couldn't breathe. The ice had closed around her. She was dead, drifting like all the other corpses, a barrier between Iskalon and the Svardark.

Stasia sat upright, gulping huge breaths of air. It took a moment for her to orient to her room, dim and blue and cold. Like the burial ice. No. It was her room, with her wardrobe, her dressing table, her window overlooking Iskalon, her molebear skin rug. Her bed, a huge slab of moist ice covered in chirat fleeces, radiated cold, chilling her whole body to the core. She drew T'Jas, soothing herself.

"I'm not dead," she told herself out loud. But was she going to die? She did not know enough to tell when the Dream was prophetic and when it was merely symbolic. If only there was another Dreamer, she might be able to learn from them, but there was no one alive who could guide or train her. Dreaming was a rare talent, legendary, and there was no record of a Dreamer in Iskalon since Queen Cataya.

She thought of her trek to the burial chamber yesterday, and Glace retrieving her, and the memory hit her like a rockfall. War! Chraun was going to attack, and Iskalon would truly be going to war. Stasia pondered what that would mean to her. She felt in her bones that the Dream was important, even more important than the war. Surely Iskalon would defeat the Flames easily, aided by the cold of Lake Lentok. Their fires would splutter and die in the frigid air. There would be a few casualties, Warriors mourned, tunnels to rebuild, but surely one princess more or less would not make a difference. Her Dream held the key to finding V'lturhst. She was close, closer than she had ever been before. Perhaps if she could return to the burial chamber, with Glace's iceospectacle, she could find a clue she had missed the day before.

But this time she would be better prepared. Stasia stood and pulled on her websilk undergarments, then went to the wardrobe and took out her armor. It was made of thick chirsh wool from the fleecy chirat, light yet strong, resistant to extreme heat and fire. The deep purple, almost black wool covered everything but her hands and feet and head, and she tugged on sturdy leather boots to protect her feet. The armor was sewn in two layers, with a thousand tiny pockets between, and before she left the city she would immerse herself in the lake, filling the pockets with water that would freeze to ice and protect her even further, and give her cold to draw on in the hot tunnels.

She crept to the door and opened it a sliver, peeking out. Glace's broad back greeted her, his sandy hair standing up as though he had been rubbing his hands through it. He bristled with weapons, and muscles in his huge arms were tight, coiled like a pitviper ready to strike. Had he truly spent the whole night out there?

"Glace!" she whispered, and he turned, positioning himself so he could face her and see down the hall at the same time.

"Yes, Princess?"

"Glace, we have to go back to the ancient burial chamber! I had another dream."

"Princess, Prince Casser's orders were—"

"Forget that! This is important! I think there is something I missed yesterday. I had another dream, and I think I'm close to finding the answer to V'lturhst. But we have to act now, before the war starts. Do you have your iceospectacle?"

Glace's shoulders shook with temptation, and though Stasia needed Glace on her side, she felt a moment of guilt for making him choose between duty and passion. She knew that he wanted as much as she to take a closer look at the burial chamber, if for different reasons.

"Absolutely not, Princess. Even if we were not about to go to war, even if I was not under strict orders to get you to the council meeting today, I would not take you back to that place. Casser would—"

Stasia never found out what Casser would do because she slammed the door so hard that her dressing table shook, all her jewelry clinking where it hung. Guilt melted away, replaced by iron anger. She began to pace. She had to find a way to distract Glace and sneak out. She could step out her window and float to the ground, but there were rules against that; Icers were supposed to use the stairs, so as not to flaunt their power over the city. She would be noticed and stopped before she'd crossed the bridges. Her father would be informed, and then she would be twice in trouble.

"There has to be a way," Stasia said to her wardrobe. "I have to find V'lturhst. If I'm Dreaming of it, it must be more important than the war." A thought dawned on her. Perhaps V'lturhst was related to the war. If she could find a hint about V'lturhst in the burial ice, then perhaps she could use it to help Iskalon win. She could be truly useful, instead of merely another body in the debates. Helping Iskalon win was worth whatever punishment Father decreed.

A heavy tapping sounded on her stone door. Was Glace trying to make amends? Stasia ignored her own curiosity and continued pacing. Let him stew a bit. She stopped by the window and stared out, looking across the lake. A few early fishing skiffs were poling along on the water. The rapping came again, more persistent.

Stasia heard the door scrape and turned to see it swinging open. A verbal thrashing died in her mouth as Lady Larc Chan stepped into the room, smoothing her long dark bangs across her forehead.

"Stasia! Didn't you hear me knock?" Her voice was deep and musical. Tall for an Icer, and dark, Larc was gorgeous. Though Stasia was a princess, and Larc only a Lady, Stasia had always seemed to be in Larc's shadow when they were together. Most Icers were pale and petite, but somehow Larc had been born with the physique of a human, big boned. She filled out her opal-speckled websilk dress with pleasant curves, and her round face was both beautiful and bright. Her glowing blue vaerce lit up her tan skin. She had more of them remaining than Stasia did; Larc was as conservative with T'Jas as she was with everything else. "What are you doing in armor? Do you know what chime it is?"

Stasia strode forward and pulled Larc further into the room, out of Glace's hearing. She left the door open, so she could keep an eye on her warden where he stood in the hall. "I'm so glad you've come, Larc," she whispered. "Listen, you have to distract Glace for me. I need to slip past him and get out of Iskalon."

Larc regarded Stasia with a brief, baffled look. Then her eyes brightened with understanding. "Stasia," she said quietly, "Is this about V'lturhst?"

"It is, Larc. I had another Dream last night, and I have to investigate. Please, will you help me get past Glace?"

"But Stasia, this is the most important Council of our lives! We will find out today if the King will declare Martial Law! We are going to war with Chraun!"

Larc's voice rose on every sentence, and Stasia glanced at Glace. He was still where he had been, unmoving. She pressed a finger to her lips. "I know, Larc. I want to know the outcome of the meeting as much as you do. I just don't want to sit there on the benches waiting all day while the councilors eat up my time. And if war is coming, all the more reason why I must do this now." She explained briefly about the location of the burial chamber and what she had seen there, but Larc was shaking her head.

"Stas, I think you should spend some time with the Heritage. They could help you with your problem. There is a meeting after second chime, in the nearest burial chamber. Come with me. Please?"

Stasia stared sadly at her friend. Larc still did not understand. "You know I won't do that, Larc. We've had this argument before." Once, Larc had accidentally looked into Stasia's mind and seen the dreams of V'lturhst there. Since then her friend, a staunch Ancestorist, had been trying to get Stasia "help" for her "problem."

"But you must do something, Stasia. Can't you see that this will destroy you? The people whisper about you behind your back. The Heritage are worried about you. And these Dreams are shortening your life. Look at your hands compared to mine."

Destroy her? Stasia thought of the feeling of being dead, entering the burial ice. Of course, she wasn't really going to die, wasn't really going up into the ice. She looked down at her hands. There were hardly any vaerce left on them, compared to Larc's palms, thick with blue dots. "How could a Dream destroy me, Larc? The Heritage won't help me. They will just tell me that everything I've been Dreaming is evil, an illusion, the work of the Svardark seeping into Iskalon to wreak havoc."

Larc was silent, and the tension between Stasia and her friend created a gap as wide as Lake Lentok. "If you aren't going to help me, you might as well go on to the Council. I'll have to find another way—"

Casser appeared suddenly beyond Glace, coming up the Hall. Stasia squirmed in her chirsh armor, then forced herself to be still, determined to meet her Uncle with dignity. Behind her, Larc's websilk dress rustled as she curtseyed.

Casser stood quietly on the threshold, staring at Stasia's armor. The silence grated on her nerves. "I was just getting ready—" she began, preparing a convincing tale to explain why she was wearing armor. Casser's gaze did not change, but cold perspiration broke out on Stasia's forehead and soaked her eyebrows.

"To go exploring," she finished truthfully, relinquishing

the lie she had intended. "Casser, this is imperative! I had another Dream last night. That burial chamber I found yesterday holds the key, I'm sure of it. I'm so close, Casser. Please. I never say anything in Council anyway."

He didn't scold her for not being dressed. He didn't allow or disallow her request. Instead he said, "Lady Larc, hurry along. The Council has started, and your presence there will be missed."

"Yes, Prince Casser." Larc curtsied and scurried to obey without so much as a glance in Stasia's direction.

Casser stepped out of the doorway to allow her to pass and continued until he stood within a foot of Stasia. She lifted her chin, refusing to cower.

"Do you know what would have happened to your father if you had been captured in the Spiral Tunnel yesterday?" There was still no reproach in his tone.

"To Father? Why, nothing. I'd be dead, but he would be safe and sound here. I'd be surprised if he even missed me. He'd have to lose the other twelve, to notice my absence." Stasia startled herself with the bitterness in her voice.

"If you were captured, Stasia, your father, who loves you perhaps more than any of his other daughters, would be forced to make a terrible choice. The Flames would not kill you, they would keep you hostage and milk their power over your father like a breeding molebear's tit. Krevas might be able to bear your death. But your torture? Flames have been known to send back hostages piece by piece. How many fingers, how many toes would it take before Krevas was no longer fit to rule Iskalon? And could your sisters bear it any more than he?"

Casser's voice lowered, his eyes held Stasia's gaze firmly. "I know I couldn't't."

Stasia said nothing. Part of her could not believe him, could not believe that her father cared that much. He had never shown it. And it was hard to imagine that the Flames would do something so horrible. Yet, something in

Casser's eyes told her he was telling the truth.

"I have no wish to scare you, niece. But if it is the only way to keep you safe, I will do it. And I will tell you this, though your father ordered it kept secret: even here in Iskalon, there have been attempts by Chraun to capture your sisters."

Stasia remained silent. She had not known that. The Gendarme must have kept it very quiet, for rumors not to reach her ears. She thought again of almost running into the Flame in the Spiral Tunnel. She hadn't told Glace about it. Had she come that close to captivity and torture?

Casser was still talking. "I've come to ask about your dreams last night."

For a moment, Stasia was tempted to lie. She knew what Casser wanted to hear—that she had Dreamed something that could help Iskalon know Chraun's intentions. Could she spin her Dream of the burial chamber as if it were somehow helpful to the war effort, and insist that Casser take her there? No. She thought there might be a link, but she couldn't be sure without more information. The prospect of war was too serious for her to dissemble. And, try as she might, Stasia just couldn't lie to Casser. "I Dreamed of the burial chamber, nothing else."

"A pity. When you Dreamed of the raid on the fungal caverns, we were able to reduce losses by posting guards in the right places. The right Dream just now could make all the difference for our defense in this war. But I suppose you can't control what you Dream. Now. Put away that armor and get dressed. The Council is starting, and we are late already. I will escort you to the meeting along with Glace."

Casser waited in the hall while Stasia divested her armor and pulled on her second best websilk, opaque and sewn with tiny ghost-mollusk pearls in delicate patterns. Woven by carefully trained neithild spiders around a clay cast of Stasia's body, the dress fit every inch of her precisely. She put her hair up in an elaborate braided bun, towering a foot above her forehead. She took her mother-of-pear tiara from her dressing table and secured it at her hairline. Now she looked every bit the dutiful princess. As she glided down the hall, she was framed by Casser and Glace like a dangerous prisoner. There would be no returning to the burial chamber today, probably not before the war began. She would have to wait until after the war to return. So she resolved to apply herself to helping Iskalon win a quick victory. The sooner the war was over, the sooner she could solve the riddle of her Dream.

Larc

The second she was out of Casser's sight, Larc began to run. She ran through the icy halls of the Palace, down the steps and across the long King's Bridge, through quiet streets and the bustling Market. She kept running until she reached the steps of the Council, where she paused to incline her head briefly to Cataya's statue and nodded a greeting to the Heritage acolyte standing watch. Once inside the building, she walked as briskly as decorum would allow up the wide, imposing halls of the Council Hall. She hadn't realized she was so late. She could not miss this, the most important Council meeting in years, perhaps of her entire life. She wanted to know if Iskalon would go to war, if the King would assume martial law, if the Guilds would give way, if they would fight it.

The Council Hall was full to bursting, and Larc had to push her way through aggressively. Bodies pressed together to make way for her. A nasal voice droned above the white noise of shuffling people. The benches were full, so she stood just inside the door, behind the blue tiled columns that ringed the room. She had never seen the Council this crowded.

Councilman Wyfus stood in the center of the room, speaking slowly. His robes were made of gleaming lakehide. The Fishing Guildsman was old for a human, his skin hanging in wrinkles over his wiry frame, his thin white hair sticking out haphazardly from a blotchy scalp, but he was far from senile. As Speaker for the Council, Representative of one of the strongest Guilds in Iskalon, he wielded his power with ruthless cunning. He could speak for chime after chime about nothing at all, simply to wear down his opponents. Larc disagreed with the old man often, but she could not help but admire his technique. It appeared doddering; it appeared unintentional and ineffective. But it almost always worked exactly as Wyfus intended. Often when the benches were opened for debate, no one even remembered what topic had been presented at the beginning of his speech. Today, already, yawns and shuffling noises came from the benches.

" . . . give only three precedents for this sort of thing. The first was two centuries after Her Majesty Queen Cataya's reign, during the Red Raids . . ."

Larc strained on her tiptoes, trying to see who was in attendance. Every one of the thirty-five stone chairs was occupied by a Guild representative, a rare occurrence. The powerful Councilors, like hulking Mowat of the Livestock Guild, and willowy Cygnet of the Gem Guild, sat up front. Zerid of the Weaver Guild whispered to Jold of the Tanning Guild. Mayl of the Heritage, not a true Guild but represented in any case, had a place of honor beside Wyfus' vacant chair. Further back sat the scribes, water-clock engineers, cooks, miners, fungal farmers.

" . . . argue that the same division is not present. . ."

Though the Icers were considered a Guild, the King was officially their representative, so no Icer sat with the Councilors. On the opposite side of the room, in the center of a raised dais, King Krevas sat on the most elaborate chair, cushioned with powder ice, wearing the mighty crown of Iskalon, its tall blue diamond spires catching the lights in the room and sparkling like ice. Websilk robes hugged his lithe form. General Zental sat to his left in chirsh armor, Casser's seat next to him empty, and to his right sat the two elder Princesses, Maudit and Jelina, resplendent in websilk dresses and sparkling tiaras.

Someday, when she had put in her time on the benches and risen in the political ranks, Larc hoped to be an advisor, sitting behind the King and murmuring secrets into his ears so he would know what he faced in the opposition. More than anything, she wanted that role. She wanted to pry out secret dealings, to organize networks of spies within the Guilds, to understand where all the Guilds stood on every issue. She wanted to dwell in the center of Iskalon politics.

" . . . a question of succession; the previous leader died and the inheritance was unclear. . ."

King Krevas' attention did not waver from Wyfus, but his advisors were scanning the crowd, looking for reactions and revelations on the faces of the people.

" . . . I do not think there will be a question of succession here, Majesty. Unless I am mistaken, at least one of your thirteen lovely daughters will be Queen."

That drew a few chuckles from the council. Krevas' patient face did not change, but Maudit glared at the room. Larc strained to see over the heads in front of her. Had dry, shriveled up old Wyfus actually attempted a joke?

"The last . . ."

A susurration of websilk shuffles announced the crowd parting for Stasia's arrival, and Larc looked up, distracted, as her friend was escorted to the benches by Casser and Glace. A Lord in lapis-speckled websilk robes stood so Stasia could take his seat. Casser walked behind the council chairs and quietly slipped in beside Zental, and Glace retreated and leaned on a column opposite Larc. Their eyes met briefly and Glace nodded a silent greeting.

Larc looked over the crowd on the benches with the eyes of an advisor. They were a mix of petite Icer Lords and Ladies in their finest websilk, and lesser Guildsmen, in an array of leathers, lakehide, and fine-spun chirsh. The other nine princesses sat beyond Stasia on the first benches, their tiaras distinguishing them from the ordinary Ladies.

Larc did not linger over what gems were worn by whom or which Lord was flirting quietly with which Lady, as another observer might. She was gauging reactions to Wyfus' monologue. He was actually addressing the topic at hand, martial law, and he seemed to be succeeding in swaying the public opinion. Even his usual opponents were nodding their heads, not out of impatience but agreement. Many of the yawners and shufflers on the benches had decided looks on their faces, as if they knew where they stood already. King Krevas revealed nothing in his solid, kindly face, merely listened attentively and politely, perhaps a little indulgently, as if his grandfather were relating a tale of his youth. Set slightly behind him, his advisors leaned in to whisper to him from time to time. Larc's heart burned with envy. What would she whisper in his ear, if she sat on the dais? Would she tell him to forget about martial law, and, when the time came to make the ruling, accept the apparent wishes of Iskalon? Or should he take control without heeding the people; should he simply act? The second choice might set him up as a tyrant. Tyrants, in Iskalon history, had been dethroned. But if he did not declare martial law, could he garner the support he needed to defend the realm?

It would be hours, perhaps even days, before they would know. Krevas and his advisors must remain silent, other than quiet whispers, until Wyfus and the other councilors had presented their arguments. Then the benches would be opened, and any Guild member allowed to share his or her opinion. That was Larc's favorite time, because it meant she could participate, and her strong voice helped her speak above all the others in the debate. It was a time of chaos, confusion, excitement. Once the issue had been thoroughly debated, the Council would carry the proposal forth to the King for a ruling. Krevas could rule any way he wished, and Iskalon would obey. However, if he ignored the outcome of the debate, if he ruled against the wishes of the majority, he would face increasing resistance and obstinacy from the council. Longer and longer periods would pass without proposals being carried to him, and he would find the political wheels of Iskalon clogged, just like the gears of the waterclock sometimes clogged, stopping time. If he ignored the people too often, he would end up with rebellion. Larc envied his advisors, but she did not envy him in the least bit. She would not have wanted to make the final decisions that could keep the realm together, or rip it asunder.

All too soon, Fifth Chime sounded, and the Council broke for lunch recess. Larc clung to a column as a wave of bodies pressed together, hurrying out to Market to buy lunch from the Cooking Guild stalls. She saw Stasia rise, looking a little bleary. Had she been sleeping? Glace shadowed his charge as the crowd parted for her and the other princesses. The councilors filed neatly out a door in the back of the King's dais, and the King and his advisors stood and stretched as Palace servants brought in covered platters. Larc watched the benches, too excited to leave. As soon as a spot in the front row opened up, she pounced on it, sitting firmly, hoping a princess wouldn't demand it from her. She cared little for sitting, but when the floor was opened to the benches, she could stand on it for extra height, to add strength to her argument. That was well worth missing lunch.

Her stomach grumbled and she focused her mind, preparing herself to argue. Iskalon must be defended, must be united. The King could not wait through endless Council meetings in order to get permission to move troops here, to take prisoners there, to set up barricades in that tunnel. The Flames would not wait on a Council to make their moves. Sitting straight on the hard bench, nearly shaking in anticipation, Larc noticed Krevas watching her from the dais as he picked at a bowl of pickled fish with slender golden chopsticks. She acknowledged his gaze by standing and giving him a neat curtsey. When she sat again she brushed her bangs out of her face. The King set his chopsticks in the dish and returned her gesture with a salute, single fist to his heart. A wave of confidence washed from Larc's toes all the way to her throat. The King noticed her. He had saluted her like a warrior. He knew she was coming to battle for him.

The King had picked up his lunch again, and Larc looked away politely. She felt invigorated and reassured. The King himself knew she was a warrior. She would fight with her voice.

The hall filled again, and the benches grew crowded. Stasia entered, and gave Larc a smile and a wave before sitting. Larc smiled back and glanced down the benches. All the princesses had their seats; hers was secure.

Wyfus started right where he had left off. Larc listened carefully, arguing his points in her mind. True, martial law could weaken the foundations of Iskalon. But if it was not declared, there might not be an Iskalon left. And it was temporary. Krevas had never acted as a dictator, never overstepped his power. There was no reason to believe he would not return control to the Council once the threat was defeated. She argued so vigorously in her own mind that she nearly spoke out loud.

All at once the crowd behind her shuffled loudly, skirts rustling and jewelry clinking. She glanced back, and saw that someone was pushing through the crowd. Another latecomer? As he passed the benches Larc saw that it was Colonel Kiner, with one of his scouts in tow. Larc liked Kiner; he had an infective laugh and a jolly personality, though he did not have much patience for incompetence. He had started as a scout, and risen quickly to Colonel. Kiner did not stop at the benches, but walked right onto the Council floor, through the seats of astonished, indignant Councilors, pausing to give Wyfus a quick, apologetic salute, and knelt in front of Krevas. Wyfus went silent, too shocked to protest. The King regarded Kiner coldly. Larc shivered. He had better have a good reason for interrupting.

"My King, councilors, Ancestors, please forgive my intrusion." Kiner stood, still facing the King. "Scout Terean comes from the furthest post in the Spiral Tunnel. Please listen to his report." He nudged Terean forward. Larc could only see the back of the scout's head, but she could imagine his fear, at addressing the King in the middle of a full Council.

"The Flame army is mobile, Majesty. They are coming up the tunnel swiftly, and they are—they are on fire, my King."

"On fire?" Krevas spoke quietly.

"Their bodies burn as they walk, Majesty. I could not get close enough to see more. The heat was great, and they smoked, a choking, hot, black smoke."

Krevas turned and addressed General Zental. "Send a platoon down the Spiral Tunnel. I want regular reports on the Flame army's progress. Do not engage unless they see you and attack."

Before the King had finished speaking, Zental was on his feet. He and Kiner and the scout exited the Council Hall together, through the back. Larc could see them running down the hall before the door banged shut. An invasion. Despite the fact that it was all the council had talked about for the last few sessions, Larc could scarcely believe it. Looking around at the stunned faces, she knew she was not alone. She could almost feel the fear rising from the crowded council. She had never heard this room so silent. She thought she could hear her own heart beating. Across the floor, a scribe's gold plates clinked, and the sound echoed throughout the hall before the scribe silenced it.

Krevas turned to face the Council again. He was silent, but his expression was clear. His eyes bored into Wyfus.

Larc thought she would have collapsed on the floor, under that gaze.

Wyfus did not collapse. He stood his ground. He turned away from the dais, and looked over the Council and the benches. Larc caught a glimpse of his face. Normally dull and unexpressive, a foreign emotion rested there—his face was pinched in terror. He turned again, walked forward and knelt in front of Krevas.

"Majesty, the Council brings forth the proposal that martial law be declared for the duration of the invasion. Let it be noted that this proposal has not received full debate on the floor. The Speaker assumes unanimity. If any wish to withdraw the proposal for debate, let them speak now."

Only silence met his words.

"The Proposal is set forth." Wyfus withdrew, returning to his seat, to await the King's ruling. Krevas stood. This was his chance to speak. When he did, his voice was loud, clear, and strong.

"From this day forth, martial law is in effect. We are all part of the Warrior Guild. Go, gather your families, and prepare to fight, to the death if need be, to defend the realm."

And that was all. Krevas stepped from the dais and hurried from the room, shadowed by his advisors. Larc sat on the bench, watching people file out, looks of numb horror on their faces. Some people were chanting verses about Iskalon's greatness. She had still not adjusted to the idea that Iskalon was actually being invaded. She felt deflated. She had been ready to fight tooth and nail for martial law, and it had happened without her help. She was a Warrior in Council, but in real battle she was useless. Like all Icers, she had served her mandatory year in the Iskalon army. It had been uncomfortable at the best of times, terrifying at the worst. Her talents lay in healing and debating, not fighting.

She glanced down the bench, and saw that Stasia was

sitting a few paces away from her, staring at the empty council chairs. She would have expected her friend to take the first chance to leave. Larc slid down the now empty bench and sat next to Stasia.

Stasia looked up and Larc saw a thrill shining in her eyes. "Can you believe it, Larc?" Stasia took her hands, and Larc held her fingers, amazed by her friend's reaction. "A chance to really fight. They will need all the Icers they can muster, to protect the Kingdom. We will send those Flames back to their tunnels with their tails between their legs!"

Larc shook her head at her friend's innocence. As if the King would allow his own daughter to be endangered by actual fighting. Still, it was hard not to be swayed by the glow in Stasia's yellow-green eyes. Larc glanced up at Glace. His scarred face was hard as the stone column he leaned against. Larc pitied him his task. Stasia would not make it easy for him to protect her.

Already, the princess was standing, ready for action. "Come. Father will be convening a war council. We must be there! I'll try to sneak you in; everyone will be too distracted to notice."

Larc allowed herself to be pulled along. She kept her misgivings inside. Stasia did not seem to understand just how dire the situation was. When they left the hall and walked through the crowded Market, the lights on the Palace seemed dim. There was a quietness to the conversations they passed, an oppressiveness hanging in the vast cavern of Iskalon. Larc remembered the one other time she had felt this way—she had been sixteen years old and her mother was lying ill. The same bleakness had hovered in the sickroom before Mother succumbed to the exhaustion sickness that took all Icers once their vaerce were gone.

Larc hummed softly to herself, a simple victory tune, and the darkness seemed to lift a little.

Medoc

General Medoc was covered from head to toe in greasy flames. The black, sticky, sweet smelling Fireblood coating his armor was similar to cababar fat, thick and flammable, but it was far more volatile; cababar fat burned with a gentle, clean flame, but this burned as if it would explode at any moment. It matched the mood of the troops as they approached Iskalon and their blood surged with adrenaline.

Medoc marched at the head of the ranks. The tunnel was wide enough for four to walk abreast. They had left the sloping Spiral Tunnel behind just now, and walked along flat, smooth, well-swept corridors. The air might have been cold; he could not tell. Here and there ice sparkled on the walls, melting away with their passing.

Behind him, twenty more Flames marched, Officers all, and behind them, a vat of Fireblood was pulled by two groaning cababar. Getting the thing up the steep tunnel had been a feat; the Semija had whipped the cababar nearly senseless. Medoc wondered how the other vats fared; there was a team of cababar for every twenty bodies in the throng that stretched all the way down to Chraun, over five thousand Flames strong. Marching beside their Flames, the Semija Warriors numbered nearly seven thousand. A strong army, with enough Fireblood to make Iskalon burn forever, as the King had ordered.

Medoc ordered a halt when they came to the place the scouts had reported, a widening of the Spiral where it branched into several different tunnels. A scout stood at each entrance. They snapped to attention when Medoc stood before them, waiting.

The nearest scout approached Medoc and bowed to his waist. Eagerness shone in his dark young eyes, and his lip had a permanent sneer. Medoc inclined his head briefly. "Report."

"A barricade waits, General. They have sealed all the

tunnels ahead with sheer rock."

"How thick?"

"At least several feet, General."

"What else?"

"The tunnels all lead to the lake. The furthest left is the most direct, General. It also goes through their fungal caverns and stock dens."

Medoc nodded a dismissal. The scouts disappeared into the rest of the army, and fresh scouts emerged to take their place. A barricade. No telling what forces were amassed on the other side. Medoc turned to face his troops. Only the first few would hear the address, but it would be passed from mouth to mouth down the line, all the way to Chraun.

"The time for War has come! Our King has willed it. The Fire Spirit wills it. He commands us through our holy King."

Medoc paused, and wondered if twelve thousand bodies would be sufficient. He wondered how many would die, and how long it would take new recruits to fill the holes in his army. Iskalon's total Icer population was only about five thousand, but they would have at least ten thousand Warriors. And the battle would be fought on their ground. His Warriors would be wondering the same things.

"We may face a fiercely guarded city," he continued. "We may be surrounded by icy cold waters. Some of us, it is true, will not return. Some of our lives will be shortened beyond repair. But we will be protected by the Blood of the Fire Spirit, which he has given to us for victory! With Fireblood, no cold will stop us! No water will drench us! No ice will pierce us!"

The troops cheered so loudly that they sounded like the roar of the lava river. For a moment Medoc imagined that the lava river had followed him up the Spiral Tunnel and awaited his commands. It was a comforting thought, to have the river at his back in this icy place.

"We will swoop into Iskalon like a tunnelfire, and destroy everything we do not capture or steal. We will take all their jewels. We will take all their Semija. We will plunder their mines and loot their sacred ice shafts! We will burn their houses and leave them crippled so that they can never threaten our realm again!"

As he spoke, thoughts that he could not speak out loud to his Warriors loomed in the back of his mind. Threaten the realm? The idea was absurd. There were twice as many Flames as Icers. And as far as Medoc knew, the Icers did not have anything that could keep them cold in Chraun. The neighboring kingdom might occasionally raid the outer Semija caverns, but that was practically a boon when Chraun was overcrowded.

His words traveled down the line of Warriors, and cheers and yells of agreement continued to well up from the tunnel, growing so loud that Medoc could barely hear himself. They were ready. "Come win Glory for the realm of Fire!"

He turned on his heel and marched stiffly. The roar behind him cut off, followed by a moment of silence. It was so quiet that he could hear his thick metal boots clanging against stone. Then the ring of the boots of the Flame behind Medoc joined his, then the next, and the next, until the tunnel was filled with the uniform sound of the army's march. A warning for the Icers, but it did not matter. He had seen their scouts, knew they watched his army's every move. It did not matter. Their ice would be no match for his army of fire, his lava river.

As he marched, Medoc pondered the King's command to take the princesses alive. Dynat had always had some strange obsession with them. He had ordered Medoc to attempt raids in the heart of Iskalon, even sent in Semija posing as escapees. All those attempts had failed miserably. Was this whole war just to capture the princesses? Medoc would have expected to capture a few of the members of the Royal Family for questioning, and to help keep the other prisoners under control, but Dynat's command to kill the king but bring in all thirteen princesses alive made no sense at all. Did he wish, as Medoc had inferred to the troops, to make Semija out of Icers, and have a bevy of royal attendants? Then why not the Ice King himself? Did Dynat intend to lie with the Ice Princesses? Chraun would disapprove, if that were the case. The thought of a Flame and an Icer bedding was revolting to any decent person.

Medoc pushed away that disgusting thought. It was not his duty to question orders, but to obey them. He reached the barrier; it was time now to put all questions aside and act. He ordered five Flames forward. They placed their hands on the wall. He could almost see the T'Jas flow from their hands to the rock. The rock melted away like ice, pooling at their feet and receding into the tunnel walls. When the stone opened completely, Medoc could see only a cave full of ice fog. The air smelled sweet and musty. This was the fungal cavern the scout had reported. The troops could eat after they had taken it, before moving on toward the lake. He stepped forward, raising both flaming hands toward the ceiling, drinking T'Jas deeply from his lava and his coating of fire.

"Company, advance!" he shouted. In spite of his doubts, the thrill of battle sang in his veins. He heard the swell of bodies behind him, moving forward, propelling him eagerly toward the waiting cold. The world erupted into a chaos of fire and ice.

Chapter 3

Sealed for Siege

Stasia

"Seraph, you will command the fifth battalion, which will be placed in the inner ring of the city." Krevas's voice rang out in his spacious throne room. "Lotica and Pasten, you will take the non-fighting citizens to the Burial chambers and protect them there should the city fall. Stasia, you will remain in the Palace under guard until the fighting is over. That takes care of the Royal duties. Now, for the Tanning Guild. We will need even more armor . . ."

Stasia pressed her lips together so hard that they went numb. She was so angry that she could not hear the rest of her father's words. Every imprisonment, every time Glace had dragged her back from the Outer Tunnels, every restriction seemed to pale before this. She could scarcely even think, she was so angry. All she could do was stare down the long oval table, past her sisters and the Officers and Guildsmen on the War Council, stare at her father as if she could will him to change his mind.

Krevas's massive throne, constructed from a cascade of ice that seemed to pour from the tall ceiling, would have made any other man appear small, especially an Icer, but

Krevas' presence towered over the table. He had changed from his websilk robes to a fine, dark chirsh ice-armor, and he looked more like a General than Zental, who sat to his right. He was no longer the quiet, considering man he had been in Council. With martial law in effect, he was in charge, moving the meeting along rapidly and effectively. His lined face was implacable; Stasia knew without speaking that he would not be moved. The great crown of Iskalon, its jagged blue diamond spikes emulating ice, sat heavily on his head, digging into the creases on his brow.

Stasia took a deep breath, trying to quiet her anger. Under the table, her twin sister Pasten squeezed her hand in sympathy, and Stasia felt a little better. It was a shame she had not been able to get Larc in; her presence would have been a comfort as well. She took another breath, and though her anger still burned low in her heart, she could focus on the council again. She had to. If, Ancestors forbid, something happened to her father and every one of her sisters, she would need to take charge of the battle.

Maudit, nearly as imposing as their father with her arms folded over her wide bosom, was asking Krevas something about the bridges. She would be Queen after him, and sometimes she acted as if she ruled by his side. Jelina, practically lounging in her chair, leaned toward Zental and whispered to him but broke off at a sharp glance from Casser. Up and down the long table, Officers shifted, exchanging glances that conveyed worry, and scribes pressed furiously into gold plate, recording Krevas's decrees so that they could be carried out. The Guildsmen fidgeted unless Krevas was addressing them directly, impatient to be getting back to their Guilds and preparing them for the war.

The Guildsmen would all be participating; every able-bodied citizen would, except Stasia. Only she had been relegated to the Palace, denied the thrill and glory of the front lines—of any battle at all. Even Pasten was to be given the important duty of protecting the children and infirm. Stasia would be treated like a delicate sculpture, packed away in the Palace.

" . . . We are also bringing great vats of water from the lake to the tunnels." Zental was speaking now, reporting the latest from the scouts. "We will try to drown them out of the fungal caverns. That is where the fighting is heaviest."

Stasia longed to be there. She was a powerful Icer, fully trained as a warrior. Not letting her fight was simply a bad decision. Speaking out of turn in a private council meeting was foolish, rude, and one of her Father's greatest pet peeves. But she couldn't help herself.

" . . . Fifty-one reported Icer casualties, but the numbers are coming in on the chime. There is not an accurate count of human casualties yet. The best—"

"Father, may I speak?"

Twenty or so pairs of eyes swiveled to stare at Stasia. Zental looked startled and annoyed. Krevas's blue eyes burned. Stasia took silence for acquiescence and stood.

"Could I not join Pasten and Lotica in protecting the citizens? I would be as safe there as in the Palace, and then I would be useful."

Silence followed her words, punctuated only by some nervous rustling of garments and the clinks of gold plate as scribes used her interruption to catch up in their furious scribbling. Krevas leaned forward, folded his hands together under his chin, and gazed down the table at her. The rest of the eyes looked away.

"Apart from today, when was the last time you attended a full council meeting, daughter?"

"I know I've been errant lately, Father. I apologize. But—"

"When?"

His tone left no space to evade. Stasia began to regret her outburst. "I am not certain, Father."

He leaned back, folding his arms across his chest. "And yet you think you know enough about this situation to speak out in a War Council? Have you had a Dream about the war, Daughter? Something you neglected to tell Casser this morning? Some reason why you should be speaking now?"

Stasia's anger dissolved into a sweeping sensation of self-doubt. She had not Dreamed about the war, much to her frustration. All of her dreams of late were about that same, Ancestor-cursed burial chamber. "No, Father."

Something moist glinted in Krevas's eyes. Stasia realized that he was sad. It was unusual for her father to show any emotion at all, much less in front of so many people. The glimmer disappeared swiftly, replaced by a brow furrowed in disappointment.

"Stasia, this one time, you will obey me without question. I have been patient, I have indulged your flights of fancy, even defended you to the Heritage. But I don't have time for this. I have a war to fight, and you must accept your role. If there was a safe place to keep all of you until the war was over, I would put you all there without a second thought. But my only choice is to scatter the royal family so that if one location falls to the enemy, someone is sure to survive in another. Zental, please continue."

Zental went on with his list of figures and facts as if he had never stopped. Stasia did not hear him. Why had Father looked so sad? Surely there was no way for Iskalon to fall. Here there was infinite cold to draw upon, and nothing for the Flames. Her anger rose again. Father must be mistaken. It would not hurt for her to fight in the city; surely the fighting would not even cross the bridges. She balled her hands into fists and stayed silent for the rest of the meeting.

As soon as her father dismissed the war council, she leapt from her seat and hurried from the room. Glace caught up with her in the hall leading to her quarters. She blinked rapidly, trying in vain to stop her useless anger from turning to tears of frustration. The tears leaked through and she smoothed them away with the back of her hand.

"You should not antagonize Father so, Stas." Pasten was approaching down the corridor, her golden locks glowing almost green in the blue icelight under a tiara of teardrop emeralds. Older than Stasia by mere minutes, she was her favorite sister. Larc walked beside her, dark and voluptuous compared to the pale, slender princess.

"I had to try, Pasten. Care to trade places with me?"

"Even if I cared to, Father would not allow it." Pasten placed her slender fingers on her hips. "Try not to think of it as being protected, sister. We are the future of the Kingdom. We have a duty to survive."

Stasia let her breath whoosh out of her nose like an angry molebear. "Then why not Jelina, or Maudit? Or even Seraph. They are the eldest; they have been trained to rule. Why are they allowed to fight? Aren't I more expendable?"

"I'm sure the King does not think of any of his daughters as expendable, Stas." Larc brushed her bangs away from her eyes. Why didn't she just trim them shorter?

"And you, Larc? Have you been bundled away to safety as well?"

Her friend ignored her question. "Your elder sisters are to organize the Guild members into a secondary army to defend the city, if the fighting crosses the bridges. They will direct from behind the lines."

"I—crosses the bridges? They think the Flames will really reach the lake?"

The two women exchanged a glance over Stasia's head, a difficult task when Larc was taller than her and Pasten shorter. "This is what you have missed by being absent, Stasia. This is not a simple raid, or a valor battle. The force the Flames have sent is meant to destroy Iskalon forever. They have filled every tunnel between us and the realm of fire with their army. They have a new substance that enables them to apply fire to water. It will take all the resources we have to defeat them."

Pasten's words sobered her. Was the situation really so

dire? If so, all the more reason why Stasia should be fighting on the front lines. They needed every single Icer they could muster.

"Sometimes, even we must take orders, Stasia." Pasten's calm acceptance only prickled at her ire again. "Come, Larc. You are a talented healer, and I would like you to help me. We must choose out our Icers, and begin to organize the people. Zental's last report put the fighting in the stock caverns. We haven't much time."

Her sister turned and swept down the corridor. Larc gave Stasia a sympathetic look, then followed. Stasia stared after her. The stock caverns were close to the tunnels where the guildless lived. Had anyone thought to bring them into the city? Or had they been left to their own devices?

"Princess?" It was Glace. Stasia took a deep breath.

"Yes, Glace. I'm going." She stepped forward, headed for her quarters. Glace trailed faithfully after her, unprotesting as the slink that shadowed him. Musche was missing, she realized, and when she asked Glace, he told her he'd sent the creature to the Outer Tunnels. "He'll be safe there. He can hunt, and the things that are dangerous to us are less dangerous to him. Here, if the worst comes to worst, he'll be trapped."

Even Glace seemed to think the Flames would breach Iskalon. Stasia returned to pacing her room, which seemed smaller and smaller as more time passed. She stared out the window for a long while, watching as all the bridges except the Bridge of Ancestors were sunk, one by one, into the icy lake. They were jointed suspension bridges, designed to be sunk, but Stasia did not think they had been lowered in centuries. The metal gears groaned and squealed, echoing across the lake. The city below her window hummed with activity, and if she did not look closely, she could almost believe that it was an ordinary day, that the Market was thriving and the streets were full of cheerful people. When she looked closely, though, she could see that Market Avenue was filled with Guildsmen lining up in rows like Warriors, that the shores by the lake were covered with brigade after brigade of trained warriors, and that the streets were empty except for messengers running on their swift little raihan from one force to another. A long line of people, molebear and carts slowly made its way up the Bridge of Ancestors, the non-fighting citizens being led away by Pasten and Lotica and Larc. Stasia wondered if Father had been forced to bribe or cajole the Heritage; the ghostly burial chambers were their domain, and they could not be pleased at the prospect of being over-run by refugees.

Stasia turned from the window and resumed her pacing. She could not fight. She could not protect Iskalon. She could not—she stopped herself mid-stride. She was tired of thinking of what she could not do. There had to be something she could do. She opened the door and saw Glace's shoulders tense.

"Don't worry, Glace. I don't intend to disobey Father. Who is left in the Palace?"

"Only you and I and your Guard," Glace replied. "The able servants and Icers have all been conscripted, and the rest of the Royal family is scattered through the city. The King is in the Council Hall with his Guard."

Stasia pursed her lips, thinking. She had thought she might at least be able to gather the servants and comfort them, or send a messenger to Larc to find out what was going on there. There truly was nothing she could do in the Palace.

Except Dream. If she had a Dream about the war, she might be able to see what the Flames were up to in the regions where scouts couldn't go. Though she could not see rapid changes in the Dream, she might get a glimpse of the Flames' strategy, to see if they were building siege engines or making explosives. If she had a Dream that could help in the war, then she would still be of some small use. "Glace, will you watch the city from my window?"

"Princess?"

"I am going to try to sleep. Perhaps if I can have a Dream about the war, I can gain some information for Iskalon. I want you to wake me if anything important happens." She could not say it, but she meant, if the cavern is breached.

"As you say, Princess."

"Glace. Will you do something more for me?"

"Anything you ask that does not contradict my duty to your Father, Princess."

"Will you please call me Stasia? And look me in the eye? Will you be my friend as you used to be?" She had wanted him to be more than a friend, before he was sent away. Now, she would settle for him to simply be open to her, rather than the stranger he had become.

He was quiet a long time, and then he looked up at her and met her eyes. "I'm not supposed to be familiar with you, Princess. I'll be reprimanded. It isn't proper."

Her heart sank, and she found herself growing angry again. She could order him to call her Stasia, but that would defeat the purpose. "Never mind," she muttered. Glace dropped his eyes again, and went to the window without another word. Stasia rolled over on her slab of ice and tried to fall asleep.

Larc

The burial chamber was so crowded that Larc could barely breathe. Children and cababar covered the floor, makeshift sickbeds lined the walls, and elderly humans wandered through the mess, confused about where they were. Six days had passed since Krevas had ordered the non-fighting citizens to retreat, and the pit alcoves to the back were beginning to fill, causing the whole cave to reek of refuse. Above, the ghostly purple glow of burial ice cast a funereal light on frightened and uncertain faces. Larc wished she could say or do something to soothe the people. A song would have provided a nice distraction, in ordinary times, but in the face of grief and suffering, singing seemed in poor taste.

Normally, the burial chambers were silent, sacred, solitary caverns. This cluster of more than fifty large chambers, the nearest to the lake, had been linked by wide tunnels, shaped by Icers more powerful than Larc, and the chambers themselves widened to accommodate nearly twenty thousand people, about a fifth of the population of Iskalon. No amount of widening could accommodate such vast numbers, and Larc resorted to drawing cold from the air and hovering above the humans in order to move through the caves. It seemed a waste of vaerce, and it was hardly polite, but war did not make politeness or distant moments of old age a priority. Her ice-armor was heavy, and she carried a leather satchel with rags and some of the medicinal fungi that aided her tasks, so she did not rise very high. She floated to the nearest wall and waited patiently while children playing a constricted game of bladderball moved even closer together to give her room. After six days without bathing or changing, their skin and leather clothing were covered in grime.

An elderly man coughed ceaselessly on his molebear hide. Larc knelt and placed her hands on his chest. T'Jas flooded into her, strengthening, reassuring. She hummed softly, a lullaby her mother often sang, soothing him as she reached deep into his chest with T'Jas. She found the source of pain and healed it, then moved quickly to the next patient, leaving the man in a quiet, deep sleep. He coughed once from that sleep, then stopped as his chest realized the pain was gone.

She went from person to person, stopping occasionally to draw more T'Jas from the icy walls, humming under her breath all the while. Each life she extended would take a little time off her life, but she hardly cared. The average Icer lived twice as long as a human, and she was willing to trade a few years so that hundreds might live today. With only ten Icers to care for several hundred infirm, many of the elderly and chronically ill had worsened. And the constant shuffle of wounded, humans and Icers both, up the tunnel from the battle caves, had only taxed the Icers further. Larc had been forced to make the decision not to heal more than one Warrior who was past her help. She knew the other Icers were just as demoralized by those painful decision as she. The cramped conditions, and limited rations, did not lift anyone's spirits.

In spite of her utter exhaustion at having T'Jas running through her almost constantly, Larc was glad that there was something she could do. Healing was her strongest ability with T'Jas. At least she had not been assigned to collapsing tunnels or shaping out new alcoves; she was hopeless at working with rock.

She was leaning over a pregnant woman, exploring her belly, when Pasten approached. The woman's child would have been a girl, but it was dead inside of her. She was shaking and moaning, and blood was seeping from between her legs and pooling on the floor around her. This was the third miscarriage Larc had seen in as many days, but it made her want to weep as much as the first had. At least she could save the woman's life; without healing, she might have bled to death. Larc placed both hands over the woman's navel.

"I've received a command from the city, Larc." Pasten looked haggard. She had not slept any less than the rest of the Icers, but it showed more strongly in her pale blue eyes.

"Have you, Princess?" Numbness washed over Larc's grief. Focus, she told herself. Her T'Jas weakened a little, and she drew more cold from the walls. Within the woman's belly, the dead child began to dissolve. The flow of blood began to staunch as Larc helped her body reabsorb the tissue. The patient stopped shaking and the horror of what was happening seemed to come alive in her eyes. "No," she whispered. She tried to sit up as her stomach sank, and Larc gently urged her to lie back while she continued the healing.

"All Icers we can spare are to report to the city. The wounded must be healed there and sent back to the lines."

Larc closed her eyes and concentrated on the healing. When it was done, she began to stand, but the woman grasped her arm. Her grip was strong, her color healthy, but her eyes were empty. "You could have at least let me bury him."

Larc almost corrected her, stopped herself just in time. She pulled the woman's hand, her grip weakening quickly, from her arm, squeezed it gently, and released it. "I'm sorry. This was better for your health. The babe is part of you again, at least."

She took a large piece of chamois from her bag and began sopping up the blood. "Any we can spare? We can spare exactly none, Princess."

"Larc." Pasten paused as if considering her words carefully. "I know the situation here as well as you. But if we do not keep the lines strong, there will be no one to protect the burial chambers, and all this will be for nothing."

Larc beckoned a hale woman who stood nearby and handed her a fresh rag with instructions to finish cleaning up and watch for complications. The patient lay quietly now, her face covered with salty tear streaks, her body shaking with grief. Larc thought of the innocent life that had lain there, killed by the caustic conditions of war. She thought of fire advancing up the tunnels into the burial chambers.

"Is there a plan for escape, Pasten?"

"We are working on a tunnel from here to the Outer Tunnels. I don't know if we will be safe there, but at least we won't be trapped."

Larc nodded. Best if it did not come to that. The Outer Tunnels were wild, and even if the Flames didn't follow them, there were other dangers, rockfalls and deadly animals, that the people of Iskalon were in no condition to face.

"I have told the other Icers. You are the last. You must go now. Take a raihan from one of the messengers at the cavern entrance; you will need to conserve your strength and vaerce. Report to Maudit's officers. They have set up triage in the Council Hall."

Larc curtsied and rose above the unusually solemn bladderball game. She tried to ignore the sounds of pain and suffering as she left them and Pasten behind and floated toward the entrance. Once she had passed through the narrow tunnel, she settled onto the ground and released T'Jas.

The main tunnel to Iskalon, intersecting several other tunnels from nearby burial chambers, was open, guarded by two Icers. Nearby, several Scribes with their pale, slender raihan awaited orders to take messages. Larc saluted the Icers, fist to heart. She turned to the nearest Scribe and asked him, apologetically, for his beast. The man was petite for a human, as most Scribes were, and he handed the raihan over courteously but with obvious reluctance. Messenger Scribes forged strong bonds with the animals they rode. Larc promised him she would send the raihan back with the next messenger.

Raihan were small and looked so delicate that Larc felt even her meager weight might crush them, but this one stood meekly while she mounted and gripped its upright blue horns. When they left the purple light of the burial ice behind and entered the long, dark tunnel to the city, Larc did not waste vaerce on an icelight; the raihan itself glowed with phosphorescence in the darkness. It glided like an Icer over the ground, swift and silent; Larc did not feel a single jolt from the rough stones of the tunnel.

Soon, the downward curving Bridge of Ancestors stood before her, towering magnificently over the lake. A heavy fog, mixed with dark smoke, hung over lake and city. The Guild houses and the top of the Council Hall stood in the fog like a thousand tiny islands. The Palace looked dark and empty. The air was chokingly stale.

Larc used T'Jas to create a bubble of oxygen over her mouth and the raihan's. They must have closed off the tunnels, sealed them against attack. Then she saw something that made her heart skip a beat. Straight across the lake, where the Fire Bridge had once floated, joining the island of Iskalon to the tunnels that lead downward, was only water. The same gaping absence loomed where the Bridge of Prosperity had floated, and the King's Bridge was gone as well. Iskalon was sealed up and cut off, ready for siege.

Larc could not help thinking about the fungal tunnels and the livestock caverns beyond the sunken bridges. How much had been harvested, how many cababar brought into the city, before it was shut off? Would she have to worry about her patients starving now, in addition to waiting too long for healing? How long before the food ran out altogether?

When she was halfway across the Bridge of Ancestors, there came a grinding sound, and the walls of Iskalon shook. It came again, and again. The Flames meant to breach the sealed-off tunnels. Surely, if they did, the lake would stop them. But Flames could float through the air just like Icers, and if they swarmed over the lake, they might gain enough ground on the island to do real damage. The sensitive raihan picked up Larc's sudden urgency and broke into a run. If there were not wounded piling up now, there soon would be.

Glace

Glace watched Stasia, sleeping peacefully on her ice slab. Her silver hair spread over the ice in waves. The thin sheets revealed every detail of her petite body. Her neck and face glowed with tiny dots of vaerce. Her breath was shallow; she was in the deep sleep of one with a head heavy with drink. When oversleep and sheer restlessness had made it difficult to drift off, she had turned to blissi. Glace was sure the Princess had drunk a lifetime supply in the last six days. She did not seem to take pleasure in it, but Glace wondered if an Icer could grow addicted to the stuff as a Warrior could, if he broke regimental law and drank.

He turned from her and resumed his watch at the window. Glint would be coming soon to relieve him for his own few hours of sleep. Six days had passed since the War Council, and the tide had not turned one way or another. The battle was still confined to the tunnels outside of Iskalon. One quarter of the army of Iskalon was in those tunnels, fighting desperately to save the Kingdom, sending messengers, wounded, and cartloads of bodies back up to the city. Glace had sent Serg Glint, the second in command of Stasia's Guard, down to the city for news, and what he learned was grim; the army was holding the invasion back, but barely. The wounded came back faster than they could send fresh Warriors out. Triage was being opened in the Council Hall, and the Warriors would be patched up and sent back to fight immediately.

From his vantage, Glace could see the training square, where new recruits were hacking at each other with practice swords in what looked to Glace to be a mockery of true fighting. At least, stuck here with Stasia, he didn't have to try to whip a bunch of rag-tag conscripts into shape. Training was his least favorite part of being a Warrior, though his superiors had always praised him for his skills. In Market Ave, under the stony gaze of Cataya, recruits deemed "ready" were being handed leather armor. The tanning Guild had been working overtime, but with wounded and casualties pouring up the tunnels, armor was suddenly in surplus. And weapons, too. Glace tried not to think of where those weapons and armor had come from. Death was always a possibility for a Warrior. Glace had lost friends in raids, in scouting missions, and to the wild Outer Tunnels. But he had never seen bodies stacked, as they were at Grimshore, where Icers froze them with heavy stones and sank them. Glace had watched each body slip under the dark waters and wondered what name it had borne, if he would recognize the Warrior's face, if he had ever crossed swords with him in the training square or marched beside him in a raid. They deserved a hero's burial, but sending the corpses up to the burial chambers would have created a panic in the people hidden there. *If we don't bury them now, will we ever have the chance? If Iskalon falls, will those corpses stay under the lake for all time?* Still, better frozen in the dark than burned.

He looked at Stasia again, and silently thanked the King for sending her to the Palace to wait out the war. Any amount of blissi she drank was better than watching her slender body, encased in ice, slide under the dark water. If she had been on the ground, seeing the bodies of the dead roll into the city by the cartload, Glace did not think he could have stopped her from joining the fighting.

A loud squealing noise of metal grinding against metal brought his attention back to the window. Across the lake, from all three bridge tunnels, Warriors were pouring into the city. The bridges were lifted so they could cross, their ancient gears protesting vocally. At first it seemed that the stream of Warriors was never ending, but when the last man was across and the bridges began to lower again, Glace's heart went cold. A retreat. A full Brigade, over a quarter of Iskalon's army of fifty thousand, had marched out six days ago. Glace could not count all the Warriors on all the bridges, but he knew that each bridge could hold about a hundred bodies in a standard-spaced march, so he could estimate the number that had crossed the Fire Bridge and triple it. The figure he came up with was less than a Regiment. Less than a quarter of the forces sent out, less than four thousand Warriors, retreating. How had so many Warriors died in six days?

Glace knew the answer, though he did not like to admit it. The Flames had a new weapon, and it changed the ability of Icers and Warriors alike to stand their ground in battle. *Fireblood*, the Flames called it. Glint had spoken to wounded Warriors who reported a thick black liquid, that burned and stayed burning on everything it touched, even water, even ice. Like molebear fat, but stronger, and explosive. Scribes had returned to the Palace on the third day, searching the Royal Library for any gold plates recording this Fireblood, any knowledge or advice on how to counter it. Glace could have told them there was nothing. He had read every plate in the library twice over. He was sure he would remember mention of such a powerful weapon.

As the incoming Warriors mingled with the fresh army, bringing carts of wounded and corpses up the street, Glace saw a few Icer Warriors by the entrances of the tunnels. They were sealing them, covering them completely. "Ancestors," he whispered. It made sense, though he could scarcely believe it. Iskalon was being sealed in solid rock. Would even that stop the Flames, with their Fireblood?

Footsteps announced a presence in the hall outside, and Glace turned away from the window. He knew it was Serg Glint before he saw him, but even so he had his hands on his weapons and his body between Stasia and the door before his second in command appeared in its frame. Glint saluted with a thick fist to his heart. His voice was hoarse and he did not look Glace in the eyes as he usually did. "Message for all staff, Captain. Our army was overrun in the tunnels and ordered to retreat. General Zental is— He's dead, Captain." The last came out in barely a whisper.

Glace kept his face straight. The General, dead in the tunnels. He could not quite feel the sadness of the news through his shock. The General dead. The army in retreat, leaderless. No, someone would have taken command, out in the tunnels. The retreat had been orderly. A Colonel or a Luten. Glace forced himself to focus. "What more?"

"They sealed the tunnels as they retreated, Captain. All the way from the battles. But some think the Flames can melt them just as fast." He left unsaid what they were both thinking: with Fireblood, the Flames probably could melt the barricades away.

"Or explode them," Glace considered out loud. "Flames like to fight with explosions and impacts. They are just as likely to hammer our walls until they collapse." Zental, dead. It meant Casser, the highest-ranking Brigad, was in charge of the army, until someone not of Royalty could be promoted.

"When I checked in at the Council Hall, his Majesty gave me a message for you. He says if the Palace looks to fall, we must get Stasia to the lake."

The Palace—fall? It seemed unthinkable. "Acknowledged. Dismissed, Glint. Let me know if anything else changes."

Glace watched the carts roll the wounded up the city streets. The air grew stale. The normal flow through the tunnels was blocked, and there would only be a little circulation coming from the burial chambers.

A high, grinding noise echoed through the vast lake cavern, followed by a tremor that shook the very walls of the Palace. Stasia woke and sat up, immediately alert. "What is it, Glace? What is going on?"

He told her, gently as he could, of Zental's death and the retreat. Her eyes went dark with sadness, but then sparked in anger. "And here I lay, helpless and useless. Sleeping my way through the war. And not a single *relevant* Dream to show for it."

"Still the burial chamber?"

"Every time. I have Dreamed of nothing else in the past six days. I don't understand it, Glace. My Dreams have always been cryptic, but this . . . If I could only go there. There must be something we missed before."

The Palace shook again, and Stasia joined Glace at the

window. "Ancestors!" she exclaimed.

Iskalon was dark, the lights of the Palace dimmed, and a low fog hung over the shore of the lake, shrouding the warriors who had stood there when last Glace looked. The bridges were all under water again, and not a light shone in a single house. Every street held a platoon or a squad.

Stasia looked scared, but she said, "Glace, I know you are going to say that Father told us to stay here, but I don't think we should stay in the Palace. If this shaking continues . . ."

"The Palace will hold," Glace assured her. The ice foundations were deep in the rock of the ceiling, and it would hold, at least until the Flames actually entered the city. "I want to be down there too, Princess."

She crowded closer, her hip brushing against his arm, and said, "Please, Glace. I don't want our last hours to be as master and servant. No one will reprimand you here. Please, just be Glace to me right now?"

He stared silently down at the darkened city and felt for her hand, slipped it into his. "Your wish is my command, Stasia."

It was a thing he had said to her jokingly, when they were young, and her sad smile told him she remembered it too. As they stood silently holding hands, watching the city prepare for a breach, Glace thought furiously.

His duty was to obey. *If the Palace looks to fall . . .* if the city was breached and burned, the flames would lick higher and higher and the Palace itself could melt. The Chraunian army would have projectiles, and their projectiles would be burning with Fireblood. If they attacked the Palace with those, the Palace would fall. It seemed inevitable. If the city fell, then the Palace would fall.

His duty was to protect. Once the walls were breached, anything could happen. He could not wait until the Palace looked to fall. If he acted at just the right moment, he might be able to save her.

"Stasia," he said softly.

"Yes, Glace?"

"Go and put on your best armor. Fill it with ice, and arm yourself with whatever weapons you can make from the ice in your bed."

He had not spoken to her like that, imperatively, since they were children, and he was surprised when she acted without questioning him. He watched the window and listened to the rustle of her websilk dress sliding to the floor, tried not to imagine what her body looked like in the dim light, standing nude beside her bed. It was a relief when she returned to his side, fully covered in thick chirsh ice armor. Ice crystals sparkled in the fibers like frost on a slink's pelt. She wore her hair down, but her small mother-of-pearl tiara adorned her forehead. Ice daggers hung around her waist like a skirt, and more ice weapons bulged in her pockets. "What do you have in mind, Glace?"

"I'll tell you when it's time, Stasia," he said. "Be ready to float us straight down to the city, at my word."

Curiosity burned in her eyes, but she did not ask any more questions. He did not want to frighten her, so he did not reveal his thoughts. When Glint came again to report, Glace quietly told him to get the rest of her guard out of the Palace. "She cannot float you all down, so best if you are on the ground. Look for us to come down from her window. If the Palace falls, everyone in it will be crushed. Do a sweep before you leave and make sure no one remains in the Palace."

After Glint left, Glace took Stasia's hand in his again, and together they waited for the final shuddering tremor that would breach Iskalon's walls.

Chapter 4

Holding Grimshore

Stasia

Stasia clung to Glace's hand as the entire cavern shook around her. She was not certain that the booms wouldn't shake the Palace right off the ceiling. Her head was still thick and muzzy with blissi. She could scarcely believe that the Flames had come so close to Iskalon. And Zental dead, along with thousands more. Glace had been vague about the numbers of Warriors returning in the retreat, but she knew that Zental would not have put himself in danger unless his forces were sorely depleted.

Stasia let the vision of a recent Dream slide over her normal vision so she could see through the fog over the lake. But what she saw with Dream-sight was the lake on a normal day, fishing skiffs littering its surface, raihan and people and molebear carts crossing bridges that now were completely underwater. She released the Dream, disturbed by the image of everyday Iskalon juxtaposed with what she knew was coming. Dreaming was proving to be completely useless. Stasia had always felt different, like she was something special because of her Dreams—Cataya Reborn, a scribe had once called her, half-jesting, until her father heard and put an end to it. But now she felt like a useless burden, a waste of space. If only Father had allowed her to lead troops, or assist Pasten.

The cavern shook again as the fog rolled back over her vision. The fog parted before a flicker of light in the tunnel where the Fire Bridge had once terminated. The tunnels had been breached.

As quickly as it had appeared, the fire faded. Stasia saw Icers hovering above the opening, concentrating intensively on resealing the breach. More Icers hovered over the other entrances, and even more waited to their sides, ready to pick off Flames as they walked through. Stasia grasped Glace's hand more tightly. Those Icers would be the first to die, if the Flames broke through.

The same bright lights flickered beyond the King's bridge, and then beyond the Bridge of Prosperity, then died as those tunnels were resealed. There had to be something Stasia could do, some way she could help fight off the Flames. She had her armor, she had a Warrior by her side. Whatever her father had ordered, she would not stand helplessly by and watch people die.

A great, echoing crack split her head and deafened her ears. Before her eyes, the entire wall of the cavern of Iskalon, as far around the lake as she could see from the window, broke apart and exploded into flame. Roaring, burning boulders hurled out of the walls and dove into the lake. Stasia realized that they were cababar on fire. The Icers by the wall had been thrown back by the explosion. Some were rising from the lake, others hovered over its surface, lifting the water high. Wave after wave washed the gaping, horizontal crack in the cavern wall. Steam billowed back out of the opening, obscuring the battle along with fog and smoke, but not before Stasia saw one Icer, and then another, and another, burst into flame in mid-air and fall back to the water.

"My hand, Stasia," Glace murmured beside her, not taking his eyes off the scene before them. Stasia looked down and realized she had dug crescents in his skin with her nails, she was gripping his hand so hard. She relaxed her grip and took a breath. She had never seen anyone die before.

"It is so pointless, Glace. They didn't have to die. Why are they doing this to us?" Tears were leaking from her eyes and she couldn't stop them, couldn't even try.

Glace put his hands on her shoulders and gently turned her to face him. His eyes were sad, but his voice was firm. "I know that you aren't used to battle, Prince—Stas. But I need you to stay strong right now. We have to be ready to get to the lake if the Palace looks to fall."

She took more deep breaths and found that she could be strong. "Yes. I can get us out of here. But the lake, Glace? Why?"

His expression grew strange and closed, and he said, "Because it will be cold." Then he turned back to the window. Stasia wondered for a moment, staring at him, afraid to look out the window again and see more people, probably people she knew, dying. And then she realized what he was trying to spare her. Iskalon could fall today. The city could burn and the Palace could melt, and there would be nowhere safe except the lake. And even that— how long could she maintain the power to keep them alive down there? She would have to sleep sometime, and then they would drown. But drowning would be better than burning.

She steeled herself and turned back to the window. The fog and steam had burned away, revealing fire and black smoke creeping across the lake. The very surface of the lake was burning, as if the water had been replaced by lava or firestone. Walking across its burning surface, marching calmly, as if there was no hurry or concern, were more Flames than Stasia had ever imagined existed. Their skin burned as they marched. The brightness pierced her eyes, blinding her. She squeezed them shut, blinking rapidly, trying to adjust. The pain and blindness and the thought of the thousands of advancing Flames roused a terrible panic she had never felt before. When she finally could see again, she almost wished she could not. She did not want to witness what was about to happen.

Thousands upon thousands of Flames poured out of the gash in Iskalon's walls. They covered the lake like fog. They were coming closer, closing in. Swimming, burning cababar came ahead of them. A black substance, thick like the bacterial slime that covered the bottom of the lake, poured out of barrels on the cababar's backs. The fire traveled on the black liquid, paving the way for the Flames, all around the lake as far as Stasia could see. Iskalon was surrounded.

"How is this possible?" Stasia demanded. "The lake is freezing cold. How are they doing this?"

"It is their Fireblood," Glace said, and he told her what Glint had reported of its properties.

Stasia did not feel any less awed by this fearsome weapon. "So they are not truly walking on the water—the Fireblood burns on the surface of the water and creates heat to give them strength to levitate across. The march is a show to terrify us. But they won't be able to float any higher—"

"Until the heat rises," Glace finished.

When that happened, the Palace would begin to melt. She grasped Glace's hand again. "We have to go now," she said.

He did not hesitate. "Yes. There is no point in staying. The rest of your Guard is directly below us."

Stasia drew T'Jas and lifted Glace and herself gently in the air, through the window and out over the city. She dropped straight down and landed in the middle of her nine other Warriors.

"The streets are thick with our fighters," Glint was yelling at Glace, to be heard over the din of marching Warriors, shouted orders and roaring flames. "It will take time to get her through on foot."

"Head for Grimshore," Glace shouted back. "It looked least thick with Flames. We'll meet you there."

Stasia rose above her guard again at Glace's direction, hurtling the two of them through the air. Grimshore was where the Fishing Guild processed its catch, the least appealing of the beaches of Iskalon, but the bank dropped away steeply a few feet into the water, and the lake was deep there. Stasia was over the stone houses of the Fishing Guildsmen, in sight of Grimshore, when something bright and hot zoomed past her ear, singeing her hair. Startled, she lost altitude, fought to regain it. "No," Glace shouted. "Get down. Fire arrows."

He was right. The short, stubby arrows flying through the air over the city wouldn't pierce skin, but they were coated with Fireblood. If the black liquid could make the lake burn, what were chirsh and ice to it? So she continued to descend and came to the ground in the middle of a surprised raid of Warriors. They were nearly attacked before Glace yelled, "Don't strike! She's a princess! We're of Iskalon!"

Stasia rested on a step of a nearby building, taking deep breaths, drawing T'Jas from her armor, while Glace talked to the Serg in charge of the raid. After a moment he came to where Stasia sat and said, "They are going to escort us to the lake. Can you go on?"

"Yes. I am tired, but I can continue. But Glace, Iskalon! What of Father? And Pasten, Larc, all of the people? How can I hide in the lake while they face this?"

"The King commands I keep you safe, Stasia. You must."

She nodded, but she was not certain. It didn't seem right that she could escape while others died, especially when she was healthy and capable of fighting, and so many others were wounded or exhausted. Still, she remembered Casser's words before the war, about how Flames treated their prisoners. She did not think she was afraid to die for Iskalon, but as a captive she would weaken her nation.

Glace took her hand, the squad surrounded them, and they headed for Grimshore. Warriors raised their shields to protect her from falling fire arrows. Looking down cross streets, she could see more Warriors marching parallel, also heading for the lake. Going to defend their home, not hide under the waters like cowards.

They were within a few blocks of the shore when a burning building toppled over right in front of them, covering the road and sending sprays of flames shooting toward them. Stasia's face grew warm and her ice armor moistened, but it held. The Warriors threw up their thick leather shields to protect her from the blast.

Glace swore loudly beside her. "We'll have to go around," he muttered.

Without warning, Flames and their human slave-warriors poured out of the burning building, coming at them in force. Glace roared and became a blur of whirling weapons, cutting down slave after slave. Stasia flung ice daggers. Most melted before they hit their targets, but she saw one Flame go down, pierced through the heart, watery blood gushing out as the dagger melted inside him. Still the other Flames kept coming, and balls of fire spun past Stasia's head. One of her protectors caught on fire and screamed as he burned. Firewhips lashed out, grabbing more of her Warriors. Stasia drew T'Jas and made a cold front; she pushed it toward the fires, trying to douse them.

"Retreat," the Serg yelled, and Glace shouted, "No! Keep fighting!"

The Warriors milled for a moment, confused by the conflicting orders. As a Captain, Glace out-ranked the Serg, but the Serg held command of the raid. The Flames took advantage of the confusion to press forward, and break the tenuous line the Warriors held. Her defense scattered, fighting the slaves one on one, and Stasia found herself alone, separated from Glace, faced by three Flames.

"Run!" Glace shouted. He stood in the middle of more slave warriors than she could count, whirling both of his long-swords so fast she could hardly see the blades. "I'll catch up!"

She stood frozen in place. Even with ice armor, she was no match for three Flames in this inferno. Glace was right. There was nothing she could do for him, she had to get to the lake and save herself. But Glace would never catch up; even if he defeated his opponents, he would be killed by the Flames as soon as she was gone.

Stasia drew a globomb from her armor. A smooth, shiny ball of ice, it looked beautiful and innocent. Then she broke one of the greatest taboos in Iskalon. She reached into Glace's mind. He could not share her thoughts in the same way that another Icer could, but she could read his thoughts, and press the shape of a thought into his mind. Hopefully it would be enough. She felt his tiredness and the pain of the small wounds he had taken, his fear for her. She pressed an image of the globomb into his mind, hoping it would come across and that he would understand.

She threw the shiny ball toward the Flames. It hit the ground halfway between her and them and rested there unbroken. She followed with three snapping iceropes before the Flames could think about it too deeply. They grinned and sent their own firewhips after her ropes. The flickering fire met the brittle ropes of ice and melted them away. Stasia backed up, keeping more iceropes coming, and the Flames followed. When they stood over the globomb, she ducked around the side of a tall stone building.

The explosion was so loud that a trickle of blood leaked from Stasia's ears and she sat down hard on the paving stones. The firewhips disappeared. Stasia did not get up for several moments; she held her ears and took deep breaths and pleaded with the Ancestors that Glace had understood what she planned. Finally she rose and peered back around the house. Nothing was standing in the street. The Flames lay dead in pools of watery blood, their fire extinguished with their lives. A few shards from the globomb were still solid sticking out of the corpses, and Stasia drew them back to her armor, blood and all. "Glace?" she called softly.

There was no response. She did not see his body among those of the Warriors who had fallen protecting her, or the Semija Warriors they had been fighting. He must have gotten her message. He had seen her intention in his mind and fled, she was sure. Stasia turned and ran down the street, around the burning building, toward the lake. She knew the streets, and though they were filled with scattered, retreating Warriors and advancing Flames, she knew the shortcuts to the lake. If Glace lived, he would meet her at Grimshore.

Larc

Larc rode in the back of a cart, bouncing against the hard leather seat as it creaked its way up Iskalon's steep hills toward the triage camps in Market Avenue. Eleven Warriors rode with her, stacked nearly on top of each other in the tiny cart, unconscious. The one she had her hands on now was barely breathing. She was trying to heal him, but the jolts of the cart kept wrenching her hands from his chest and breaking her concentration.

They rode from Grimshore, where the fighting had just broken through. All the other beaches had been overrun, and Casser—General Casser, now, she thought dully; the news of Zental's death had disheartened everyone—held Grimshore firmly. Only those who couldn't stand were being sent up to triage, and someone, perhaps one of the princesses, had espoused the idea that an Icer should go down on the carts and meet the wounded, to start healing them on the way up. It hadn't been said, but Larc understood the unspoken implication: the faster they were healed, the faster they could be turned around and sent back to the front. If she could get the

Warrior she was trying to heal moving again, he would hop off the cart and go back, perhaps to his death. The whole thing seemed futile, and Larc would have resented the rapid disappearance of her vaerce if the situation hadn't been so dire. Or if she hadn't already seen the dead piled high on carts. What was a week, a month, a year of life compared to fifty years or more for each one of these Warriors?

"Stop the cart," she yelled to the driver, loud enough to be heard over the distant explosions, the yells of commands and not-so-distant clash of weapons.

"My orders, Lady—"

"I don't give a pile of fungal fodder for your orders! You will stop this cart until he is breathing normally."

The driver muttered to himself, but he pulled on the reigns, and the two molebear came to a plodding halt, stamping their feet and swinging their shaggy heads side to side. "I trust you'll hurry, Lady. This area could come under attack. I've reports they've breached the shores in several places."

Larc did not answer, but she did hurry. She grasped the dying Warrior and pulled as much T'Jas as she could hold from her ice-armor. When he opened his eyes and took in a shuddering breath, she remembered to breathe as well.

"Go ahead," she called to the driver.

The driver yelled and cracked his whip, and the molebear started again. They seemed to be going faster than before, and hitting all the bumps deliberately. Larc continued trying to heal the Warriors, but it was impossible to focus with the jolting. She would have to wait until they reached Market and the triage tents there.

The air around Larc became oppressively hot in a matter of seconds. She turned and saw an army of Flames advancing up the street. They wore fire on their bodies like clothing, and carried long, burning whips. Larc trembled with fear. The cart was moving fast, but the Flames were faster. She watched them gain ground, and it was as if time had slowed down but she had frozen stiff. They were three houses back, then two, then one, then they had passed the edge of the nearest lawn, a river of fire pouring up the street, lapping at the cart. She yelled to the driver to hurry, but there was no response.

The air around her burst into flame. The cart jolted to a halt and she fell to the bottom. The Warrior she had just stabilized fell on top of her. She did not move, but huddled underneath him, his body a slim protection as fire enveloped the cart. She squeezed her eyes shut, blinded by the fires, and listened intently, trying to deduce what was happening by sound alone.

After a time, all she could hear were distant sounds of battle. The voices and the roar of flames surrounding the cart seemed to have died away. Everything was hot, but her ice armor still held. It was sodden, but cold.

She gently lifted the Warrior off her chest. The others lay still in the bottom of the cart. Terrified, Larc poked her head over the edge of the cart and looked into the street.

It was empty. The Flames had moved on, leaving the wounded to die. All around, houses and buildings were burning. Someone's garden lay in ashes just beyond the rim of the cart.

"Let's go," Larc said. "They're gone."

The driver did not answer. Larc peered forward—and leaned over the side and retched a stream of slimy bile. The driver was a pile of charred bones on the cart seat. The molebear were no more than heaps of cinders, though the harnesses, made of metal, still protruded from the cart.

Larc tried to spit the bitterness out of her mouth and slumped back to the bottom of the cart. She was numb and tired. She should be healing the wounded. That was what she was doing, healing the wounded as they came back from the battlefield. Healing them so they could go back and die. I'm in shock, Larc thought to herself. I need to heal myself, first. But she could not seem to move. Her limbs didn't want to work. You're just tired, she told herself. Move. She drew T'Jas and tried to heal her own shock away. But T'Jas was as stubborn and immovable as her limbs.

Stasia . . .

Why did I think of Stasia? Larc wondered. She is safe in the Palace.

"Stasia!"

It wasn't a thought, it was a real voice, calling to Stasia. Glace's voice. He was running past the cart. His blonde hair was dark with soot. His armor was cut in places, and dark circles hung around his eyes. Why was his face covered with blood? "Stasia!"

"Glace!" The familiar face intruded into Larc's shock and she stood shakily in the cart. "Glace! It's Larc!"

He stopped at the edge of the cart and turned, looking up in surprise. "Larc! Come with me! You have to help me find Stasia. We have to reach the lake."

"Stasia is in the Palace," Larc said. Her brain was sluggish. "Why aren't you there, guarding her?"

Glace looked at her strangely, and he said, "Larc, you must come with me. I don't have time to explain. I will get you to the lake, too."

"I have to stay and heal these people," Larc said. "That is what I'm doing, healing Warriors so they can go die."

Glace looked over the sides of the cart and cursed. "They are dead. Can't you see that?"

"Dead? No, they are only wounded, Glace. They can't be dead. I have to—"

Suddenly he was at the edge of the cart, reaching for her. She felt her body lifted into the air and flung over his shoulder. "Glace! What, by the Ancestors—"

"No time for this," Glace gasped. "Taking you to the lake. You're in shock."

"I know that!" Larc kicked and tried again to draw T'Jas from her armor. It slipped away like water between her fingers. Glace began to run, and her cheek bounced against his broad back. She pounded him with her fists, but he did not pause. She was more and more ill as the ground, littered with corpses, sped by beneath her eyes.

Stasia

Stasia stood on Grimshore and looked out across Lake Lentok, watching the normally still waters ablaze with fire and Flames. She drew cold from the icy depths, drinking in T'Jas, filling her reserves. The smooth, slimy stone was littered with fish guts and bones. She was surrounded by Icers and Warriors. The pocket of fighters held a small section of the shore, and continued to hold it, though the city burned behind them and the lake blazed before them. A few others, like Stasia, had made it to this haven; she had seen Icers replenish their T'Jas and join the ranks, and she had seen wounded pulled to safety under the surface.

"Ranks, stand!" The strong command came down the line. Stasia thought it was Casser's voice, but she wasn't sure—the roaring fires on the lake and the falling, exploding buildings behind, and the clash of weapons as warriors fought to protect the shore from the Flames in the city, obscured all other sounds. Stasia stood her ground along with the rest. Surely Glace would make it through the battle in the city and find her here, but until he did she would wait, and help hold the shore.

"Wave!" It *was* Casser up there, issuing commands. Stasia thrust her hands out, pouring T'Jas into the lake, pulling the water up. Up and down the ranks, other Icers were doing the same. A wall of water rose high above them, obscuring the Flames.

"Release!" Casser's command was echoed around the shoreline. As one, the Icers let the wave roll back, pouring thousands of tons of freezing water onto the Flames.

When the wave finally fell and the surface of the lake reappeared, the fires had darkened. Stasia felt a moment of relief, though she knew it was temporary. Her eyes welcomed the rest from the piercing light.

Then Lake Lentok was ablaze again, suddenly, furiously. Dark, dead bodies of Flames, drowned as their fires were doused by the ice-cold water, rose and burned. Pockets of Fireblood re-ignited under water, exploding into steam. Once again, a wave of fire and Flames rolled forth from the gap in the walls of the cavern.

These Flames carried fire arrows, and they shot a volley of them, not into the city to burn the houses as they had before, but straight at the force of Warriors protecting the shore. Before the arrows had landed, Casser's mind entered Stasia's with force. *On three count, send a barrier of cold air above the shoreline.* Just as quickly, he was gone from her mind. Stasia prepared her T'Jas to cool the nearby air. As she made it dense and hard enough to repel the missiles, the Icers around her did the same. The missiles hit the barrier and fell to the lake, igniting it in more fiery explosions. At the same time, the Flames advanced across the lake, pushing the cold air back, shoving their heat forward in an invisible wrestling match.

The heat became too much. Stasia felt the cold suddenly pushed back into her body, as the Flames marched forward, onto the shore. Stasia struggled to hold her ground, but the heat forced her back. All along the shore, the army was retreating back a few steps. The barrage of fireballs began again, and the houses behind them erupted into fire. Smoke rose toward the Palace. Two Flames opposite Stasia came forward eagerly, raising their hands, ready to incinerate her.

Stasia drew upon the cold in her ice armor and hurled an icy blast of air at the Flames. It doused their fire and disabled their lava, turning it to solid rock that cracked and fell away from their skin in bloody chunks. The Flames reacted without hesitation, drawing on the heat from the flaming lake to blow away the fog that shrouded her. The heat from their blast only caused the ice to create more fog, and Stasia, still drawing on the cold of the pockets of water that remained of her armor, pushed forward her own icy front. It held their heat away from her body, between her and the Flames. Stasia pushed as hard as she could, knowing that one more blast of heat would evaporate her water and start the chirsh smoldering.

Her cold front slid back a hair. The heat crept closer. She was no match for two Flames with plenty of heat to draw upon. She slipped further. She could not get to the lake. She thought of Glace. Had he survived the city? Would he find her body here on the shore?

The heat was moving faster. It was inches from her now. Her mind ticked off the seconds before her armor would burn away and the heat would sear her bare body.

A silver blade flashed red in the light of the fire and plunged into the neck of one of the Flames. Blood spurted from the wound, splattering Stasia and landing in the slimy mud at her feet. A huge, spiky mace swung out on its chain and smashed in the skull of the other, sending a spray of blood, brain and bits of skull everywhere. The pressure and heat faded for a moment. "Retreat, Glace!" Stasia screamed. He had saved her life; now his would be forfeit when another pair of Flames closed the gap. Already, more were stepping forward. Stasia used the moment to reach for the Palace and draw cold from the very ice that hung over her head. She was not alone; all down the shore cold settled over the ranks. Cold pressed against her back.

"Stasia? But you are safe in the Palace." Larc's voice, strained and tired. Stasia held her ground. She was in the front rank; for her to retreat now would weaken the force, break the lines and let the Flames through. "Larc, get out of here." Her friend had served her year of conscription, but she was a terrible Warrior. From the feel of the cold behind her, Stasia guessed that her friend's ice armor was melted too. "Both of you, retreat. Find another place on the lake to get under."

"I have to heal the wounded, Stasia." That did not begin to make sense. How was Larc even here? She should be with Pasten and Lotica, in the burial chambers.

"I swore an oath to protect you," Glace said. "If you will not come, I must carry you." She felt his strong hands on her shoulders.

"Don't," she hissed. "If I release my cold, they may incinerate us all."

"The city," Larc said softly. "Oh, Ancestors, look at the city, Stasia."

She turned for a brief moment, holding her cold front tightly before her. The Flames crept closer. Behind, the city was burning. Not just a building here or there—the whole city. Smoke filled the air; Stasia spared a trickle of T'Jas to keep the air clear around their heads so that she and Larc and Glace would not be smothered. The Council Hall on the hill was a font of flame. Glowing ashes drifted up, racing the sparks to the Palace. "Father," she whispered.

She could do nothing for him or her sisters, trapped between the advancing Flames and the burning city. Already, heat was bearing down from behind. The ranks behind her had turned, and now their forces were divided between the onslaught and the fire. Glace and Larc would die with her. Her skin prickled, thinking of Pasten and all of the defenseless people in the burial caves. When the city was destroyed, would they be taken as slaves, or merely slaughtered?

Casser's voice entered her mind again, commanding and reassuring. *Reach past the fire, into the lake. Raise a wave and sink them. Don't do this unless you can maintain your cold front.*

Stasia did not hesitate. It was difficult, to divide her forces between keeping the air cold and hard before her and reaching with T'Jas into the lake, but she could do it. The hardest part was getting past the flaming surface, but she did that with a will, pouring her T'Jas in. She could feel a few others down the line joining her in the water, but they were not many. Casser was one, she was sure. Larc was helping with the cold front, using her relatively meager power to add just enough to make a difference. Glace crowded close behind her, ready to rush forward if the cold front broke. He would die first, unless she could stop it from happening.

The dark waters of the lake swelled up from the very depths. Stasia felt as if every molecule in her body was water. She pulled, drawing the water up toward the fire, up through the Flames. When the wave broke, it flung fire and Flames high in the air. The Flames on the shore continued to maintain their front, but those on the water behind them sank. Some did not resurface, and some sank and rose again, bobbing lifelessly in the current, but some shot up, thrashing in the swell, drawing power from the fire on the lake. Firestone would have waterlogged and sunk long ago, but the black liquid floated, and the water could not disperse it. Stasia's cold was fading, and with it T'Jas. She barely had the strength for another wave, and if she did not, neither would the rest of the ranks.

Casser must have realized the same, because his command was less reassuring this time. *Retreat,* came the thought. *Move in an orderly way, and keep the Flames distant. Retreat to the foot of the Bridge of Ancestors.*

Just like that, the city had been given over to the Flames. In spite of Casser's command, the organized line at the lake turned into a chaotic stampede. Screams and shouts from the Warriors at the city front burned in Stasia's ears; she knew distantly that they were being pushed into the Flames they fought by the retreating Warriors from the lake front. Stasia was jostled and pushed as the army rushed to get out of the way of the Flames on the water. Glace came near, protecting her and Larc from wildly swinging weapons with his shield. *The lake,* Stasia thought. *We have to get into the lake. It is the only hope.* In what seemed like no time at all, Stasia stood alone on the shore, with only Glace and Larc beside her, facing a line of Flames. Heat rushed in, pushing away her cold front.

The Flame before her sent a wave of fire hurtling toward her body. She screamed as it flash-incinerated her wet armor, leaving her skin red and bare. Her T'Jas faded completely. Glace rushed forward, both swords drawn, a knife in his teeth. The Flame flicked a wrist, and the huge Warrior was flung back. Stasia heard a crunching sound like broken bones. The last of her cold gone, Stasia choked on the overwhelming smoke in the cavern. The Flame raised a hand high above his head, fire on his fingertips pointed down at her eyes, and Stasia turned to run.

"That's one of the Princesses! Take her alive!" Another Flame joined the one about to deliver the killing blow.

"How can you tell, Serg?" Stasia felt fire on her feet, around her ankles—they had lashed out at her with a fire whip. It wrapped itself around her shins and tripped her up. As she fell, rolling onto her back, trying to break the fall with her hands, she saw Larc watching helplessly. Her friend was red, her armor half burned away, her thick hair charred and smoking. Stasia's stomach churned as the firewhip pulled her over the slimy shore toward the Flames.

"The tiara, hippole-brain."

"Anyone can wear a tiara. How do we know she's really a princess?"

"The silver hair and the eyes match the sketches. Take her back over the lake. See that no harm comes to her until she's safe in Chraun."

"Yes, Serg."

How did they know what she looked like? The thought was distant and confused. The firewhip wound around her ankles, and the Flame scooped her up and put her over his shoulder. Her flesh scorched by the burning black stuff and the lava mesh coating the Flame's body, her brain smoldering with heat, Stasia was dimly aware of Larc screaming behind her. She thought she heard Casser's voice.

"Get to the lake," she tried to shout, but it came out in a muffled whimper against the Flame's back. So hot. Stasia struggled to think through the haze of heat and pain. She thought of Casser's warning, that as a prisoner she could be used against her father. Was Father even alive still? Her sisters, she would be used against her sisters. Pain, digging into her skin, penetrating to the bone. They would enter her mind. Everything she knew about Iskalon would be theirs.

No. There was one way to fight. Stasia could die, and her secrets would die with her.

The decision terrified the part of her that wanted to live, but it was fading, overwhelmed by agony. Just a little more pain, and then death would bring cold relief. Stasia placed her hands against the Flame's lower back and the nerves were seared off her fingertips. She heard the crinkle of burning flesh, felt the lava digging into her. As she had been taught long ago, she began to pull the heat from his fire, from his lava, from his very body. All Icers could draw heat as they could cold; to draw heat meant pain instead of T'Jas; to draw too much meant death.

The Flame shouted and tried to throw her down. Stasia gripped his flesh with white knuckles, pulling more and more heat. The burning black ooze snuffed out on his skin, sprang to life where it coated hers. She saw the lava on his back go dim and solidify into rock. Rock cracked apart into thousands of bloody pieces and crumbled to the floor of the cavern. Still she held on.

Her body blazed with fire. The distant part of her mind that could still think was sure she should be dead by now. Thought faded, replaced by fear, anguish, white-hot rage, then surrender. The Flame dislodged her; the hard ground caught her. She did not feel it. She was beyond feeling anything but fire.

The heat did not stop coming. T'Jas filled her core. Not soothing, gentle, cold T'Jas. Ruinous, angry, hot T'Jas. It burned her away as it filled her up. Her veins ran with lava, her bones smoked, her flesh was molten. There was only heat and pain. T'Jas kept her alive, but the pain—the pain built until it exploded and there was nothing left of Stasia but fire.

Larc

"Stasia!" Larc screamed, as she saw Stasia fall to the ground burning. The Flame clawed at his lava, chilled and vulnerable. Her friend's skin began to blacken and split, angry red lines opening on her back. Stasia was burning to death before her eyes, burning up. Soon she would be ash. Larc stopped screaming and tried to think. Flames swarmed past her, ignoring her; scorched and down, she was no threat; they would pick her off later. They were taking the city. Iskalon was falling behind her, and her friend was dying in front of her. What could she do? She didn't know how to fight. Even if she did, her armor was gone. There was no cold she could draw from. She experienced an overwhelming sense of failure. In the moment when her friend and her kingdom needed her most, she had succumbed to shock.

"Heal her!" a voice shouted in her ear, and for a moment it didn't register. Then a wave rose from the lake and doused Stasia and the Flame with cold water. The Flame, his lava already hardening, cursed and spluttered. Stasia lay still on the ground. Was she unconscious, or dead?

Prince Casser pushed past Larc, a blessed breath of cold amidst the hot press of Flames and fire in the great cavern. He still wore his ice armor, but it was soggy with melt. He flung a knife of ice into the Flame, finishing him. Blood welled from the wound, but the dagger did not melt all the way, and the Prince withdrew it, tossed it to Larc. He knelt by Stasia. "Quickly! Help me heal her. We must get her to safety."

The little bit of cold spurred Larc to action. She drew

T'Jas deeply and rushed to Stasia's side. The Flames were gone from the shore; they were all in the city now. Larc did not look toward the burning buildings, tried not to hear the screams. She thought of the burial chambers and the people trapped there. Had Pasten ever finished her passage to the Outer Tunnels?

"She's too hot to touch. Melt it all!" Casser snarled. Larc reached toward her, hoping to at least determine if she lived, but the Prince was right. The heat in her body nearly burned Larc's hand, and she withdrew sharply. The little bit of cold she had began to melt and fade.

Casser was looking toward the far shore of the lake. Larc followed his gaze. For now, at least, no Flames were coming from that direction. They were all in the city. "Go heal Glace instead, Larc. We need a human to carry her. Hurry."

Larc scurried to obey. At least there was something she could do. Glace was unconscious, and several of his bones were shattered. Exhausted as she was, Larc was able to knit the bones, soothe the pain, and give Glace the strength to wake. "Stasia," the huge Warrior asked as his blue eyes flickered open. Larc helped him to his feet. They both turned to the shore, where Casser stood over his niece's body, still watching the other side of the lake.

"Does she live?" Glace asked.

"No time," Casser muttered, shifting his gaze to the city. "There is another wave of Flames approaching. We have to get out before my armor is melted away. Glace, you must carry her. She's boiling with heat." Glace scooped Stasia up in his arms, wincing. The heat would not make him ill like it would Casser or Larc, but it could not be comfortable. Stasia did not stir. "Stay close. Breathe as little as possible. Larc, do you still have some cold?"

"Yes, Majesty."

"Then use it to make us an airshield. Squeeze my hand twice if it falters. Once we are below, you can draw cold from the water. I must conserve my strength for the tunneling."

Larc took Glace's free hand, then Casser's. Together they followed Casser into the lake. All along the shore, others were fleeing for the lake, diving under just like she was. Some of them were Icers, and would survive. Others were humans who would likely drown, unless the Icers joined them. Some were on fire, screaming. Just before Larc's head fell below the surface, she saw more Flames approaching across the fiery water.

Under the surface of Lentok, everything was dark. Larc formed an air bubble around their faces. It took every bit of strength she could muster. Glace's hand was rough and heavy, Casser's smooth, his grip firm. Glace held Stasia in his other arm. Was it Stasia he held, or her corpse? Larc could not be sure. The older Icer led, though Larc didn't know how he could tell where he was going in the murky darkness. Casser made an icelight, but close as she was Larc could barely see it through water thick with ashes, mud and blood. A ripple pushed against her air bubbles, and a corpse drifted down toward them. Larc pulled Glace closer to avoid it. She couldn't tell if it was a comrade or a Flame.

After what seemed like hours, they reached the other side, a vertical rock wall that contained the lake. Casser drew them to the surface and helped first Larc and then Glace, still heavy with Stasia's body, onto a tiny stone ledge above the water. There were no Flames in their immediate vicinity, but Larc could smell the smoke from their fire coming off the lake.

"She's breathing," Glace whispered, amazed. Her body blazed with heat, even after being immersed in the cold water. Larc still could not bear to touch her.

"We'll make for the Outer Tunnels," Casser said. "There is some cold there, and likely no Flames."

"No," Glace said. He sounded bone-weary. Larc could hear her own loss reflected in his voice. Even if she still breathed, Stasia could not last long. Not with all that heat.

She would try to heal her, but no Icer could withstand what Stasia had taken in. "There is another place. A better place."

Larc felt like sobbing. She looked out over the lake, and saw the city burning. She should have been able to see the top of the Council Hall from here, but it was not there. She did not know how Glace could speak without crying. But when he spoke again, his voice was strong and steady as ever. "A burial chamber."

Great chunks of ice, wings and rooms and balconies of the Palace, began to fall from the ceiling, crushing what few buildings remained standing, creating huge waves where they landed in the lake. A little wake stirred against the shore at Larc's feet. Casser began to tunnel into the rock wall at Glace's direction.

Iskalon had fallen.

Part 2 ~ Exile

After the torchlight red on sweaty faces
After the frosty silence in the gardens
After the agony in stony places . . .

The Waste Land, T. S. Eliot

Interlude

Khell, Seventeen Summers Prior

Maia

Maia ran over ice, its sharp coldness digging into her feet. Her doal-hide moccasins, made for scampering around the summer camp, were wearing thin. Her furs no longer felt warm; she had been too long without shelter or a fire. Her stomach writhed with hunger like the windblown clouds above.

The clouds were gray, almost black, threatening a storm. The storms rolled off the water over the endless ice plain all summer. If hunger didn't kill her, the storm could, with its piercing cold winds and sharp flakes of ice-snow. The ice was dense under her feet, but a mountain range rose ahead. If she could reach it, she could burrow into the soft snow on its flanks and live. If she did not collapse from exhaustion first.

She ran over ice, images flashing through her mind. Dhuciri, reaching toward Grandmother with long pale fingers. The camp in disarray, the people in a long line before the dark birds. Dust like ash covering every surface. Everything and everyone she had ever known, gone. She was really, truly alone, on the vast sheet of ice.

Alone, but alive. The wind blew to her back, from the water, not the mountains. A summer storm. A winter storm would have killed her. She ran on.

The way grew steep, and snow began to collapse under her feet just as the first flakes of ice fell from the sky. She had reached the mountains. She stared out at the plain for a moment, gasping for air. The snow looked dirty to her, like the dust of her tribe had been swept up by the wind and carried here to haunt her. She turned and scraped at the snow with raw, cold hands. She burrowed far below the surface, escaping the storm.

In her constricting snow cave, she pulled out the pouch and felt its contents. Ten finger bones lay huddled together within the soft leather. Some were rough, others smooth. They were different lengths, some long and skinny, some short and stout. She considered trying to eat one, and decided against it. Grandmother had trusted her with them. They were sacred. Hungry as she was, she could not eat them.

Instead, she dug further into the snow. Her hands were bleeding and cracked, but she found bare rock within a few feet, supporting tiny patches of frozen lichen. She knew they would not keep her alive, but they eased the cramping in her belly when she chewed them up and choked them down.

The storm passed. Maia stood on the ice again, blinking in the blinding sun, staring at the mountains, wondering if it would be better to scale them or keep to the plain. She needed meat desperately.

What had Grandmother said about the mountains? The summer storms blew in from the Stormbirth Waters, and in the summer, the far side of the mountains sheltered great flocks of gwenwing and wild doal and even inland boareal. If she could cross the mountains, she might find something there she could kill and eat. She set her feet on the slopes and tried to stomp out stairs. The snow was too soft, and she floundered. She could not keep above the snow pack, and she was too weak and hungry to swim though it. She had no choice but to continue on the plain, walking beneath the mountain ridge. Perhaps she could find a low pass or another tribe's trail.

It was difficult to walk. Her moccasins, made for scampering around camp, not long treks, were worn through. Her feet were swollen and black, and she could not feel her toes. The sun pierced her *with its brilliance. The mountains never changed, no matter how long she walked. The sun set and she walked on through the dark. It was too cold to stop moving. She walked under twinkling stars until black turned to grey and grey turned to blue and blue turned to all-encompassing white.*

Maia's gait grew slower and slower. Her feet and legs grew so tired that they could no longer hold her up and she fell to her hands and knees and crawled over the ice. Then her knees and arms gave out and she collapsed on the ice and died.

Death brought blackness and an eternal stillness. The stillness was broken by strange noises, a shuffling and scraping like hides over ice. Blackness faded and she saw the long, slobbery snout of a giant boareal snuffling toward her. Its razor-tusks flashed inches from her face. She was not afraid, because she was dead. They were spirit boareal, coming to take her home.

The tusks passed by her, and a human face looked into hers. She was flung across the boareal's huge, bristly back, covered in warm furs, rubbed with snow, taken into tent-like traveling egla, fed hot broth and warmed by a fire.

"I am Hakua of the Liathua Khell," said a smiling young face. "What is your name?"

"I was Maia, of the Nuambe Khell. Now I have no tribe."

"But Maia means Lost One," Hakua said. "You are no longer lost. You are welcome to live among us, if you like."

Then a large man pulled Hakua out of the egla, away from Maia. "Don't speak with the prisoner, Hakua. She will save one of us from the Dhuciri tithing, but you must not grow attached."

Chapter 5

Whispers of Treason

Dynat

Success, the Fire Spirit whispered into Dynat's mind. Its face shone clearly, all of its features flames, eyes glowing red hot like lava. *Successsss,* the flames of its lips hissed. Dynat basked in that voice, sank into the heat. He could almost see the Lava Lake beyond the burning ears.

" . . . Complete success," Medoc said, snapping Dynat out of his trance. The General stood stiffly in clean steel armor, his lava mesh glowing in sharp hexagonal patterns. "The lair of the Ice fairies belongs to us, Majesty."

"That is not entirely true, My King." Bolv's eyes shone with glory and anger, nearly as bright as her feathery lava mesh. "Many of the Icers and their humans fled the city through the lake. They hide in the Outer Tunnels. It will take time to gather them up."

"We must find them," Dynat said. "They will scratch away at us until we bleed." So the Fire Spirit whispered to him, and he knew it to be true. "What of the prisoners? Have we the Princesses?"

"They await questioning in the Pit Dungeon," Medoc

said.

Gooood . . .

"Good. And they have not been questioned yet?"

"We have been organizing the prisoners, and counting our own dead." Medoc sounded tense. Perhaps he needed a rest, a time spent in the baths. "I did not think them an urgent matter."

Dynat stood, considering the forest of stalas that led to the entrance of his throne cavern. "You both have worked hard, winning this war. You will have until tomorrow to rest in the baths. I will handle our special prisoners. I do not want them questioned by anyone but myself."

This was the Fire Spirit's command as well, and it was odd—Dynat had never questioned prisoners. The army had Officers trained to interrogate. Even if the information were sensitive, Bolv would be assigned the task. Indeed, Bolv was looking at him strangely now. But the Fire Spirit was explicit in his hissing voice. No one except Dynat was to speak with the Princesses.

"I will relay the order, Majesty."

"Good. Go. You have both earned a respite."

Medoc saluted stiffly and marched out of Dynat's presence. Dynat's Kinyara gave him a wry look, then turned on the pointed metal heel of her shoe and swayed away. The Prince of Flames watched her hips swing as she left his presence.

She isn't here, the Fire Spirit whispered in Dynat's mind. *Find her.*

Dynat brushed the words away and tried to focus on the dim, circular pit before him. Only nine princesses huddled there beneath his stone ledge. The air simmered with heat, and lava trickled down the wall at Dynat's back. The heat would keep the prisoners from using their powers, and break their spirits, making questioning easy. Several of them seemed dead already, fainted or swooning on the sharp, hot rocks that lined the pit. Swirls of steam rose in several places where some had vomited. A few were still coherent enough to look up and glare hatred at Dynat. Each wore a slim tiara that glittered in the dim light.

Their skin was bright red. They were bigger and more sturdy than Dynat had imagined Icers would be, though still much smaller than any Flame Dynat had ever met. The nearest one opened her eyes, and they were deep silvery blue, bright and moist, beautiful and fascinating. She pushed back wilted pale hair, and pierced Dynat with accusing eyes.

Something deep within Dynat flickered and tried to feel a long forgotten emotion. Sorrow, guilt, remorse, and empathy paraded like shadows against the back of his brain. They flickered once, twice, three times and guttered out, dead flames leaving not even soot, swept away by the rush of voices that coalesced into one, the Fire Spirit. He burned with a fury in Dynat's head, whispering until Dynat thought he would go mad. *Where is sssshhhheeeeee? Where is the Dreamer?*

Dynat spoke to one of the guards manning the pit. "There were supposed to be thirteen of them."

"Yes, Majesty. We recovered three tiaras on bodies in the wreckage. We assume they were killed in the chaos. One princess appears to be missing."

"I see," Dynat said slowly, struggling to contain the fury of the Fire Spirit. "Bring the tiaras. We shall try to see who escaped our net."

It had been a simple command, had it not? Destroy Iskalon and capture all thirteen princesses alive. Dynat knelt carefully by the edge of the pit. The pale haired one who had been glaring raised her hands in the air in an imploring gesture. Her face, which another Icer might once have considered beautiful, was pinched in pain and dripping sweat. "Please, Fire King. Do what you will with us. But our people have done you no wrong. Have mercy on them."

Mercy? Mercy? We will show them mercy. The Fire Spirit ranted in the back of Dynat's head, making it hard to hear her faint voice. *Find the Dreamer. Kill them all. Kill them all. Kill . . .* Dynat struggled to focus as he looked into her silvery eyes. "What is your name, little ice fairy?"

"Pasten, Fire King." Her arms drooped to her sides, but she continued to look up at him.

Three more Flames entered, each carrying a large basket woven of jewelsnake skin. They set these down above the pit, and took off the lids. "Look closely, Princess Pasten," Dynat said. "Do you recognize what you see?"

All three Flames held their hands over the baskets, and a jumble of charred bones rose from each. The princess looked confused. When the blackened skulls, still decorated with sooty gilt tiaras, rose into the air, recognition glinted in her eyes, and she squeezed them closed, determined to see no more. Steamy tears rolled down her cheeks and a sob escaped her lips. Another princess, with a bosom to rival a Flame Lady's chest, her tiara in her hand, put her arms around the writhing Icer's shoulders.

"What is your name?" Dynat asked.

"I am Maudit, Queen of Iskalon." This one had more strength in her voice, and more meat on her bones. "What do you want from us?"

Dynat gestured toward the pit. "Bring the pale-haired one."

Needing no further instruction, one of his Flames reached in with T'Jas, and out drifted Princess Pasten, until she hung limply in the air before Dynat.

"Watch closely, Queen of fairies," Dynat said. "This will continue until you answer my questions."

He made a firewhip from the heat in the room and let it travel through the air and wrap itself around Pasten. Her face was red and clenched, her lips pressed together firmly. Without warning she spat into the air between them. The glob of spittle fell far short of his feet. Dynat's impulse was to chuckle at her anger, but the Fire Spirit blazed alive suddenly in his chest. The instruction was clear, and Dynat wasn't sure if it was he who poured the heat into the princess or the Fire Spirit working through him.

Her scream had a musical quality, horrible as it was. She writhed and choked. Dynat heated her further. She made a retching noise that was completely unmusical and vomited all over herself. Dynat felt as though he hung in midair, suspended between great anger and not caring. He did not feel the anger that he acted on, merely observed it from a distance. Maudit and the other princesses shouted and pleaded for him to stop.

The Fire Spirit went silent and the flames subsided from Dynat's mind. The princess's eyes closed, as though she was losing her grip on consciousness. He pulled the heat back out slowly, and let her fall flailing to the ground, by the rim of the pit.

"Maudit," he said, as Pasten ceased thrashing and lay gazing in quiet disgust at the vomit under her cheek. "There are nine of you here, and three tiaras which you surely recognize. Who is the Dreamer? Is it one of you? One of those dead? Or is it the missing princess? Tell me, or her torture will continue."

"Stasia," Maudit spat out. "Ancestors send she is safe. You will freeze for this, chirat dung. Burning chirat dung. Smoldering, rotting fish carcass. . ."

Dynat could not hear the rest of her curses because the Fire Spirit began whispering, low and solemn, almost like a breath of air through his head. *Stasia, Stasia, Stasia* . . . Dynat struggled to focus. He forced a smile at Maudit.

"And who will freeze me, little Ice Fairy? Your father's charred bones at the bottom of your lake? Those baskets, there? Stasia the Dreamer, who somehow has escaped my Flames? Or you? Do you have some ice hidden away in your pocket?"

She fell silent and looked away. Dynat nodded curtly toward the pit. The Fire Spirit continued to whisper *Stasia* over and over in his head. Dynat felt that he would go mad if the voice continued. He must not doubt the Fire Spirit. It had led him to victory. This Stasia must be an important part of his victory. He would find her.

As his Flames lowered the burned Princess back into the pit, Dynat barked an order at the highest ranked among them. "Roust Medoc from the baths. He is to attend me in the Throne Room immediately."

The Flame bowed low and said, "Yes, Majesty."

Dynat glared at the pit. The constant whispering was building a pressure in his head, and he felt like he might explode. A simple command, and they had botched it. The Dreamer had slipped through his fingers. Someone would pay.

Medoc

Medoc lay in a pool of soft, hot water, feeling the tickle of bubbles against the hairs on his skin. At the far end of the pool, a Semija played a soft rhythm on a tanka drum, a sound like dripping water. As he laid his head back on the cushioned ledge, another Semija placed something in his mouth. It was juicy, salty and crunchy when he bit through tiny bones—a stuffed flat, flash-roasted. He closed his eyes and tried to give himself over to the pleasure of decadency. Yet another Semija leaned over and wiped Medoc's chin with a soft piece of hide.

The pool was crowded, full of the most beautiful young Ladies the Kingdom had to offer. They lounged nearby with sharp eyes, ready to swim over and wait on him, subservient as a Semija. Though Medoc was married, it was not uncommon for someone of his power and wealth to take a mistress, or even a second wife. Medoc had no desire for it; the first wife was trouble enough. His duties left him little time for dallying. Still, he let them stay; it would have been impolite to ask them to leave. They might wait on him like Semija, but they were the daughters of the most powerful noble houses in Chraun. It would not do to offend them.

Normally the bath was a sheltering space, and he could shut off his mind for a time, let the drumming and the heat take away his inner fury of thoughts and feelings. This time, that peace would simply not come. He gestured for the oldest Lady, a widow with thin, arched eyebrows, and she came quickly to his side. He sat upright on the padded ledge under the water and let her slip behind him. Her fingers were warm and experienced, and her T'Jas strong as she healed his aches and pains. Still, she could not heal away the turmoil running through his mind, and he sent her back to the other ladies after a time. She took the rejection gracefully, masking her disappointment under a tight smile.

Medoc had done as ordered, and razed Iskalon for his King. The mission had been more than successful; their lake was still on fire, their great Palace melted away, and their city destroyed. Sure, a few thousand Icers and their humans had escaped, but they would be scraped away in time. In fact, it was almost a boon to have them; the Flames would have something to ease their restlessness in times to come, once the glory of this battle had worn thin. No, Medoc had done better than might have been expected. So why did he have this grim feeling, a tightness in his stomach, a sense of urgency that would not let him relax?

He thought of the enormous task of counting and identifying the dead. He had lost men, a lot of good men. And women, several of the few who served in the army. He saw in his mind the great, horrible wave sweeping over the lake, slamming against the T'Jas shield bubble he stood under as he commanded the battle. He imagined sinking under the icy, dark water, feeling his lava harden, feeling the cold leech T'Jas from his very body, unable to create a breathing shield, choking and suffocating to death. Medoc had once watched a Semija drowned in the baths for a

Flame Lord's pleasure; the man had struggled mightily. Would Medoc have struggled to reach the surface, or would he have merely sunk like a stone?

Many of the bodies of his Flames had floated, later to be scooped out with the Icer's nets and carried back down the tunnels to be consecrated in the lava river. Yet even more must have sunk; there were still hundreds of Warriors unaccounted for. Chraun did not have the means to dredge the lake, and so they would never receive proper consecration in the Lava River. Medoc had grieved as befitting his station; he had shed tears of fire, and thrown in firedrops and rubies after the bodies as the lava rushed up to meet them, and prayed to the Fire Spirit to shelter their souls in the Lava Lake. His Warriors had merited grief, and he had given it.

There was no reason to dwell upon the matter now. But the numbers kept swirling back into his mind. Two thousand Flames unaccounted for or consecrated, a full quarter of his army. Two thousand good men and women, some young, others experienced officers, many of whom Medoc knew by face if not by name. Another five hundred would die soon of exhaustion, their life force battled away through T'Jas use. The Semija losses were not as personal, but just as staggering—more than twenty thousand gone. It was a small percentage of the over-all population, but a large percentage of his war-trained Semija. Even the cababar used in the lake were a loss, nearly five hundred.

And what had that great price purchased? The looting had filled the Royal coffers and those of the highest Nobles with zirc and gems. The armory bristled with looted weapons. The stock caverns were overrun; and the more daring of the Nobles feasted on charred fish that had washed up on the shores of the cold lake. Everyone who wanted a Semija had one, though the new ones were so ill trained as to be useless. Beyond the material gain, there was increased morale, the joy of victory, and glory-medals for the heroes of the fight. But the King himself had not seemed pleased at the great victory, had not thrown a feast of rejoicing or given the folk a holiday or any of the normal things a King did at even a minor victory in a raid. Instead, Dynat fixated on questioning the princesses. He was like a man driven, and he did not seem to have the control a King should have. Medoc had asked Bolv, on their way to the baths, what she thought of her King's obsession. She was closed mouthed, but she did not seem pleased, and she seemed even less happy to be, as she put it, "dismissed to the baths like a Semija given a free-day."

It was the first criticism Medoc had ever seen her offer Dynat. The man was more attached to his Kinyara than was appropriate, though Medoc would never tell Dynat that to his face. Kinyara was an ancient and sacred role. Ever since King Khanten and his cousin Zedya had come from the Lava Lake and founded Chraun, it had become tradition for the King to take his closest female cousin as lover and advisor. If a man did not have a female cousin, he did not become King. Often the Kinyara bore the King children, and their children were not considered royalty but sacred; at a young age they joined the Acolytes of the Fire Spirit on the other side of the Lava River. This sacred relationship was never intended to be a marriage, but Dynat lived with Bolv, treated her like his wife, and did not take a Queen to beget true heirs. At least the King did not lie with Semija, like the King before him had. Medoc had watched five Kings rule and fall in his fifty-one years. Five kings, five decades.

Once again, numbers rolled through Medoc's mind. Only about five hundred Icers had been captured, but nearly fifty thousand new Semija were being housed in the outskirts of the mines. They were no replacement for the twenty thousand warriors he had lost; it would take years to train them, and some would never be truly loyal. The crowded conditions were ripe for a riot. Medoc wondered how many he would have to order thrown into the river simply to avoid an eruption of violence. And would they go meekly into the lava? Of course not. It would be another battle just to herd them to their deaths.

The more Medoc thought about it, the less the numbers added up. The price had not been worth the gain. Medoc had studied the scout's reports from the past several years. The Icers were cowards. They had never posed a real threat to Chraun. They would not have attacked, and even if they had, they wouldn't have been able to fight in the heat. Their ice-armor was nothing compared to Fireblood. Twenty-five hundred good Flames, for what? The King's entertainment? And how many more would Medoc risk so that the King could have every last Icer in the Outer Tunnels?

Medoc pushed away the thoughts. They were not the sort of thoughts a General should be thinking about a King. Dynat was chosen by the Fire Spirit to rule Chraun. What he wanted was right. No matter what the numbers said.

Medoc leaned back and accepted another morsel, cababar liver pickled in rocksalt brine. It was sour and juicy and made his mouth pucker. He gestured to a younger Lady, the tops of her bare breasts gleaming in the torchlight, and she swam over eagerly. Perhaps her soft hands could relax his muscles and help him forget the numbers for a time.

"General Medoc, I bring orders from the King." A Cadet stood in the doorway. Cadet Tejusi, if Medoc remembered correctly. Young still, with much promise. Five new valor-medals decorated his scale armor. He would be promoted to Officer soon, replacing one of those lost in the war. His words registered suddenly—orders from the King?

"Well?" Medoc rose from the water and a Semija stepped forward to wrap a soft, absorbent hide around his shoulders. Steam swirled around his body, and water sizzled and danced over the patterns of his lava.

"You are to attend him immediately in the Throne

Room, General."

Medoc stood by the bath as the Semija dressed him in steel scale armor, watching the Ladies make a pretense of lounging and relaxing in the waters. The woman he had summoned was hiding a look of disappointment behind a casual yawn. They would scatter the moment he left the cave, and some other high-ranking Lord would get their company.

Medoc did not mind the interruption of his bath, but he did feel a sense of misgiving. Why should Dynat demand his presence so soon after sending him to rest? Was something wrong? Perhaps the Icers who had escaped the war were attacking. Or perhaps those Semija riots he worried about were starting already. The Icers in the dungeons—could they have escaped somehow?

Tejusi saluted as Medoc exited the cavern ahead of him. As they left the crowded tunnels by the bathing caverns behind, the young Flame spoke again, in a low tone. "He seemed—very angry, General. Apparently not all of the princesses were taken alive, and one is missing yet."

Medoc frowned in the solemn torchlight. He did not alter his pace, but his misgivings increased. One single little ice fairy, huddled in a tunnel anywhere from here to Iskalon, or even dead at the bottom of the lake, *that* sparked the King's ire? When hundreds of Icers were held in overflowing dungeons with the barest security he could afford? When tens of thousands more untrained Semija might riot any day? A flare of white-hot anger rose in his chest.

He had suppressed it again by the time he reached the Throne Room and was admitted. Perhaps the Cadet was exaggerating, and Dynat had called him to an audience for some completely different reason. But when he entered the vast, hot cavern, it was clear that the King *was* angry. Dynat sat on his throne, glaring down in the dim light. His gold crown with the emblem of his house, the crouching slink, glinted red. The lava river roared in the background, an echo of the anger on Dynat's round face. Flames danced in his yellow eyes. Medoc bowed low and said, "You sent for me, Majesty? Is something wrong?"

"I gave a simple command," Dynat said. "Attack Iskalon and bring me all thirteen princesses. Alive."

"Yes, Majesty."

"Can you tell me why there are only nine princesses in my dungeon? Why three are dead, and one still runs free, mocking me and you and Chraun and the Fire Spirit?"

"I am sorry, Majesty. I myself was only informed of this moments ago—"

Dynat made a choking sound and Medoc went silent. He had never seen the King so angry. He reminded the General of a petulant child denied a toy or a sweet. But this petulant child could have his head with a word.

"Only now informed? Tell, me Medoc—" and the King leaned forward, his voice rising "—are you not the General of Chraun? Is it not your duty to know whether our commands have been carried out?"

"Yes, Majesty." Medoc was not sure what else to say. He was completely baffled by his King's anger.

Dynat leaned back. Medoc watched him closely. His face seemed to change, the anger fading, but his eyes grew dangerous. When he spoke again, his tone was bland, as if he was discussing taxes or tunnel construction.

"You will find this missing princess, this Stasia the Dreamer, and you will bring her to me alive. Your fate is tied to hers, Medoc. If she dies before she is brought before me, you will die too. The Fire Spirit has willed it."

"Yes, Majesty." Again, there was nothing else Medoc could say.

"Dismissed."

Medoc bowed again and marched stiffly out of the room. When he was well down the tunnel, away from the King's Honor Guard, the portcullis shut behind him, he took a deep, shuddering breath. His pulse was racing and sweat beaded his brow. Anger and fear lanced through his chest. He leaned against the wall and took another deep breath, then another, trying to calm himself.

He heard footsteps and looked up to see Tejusi watching his face. The Cadet had waited in the hall and heard the entire exchange. Medoc straightened and wiped the sweat off his brow. "Cadet, return to your duties."

To Medoc's astonishment, the young Cadet hesitated. He stood with a straight spine and looked Medoc right in the eye, as if he wanted to speak but feared to. At last he said, "You will no doubt punish me for what I have to say. Some of the men have been talking. If the King were to fall to some harm, there are few among us who would not support you, General."

Medoc stroked his mustache to keep his mouth from dropping open. Such outright treason could not be tolerated. Punish him? Medoc should cast him out of the army, put him in a dungeon and question him to discover the Flames who had spoken so. Tejusi should be thrown into the lava river as a sacrifice to his King.

Yet watching the young Cadet's bright, earnest eyes, Medoc was reminded of himself as a boy, many years past, when he supported Lord Rodev, brother to the former General, in his overthrow of the man who was then King. And after that, Medoc had campaigned within the army to gain General Ticol support in his coup of King Rodev's throne. His mind ran over his conversation with Dynat again. The King had just threatened to kill him, Medoc, the General who had served him faithfully for years, if he did not find this Icer princess. Dynat was not in control of himself. How could Medoc punish the Cadet for something he himself had considered? Yet he must do something. Treason would fester, and it would become rebellion . . . But Tejusi said they would follow him. Perhaps . . .

"No." Medoc was startled to find he had said the word out loud, and struggled to gain control over himself. "Do not speak of this again, Cadet. If I hear even a whisper, I will be forced to act. Go, now."

Tejusi bowed low, as low as an Officer in his position would have bowed before the King himself. Medoc let his breath out in a soft growl once the Cadet was out of sight. As he resumed his journey down the tunnel, strange words swirled in his mind. Treason. Rebellion. Overthrow. Madness.

Stasia

Stasia lay suspended between great heat and frigid cold. Her front roasted, blazed, burned. The back side of her was icy. Even with her eyes closed, she could see fire. Red and orange and yellow shapes flickered and danced. Her front ached. She opened her eyes, and they hurt from the sparkling brilliance of yellow light that assaulted her from above. She was floating on a vast lake of water, under a huge ball of yellow fire.

She rolled over in the water, and her breasts and belly were soothed and cooled. Soon, though, her back began to burn, and she folded her body at the waist, grasped her shins with her hands, and dove down beneath the surface, away from the bright light. She sank further and the light faded, until she reached a murky darkness. She rested there, cool, dark, lifeless.

" . . . Can't heal her while I'm running . . ."

"—No choice, have to keep moving—"

A flicker of noise echoed toward her and she started to rise again. The light grew brighter. As she rose, the burning began again. When she reached the surface, the water disappeared and flames took her.

" . . .ok, Stas, it's ok. Shhh." Larc's soft voice and cool hand broke through the flames.

"—Keep her quiet, they'll find us—" Casser's stern and commanding tone cut through Larc's gentle hush.

"Will kill every one of them for this. Every last Flame!" Glace, his voice so full of hatred she almost didn't recognize it.

She was suspended in midair by Larc's cold, moving rapidly through a tight tunnel. Even surrounded by cold she burned as if she was still in the Flame's hands.

"Glace," she tried to say, but Larc shushed her. She wanted to be taken to the ancient burial chamber that she had found before the war began. She wanted to be buried there with the copper-clad lady, protecting Iskalon for all eternity.

"Shhh, its alright, he's here."

"Got to keep her quiet. We are close to the Spiral Tunnel."

Larc's hand touched her forehead, and Stasia sank back into the dark water.

Flames sprang to life again, and Stasia woke from the darkness to find herself in a giant, empty cavern. The ceiling was blue, the floor was bright and dusty, and the piercing yellow light shone at its zenith. She was in V'lturhst. She was hot and thirsty and weak.

"Why didn't you save me at the lake?" Glace asked, appearing before her. He looked at her with his blue eyes accusing.

"You failed me." His face melted and became her father's face, scorched and burnt like half-cooked meat.

"You're a Flame and a traitor." Her father lit on fire, burned down to the ground, and she was surrounded by the people of Iskalon, all covered with dancing flames.

She raised her hands to her face to cover her eyes, and too late she saw that her own hands were flames. She burned to the ground like her father. She lay on the parched ground, ashes, surrounded by the ashes of her people.

The bright yellow light faded, and the blue ceiling grew dark and grey. Water began to drip from it. A darkly handsome man stood over her ashes. She could see him clearly; the lines of his square jaw and close-cropped hair were sharp against the grey walls of the cavern. His face burned into her mind; she saw the pores on his nose, the mole on his right cheek, the tuft sticking up from his left eyebrow. He raised his face and looked up at the ceiling. "Looks like rain," he muttered. He drew a long, thin object from his black suit and pressed a button. The object made a whooshing sound and grew into a miniature ceiling. The man walked away beneath it, whistling.

The water from the ceiling pooled on the floor, and Stasia's ashes began to float.

Stasia opened her eyes to cold. Who was that man? She had never seen him before, in Dreams or in Iskalon. The thought fled her mind when she realized that she was encased in ice. A soft purple light surrounded her. She no longer burned. Above, the bodies of her ancestors floated in burial ice. The woman with red hair and a copper dress looked down on her, beckoning. So this was death. She did not feel much different. Everything was still, silent. She was peaceful. Her lungs hurt.

Her lungs hurt? How could anything hurt, if she was dead? She had always thought that pain would not follow into the burial ice.

Then ice peeled away from her body and she realized that she lay on a cold slab. The ancestors still hovered, but far above, too far to see their features. Larc's face came into view, then Casser's, then Glace.

"Stasia?"

She wasn't sure which one spoke. Perhaps it was all of them at once. Slowly, she sat up, looked around, came back to herself. She reached into the ice below and drew strength from it. She still felt an unfamiliar heat in her core, but it did not hurt anymore. Her armor was gone, and she was draped in a soiled piece of chirsh. Glace's jerkin, she realized after a moment, clutching it against her chest. There were vaerce missing from her arms. It seemed like a lot were missing but she couldn't quite remember what they looked like before. She struggled to remain focused on the situation at hand, to think of something to say.

"How long?" she asked at last.

Three pairs of eyes exchanged glances above her head. "Hard to say without a water clock," Casser said finally. "I'd say two, maybe three days."

Three days. "Food?" She had not eaten in three days, which would explain why it was difficult to sit up and why her thoughts were so scattered. Glace stepped forward. She expected fish, with its rich nutrients, best for a recuperating Icer, but what she got was dry, stale cababar. She did not complain, but chewed on it thoughtfully. As the meat began to hit her belly, she was better able to think.

"If I'm not dead, why are we here?"

More glances. Larc spoke, sadness in her eyes. "It was Glace's idea. We thought you would—need a burial chamber. We—well, Casser—tunneled here from the lake. It is cold here, and the Flames don't seem to know of this place."

"Iskalon?" Stasia dreaded the answer. She remembered a few things, the lake on fire, the houses burning behind her.

"Demolished," Glace said. He was leaning against the wall, sharpening his dagger on a stone in his palm.

"The people, Casser? Why did you leave them?"

Darkness passed through her uncle's gentle eyes. "You may be the last member of the royal family alive, other than myself. I didn't know where the other Princesses were, but I had a chance to save you, and I took it."

Perhaps, if she had gone straight into the lake instead of waiting for Glace to reach her, Casser would have been free to rally the people, or to save other lives. Perhaps. "My father."

The scritch-scratch of Glace's blade on the stone grew louder in the silence, and at last Larc answered sadly, "After we crossed the lake, we saw the Palace fall onto the city. I couldn't see the Council Hall, but whatever was left of it was crushed."

Stasia looked up at her ancestors. Her father should be floating up there, protecting Iskalon for all time. If he had been killed by Flames, his body would be gone, burned.

She could not believe it. It could not be true. Any moment now, Glace would chuckle, scoop her up in his arms and carry her back to Iskalon, deposit her in her quarters. Father would stop by and scold her for running away again. Maudit and Lotica would shake their heads and tell her she was foolish and disobedient, and how could she break Father's heart so? She looked down, studying the faces around her. Glace, anguished and angry. No, he would not chuckle at her for a long time, perhaps never again. Larc, dark circles of grief around her eyes. Stasia wondered what had happened to Larc's family, her father and brothers—were they as dead as Krevas?

And Casser. His eyes were kind, compassionate. He had lost just as much as she had. Everyone had lost so much. It was almost more than Stasia could bear. Were they the only survivors in the whole Kingdom?

"Have you found anyone else?"

"We have not looked," Casser said. "I sent Glace to find food, but Larc and I were needed to tend you. We wanted to wait until—until we were sure."

Stasia stared at him, confused. Until they were sure of what? Surely Larc could have done whatever healing was needed. Casser should have been keeping busy the last few days, looking for survivors. There had to be others. Of her twelve sisters, some must have survived. They would be gathering, hiding in the Outer Tunnels. The survivors must find each other and band together. Iskalon would continue in Exile. Stasia looked down at the remaining meat in her hand. When they had enough Warriors, they could raid supplies from the outskirts of Chraun. Why had Casser not taken action?

"Stasia," Casser spoke again, and his voice was gentle. Too gentle. "There is a very good chance that all of your sisters are gone, Stasia."

"Nonsense," Stasia said sharply. "If we survived, some of the others must have. My sisters would have had a full Guard surrounding them, unlike myself."

"Whether they survived or not, none of them are here now. Only the four of us are. And of the four of us, you stand highest rank. Which makes you Regent."

"A formality," Stasia said. She knew all about rank within the Royal Family. "You are clearly more suited to the task, Casser. I abdicate my rank to you." Perhaps before the war, she might have jumped at a chance to rule, to be able to act without any restriction. But the reality of war had sobered her. Had everyone in Iskalon known what was coming? Larc had tried to tell her, she realized, and Pasten. They had known what they faced. Only she had remained willfully blind. Only she had scorned the Council meetings as a waste of time. She was not fit to rule.

"I do not accept." Casser's tone was firm. Stasia looked at him; his face was set, stubborn. "If we are the last of the Royal Family, there must be no confusion about who is the Ruler of Iskalon. That kind of uncertainly can tear a Kingdom into civil war. I must accept your rank, and you must accept your place as Regent."

Stasia looked away. "How could you just sit here and wait?" she asked, angry. "Three days. You could have found my sisters, by now. You could have saved lives."

Casser's expression did not change. "Stasia, when we carried you out of the city, you were burning up. Not just burned, but actually producing heat. I could have lit a Flame's torch off your breath. It was all Larc and I could do to get your temperature back to normal. I didn't know if your sisters were alive or dead, but I did know that you lived, and I decided to stay with you until you were healed, or until we placed you in the burial ice."

"Still," Stasia said weakly. "Iskalon needed you."

"Instead of worrying about my responsibility, you might want to concern yourself with your own, Stasia. Iskalon needs you."

"But you are far more suited for the task, Casser. It does not matter which of us outranks the other. You will succeed, while I—"

"You can do this, Stasia." That was Larc. Stasia turned to her.

"Even you would be better suited to this than me, Larc. You know more of politics than I do."

Casser said, "We will be at your back, Stasia. We will help you make decisions. But I will not hold you up like a puppet. Iskalon must have a strong ruler. You will be more capable at this than you think. Trust me. I have known you all your life. I have never seen you shrink from a challenge."

Stasia looked at the ceiling. The deaths of her father and so many of her people weighed on Stasia like the ice in the shaft above her. She would have to set that weight aside until the rest of Iskalon was free and safe, restored to its former glory. Once her sisters were found and the war was won, Stasia could grieve. Oh, she could refuse, force Casser to take charge. But he was right. She had a responsibility to her people. She could not simply pass off her duty. She looked back down.

"This is a good place to start," she said. Three pairs of eyes stared at her. Casser looked satisfied, as if he had never doubted that she would take the mantle of leadership. Larc looked traumatized, as if she had seen too much. Glace looked the way he did when he bowed before Cataya's statue—admiring, almost reverent. "There is cold, here, and this place is well hidden. No one else in Iskalon knows where it is, so they won't find it by questioning their prisoners. The back of the cavern is riddled with ice that can be shaped out and used to form small dwellings. We will find other survivors and bring them here. This will be Iskalon in Exile.

"Glace, Larc, are you rested and fed?" They nodded, and Glace saluted her with his fist to his heart. "Good. Then start searching for survivors. Stay together and don't take any risks. Don't fear, Glace, I will not leave this place until you return." Glace nodded and turned away, once again not meeting her eyes. So he was back to being distant; Stasia chafed at that, but she did not have the time or energy to confront it. Larc saluted her less assuredly and caught up to him at the entrance to the Burial Shaft.

"You know I should have died," Stasia said to Casser. She chewed on more of the meat. The little bit she'd eaten already only served to make her ravenous. "I had every intention of dying. Why didn't I?"

"You should have," Casser agreed. "You were hot as a Flame. Glace had to carry you; neither Larc nor I could get close until we got you under the water in the lake. No Icer could have withstood the amount of heat you took in."

He looked troubled. No, troubled wasn't the right word. His brow was furrowed, but his lip was curled back like he had tasted a bitter fungus.

"Tell me what it is you know, Casser."

He looked down at his hands, turning and spreading them, tracing the fingers on one nervously. "Your father ordered the secret kept, and we kept it. Only five of us knew: your father, myself, your two eldest sisters, and your mother. The rest thought she was a human who caught your father's eye."

"What human?" Stasia suffered a familiar pang at the mention of her mother, who had died giving birth to her and Pasten. Krevas had never remarried, after Queen Rashesh's death. Stasia had always wondered if he blamed her for killing Mother.

"Your father commanded us never to tell you. He thought there would be no consequences other than his broken heart. But I cannot believe that he would keep the secret, knowing what I know now."

Stasia huffed in frustration. "Enough riddles, Uncle. Tell me plainly what you know. My father is dead—" the words did not choke her as she had expected "—and until we find my sisters, I am your Regent."

Casser smiled sadly. "You will make a better Queen than you think. Already giving orders. Queen Rashesh died shortly before you were born, Stas. Your sister Pasten's birth alone destroyed her. To the very end, Krevas and Rashesh were married for convenience, though they were great friends. His true love was your real mother, Lianda."

"Lianda? I don't understand. Pasten is my twin. Rashesh was my mother." What was Casser saying?

"When you were born so close to Pasten, it was easy to spread the story that twins were too much for Rashesh to bear. Lianda was a close kept secret. He saw her only in private, accompanied only by his most loyal guards."

"I don't understand, Uncle." She didn't, but his words were still running over her, contradicting everything she'd ever known about her life.

"She came from the Flames. A Flame herself, of their Noble class, brought low when her house made a grab for the throne and failed. Lianda would have been executed by the King who ruled Chraun then, but she fled to Iskalon and begged Krevas for asylum."

Stasia stared at Casser, cold sweat running over her body like icy fingers. "What are you saying?"

"Your two eldest sisters, the only others who knew she was here, wanted your father to send her back to Chraun as a sign of good faith to the Fire King, to improve our relations with the Flames. But Krevas took pity. No, it was more than that. He fell in love with her, Stasia. Even if she was a Flame, your father loved your mother very much."

"That's impossible," Stasia said. "How could he keep her a secret? How could a Flame even survive in Iskalon?"

"Those who knew her thought Lianda was a human, an escaped Semija. Some whispers got around, but your sisters clamped down on them, not wishing to see your father shamed. And you know as well as I that it is not uncommon for Lords and Ladies alike to take human lovers. No one would believe they could have gotten a child together, since no child has ever come of a union between human and Icer."

Stasia stared at Casser, thinking furiously. It almost made sense. If Lianda had been human, it would have been impossible for her to bear Krevas's child. But if she were a Flame . . . No. It was unthinkable. Disgusting. But, why would he lie about this? She resisted the urge to grasp his mind and see the truth.

Casser looked into her eyes, and she saw that he knew what she wanted to do. "Go ahead, little niece. You should be able to see your mother. She was beautiful, in her own way."

Stasia nodded, taking a deep breath, and plunged her mind into his. She knew he would gain all of her knowledge, her experience, her dreams. She opened her eyes to his.

She saw her mother as he had seen her, her chirsh clothing covered in a brilliance of gems, veils sewn thick with shimmering fish scales covering her face, disguising her so she could go among the people without her lava scars revealing her. The people had thought her opulent, vain, aloof. She had not chosen any Guild, and that made her no better than the guildless, an outcast. Only Casser and Krevas had seen her uncovered, her dark skin crisscrossed with tight, lighter scars, the ghost of her lava mesh. Her eyes were dark, almost black, reflecting the icelights over Lake Lentok perfectly. Her straight, long hair hung over her shoulders, framing a smile that lit her whole face and made her lava scars seem to fade to nothing.

Stasia gasped. She had seen that smile before, staring back at her from the polished ice mirror in her bedroom. This Lianda wore her smile. This Lianda, this Flame, was her mother. "My mother was a Flame . . ."

"Yes," Casser said. "And Lianda died shortly after your birth. With her gone, it was easy for the people to forget that she had even existed. When Rashesh bore her last child in such a difficult birth that not even the strongest healers could save her, Krevas gave Pasten to

Lianda to nurse. Lianda was so isolated, it was easy to proclaim you twins, born of Rashesh. Especially when you began to exhibit the powers of an Icer, and a very strong one."

Stasia pulled herself out of his mind, away from that smile crossed with lava scars. "How did she die?"

Casser started as the link broke. Then, he initiated another link, pressing memories into her mind. Lianda, speaking of the family she had left behind, a Flame husband and a son in the Fire Kingdom. She told Casser of her constant fear of what the Fire King would do to them to get her back. There was a secret council between Krevas, the two oldest princesses, and Lianda and Casser. Whispers of an impending attack on Iskalon, demands from the Fire King to send Lianda back. Arguments from the princesses. Refusal and anger from Krevas. Quiet reasoning from Casser, laced with sorrow.

"She stole away," Casser said out loud, and Stasia, still linked, saw Krevas's bitter rage, saw him confronting Casser in fury. "She told me before she left, but not Krevas. She feared for his life, for the lives of the Icers, and for the lives of the husband and son she had left behind. She told me she had been selfish, thinking she could cheat death. Then she left you on your eldest sister's breast." And Stasia saw it as he spoke, saw her mother holding a small bundle, tears running over her scarred face. "Protect my child," she whispered to Casser and Maudit as she handed her over. "Tell no one what she is."

"What does all this mean?" Stasia asked, pulling herself out of the past, and the sorrow of the moment, and back into the present, into the cool air and the soft blue light of the Burial Shaft. She thought of her father's constant disappointment in her. Had he always looked on her with disgust?

She thought of her battle with the Flame at the end of the war, of taking in the heat. He was taking her alive because she was a princess. Did someone in Chraun know about her heritage? "Ancestors," she breathed. "Oh Casser. I think they want me back. I'm the last survivor of this Flame family. This whole war—Casser, did they raze Iskalon just to find me?"

"It's unlikely." Casser was frowning. "The King who rules in Chraun today is different from the King who ruled in Lianda's day. King Ritnu killed her family, and since then the throne has passed from Ritnu to Bretle, and to Bretle's son Dynat, the current ruler. Alliances shift so quickly among the Chraunian Nobles, it is possible that Dynat has never even heard of your mother's family."

"But if he has . . ." Stasia looked back up at the Burial Shaft. She could almost see the expression of the copper clad woman's face. "The fire I took in should have killed me. If the Flames know that I bear some protection from their power—if Lianda told them of my existence—they would want to find me."

Casser shook his head, slowly coming out of memory himself. "I doubt that Lianda would have betrayed you. But I do think you bear more than protection from fire." He stood, stretched, and looked up at their ancestors floating above. Then he looked down at her, and his eyes were full of awe. "Your ability with heat is untrained, undeveloped. However, I think that with effort, it could become strong.

"In time, Stas, you could be an Icer and a Flame, as well as the only Dreamer since Cataya."

Chapter 6

Council of Exiles

Glace

Glace did not want to leave Stasia in the Burial Chamber, so close to Chraun. It had been hard enough to leave while she was still unconscious, to seek food; now that she was awake he wanted to drink in the sight of her, to tell himself over and over again that she was alive. Alive, though Casser said she should have died. Glace turned away from that thought. She was alive.

He and Larc felt their way through the dark Spiral Tunnel, listening for Flames coming through. He would have avoided the Spiral if he could, but the tunnel Casser made went to the Lakes, not the mines, and there were no spurs this far down that were not dead ends. If they found more Icers, they could start to shape tunnels around the burial chamber, make safe passages that could be hidden from the Flames, but for now there was only he and Larc, and Larc admitted that she had no affinity for stone.

The patrols in the Spiral were thick, and more than once they saw the telltale glow coming around a bend. The first time they were near a spur, and thankfully the Flames did not follow them into that cobweb-filled crack. The second time they had to backtrack quickly to the nearest spur, and hide in an alcove when the Flames checked the spur with their torches. Glace's fear for Stasia increased; if they were checking the spurs, what would keep them from finding the burial chamber? But there was nothing he could do for her now.

When they drew near the top of the Spiral where the tunnel branched, the distant glow of Flame torches blinded them both. Glace pulled Larc into another dark spur. If he remembered correctly, this one went through to the mines, bypassing the busy tunnels by the lake. As he padded silently through the narrow tunnel, Larc's websilk rustling against the sides, images of the battle rose and flickered through Glace's mind, playing over and over. Houses on fire, bodies filling the streets, blood and ash coating everything. He had bathed in a spring near the Burial chamber, but he could not wash the slimy feeling of blood off his skin. Larc's breathing grew heavy, and he realized she must be remembering, too. He reached back and grasped her hand.

They said nothing, just walked awkwardly with hands clasped. Glace pushed through giant, sticky webs of wild neithild; it did not seem the Flames nor anyone else had used this tunnel for a very long time. The ground sloped gradually upward, a good sign that they were headed for the mines. Glace hoped that it was the tunnel he remembered, that it really did have an exit at the end.

"At least Stasia lives," Larc said once, hollowly. "And Casser. At least we have that much."

Glace said nothing. He agreed, but the immensity of loss was too much to bear thinking about. He saw blood again, and chunks of ice falling from the ceiling as he carried Stasia into the lake. His home. What if the four of them were the only survivors? Would they live out their days in the Burial chamber, sneaking food from the Flame's stores? Glace could not imagine such an empty existence. He still could not believe his home was gone. The Council Hall, Market, all the people, the lake—he would never again saunter onto the training square and engage another Warrior in a spar.

A sound echoed down the tunnel and Glace froze. Larc bumped into him from behind and stayed close and quiet. Glace gripped the handles on his mace and axe. There would not be much room to swing them in this tight tunnel, but drawing his long-swords would be impossible. He would throw the mace with all his might, follow it with the axe, then draw his dirk for a close attack.

The sound continued, a faint snuffling, almost too faint to hear, a rock dislodged here and there. Glace could feel the air change slightly as Larc drew T'Jas. He wished he could talk to her, to coordinate their attack, but talking would only give them away too soon.

Glace blinked, trying to prepare his eyes for the burst of light that must be coming. The noises grew, but the light did not appear. A strong smell washed over Glace and joy exploded in his heart. In the same moment, Larc giggled and made an icelight.

A pair of eyes, low to the ground, glittered in the blue light. Glace cautioned himself. It was probably a wild slink, migrating to the warmer tunnels to mate. He let go of his weapons and stepped forward slowly. He saw a notched ear hovering in the light.

"Musche!" He cried, hurrying forward. The slink became a wriggling ball of fur in his arms. Glace held him, then backed up and looked at him.

The slink was worse for the wear. His ears had a few more notches, and his fur was burned off in patches. Blood leaked from a gash on his flank. Glace wondered if the Flames had done all the damage, or if he'd fought other slink in the Outer Tunnels.

"Phee-ew!" Larc exclaimed, catching up. "Only you could love a male slink, Glace. How is he?"

"Alive," Glace said. "Save your T'Jas, Larc. There will

be human survivors, and they will be wounded."

Larc ignored him completely. She knelt on the rough ground and petted Musche. He began to purr and reached around to lick her fingers. Glace watched the gash close up, saw his pelt grow thick and strong. "I can't do anything for his hunger, though. He must have forgotten how to hunt, eating your table scraps. But Glace, how by the Ancestors did he find you?"

"He always finds me," Glace said, standing. "Come. We must go on. If he survived, there must be people in the mines and Outer Tunnels."

The mines were dark and cold, with no evidence of Flames except the smell of Fireblood and sooty air. The Flames had attacked here, but moved on. The forges were cold, the ore carts empty. Apparently the Flames had also looted. Musche led the way now, nosing across the echoing caverns and up through mining veins. Glace followed him, trusting the animal's sense of smell to lead them true.

His faith was well placed. Larc kept her icelight shining, and just as they entered the outskirts of the Outer Tunnels, an icelight appeared down a branching tunnel, greeting them. "Careful," Glace warned. "It could be a trap."

A lone Icer greeted them, a short blonde man with wary eyes. Glace had seen him before but did not know his name. Larc did.

"Ujune! You're alive! Are there others?"

"Larc? Is that you? And Stasia's Guard? Are you alone?"

There was a moment of silence, and Glace felt the terrible irony, that they had found their first survivor and instead of reunion there was a sense of distrust on both sides. Lord Ujune thought they were sent by Flames to roust survivors, and Glace could not help but suspect the same of him, that this was all a trap, that Flames were waiting to kill them—or worse, follow them back to the

Burial Chamber and take Stasia.

"Oh, Ancestors melt me," Larc exclaimed into the awkward silence. "Here, Ujune. Search me. I don't care what you learn, if it's the only way past this impasse."

It took Glace a moment to realize that she meant to link minds with the other Icer, and he looked away politely while they joined. He experienced a moment of sheer loneliness. What would it be like to do that with Stasia, to see her mind, to really, truly know her? He would never know. Even if she entered his mind, he could not reciprocate, could not delve into hers. For all he knew, she might have entered his mind without his knowing. He did not think his mistress would do such a thing; it was expressly forbidden, and she was respectful of him if not of the laws.

The two Icers embraced, their cheeks wet with tears shining blue in their icelights. "Come," Ujune said, grasping Glace's hand in a gregarious gesture of shared sorrow mingled with joy. "Come and see the others."

The others were more numerous than Glace could have hoped. They were scattered throughout the Outer Tunnels, holed here and there in meager pockets, the humans too cold, the Icers too warm, and everyone very hungry. The wild animals in the Outer Tunnels were full of poisonous metals, and catching and purifying them took more vaerce than it was worth.

Because Ujune had taken in Larc's knowledge, they did not have to explain about the Burial Chamber or Stasia's survival. "They have not found any of her sisters, dead or alive," Larc confided to Glace as they walked through a narrow tunnel crowded with guildless, Guild members, and Icers side by side.

"And Krevas? Was he truly in the Council Hall when it fell?"

"All accounts put him there. And—your father, Glace. Oh, Glace. I'm so sorry. He was there too, protecting the King."

Glace was sorry for his father's death, but no more so than he was for Krevas' death. It would have been worse if Krevas had died and his father survived; Dalen had died doing his duty, died for his King. As Glace would someday die for Stasia.

The thought reminded Glace of how close he had come to outliving Stasia, and he felt a strong urge to be by her side again. "We should start moving these people to the Burial Chamber," he said to Larc. "These tunnels are not safe. I will take a party down."

"I will stay and organize the healthy ones to seek out more survivors," Larc answered. "Take heart, Glace. As long as some of the people live, Iskalon lives."

Glace nodded, but he saw the tightness around her eyes. He wondered if there had been any word of her father or brothers. He had not seen them among the refugees so far.

"Poor Stasia," Larc said, just before they parted. "Perhaps her sisters will turn up. But in the meantime— she has to decide what is to be done. I don't envy her the task."

Glace did not either, but in a way he was relieved. She could no longer struggle against her role in Iskalon. As Regent, she could not take risks, and his job of keeping her safe would be easier. He had a sudden flare of grief, an experience of the depth of loss. He wished that she had just gone traipsing off again and he could chase her down and bring her back and they would be in the Palace and everything would be normal.

He pushed the feeling down hard. Stasia lived, but she was not out of danger yet. Even now the Flames could be rushing the Burial Chamber. He was Captain now, not just of Stasia's Guard but of the whole Gendarme. Duty must come before grief.

Stasia

First in a trickle, like water dripping down a tunnel wall, then in a deluge, as more and more people searched and found pockets of survivors hidden away in the Outer Tunnels, the ancient burial chamber began to fill with Icers and humans. The first few parties that Larc and Glace returned with gave Stasia heart, and purpose; she set to work immediately setting up homes for them in the ice caves at the back of the cavern, healing the ill, and portioning out rations from the little food Glace had stockpiled. But as more and more people poured in, she began to feel overwhelmed.

She searched every new face, looking to see one of her sisters, but they did not appear. It seemed that every time she turned around, someone needed her. And then every time she turned around, five people needed her at once. The crowd grew more and more difficult to organize. Then suddenly ten, fifteen, twenty surviving councilors stood before her, each clamoring for her attention and pressing their needs. Wyfus wanted a party of warriors to go back to the lake, to see if it was still patrolled. Mowat, the heavy councilwoman representing the livestock Guild, wanted a party to go to the Outer Tunnels to capture wild molebear. Every other Guild wanted their Guild's needs met now, first, before all others. All the Icers wanted to know who to heal first and where to shape the caverns and whether to conduct raids. Casser stood quietly by her side, waiting for her to act. His passivity made Stasia want to scream. And still more wounded and hungry people poured in, wandering confusedly around the cavern. There was no order to the chaos.

"SILENCE!" Stasia used T'Jas to project her voice over Wyfus and Mowat's shouting match. "HEAR ME!"

The cavern went blessedly silent, and Stasia realized that she had to say something, had to make a decision, had to somehow make everyone happy. She had to speak now, before the arguments erupted again.

"Is there a member of the Timekeeping Guild among us?" she asked. A small, balding man in scorched woolen clothes stepped forward. He was stooped and unassuming, but his voice was steady when he bowed and said, "I am Ivare of the Timekeeping Guild, if it please your Majesty."

"Thank you, Ivare, it pleases me very much. What would you need to make a waterclock here in this cavern, Ivare?" She was aware of tapping feet and impatient glares, but she kept her attention on the Timekeeper.

"A bit of scrap metal, and welders to shape it, Majesty. An Icer to fill the reservoir and help with the finer parts of the mechanisms. A few people to hoist the pieces into place."

"Then I command you to make us a waterclock, Ivare. Ask for what help you need; by Royal decree, it will be yours. We may be exiled from our home, we may be full of grief and shock, but we can continue to live orderly lives. A waterclock will give us all a bit of normalcy."

There were mutters at her order, but also a few nods of approval. Casser smiled at her; reassured, she continued. "As for the rest of us, the first step will be reorganizing ourselves into Guilds. I want one member of each Guild to meet in a closed council with me. We will work together to determine our priorities. Your Guild may be reassigned, your members may be recruited for other tasks. We must make sure everyone has shelter, food, and healing. After that we can resume open Council meetings and look to the future of Iskalon."

To her surprise, everyone hurried to obey. The waterclock was erected before the Guilds had even assembled for the closed council. The chimes were tracked, and time began to pass again. At the order of the council, the back of the burial chamber was hollowed into a network of tunnels and little caves, where people slept cramped together, stacked on top of each other with a thin barrier of rock between their bodies. The remnants of the Warrior Guild were reorganized, and raids on the Flame's outer storage caverns began, and a little food began to trickle in to feed the masses of people.

The time for the first real Council Meeting drew near, and still Stasia's sisters did not appear. She remembered with apprehension the words of the Flame that had almost captured her, to take the princesses alive. Had they all been captured? It seemed impossible. Surely at least one of them had made it into the lake. They had to come back. She could not bear to face the Council Meeting, where so many times she had sat with all of her sisters on the benches. What she had done here so far was simple, basic survival; the priorities were clear. In Council, though, she would have to actually govern the remnants of the nation. She did not know how she could bear that weight alone.

Larc

"Enough food, Lady?" The woman cradled her tiny bundle against her chest. The way she bounced it slightly up and down to hush the cries made Larc ill. "We get the same ration as everyone else."

Tunnel fungi, less than a handful, and the occasional piece of dried molebear. The baby began to wail again, and Larc reached out and healed it. The healing would not keep; in all likelihood she was wasting her vaerce. As the baby quieted and fell into shallow breathing, Larc straightened and backed out of the tiny alcove where the new mother slept. She could see the woman more clearly, with the icelight shining through from the burial chamber. Her hair was long and black and may once have been beautiful. Now it was dull, crusted with dried sweat. Her eyes were wide-set in a shrunken face, and her stomach was swollen with malnutrition under torn, grimy lakehide garments.

She, and the babe, and thousands more, might not survive to the next day. The people needed food, urgently. Ten days had passed since Larc and Glace had discovered the first refugees in the Outer Tunnels. In those ten days, twenty-five hundred Icers and over ten thousand humans had been rescued from their hiding places and moved to the Burial Chamber. They were found in the far reaches of the Outer Tunnels, hiding down mine shafts, and scattered in the spurs of the Spiral. In the tight, noisy, smelly alcoves, stacked on top of each other up the high wall to the ceiling, ten thousand seemed like a huge number, but it was chillingly small compared to the hundred thousand people who had populated Iskalon. Lake Lentok was patrolled by Flames, so there was no way to tell if the missing were dead or captured.

Larc held out hope for her own family, though it was a hollow, weak hope. Her brother Bralon had survived, and as a Luten was commanding scouts now, but there was no word of Father or their younger brother. When either of them had time for sleep, Larc shared an alcove with Bralon, and they clung to each other. Sometimes he cried in his sleep, but Larc had not cried yet. She thought perhaps she was simply too exhausted to cry.

She squeezed the woman's hand. "Your babe will be well," she said. "The scouts will find more food, too. All will be well."

It was hard to say because part of her did not believe it. She left the alcoves and reentered the main chamber, aglow with purple burial ice. The chamber had been widened by Icers to four times its original size, and twenty young warriors stood before Glace, taking up half of the space, swinging weapons taken in raids on Chraun's outer store-caves. Most of the warriors were newly recruited from the fishers, miners, and stock tenders who no longer had their own Guild's work to do. Their actions were stiff and awkward compared to Glace's smooth coordination. Larc gave Glace a quick salute, and he returned it with barely a pause in his drill.

On the other side of the enlarged chamber, the Council was preparing to convene. Larc headed for the

raised dais where Stasia sat already, looking so regal that
only Larc could have guessed how nervous she was. A new
circlet had been made for her from scavenged metals, and
it was fitted with a drop of mercury held in an oval of
quartz, a symbol of the temporary status of her reign. She
wore a borrowed websilk dress with a smattering of pale
emeralds and very subtle patching. Casser sat behind her in
full chirsh armor, glistening with ice crystals, and beside
him was Kiner, now General of Iskalon, also in armor, his
medals on his lapel. Larc hurried her steps. She was late.
When she reached the dais, nearly all the councilors had
taken their seats. Larc leapt up and slid into her spot
behind Stasia. As she sat, Larc remembered the last council
before the war. She had dreamed then of sitting where she
sat now, of whispering advice into her ruler's ear. Now she
had her dream, but it was more bitter than sweet. She
would give it up in a heartbeat to have Iskalon and all her
people back.

Speaker Wyfus had survived the war somehow,
probably hiding like a cababar cub in a burrow. Larc
herself had healed him, but she could not heal away the
drooping of his flesh from hunger. His heavily patched
lakehide robes sagged over gaunt bones as he began the
first address of the Council of Iskalon since the war. It
sounded just like any other address he'd ever made, as long
winded and dull as ever, and Larc felt unreal, sitting in a
strange cavern so far from home, hearing his familiar
words. After quite some time, he got to the point.

" . . . matter of security; if another royal person falls
into Flame hands, every one of us is compromised. At
least until we find more members of the Royal Family, we
suggest that Princess Stasia be restricted to this cave and
not allowed to venture out in the raids. The floor is open
to discuss this suggestion and form a proposal or negate
it."

"Even if the other princesses are found, I believe we
must value Her Majesty's safety above all other things."

Councilwoman Mowat, representative of the livestock Guild, was big as a molebear herself, her girth sagging under an ill-fitting leather dress. The soot had been brushed from the hide, but it still bore scorch marks. She barely waited for Wyfus to finish speaking before she stood. How that horrid woman had survived, Larc could not guess. Perhaps the Flames had captured her and then thrown her back. "She is the hope of our future. The Ancestors speak to her. See how she found this ancient cavern, and made it a home for us? We must protect her at all costs. She will lead us to victory, but that cannot happen if she should be killed in a raid. She will . . ."

What was the woman playing at? She had never loved the Royal family; in the past she'd fought tooth and nail against just about anything Krevas had supported. Did she hope to win favor with the new regent by this flattery? Stasia's back was quivering; from her angle Larc could see the tension in her jaw. Nothing would enrage her more than being told to stay put. Larc leaned in and whispered. "She is trying to bait you. Be ready, the conversation may shift. But on this point, I would advise conceding. It is a small point and can show that you will compromise."

Some of the tension seemed to leave her friend; Larc took a deep, silent breath. Casser gave her a quiet nod. He was close enough to hear her whisper, and he approved of her advice. She wondered if she had overstepped; perhaps she should be quiet and let him do the advising; he had sat behind King Krevas many times.

Mowat finished at last, and the debate rolled around the floor. Not one single person spoke against it. Stasia had few friends on the council; they did not know her well, since she had rarely attended the meetings. And how could anyone argue against the Regent's safety?

Larc wished they would end the matter, and move on to more pressing things, such as how food would be obtained and distributed, and how they were really going to survive and take back the lake. The debate droned on, until at last Councilwoman Cygnet, of the gem Guild, rose to speak.

"I would like to propose an additional clause to this proposal." She was skinny and pale in a once resplendent, now dusty dress of diamond-sewn websilk. "Even if she is retained in this cavern, there are still dangers untold for the Princess. She might fall ill, or the Flames might slip in an assassin, or an accident might befall her. I propose we add a clause, that the Princess be paired immediately with a suitable Icer male, to perpetuate the royal line."

Larc could not see Stasia's face, but her back stiffened again, and anger glinted in even Casser's serene eyes. She understood that; they might well make the same demand of Casser. It was a ridiculous proposal; the last thing that Iskalon in exile needed was another mouth to feed. How could Stasia lead them to victory while pregnant? It was horrid, proposing to breed the Princess like she was a molebear. No, Cygnet and the others could not believe that Stasia would accept such a ruling, could not even believe it wise. Cygnet had merely used it as a distraction, to shift the focus from the main proposal. When it came time for Stasia to make a ruling, she could either refuse the entire proposal and look like a tyrant, or accept the proposal without the breeding amendment and look like a wise leader who knew how to compromise. Indeed, Casser was leaning over, whispering as much into her ear.

Debate was beginning to rage on the floor. Larc's heart swelled with the usual surge of adrenaline. She almost wished she were down there, rather than up here, bound in silence as an advisor.

" . . . Surrender . . ." The word rose above all the others, creating a hush in the cavern. Larc focused on the floor, trying to determine which mouth that word had come from. She could feel Stasia's rage. She prayed to the Ancestors that her friend held her anger; for Stasia to speak out of turn for no reason, in her first council ever, would be political disaster. She would never recover from the diminishment of respect.

There it was. Capris, representative of the fisher-net weavers, a small but strong Guild intricately tied to the fishing Guild. He was newly raised; the old councilwoman had not been among the refugees. His neithild spider had survived; it perched on his shoulder, all eight eyes surveying the council with disdain. " . . . Are starving. We could not defeat them at full force on our own lake; how can we hope to defeat them with a starving population and a fraction of our army? Surrender may be our only choice, and I say the sooner the better."

Whatever words Capris spoke, Larc could be sure they had been placed in his mouth by Wyfus. She opened her mouth but Kiner was already leaning in, whispering, "This kind of talk must be quelled. It will damage morale if the Warriors think we may be fighting for nothing." Larc added, "It could be more bait. Don't rise to it, just quietly acknowledge it and deny the proposal if it comes before you." She did not tell Stasia what she truly thought, that Capris might be right. Living as slaves to the Flames might be better than dying of starvation in this cavern.

The debate rambled on. Surrender was discussed more seriously than Larc had ever seen an issue taken. Even Guilds that normally stuck together on issues disagreed. Wyfus kept quiet, apparently happy to have Capris argue for him, but Cygnet actually spoke up against surrender. "Do we even know if those taken prisoner still live? They may kill us just as quickly as starvation. At least here we have a chance."

And Fickus, of the scribe Guild, agreed: "The Flames put all their resources into making this war happen, into destroying Iskalon. They will be short on food as well, and they have historically taken drastic measures when their population exceeded the capacity of their stores. Their human slaves were murdered wholesale, but at one time they went so far as to kill newborn Flames. Surrender to them will be certain death."

The debate was so fragmented that surrender was never formed into an official proposal. Just before Fourth Chime, Wyfus put forth the proposal to keep Stasia confined to the burial chamber, along with the amendment demanding an heir. Stasia stood on the dais, looking down at the council with palpable anger.

"I shall accept your restriction to stay out of raids, and away from the fighting. I will not be confined to this cavern, but I shall never leave it without a Guard, and only at great need. My choice in a mate and childbearing will not be dictated by your council. If I die, Prince Casser will be your Regent, and if he dies, then Lady Larc shall rule Iskalon until my sisters are found, or another family is chosen by unanimous Council vote."

She paused. The ring of metal on metal echoed across the chamber from Glace's training, penetrating the silence of the Council. Larc was stunned. She should rule Iskalon if Stasia and Casser died? A terrifying thought, one she had never considered. And the way Stasia had approved the proposal, without approving it at all—she wasn't certain if it was mad or brilliant. It certainly hadn't made the Princess any friends, if the looks from Wyfus and the rest were an indication.

"Now, as to the matter of surrender." Larc started— surrender had not been put forth as a proposal; Stasia should not be ruling on it. "If the word surrender is ever mentioned in my presence again, it will be considered treason against the Royal family, with all the impending consequences of such treason. This Council session is closed. We will reconvene at Fifth chime; I hope you will have something more important for me to rule on than my choice of mate."

Chapter 7

Dreams of V'lturhst

Glace

Glace sat in a cramped, dim cave with Stasia, Larc, Kiner, and Casser. It was a small King's Council—Nay, Queen's Council, for Stasia was sure to be Queen. Glace was among those who believed that if the other princesses had survived, they would have been found by now. He could not say so to Stasia, though. She still spoke of her sisters as if they were alive.

In spite of her inexperience and her previous lack of interest in politics, Glace thought that she was doing well as Regent. She had organized the Guilds, put a system of raids and rations in place, and maximized the small space in the burial chamber. She had appointed her own advisors, Casser and Larc. Kiner had survived the war as the highest ranking Icer other than Casser, and she had promoted him as such to General. Since Stasia was the highest ranking Royal, and the Gendarme outranked all other positions in the Warrior Guild, Glace ranked now as the highest Warrior, High Captain of the Gendarme.

Glace hated being High Captain, mainly because it

kept him from Stasia's side. Other than these brief councils, he was constantly training and organizing recruits, planning raids, counting warriors. Sometimes he thought he had been promoted simply to keep him occupied. Of the rest of her Guard, only two men had survived, Glint and Fedor. Glace had pulled seven more from the most promising of the recruits and filled out her Guard with them, but it still irked him not to be by her side more often.

At least this council session had granted him a bit of relief by restricting her to the Burial chamber. Stasia, of course, was livid. She sat on her stone stool, hands gripping the edge of the table so tight that her knuckles were white, venting her anger in a loud and animated tone. She looked beautiful even in anger, with her hair done up high in elaborate silver plaits. Her yellow-green eyes could have shot sparks into Casser, who sat opposite her. The elder Icer's eyes were not calm either, though his anger was more subdued. He sat silent, letting his niece rage on about the council. Kiner, sitting beside him, was nodding fervently at Stasia's expletives. Larc sat opposite Glace, next to Stasia. The too-pretty Icer appeared calm and collected, although Glace detected a hint of anxiety behind her demeanor.

"How dare they? I have a mind to get with child from one of the guildless refugees just to spite them. Thinking they can breed me out, like a molebear fem in heat. Curse Wyfus! I should have him conscripted, see how well he can manipulate the council after he dies in a raid. Fish slime!"

Duty and deference, Glace reminded himself. She had a duty, as much as he did, and hers was to provide heirs to the throne. Her duty had been less urgent when she was thirteenth in line, but now it would be imperative. His mind said that, but hot jealousy crept down his ribs to his gut. When he had heard Cygnet's proposal during council, he let his anger out through his axe, hardly noticing what he was doing until the fisher he was training squeaked,

"Yield, yield!" Then he realized that he had backed the man against a wall and was hacking at his shield with the axe. Duty, he reminded himself now, taking a deep breath. Duty and deference.

Stasia's curses continued, and at last Casser interrupted in a commanding voice. "We cannot sit here and rage all chime, Stasia. It is good to let off steam, but we must speak before the Council reconvenes. Do you need to hit something?"

Stasia's rage dissolved into a disgruntled expression. "I—hit something?"

"Your father would often take a practice sword and spend the chime between sessions in the Warrior's yard. It helped him stay focused during the next session."

A look of incredulity crept over the princess's face. Had she never known this about her father? From time to time Glace had been called to mock-battle with his own King. It was good training for a warrior; Krevas would suppress his T'Jas, to make the fight fair, but he was a worthy opponent even so. Glace felt a glimmer of loss; he would never again see Krevas march angrily into the training square, pick up a dull-tipped blade, and make the challenge stance. He pushed the feeling down, and focused on Stasia. She was trying to regain her fury, but wasn't succeeding.

"I do not think I will need that, Casser, thank you."

Casser drew himself up; he was tall for an Icer, and though Glace was much taller still, the older man dominated the table. Stasia looked slightly sulky, as if she knew a lecture was coming.

"Your ruling today was highly unorthodox, niece. It may have seemed clever at the time, and perhaps it was, but you will pay for it. You have not made one single friend on the Council, and those who might have been swayed to support you now fear your power. What you did in there was no compromise; it was completely undiplomatic. You showed the Council that you will rule as you please, no matter their wishes."

"But Casser, don't you see how absurd it is for them to restrict whether I can leave this cavern? What if we are attacked here? Do I have to wait for a ruling before I can flee? If I am taken prisoner, am I to say to the Flames, 'you will have to wait for our next council meeting, I am not allowed to leave?' The very proposal was insulting. The Council was telling me they have no faith in my judgement."

"It was a test, and you failed, Stas." Larc shifted her feet as she said it, but her voice was strong.

Glace admired Larc's bravery. He had seen the same thing, in what little he had heard of the Council from the training square, but he would not have been able to tell Stasia that to her face. Larc went on, "They gave you a small matter for the first proposal, so that they could judge your response. Now that you have taken the hard line, they will resist you at every turn."

Casser spoke before Stasia could explode again. The Regent was glaring daggers at her friend. "And that does not even speak to your bringing up surrender. That was a clear breach of the charter, which states that the monarch may not debate any proposal before it is laid before them. You did not merely debate it, you refuted it before it even became a proposal. Treason to speak of surrender? Will you have Glace arrest me now, because I have spoken that word twice?"

Glace hoped Casser did not underestimate his niece's brashness. He did not want to have to arrest the Prince; Casser might be the only one to whom Stasia might occasionally listen.

"Don't be absurd, Uncle. You know I will not. Surely you can see that I had to stop that kind of talk. How can we wage war if half the people are ready to simply give up? We must have a strong Iskalon. The charter is absurd. Why should I not be able to speak my piece, like any other citizen?"

"Because you are not a citizen, you are royalty." Glace was startled to hear the words leave his own mouth. The other three swiveled to stare at him, and from the sharpness in Stasia's eyes, and the impatience in Casser's, he regretted speaking, but he could not stop now. He had studied the history of the Royal line of Iskalon in great depth, read every gold plate on the subject, and Stasia needed to know what he knew. "When the Great Cataya united the people of Iskalon under herself, a single monarch, she knew that without balance, her power could be as harmful to the people as she meant it to be good. It was your own ancestor who created the council system, asking the people to elect representatives from their craft groups, for this was before the Guilds. She pledged that although she had absolute authority to make decisions, she would hear the people's position on every matter before she ruled."

When he stopped, there was silence. Stasia's features had softened somewhat, Casser looked a little more attentive. Larc wore a tiny smile. Glace looked his Queen in the eyes. He had often gazed on the sculpture of Queen Cataya that stood before the Council Hall—had stood; the Flames had likely rendered it to dust. Stasia bore more than a passing resemblance to the great monarch, although the wisdom and peace the artist had captured in Cataya's eyes were eagerness and impatience in Stasia's. He expected a reprimand, or a shift in the conversation back to the council meeting at hand, but instead Stasia said, "Go on," in a cold but contemplative voice.

Glace needed no further prodding. He launched into as brief an account as he could manage of the evolution of the councils after Cataya's mysterious disappearance. How to explain the increasing power of the representatives without describing the entire shift of the craft groups into Guilds? How to convey the importance of the silent monarch to the people, without detailing the ten great rebellions, and the shifts in royal family that made Stasia's ties to Cataya's line tenuous at best? As he spoke, he could not help wondering why they allowed him to eat up the precious time before Fifth with his histories. Didn't Stasia know these things already?

"The last great rebellion was more than three hundred years before Krevas's rein. We have few records from that time, because the people stopped mining, and no gold plate was made. We do know that the entire royal family was killed in their sleep, before anyone knew there was a problem. Supposedly a distant cousin survived, and carried the blood of Cataya on into the next monarch, but for many years Iskalon was without any ruler. It is believed that the King who precipitated that rebellion, King Lentel, did so by disbanding the Council and ordering the representatives beheaded."

Larc shuddered. Casser said, "Thank you, Glace. I believe that is all we have time for, at the moment. Stasia may rely on you for your knowledge later. It is fortunate that some of what was lost in our royal library is carried on in your mind.

"Do you see now, Niece? Without you, Iskalon shall be a boat with no pole in the midst of the lake. But you must steer her where she wants to go, not where you alone will."

From the look on her face, all of the Stasia's rage had faded into regret. "I see that I am unfit, Casser. I have been foolish and selfish. I will be the most meek, quiet Regent there ever was, until my sisters are found." She looked at her hands, and Glace felt her loss of heart keenly.

"You won't be alone, Stasia." Larc reached for her friend's hand. "We will be here to advise you."

Stasia let Larc clasp her fingers, but her eyes went to Casser. "Am I to be a figurehead, then?"

Again, Glace's mouth opened of its own accord. "You are to be a Queen."

She looked at him in surprise, as if she had never really

considered the notion. She raised her chin and drew herself up taller. In the distance, Fifth chime sounded, clear and sweet, echoing into their tiny alcove. Stasia stood first, smoothing her garments and straightening her Regent's crown. Her shoulders were straight, and Glace could almost see the duty pressing on them. For the first time, Glace saw her not as a rebellious princess, defiant and childish, but as the Queen, regal and wise, an echo of Cataya.

"Let us go," she said, and her voice was not resigned, it was almost eager, "And hear what the people of Iskalon want."

Stasia

Stasia tossed and turned on her slim pallet of ice. In the dark tunnel beyond her small sleeping alcove, she could hear the quiet sounds of Glace polishing his weapons and his slink, washing itself compulsively. When did her High Captain sleep? How could he watch over her all through the night and then stand and train recruits for another full day? Beyond Glace, she could hear the sounds of shuffling, cries of babes, moans of sickness and hunger from her people echoing through the dark alcoves. Sleep was impossible, had been impossible since the refugees began to fill the spaces shaped out of the back wall of the burial chamber.

The afternoon council had been long, boring, and unresolved. No more proposals were laid before her, and she was almost relieved. She was beginning to realize that she could not storm into Council like a Warrior into battle; she had to tread lightly, and be patient, to whisper when she wanted to shout. She was completely inadequate for the role of Regent. If only her sisters would return. Queen, Glace had called her. Stasia knew she was not fit to be Queen; she had seen that in Casser's and Larc's eyes. There had never been any question of her destiny before the war;

she was to be a princess forever, and the youngest princess, free to choose her own path.

She rolled over. She could not get comfortable in this little cave; the pallet was thin over the rock, and she was ill with anxiety. Surrender. How could they win, when they could not even defeat the Flames with the full forces of Iskalon? How would she feed the people, let alone lead them to victory? For every ten refugees brought in, four died of starvation, Larc said. Even the Icers could not prevent the deaths. They had to take back the lake. The scouts said the Flames still patrolled it heavily. Could Iskalon simply wait until Chraun grew bored with its conquest and left? It was not likely. But how was she to retake the lake with starving Warriors?

Perhaps because dreams of V'lturhst were easier to think of than the destruction of her Kingdom, her thoughts drifted there. She saw an endless expanse of green framed by the bright blue ceiling of lapis. Drawn by the image, she slipped into sleep, and Dreamed.

Stasia stood in the middle of the burial chamber, staring up at the long blue ice shaft above her head. In her hand she held a Flame's torch, burning hot. She drew T'Jas from the heat and drifted toward the ceiling and the surface of the burial ice.

When the fire of the torch hit the ice, it melted away, dripping down over the council assembled on the floor of the burial chamber. The representatives all looked up and started yelling at her. "Heretic!" They screamed. "Blasphemer!"

She held the torch higher and drifted up into the opening it made in the burial ice. "Flame!" the voices below shouted. "Kill her! She's a Flame, she's the enemy!"

The ice sealed behind her, and she rose through the shaft, the torch melting away the ice. Water dripped over her, cooling her warm body. She closed her eyes, and when she opened them, she stood on a carpet of waving green stems. They tickled her bare calves. A soft, warm breath from some giant creature enveloped her whole body, and the stems moved, blown by the same breath. The ceiling was dark and covered with millions of tiny pricks of light, as if a cavern above was blindingly lit, and that light was filtered down through tiny cracks and holes in the ceiling. One large hole, perfectly round, let through enough light so that she could see the floor of the vast cavern. The carpet beneath her feet stretched endlessly.

The breath grew stronger. It tore at the stems, pulling the long strands from the ground until the carpet drifted away completely, leaving her standing on bare rock under that immense ceiling. The lights winked out one by one, until nothing but darkness remained.

Stasia woke with a start. First chime was sounding softly, echoing on the walls of her tiny room. Somehow, she had slept. She did not feel rested, though. *She's a Flame. She's the enemy.* Often she doubted the clarity of the Dream, but this one at least seemed obvious. She must learn to conquer the power of fire, or she would rest in the burial ice before her time. Stasia stood, hurriedly pulled on a dry suit of chirsh armor, and stepped out of the cave. Two Warriors, Glint and a recruit whose name she did not recall, had replaced Glace. "Send for Casser," she said. "Tell him to meet me at the Spiral."

A short time later, Stasia led Casser past the Icers posted at the entrance to the Spiral Tunnel. Her uncle looked anxious, and well he might; a Flame could appear around the next bend at any moment. Stasia held a tiny, dim icelight, casting just enough of a glow to see the nearest tunnel walls. With luck Flames would be distracted by the light from their own torches before they saw it. Stasia was reminded again of her reckless trek down this tunnel before the war. Perhaps this was just as reckless. But it was necessary. And if she had not made the previous trip, they would not know of the Burial Chamber that had become their sanctuary. Still, if they were caught by a patrol, not only would their lives be forfeit, they would be betraying Iskalon in Exile.

Stasia went right at the exit, up the steep tunnel toward the lake. Within about a hundred paces, she led him into another offshoot. It was a quiet, short tunnel, with many high pockets of heat and low pits where cold air pooled. It was the kind of tunnel where slink nested and Flames hunted them. It was also a loop, so if Flames came up, Stasia and Casser could escape back to the Spiral Tunnel. The Warriors Glace had assigned to her remained by the Spiral, out of earshot. They would give warning if they saw torchlight.

"Perfect," she said, flopping down in a pit of cold. Casser stopped behind her, crowding her in the cold pocket.

"What are we doing down here, Stas? You swore to the council that you would not leave the Burial chamber except at greatest need."

Stasia drew deeply from the cold, then stood and climbed up the rock wall to a ledge above. It was empty, though from the tiny bones and musky smell, she thought a slink had used it in the past. The air was warm; not hot, but warm. It surrounded her body, uncomfortable, a strange contrast to the cool air. Her armor, dry and without ice, held the warmth against her skin, and it became heat. "The need is great, Casser."

"It had better be. A Flame could come up that tunnel any minute."

"We are still far from their main tunnels. But even if we had to get closer, I would risk it. I must do this, Uncle."

She heard him scratch his hair and lean against the cool wall in the dark. "You're trying to learn, aren't you? How to use your mother's T'Jas. Ancestors, you must be careful, niece. We don't know what the effects could be. The Flame life spans are short, it is said. They do not have vaerce to track their rate of decline. If you use Flame T'Jas, your life may be shortened without your knowledge."

Stasia did not answer. She held herself very still and concentrated on the heat. The memory of burning up from the inside out was fresh; Larc's cool healing had not erased it. She did not try to bring the heat inside her body. Instead she tried to concentrate the heat outside her body into one place, right above her palm. She focused for a very long time, feeling the air currents and trying to guide them, but it was like trying to sculpt lake mud underwater. She was working as hard to repress her cold, to keep it from taking over and pushing the hot air into one place, as she was to move the hot air.

At last she jumped back into the cold, and let it wash away the heat. She was exhausted. "Did you ever see my mother use Flame T'Jas?"

"Not one single time, Stas. It was too cold for her." What must it have been like, to love the heat and then be forced to live in the cold? Hatred for her mother overwhelmed her without warning. It served her right, the chirat-dung Flame. The hatred trickled over. Stasia, herself, was a Flame. Her eyes went wide in the dark. *I am an Icer! I am an Icer, and I will do what I must to save my people. Even if it means to be a Flame.*

"Did she ever speak of how they use T'Jas?"

Stasia heard the thunk of his ice-armor against the rock as he slid down to sit next to her in the tunnel, leaning on the wall. She moved aside to give him room. "She spoke mostly of her child. He was nine years old when she left. She worried for his life constantly. Seemed to think the Fire King would kill him, or worse, for what she had done."

"Surely she must have mentioned something?" Stasia pried a rock free from the tunnel floor and held it in her hand, considered throwing it against the opposite wall, then set it down gently.

"She said that if her son lived to be twelve or thirteen years, he would gain his lava mesh and begin his training. They stand by their river of lava and pull in as much heat as they can bear. Some burn out their powers this way, and some die and tumble into the river. But most walk away from the river with a lava mesh crisscrossing their skin.

From that day forth, they are Flames. So even if the King didn't kill him, there was still a chance that he would die."

"Well, that's out," Stasia said, prying out another rock and squeezing it with all her might. "If I got within ten feet of that river, the flesh would melt from my bones."

"I'm not so sure, Stas. Taking in that Flame's heat should have killed you, but it did not. Perhaps you would survive the river of lava. In any case, you couldn't get there alive. It's in the heart of Chraun."

Stasia clambered onto the ledge again, immersing herself in the hot air completely. She tried to do what she had done during the war when the Flame captured her, drawing all of the heat into her body. She sweated and her stomach rolled, but that was all. She kept waiting for a fire to leap into being inside her, as it had done before, but the only thing that leaped up was the bit of dried morchella she'd eaten last. Choking on bile, she fell back to the cold floor. Casser caught her in his arms and began healing her.

"This is not the only reason you asked me to come here, is it?"

"I need to share something with you, Casser." She was only half healed, but she withdrew and stood facing him in the dark.

He was silent, waiting, and Stasia took a deep breath and used T'Jas from the cold to enter his mind. She had wanted to try using heat for this, but it was not working, and she did not have the patience. Trying not to pry into his thoughts and feelings, shutting out all she could, she pushed her own thoughts into his mind. She gave him her dreams, her visions of V'lturhst, her endless searches, her knowledge of the Outer Tunnels. Without speaking, she told him what she wanted. When she withdrew, he was silent for a long time. She waited, patient as she could be. He has the right to refuse, she reminded herself. He is my Uncle. I will not command him to do this.

"I had hoped you had set this all aside, Stasia, especially given the duty you now bear."

"Don't you understand? If V'lturhst exists, we could find refuge from this hopeless battle. We could go to a place where there are no Flames. Find a new home. If I was not Regent, I would leave today and not stop until I had found V'lturhst."

Stasia did not need to be in Casser's mind to hear the disappointment when he spoke. "I wish you could hear how foolish you sound, Stas. Can you not see your dreams for what they are, pretty fancies? This is reality. This is what you have. You have me, and Kiner, and Larc, and the people who have survived. We are the tools you have to work with. Use us. Set aside these useless visions."

A flare of anger rose in her chest and Stasia tried to quench it. At least he had not called her a blasphemer. Was she ill in the head, like some of the guildless were? How could he see what she saw in her own mind, and not understand how real it was? "Tell me that you will at least consider my request."

"I will not lie to you, Stasia. I will not abandon Iskalon, any more than you would, to chase fancies in the Outer Tunnels."

Anger rose again, in spite of her efforts. "Then I will give you a command, as your Regent, and perhaps, Ancestors forbid it, your Queen. I command that if we must surrender our lives to the Fire King, you will flee before you are taken. You will take the images I have put in your mind and search the Outer Tunnels for the way to V'lturhst. You will find a new home for any of our people who still live."

"You command that I abandon our people in their time of greatest need?"

"I command that you save your own life, for they will surely kill you and me if we are captured, and perhaps save the lives of some of our people. Even if V'lturhst is just a dream, you will be of more use to Iskalon alive and free than dead or imprisoned."

After a long, dark silence, Casser spoke. "We should

return to the Burial chamber. Council will start soon, and we have been here too long. Promise me you will not leave the Burial chamber again, Stasia."

"I will not promise that. Iskalon may need a ruler who can resist fire, Casser. And my life may depend on it. You know that is worth the risk."

Cold quiet settled between them, and grew as they returned through the Spiral Tunnel. Glint and the other guard followed like creeping slinks. Halfway back to the tunnel to Iskalon in Exile, a sound echoed up the Spiral, and they both turned, peering into the darkness. It drew closer. Casser pulled nearly all of the cold out of the air, preparing for a fight. "It is our raiding party," Stasia said quietly. "If they were Flames, they would have torches."

"Best to be sure." He did not relax. Stasia leaned into the wall and drew cold from it. The sound of footsteps grew. It was accompanied by a louder, deeper sound, like heavy hides being dragged over rocks. Low voices echoed up to Stasia's ears.

"Oh, Casser!" Stasia barely remembered to keep her voice low in her excitement. "Do you hear what I hear?"

"Sounds like Jath's voice," he said teasingly. "And Mazol. Are you so happy to see them?"

Stasia drew moisture from the rock and sent a puff of powder ice down the tunnel, to welcome them home. Unable to wait, she raced down the tunnel. "How many?" She asked Jath, who was leading the raiding party. "How many did you get?"

Mazol answered. "Thirty, Majesty! Most are breeding fems."

Stasia sagged against the tunnel wall. Thirty cababar, of the right sex. They could butcher half and keep the rest for breeding. The relief was like a jump into Lake Lentok after running up a steep tunnel. Stasia thought of all her people, slowly dying from hunger. They would have the food they needed. She did not wait for the raiding party, but pulled in cold and flew up the tunnel, racing Casser back to the burial chamber. Mowat would be pleased to know that she could put her Guild to work again. Thirty cababar weren't many, but they were a start. They would be a symbol of hope in the hard times to come.

Interlude

Khell, Seventeen Summers Prior

Maia

Overheated by the dense tangle of sleeping bodies, Maia crawled out of the furs, oblivious to the complaints of the other children she tread on. Once she was out, she was almost immediately cold again, but she did not care to re-immerse herself in the suffocating furs. She was restless after months in the egla. The wind howled outside, beating against the thick walls like an attacking tribe.

The Liathua had reached the Doaltooth Mountains well ahead of the worst of the winter storms. They set up a permanent camp of sturdy ice egla, nestled on the leeward side, the boareal snuggled in a pile in the pens for warmth, several families together in each egla, sharing fires and stories. Maia lived in the egla of three small families, and she and the other children piled together like the boareal, along with the sled-doal, all under one big hide. No one would have guessed that she was to be given in the next tithing while they would be protected.

Part of her welcomed the sacrifice. Antahua, healer of the Liathua, had condemned her, telling the others that she was bad for escaping while her whole tribe was taken. In the eyes of the Liathua, being given to the Dhuciri in the tithing was no less than she deserved.

It would right a wrong, restore balance to the lives of all Khell. Her sacrifice was not just to save the life of one of the other children snuggled against her, but to save all Khell. Or so the healer said.

There was no way of knowing when the next tithing would occur. Chief Lubar, Hakua's father, had expressed his hope that it would not happen until next summer, when the skies were clear, the dark birds could be seen from far away, and the Liathua had more captives from summer raids to offer. If it happened during the winter storms, the birds would be obscured, the Khell would not be able to hide until it was too late, and they would only have Maia to offer in the place of one of their own. Maia secretly agreed with the Chief. A summer tithing would give her time to convince Hakua to plead for her, and it would give her more captives to hide amongst. If there were enough new captives, perhaps she would be spared.

The Liathua traveling camp had been busy, not sleepy and almost dead as this winter camp was. Every morning before the sun they rose and packed everything they owned, tents, hides, weapons, all on the backs of the sluggish boareal and on sleds dragged by teams of doal. They were moving, Hakua told her, from their summer camp at Pebble Beach to their winter camp, snug in the southern Doaltooth Mountains. The mountain range she had been hugging when they found her was the northern reach of these Doaltooth Mountains. All day, every day, they traveled over snow and ice. Maia usually walked, but they had replaced her tattered moccasins with good, thick, traveling ones. Sometimes different riders would swing her up on their boareal and she would rest.

Her life was so close to normal that the ache of losing her family and everything she'd known began to dull. She did not forget her mother's face, but it no longer turned to dust every night in her dreams. Her fear of the Dhuciri did not diminish, but she no longer saw them in every shadow. She was allowed to sleep on furs in various tents, fed when there was food, and played with other children as she had in the Nuambe camp.

Often when she walked, Hakua would escape his father's eye and scamper beside her. Hakua had become her friend in spite of his father's objections. His father was the chief, and Hakua, eldest of his brothers, would be chief when his father took his ice-journey. The chief *of the Liathua was too busy, Maia soon realized, keeping the camp organized and planning the summer raids with his brothers, to keep a firm hand on his son. At first, Maia encouraged Hakua's attention out of the understanding that he could speak for her and save her from the tithing. In time, though, it grew to more than that. While there were many children to play with, only Hakua's efforts could bring a true smile to Maia's lips. She loved him as a brother, though he was also as irritating as only a brother could be. He was only one winter younger, but he often acted much more childish. Especially when he spoke of being chief.*

"When I am chief, all the warriors will do as I say," he said after being chastised by one of his uncles.

"When I am chief, all the girls will play with me everyday," he said after being chased out of the girls' games.

"When I am chief, my father will never tell me what to do again," he said after his father pulled him away from Maia's side.

In the crowded egla, Maia trod on the broad tail of a doal, and it woke squealing. She stroked its sleek back soothingly, and it burrowed further under the hides with a sigh. Maia thought of her parents. Her father had been Chief of the Nuambe. Her mother had been the Healer. They had been rare, a healer and chief who mated exclusively. The healer and chief of a tribe were not allowed to live together, and they often took other mates, but they could and sometimes did mate. Never had a Healer and a Chief shared as much love as her mother and father. Or so Grandmother said.

They were all dust now. Maia tried to imagine that she was the Healer in this tribe, beside Hakua-as-chief. How would she counsel him? What soft words would she whisper in his ears? All she could imagine telling him was to grow up and stop being so childish. But that would surely lose her his friendship and condemn her to being given at the tithing.

She approached the fire pit. The embers burned low. A Grandfather sat beside it, nearly asleep, head drooping over, skin spotted and tough like an old hide. Maia poked his ribs, and he startled, then leaned over and wedged another boareal chip into the coals. Flames sprang up; he mumbled something incomprehensible and began to droop again.

Maia stared at the flames until her eyes became sore and dry. She looked round the egla; everyone else was sleeping. The Grandfather was too senile to take notice. She reached into her fur tunic and pulled out Grandmother's pouch. From the beginning, she had kept the pouch close and did not show it to anyone. She had heard of other tribes taking valuables from their captives and she did not want to lose it. Even though her Mother and Grandmother's bones were dust now, the pouch was still a connection to them. She hesitated, then thrust her hand inside and felt the contents.

The first thing she pulled out was a small mat folded in a tiny square, woven from the finest grass fibers, traded centuries ago from a tribe far to the north, where the lands were covered with dust and stones, not ice. She unfolded the mat and spread it between her and the fire as she had seen her mother do. The next item was a smaller pouch. It was full of a bluish powder, sea urchin spine. Mimicking her mother, she took a pinch and threw it on the fire. Flames sprang up, casting wild shadows on the walls of the egla. The Grandfather stirred, then drooped again. The flames were a myriad of colors, like the brightest seashells Maia had ever seen.

Upending her pouch, Maia shook the remaining contents of the bag into her palm, then opened her fist and stared at them.

The bones were small, each the longest bone of the littlest finger. There were exactly ten, one from each of her greatmothers. One day, it could be hoped, there would be eleven bones in the pouch. That would not happen if she were offered in the tithing.

Guide me true, greatmothers, she thought, as she rolled the bones between her palms and then cast them on the mat. Tell what awaits me.

The ten narrow, long bones fell across the mat. They were browning with age, and several of them were beginning to split, tiny flakes falling off the sides. The lay of each bone in relation to the other told a story, and only those of the blood of the bones could read it. Maia had watched her mother cast the bones since she was out of the carry-board.

The whitest bone, that of her own great grandmother, and the oldest, brownest one, lay crossed in an X at the very center of the mat. The others lay in a rough circle around the X. She could see a few things in that circle, but what concerned her most was the X.

"Crossbones," she muttered into the stillness. "Darkness coming. It is not the appointed time, but they come. On the day the storm passes they will be upon us."

Other images filtered through her mind, strange things that she could not put words to, dark wings and a hole in the earth and a fire burning in her belly. She did not notice when the images stopped and sleep took her.

When Maia came to, the Grandfather was holding her shoulder and looking into her eyes. His face was alert and aware. Why had she thought he would be oblivious to what she was doing? He began to yell for the healer to come.

She was woozy and disoriented. What had she done? She remembered taking her pouch out, colorful flames . . . Her pouch. She tried to sit up, but could not. Her eyes fell across the mat. The bones were still spread out before her. "Please don't take them," she tried to say, but her voice sounded distant even to her own ears. As if she was talking through snow. Then Antahua was standing over her, staring at the bones, arguing with the Grandfather, dousing the fire. She saw a bowl lifted to her lips and a strange broth was forced down her throat. After a moment, her vertigo passed and she was able to sit up. The Healer was watching her sharply.

"I'm sorry," Maia said. "I didn't mean—"

"Bone casting was lost to the Liathua many greatmothers past." Antahua's dark eyes were large and frightening in the dim light of the coals.

"I'm sorry," Maia said again.

"If you are truly a Seer of the bones, your art could be useful for the tribe. If the tithing comes when this storm clears, as you have predicted, you will move your furs into my egla."

Maia was silent, hardly daring to hope that she was hearing what she thought she was hearing. Living in the healer's egla meant being her apprentice. A healer's apprentice was never sacrificed.

"If, however, the tithing does not come on the day you predicted, I will not wait for it. I will cast you onto the ice. Someone who plays with such magic for her own gain cannot be anything but a danger to the tribe. Now clean up this mess and get more chips for the fire."

Maia was not made afraid by her ominous words. She had seen her mother cast the bones many times and be right. She knew she was right about the tithing. "Thank you," she said, not to Antahua but to her greatmothers. The camp was waking, the storm slowing—not stopping, she knew now that it would not stop for another five days, but slowing enough for the tunnels to the boareal egla to be cleared. Maia felt safe for the first time in many months as she scooped up her greatmothers' bones. Her place among the Liathua was secure.

Chapter 8

The Heroes Return

Dynat

Dynat pushed his hands in opposite directions with all his might. He felt slippery fur sliding under his fingers, and at last he heard a snap as the slink's neck broke. He held the limp body of the animal for a moment, then thrust it aside, sagging against the wall of the narrow tunnel, exhausted. He drew deep, heaving breaths. Sweat dribbled over his skin, stinging where it was broken by the slink's claws and teeth. One big gash on his forearm was bleeding too much, and he held the cloak over it, trying to staunch the flow. It would heal. He had defeated death once again.

It was not enough. Still adrenaline raged in his blood, still the fury of the Fire Spirit screamed in his head. The tremendous battle with the slink had done nothing to quiet the roaring flames. Snarling, Dynat kicked the feline's body, but it was dead, useless now. He knew he should bring it back to be skinned and tanned, to add another pelt to his collection. Instead, he turned and marched briskly down the tunnel toward Chraun. He needed something but he could not imagine what. Something had to satisfy his anger and passion, had to quiet the burning rage in his head.

When he reached the bottom of the Spiral Tunnel and his Guards began again to shadow his every move, Dynat did not return to his rooms to draw his lava from the crucible. With great effort, he did not drink in T'Jas from the hot air, though it tried to seep into him. He went instead to the caverns where the Semija games were held.

It was a long march to reach them. Dynat was already tired from his trek up the Spiral, and his fight with the slink. But the fire in his mind kept him going, through the mine shafts and past the fungal caverns and the stock dens, through the Semija quarters, all the way to the outermost tunnels of Chraun. The Semija games were illegal, and so they were held as far from the center of power as was possible. Dynat visited them occasionally, just to let the Lords of Chraun know that he knew what they were doing and allowed it; another King might not.

He did not intend his visit today to be political. In fact, it might hurt him politically, but he did not care. He was the Chosen of the Fire Spirit, what were politics compared to that?

At the end of a narrow, dark tunnel, a dim flickering of torches shone through the doorway, silhouetting a stout common Flame in brass plate-cloth, who held up his hand and muttered, "Private party, invitation only." Then he saw Dynat's Guards, and recognized his face, and his eyes bulged.

The Flame kneeled in haste while Dynat brushed past him and entered the room. The gaming cavern was a round, high-ceilinged cavern with only one entrance. Stone step seats had been carved in the downward sloping floor, to the pit at the center, ringing the cave. At first, no one saw him, and he was greeted only by the familiar roar of laughter and applause. Flames, both common and Noble, sat on the stone seats, looking down on a wide, open space in the middle of the cave. Metal cylinders focused the torchlight toward that space. The air was thick with the sour smell of blissi and the rich smoke of powderlux. Nobles lounged on cushions beside the center ring, and commoners sat and stood higher up. Even amid the roar of the crowd, the click of zirc coins could be heard as bets were placed.

In the center of the ring stood Dynat's objective. Two giant Semija, naked but for small loincloths around their waists, faced each other. Their meaty muscles gleamed with oil in the torchlight. Dynat's adrenaline surged when he saw them. When the gong was sounded and they gripped each other in a fight to the death, Dynat fought the urge to rush into the ring that very moment and attempt to strangle them both at once.

Both at once. In spite of the furnace in his mind, Dynat smiled. At the same moment, a Noble looked across the cavern and recognized him. Lord Binch was his name, and he stood and bowed, shouting over the noise of the crowd, "Greetings, Majesty!"

The spectators went into a quiet, slow motion panic. Nobles pulled hoods and veils over their faces. A few commoners in the highest tier edged out the door; Dynat could hear them pattering down the tunnel. The Semija continued to fight, oblivious to the danger; they were pulled away from each other with T'Jas and held on opposite sides of the ring, panting and straining to reach each other again. Slowly, the gasps and exclamations died away to silence, and Dynat walked down to stand before the ring, surveying a room full of terrified, kneeling subjects.

"At ease." No one moved a muscle. "I am not here to punish," Dynat continued quietly, "but to participate. Are these two the largest you have?" The two Semija still glared at each other across the ring.

Lord Garn, the owner of this gaming cave, stood opposite Dynat on shaky legs and bowed low. "At this time we have one larger, Majesty. The winner of this match was to fight him. He is undefeated."

"Bring him."

The crowd waited in silence while Dynat's order was carried out. There was a small commotion as a chair was offered to him. He waved it away, but he did shrug off his cloak and breastplates and hand them to one of the Ladies in the crowd. His slink scratches had stopped bleeding and were beginning to scab over. The gash on his forearm was not gushing any more, though it still glistened with wet blood. His Guards surrounded him closely, observing the crowd, ready to leap into action the second it became necessary. They would not like what he was about to do, but they would have no choice but to stand by.

The Champion was led in. He towered above his handlers. Dynat was tall, but this beast was even larger, over seven feet, and he must have been forged in the mines; his biceps were as large around as Dynat's legs, his chest a boulder of rock-hard muscle. Dynat did not hesitate. The fire in his mind raged him forward. He climbed down the stone stairs and stepped into the ring, facing Champion, making a square with the other two Semija. The walls of the arena rose just above Champion's head on all sides.

"What is it you wish to see, Majesty?" Lord Garn stood at his elbow now, bowing again. "We can order them to fight in any manner that pleases you."

"I do not wish to see anything, Lord Garn. I will fight all three of these Semija without my T'Jas. Sound the gong."

The crowd hissed with gasps. Lord Garn went pale as an Ice Fairy. Dynat was sure that no Noble Flame had ever entered that ring and demanded to fight. Perhaps a drunken commoner, but never a Noble and certainly not Royalty. Bets were being placed, halfheartedly; certainly no one believed he would win, but who could bet against their own King? The bets were small, sure losses.

"Majesty—" one of his Guards began.

"I will do this," Dynat told him. "If you interfere, I will have you consigned to the lava river. Wait outside if you think you will not be able to stop yourselves."

"Yes, Majesty." They withdrew, leaving Dynat exposed and vulnerable. Lord Garn looked as if he might have something to say, but Dynat's glance told him he was included in that order. He hurried up the steps, looking over his shoulder often, until he reached his own cushioned seat.

"Fight as you would in any match," Dynat said to the Semija in the ring. "Do not hold back because of who I am. If I think that you are holding back, your deaths will be slow and painful, rather than fast and merciful."

They prostrated, as Semija must to someone of his stature, but then they stood, ready and eager, hate in their eyes. The gong sounded, and they were advancing across the dusty ground faster than Dynat could think, Champion flanked by the smaller Semija. One of them bore the tattoo of a small Noble house, Levire, a three-pointed star, pale and faded under a bright blue miner's pickaxe. The other bore deep scars of the whip on his face; either he had been defiant in his youth, or run afoul of a particularly cruel crew master.

In the orphan tunnels, before the sweetness of T'Jas ran through his veins, Dynat had learned to fight with the only thing he had possessed then, his fists and feet. He was not as large or well fed as many of the other children, but he was lithe and clever and fast. It had served him as a child, it served him in the hunt, and it served him now, facing a rockslide of flesh.

He sidled to the left so he faced Levire's arm, and before the Semija could turn their momentum with him, he pushed as hard as he could against Levire. The Semija lost his balance and fell right into Champion. Champion shoved him away by reflex, and Levire grabbed Champion's arm and pulled, disrupting the larger Semija's balance. But Dynat scarcely noticed, for he was already dancing around the ring to meet Scars. His own back safe against the wall, he engaged the ugly creature, baiting him with fist-jabs. He landed a blow on the Semija's jaw, and another on his lower ribs, but the punches didn't seem to phase Scars. He shot back blows that seemed to splinter Dynat's wrists where he blocked them.

Then a punch got through, but it was Scars', and it landed right on the bridge of Dynat's nose. He reeled back and hit the wall. Panic rose, a trapped sensation, fear and pain threatening to overwhelm him. He nearly drew T'Jas. Instead, he found rage, and rage gave him the strength to stay on his feet. He raised his fists to throw punches, but threw a kick at Scars' right shin. The kick carried all his weight and nearly unbalanced him, which set off a new wave of fear and anger; a fall to the ground right now would be fatal; but he caught himself on the wall. The crack of the kick was swallowed by Scars' scream. The Semija fell to the ground sobbing for mercy, bones splintering through the skin on his leg.

Dynat had no time to give it, or to tend to the mask of pain his face had become, for Champion and Levire had worked out their differences and were rushing toward him. Dynat pushed himself forward to meet them, faked left toward Levire and swung an arm up through Champion's defenses, jabbing both his eyes with the tips of his fingers. The huge Semija roared in pain and stopped his assault. Dynat crashed into Levire and grabbed him in a choke-hold, using all his weight to bear the Semija to the ground without getting pulled down himself. Dynat aimed a series of kicks at the Semija's head and vitals. His face still ached; his nose was probably broken; his hair came loose, sticking to his shoulders; sweat dripped into his eyes and stung. The pain inflamed his anger and he focused so hard on kicking the life out of Levire he forgot about Champion.

Huge hands engulfed his neck and his thigh, and Dynat's head spun as he was lifted off the ground. He saw the arena whirling above as Champion turned, holding him high in a victory stance. Then everything blurred and Dynat was falling, no, hurtling, through the air. The world seemed to stop. No one was cheering. The whispers of the crowd were like the sounds of the baths from under the water. He saw something brown and bright rushing toward him very fast.

It was the ground, and when he hit it he heard a crack that raised in him a sensation he had not felt for many years: utter terror. He struggled to a sitting position. Something inside of him was broken. Champion was coming toward him fast. Something was broken. Champion was coming.

Bury the pain and get up.

Dynat could not tell if the Fire Spirit was speaking now or the voice was a memory. Either way, it woke the deeper terror of punishment for disobedience. He lurched to his feet, sending the pain to a far distant part of himself. He danced back awkwardly. He wondered if his Guards would disobey and come to his rescue. The thought made him angry, and he was able to move a little faster. He felt the wall behind his back. Champion was almost on him, trapping him against the wall.

Dynat thrust his fists toward Champion's face, and as Champion put his arms up to block, he dropped to the ground and rolled under Champion's legs and behind him. From the back, he jumped on the hulking Semija and got a killing grip on his neck. Pain lanced through his abdomen as he tensed, throwing all his weight into the Semija's spine. The beast roared with anger, reaching with arms of iron behind his back, trying to dislodge Dynat. The crowd was on their feet, drowning Champion's roar in applause, cheering on their King. The Semija turned so his back was to the wall. In a minute, he would slam his back into the wall and break Dynat completely. Dynat put his last strength into a final wrench of the Semija's head.

This time the sound of the crack was satisfying. Champion fell to the ground, a lump of shuddering flesh, and Dynat landed kneeling on his back, victorious. He screamed a primal slink call into the sudden silence of the arena.

The cavern was utterly silent. Then it erupted in a roar of applause. Dynat, panting and exhausted, jumped off Champion and gave Levire and Scars quick, merciful deaths with T'Jas. Under the noise of the crowd was a blessed silence. The Fire Spirit was appeased, for now.

A flurry of activity commenced. A chair was brought, and warm water and hides; a Semija began to clean him up while a Lady knelt and asked if she could have the honor of healing his wounds. Dynat accepted her offer without hesitation. More Semija arrived with platters, drink and smoke. The bodies of the defeated were being hauled away. The few who had placed bets collected their winnings. Dynat commanded that his lava be brought from his quarters.

He stayed long in the cavern of Semija games, watching the fights, each more brutal and perverse than the last. Most were Semija on Semija, but some were Semija against tusked male cababar or captured slink. The female Semija fights were thrilling and exotic, and the awkward, unwilling fights between newly captive Iskalon Semija often comical. Dynat lay on the softest cushions, with the best view of the ring, surrounded by his Guards and doting Nobles. Beautiful Ladies fluttered their lashes and cast him smoldering glances. He placed bets and drank more than his share of blissi. He slept on cushions in the gaming cavern, woke with Ladies wrapped around his body, rubbed sleep out of his eyes and began to drink and bet and smoke again. His head grew heavy with powderlux and he lost track of time.

Dynat was so deep in a haze in the pits that when the message came through his Guards that Medoc wished to report, he did not know if days had gone by or weeks. "Tell the General to attend me in the Throne Room," he said blearily, pushing away a Lady whose name he did not know. He pulled his hair back, splashed water on his face, ordered a Semija to fetch a fresh suit of armor. The Fire Spirit was whispering again in the back of his head. His respite was over.

"I believe we have found them, my King." Medoc stood before Dynat's throne, sturdy and solid, unchanging as stone, a pleasant contrast to the hissing, roaring flames that plagued Dynat's mind. The voice of the Fire Spirit rolled over a pounding headache that not even T'Jas could take away. "The Icers have found a cavern about halfway up the Spiral Tunnel, at the bottom of one of their huge ice shafts, where they freeze their dead."

"And the Dreamer Princess, she is there as well?" Dynat stroked the warm, smooth stone of his throne. The Fire Spirit echoed his words in his mind, hissing *Stasia* over and over.

"That I cannot say for certain, Majesty. But it is as likely a place as any." Was Medoc looking at him oddly? Dynat wondered if people could tell when the Fire Spirit was speaking to him.

"The princesses. You learned this from them?" At the mention of the princesses, the hissing echo turned to thoughts of killing.

"The princesses knew nothing of it, Majesty. I had them questioned again, after our scouts followed one of the enemy's raiding parties and found the tunnel entrance. All of their raids come from that tunnel and return to it. But the princesses seem completely ignorant of its existence."

Dynat realized he was stroking the arms of his throne almost compulsively, and he stopped, clasping his hands together in his lap. The Fire Spirit was quiet for a moment, but began to whisper about killing again. "Can we tunnel above without them knowing?"

"I believe so, My King. The shaft of burial ice goes straight up from the ceiling, about twenty feet in diameter.

Around it is solid, cold rock. We can tunnel through it to the burial ice. T'Jas will not penetrate the burial ice, but fire will. A torch can melt through it like tallow. We looted corpses in their other sacred caverns that way, during the war. Strategically, though, an attack from above is a waste of men. Better to cut off their escape tunnels and siege them out."

"But an attack from their sacred ceiling, through the very ice they believe their ancestors live in—it will break them, Medoc. You will have an easy time taking them before they recover from their shock. The Dreamer will be mine."

The General stroked his mustache and started to say something, then stopped. Dynat let it pass. Perhaps Medoc thought he was perverse—a foolish thought. How could he desire a cold, slimy little Icer, especially one he had never even seen? The Fire Spirit wanted her. That was all. The Fire Spirit would have her, and when it was finished Dynat would throw her into the Lava River, and that would be the end of it.

As Medoc turned to leave, the heavy double doors to Dynat's throne room burst open. A Cadet entered and bowed nearly to the floor. "Please forgive my interruption, Majesty, General, but I was sent to tell you immediately by the Lord of the Bathing Caverns. Majesty, the Baths—it is the Fireblood we used in battle—they are in chaos."

"He commanded you to report this to the King?" Medoc asked impatiently. "Is the Kinyara not available? The Baths are her province."

"She is there, General. They said you must come. It started in Lord Flame Barrett's pool. It filled with the Fireblood, and the heat and gas ignited it, and now the pool is covered in flames. All of his Semija were killed. But it is spreading to the other pools. The Lord of the Baths is beside himself."

"Enough," Dynat said. Surely Bolv could attend to this. She was more than capable. He had more important things to think about. The Fire Spirit cared nothing for baths; he was whispering still of killing. "This is not a matter for our ears. Tell the Kinyara to take care of the problem herself. Medoc, you have your orders. I am going to pay another visit to our royal guests. Will you have any further need of them, General?"

Medoc was slow in answering. The Cadet bowed again and hurried from the room. Medoc stared after him, then turned to Dynat. "The princesses? I—no, Majesty. I do not think they have any more information to offer." He bowed to Dynat, almost as an afterthought. He seemed distracted. Dynat recalled that he had sent Medoc to the baths to relax, and pulled him back into duty to find the Dreamer. Once she was captured, he would give Medoc a long respite. As the General left the throne room, Dynat stood. He would go and look in on the princesses before he passed down the Fire Spirit's orders.

Kill them all, the Fire Spirit whispered in Dynat's mind, the command coalescing into clarity from a maelstrom of different thoughts. There was a touch of glee in its tone. *All of them. They are useless. All we need is the Dreamer.*

A short time later, he stood above nine bedraggled Icers, languishing in their hot pit. None of them stirred. Were they dead already, then? Was he too late to say farewell?

Kill, kill, kill, the Fire Spirit still whispered clearly into his mind. No, their chests were rising and falling shallowly. They lived.

"Pasten," he said softly. The golden-haired one stirred. The others began to squirm as well, making the pit writhe before Dynat's eyes like a basket full of jewelsnakes. He looked away for a moment as a wave of nausea passed over him. Drawing deeply from the T'Jas in the room, he stood above the pit and forced himself to look directly at Pasten. She sat up, looking bravely back at him.

Once again, Dynat felt a peculiar stirring inside, shadows and ghosts of emotions long dead parading through his heart. "Your sister will be joining you soon, fairy," he said out loud. "We have discovered her hiding place."

The Fire Spirit began to rant, savoring the despair and hatred that played across the little Icer's features. Dynat pushed away the shadow of doubt that plagued his heart.

"Please be merciful, Fire King. Our people have done you no wrong. You can put an end to the killing, Great King. Please do it."

"No wrong? They have been stealing from me, Icer. I am informed that several weeks ago, they took a whole herd of cababar, and killed the Semija who tended them. More recently, they stole a large cache of weapons, and killed four of my Flames. It is they who are killing, Pasten."

"I'm sorry for that, Fire King. If you would send one of us to speak with them, I'm sure we could make them see the situation clearly."

Dynat stepped back. It was time to give the order. And then what? More slink hunting? Another fight in the pits while he waited for Medoc to bring him the Dreamer? It held no more honor to execute the princesses than it did to incinerate a slink with T'Jas. He let a smile that he did not feel stretch across his face, tightening the skin over his cheekbones.

"Perhaps you are right, little Icer. I can be merciful. Any of your sisters who battle me in single combat will be sent back to your people."

Dynat savored the look of confusion and hope that spread across the Ice Fairy's face. The Fire Spirit quieted to a background hissing. "Surely you jest, Fire King. We are in no state to fight, here."

"Guard!" Dynat called to the men standing by the door. "Escort the prisoners to the gaming pits. No, the Market. All of Chraun will want to watch this. Have my princesses healed, bathed and fed, and bring ice down from the lake. Get some of that armor they wear, if you can. And for me, Fireblood."

He walked away, pleased at the prospect of a fight with T'Jas. He had battled Flames in training before, but they were always quite restrained, unwilling to hurt the King. The princesses would be really trying to kill him, just like a slink protecting her kits. Perhaps he would take on several at once.

In the back of his mind, the Fire Spirit was laughing.

Medoc

When Medoc left the throne room, he went immediately to his second in command, Luten Renault, in the mess cave. Renault was stout, short for a Flame, but a better Luten Medoc had never known. He had been left behind during the attack on Iskalon, to replace Medoc should he have been killed. He bowed shallowly, and Medoc inclined his own head very briefly in respect.

"Have you heard of the situation in the baths, General?"

"Just now. I am headed there. I came to tell you to organize the attack on the remaining Icers. I will take over once we are ready to attack, but for now, you will start the tunneling and scouting." He outlined Dynat's plan briefly, cursing it silently as he did. It was a poor tactic. Dynat had been schooled in strategy, but that was many years ago now, and his lack of experience showed. He had never tried to interfere with the details before. Why now?

If Renault agreed with Medoc's unspoken assessment of the plan, he did not share his reservations. "I'll get this started right away, General. If I may ask, sir, have you had a chance to rest since the battle?"

"What are you now, my own wife?" Medoc growled. "See to your men, Luten, I am fine." He did not storm out of the room, but he left quickly. Did he look so bad as that? He paused in the tunnel before a long, smooth wall of obsidian, illuminated by torches. He could see his dark reflection in the wall. His mesh was in order, neatly organized in hexagons, his scale armor all coordinated and placed just right. His hair was oiled back; not a single strand fell out of place, and his mustache was trim and combed as always. Renault must be imagining things.

The baths were in chaos. Medoc was choking on smoke before he even reached the steam tunnel. He used T'Jas to make a bubble of clean air around his face. Dead Semija were being pulled past in carts. Young Flames covered in flaming Fireblood raced through the tunnels, excited by the intense heat and fiery eruptions. Older, more reserved Flames milled around, complaining about the interruption of their relaxed bathing. Living Semija crowded beside them, begging for healing of minor burns. Further in, he could hear several women wailing in mourning. Mourning for Semija? That was odd. Had a Flame died?

Medoc pushed through the mass of people in the steam tunnel to the main bathing hall. Bolv stood before the communal pool, speaking with the crying women. She left them and came to meet Medoc halfway through the crowd. "Where is Dynat?" She looked tired, shocked; deep blue circles surrounded her eyes, which had a red cast— had she been crying as well? Medoc pulled her away, out of earshot of the others.

"I am here, Kinyara, and I will have to do."

She nodded sharply. "Come. It is better if you see for yourself."

She led him past the filthy, sooty baths and up winding stone steps to the river. The Solph River seeped out of porous rock, travelled over a long plateau of thermal vents, and poured down a steamy waterfall, terminating in Lord Barrett's pool. Lord Barrett was the Lord of the Bathing Caverns; he owned most of the baths, and the other nobles paid him tribute. Medoc looked across the rushing river where it ran over flat rock, just before plunging twenty feet down. Large, dark lumps rolled in the current and disappeared over the edge.

"What is it?" He asked, peering closer. Bolv was silent, and he reached out with T'Jas and pulled one to the rough riverbank, dragged it to his feet. When he saw what it was, he felt ill.

Waterlogged and half eaten away by fishes, the face was no longer recognizable, but the build, the dark hair, and the steel armor marked the corpse as one of his Warriors. The river was full of them. One after another, they disappeared over the edge of the cliff. Medoc had an image of them being scooped out of Lord Barrett's pool, and suddenly he realized that the bodies he'd seen on the carts hadn't been Semija at all. They were Flames.

That explained the wailing, and it was likely why Bolv looked so bone-weary and sad. The bodies of all the war heroes were returning to Chraun.

"They aren't all ours," Bolv said. "About three quarters are the corpses of the Icers. Lava is too good for them. I have ordered them interred in rock in the ghost veins of the mines."

"How is this possible?" Medoc asked, staring at the lumps in the river with morbid fascination.

"Did you never wonder where our water comes from?" Bolv's tone was angry. "It is amazing that they did not use this to poison us long ago. Our scouts at their lake report rivers and streams pouring off the top of the lake and filtering through the bedrock to the Solph. Their Palace melting raised the lake level, so that anything floating on the lake went down these streams. Most of the tunnels are too narrow for a body to travel through, but the Fireblood was carried easily. We sent Flames up through the limestone to find the source of the contamination, and they opened a larger pipe-tunnel, and the bodies began pouring out."

"Why wasn't it resealed?"

"Think about it, General."

Medoc thought, and understood. The water in the

bedrock would not be hot like the baths, but it would be warm enough to allow the bodies to decompose. As they rotted, Fireblood would be the least of the contaminants in the water of Chraun; dead bodies would harbor disease. Better to clear them out all at once and gather them from Lord Barrett's pool than have their sludge leaking into the pools for months. Medoc felt ill again. There would still be corpses further up, in other, narrower streams. The whole bedrock could be contaminated.

"Have you been able to clean the Fireblood out of the pools?"

"The main bathing pools have been evacuated, and I have twenty Flames working on extracting the Fireblood and saving it in barrels. As they clean a pool out, more Fireblood comes down from the Solph, and we cannot stop the flow without leaving Chraun waterless. But the bathing pools are not the greatest worry. The poison has spread into the drinking springs, and beyond that to the pools that irrigate the fungal caverns and fill the stock tanks."

"Can it not be filtered?"

"We are working on all manner of filters, General. They clog, and then the water ceases to flow. Already the fungal caverns are drying up."

"Then there is no choice," Medoc said. "We must clean the lake, Bolv. And the tunnels between."

"That is absurd," she flared. "Go willingly into the cold? It is enough that we waste good Flames patrolling it. And how are we to clean it? Even using Fireblood, we will not have enough heat to tunnel through the cold rock, to get to the limestone filters where the bodies lay, where the Fireblood must be pooling."

She was right. Medoc let that rest while he sent orders to his officers to bring troops to the baths. He ruminated on the problem while helping Bolv set up temporary measures to decrease the impact of the Fireblood on the water supply. Together, Medoc and the Kinyara organized a team of common Flames working above the waterfall, to catch the bodies in the river and set up a variety of filtration systems. They could not keep the Fireblood completely out of the water, but they could at least catch the bulk of it before it reached the baths. He ordered teams of Warriors to patrol the baths, restoring order and giving solace to the grieving Ladies. He also sent a team of Warriors to take cababar with empty barrels to the lake for water, in hopes of finding a layer of water under the surface that wasn't contaminated.

He was talking to a common Flame, who specialized in irrigation, about the materials they would need to mine for filtration when Tejusi arrived with a summons.

"The King requires that all available Officers report to the Market Tunnel. He is staging an event to build the morale of Chraun."

"What is it, Cadet?"

"He wouldn't say, General Sir. Rumor has it its something to do with the Princesses."

Medoc's exhaustion hit him so hard and sudden that he wondered if he had reached his own end of days. No, more likely he was just tired. He had no wish to participate in whatever it was Dynat had planned, and he told Tejusi so. "He'll have a hard time finding available Officers, Cadet. Go in my stead and report to me when it's done. If he asks where I am, tell him I humbly request his presence in the Baths."

"Yes, General." Tejusi saluted and left.

Medoc finished talking to the irrigation specialist and sent a scribe with gold plate to the mines. He spent some time soothing Lord Barrett, assuring him that his taxes would be reduced during this crisis. After that, Medoc sought out Bolv. She was overseeing the removal of bodies. "The flow is slowing," she said, "a body comes down every hour or more. But the Fireblood is steady. How much did you haul up there, General?"

"Enough to make Iskalon burn forever," Medoc said

softly. Barrels upon barrels, dragged up by cababar and Semija, lifted with T'Jas when the way grew steep. For what? An empty victory. Medoc could not think of one thing that had improved in Chraun since the end of the war. And now this. Inspiration struck Medoc, and suddenly he knew what must be done.

"The Icers," he said. "We must send the Icers back to the lake, to cleanse it."

Bolv glared at him. "Dynat would never allow it. *I* would not allow it. Do you have treason in your heart, General?"

"Of course not," Medoc said lightly. "I will speak to Dynat. He will agree, I am sure."

"When you see him, bid him to come here. The people need their King to reassure them. They must see his face, and see that he grieves for the deaths of these warriors."

Medoc left the baths and headed toward Market. Surely Dynat would see the need to send the Icers back to the lake. Under guard and with a signed Treaty, of course. The King was not as fanatic in his hatred as the Kinyara. Was he?

Dynat

Dynat stood in Market Tunnel, wearing his crown and cloak, covered in flaming, greasy Fireblood. The center of the huge tunnel had been cleared, and a pit constructed. The Princesses sat in limestone chairs at one end, clad in glistening ice-armor. They were ringed by Guards who kept them under control and kept the crowd from tearing them to pieces. The whole of Chraun seemed to be gathered in the tunnel, nobles, commoners and military alike pressing close. When Dynat stepped out onto a tongue of stone above the pit, they cheered madly. He basked in their attention. He did not see Medoc, or Bolv, and that irritated him. Bolv at least should be here to see him. Her presence always seemed to add to his glory.

A Guard prodded the first contestant forward. She stood with her spine straight and head high, and Dynat hopped down into the pit to stand before her. A scribe called out her name and rank.

"Princess Lotica of Iskalon, to face King Dynat Sikur Antah, Defender of Chraun, Prince of Flames, Keeper of the Lava River, True Ruler of all Sholaen, Chosen of the Fire Spirit. Let the winner demonstrate the power of Chraun and the corruption of the Frozen Ones."

Dynat savored the hatred in the princess' eyes. She had long, dark curls and a haughty expression. Likely if the old Ice King had survived, he'd have been glad to have Dynat take this one off his hands. Almost before the scribe had finished speaking, four ice daggers flew from Lotica toward Dynat. He melted them all mid-air. Dynat shot flames at the princess to keep her defensive, while he considered how best to kill her. Fighting with T'Jas took more thought than hand-to-hand combat. She dodged his flames easily and raised a fog that made her difficult to see. Dynat heated her fog, evaporating it and revealing her. Her skin was red where the hot fog had scalded it. She threw up a barrier of cold air, and Dynat pressed forward with his own hot air. They wrestled back and forth, and she nearly pushed through. Cold air pressed on his cheek; fear and passion tingled down his spine. He pushed back wildly, driving her to the edge of the pit where her sisters looked on. He lashed out with fireropes, weaving them to get around her barrier, and she reached back with iceropes, dousing his fire.

Then suddenly her cold simply gave out; her use of T'Jas had depleted it; Dynat's heat rushed in almost against his own will. She screamed in pain as fire seared through her skin, reddening it further. Dynat reached out and touched her forehead, sent a jolt of heat into her skull to cook her brain. Her screaming stopped and she slumped to the ground, fear, pain and hatred frozen in her dead eyes.

Dynat was panting when he stood. The fight had been more difficult than he expected, and he had eight more to go. Her death did not make him feel quite the same as a slink's death. Perhaps it had been the loss of her power at the end that cheapened it. Still, adrenaline surged in his blood, fear and fire reminding him that he was alive, that once again he had conquered death. The princesses were making noise on their dais, crying foul play. The cheers of Chraun drowned them out. When a Guard came to take the body, Dynat said, "Take the head. Dump the body in the ghost veins, but keep the head intact. I promised that every Princess who fought me would be returned to her people, and I mean to keep that promise."

He demanded that the next two come in a pair. They even looked alike, Princesses Senlei and Roila, with matching, sooty hair cut short like a boy's. One wore a ruby in her tiara, the other turquoise, and they quickly put the one with the ruby behind Dynat, so that he was surrounded by cold. Senlei nicked him with her ice dagger, drawing blood, and at one point Roila got an icerope around both of his wrists and pulled him to the ground. The booing echoed off the ceiling, deafening Dynat as he struggled to his feet, drawing T'Jas from his lava and dissolving the rope. He roared as he stood, backing against a wall to force them both to his front, and cast fire ropes around the pit to grab them from behind. They doused the ropes quickly, but the next time he cast the ropes, he drew them back before they could douse them, and like fools they followed the ropes, separating from each other. Dynat let Senlei douse his rope while the rope Roila battled grew white-hot, penetrated her cold, and strangled her.

When Senlei saw her sister dead on the ground, she went to her knees and pleaded for mercy. Dynat, still enraged from the blood she had drawn, gave it to her in the form of a quick death, a jolt of heat to the brain.

After that the battles became a blur. Each pair of princesses tried a new set of tricks to trap or distract him, and he defeated them all. They came at him with ice daggers, with ice ropes, with fog and cold air, with pellets of ice shot so fast they would have torn through his organs if he did not melt them away. They came at him with floating globules of water meant to douse his flames. They came at him bare-handed and pleading, only to bristle with icy weapons when he approached. He defied them with fire while the Fire Spirit reveled in their deaths. He remained strong with T'Jas, but his body was beginning to tire. Blood leaked from cuts across his skin where daggers had struck. The Guards who came to get the bodies asked to give him healing, but he refused it. The blood told him that he was still alive.

At last only the oldest and the youngest, Maudit and Pasten, faced him. The rage and sorrow and hatred in their eyes alone could have killed him. They behaved differently from the rest. Perhaps they realized that no matter how bravely they fought, they would die today. They stood together, arms crossed, faces regal. They did not raise a cold front, did not lash out with iceropes, did not cast daggers at his face as he approached. They stood still and did nothing. Dynat smiled at them.

"Wiser than your sisters?"

They did not reply, only stared at him.

"If you don't fight, it's back to your pit for more suffering," he lied. "This is your chance for a clean death."

"There is nothing clean about this, King of Fire." The eldest spoke. She looked like a common Flame-wife on a bad day. How had the Ice King managed these women? "Your kingdom is soiled."

"We would have given you generous terms in a surrender," Pasten said sadly. "You did not have to destroy us. You could have ruled Iskalon and Chraun both. Instead you will rule ghosts."

They still did not move. Dynat reached out with firewhips to strangle them both where they stood. He'd given them ice and armor and a chance to defeat him if they could. It was not his fault they were too cowardly to take it.

As his firewhips drew toward them, each princess reached into her pocket and drew forth a perfect white sphere.

Too late, Dynat tried to snap his whips back, away from their weapons. Globombs—these could be nothing else—would explode when they encountered heat. But the whips were already past the point of no return. When the fire touched the princesses, they exploded. Shards of ice raced toward Dynat, piercing his skin. The Fire Spirit surged in his mind, and Dynat saw flames racing out from his own skin to meet the ice. His ears rang and the world went black and he felt cold, then nothing.

Chapter 9

Iskalon Stands

Medoc

The Market was in even greater chaos than the baths had been and Medoc felt his exhaustion keenly as he watched it from the upper entrance. Shoppers and Semija swarmed past him, leaving the open cavern in a hurry, and more huddled behind the stalls, where the shopkeepers complained vocally about the mess. A large pit had been dug in the middle and was thick with his own Warriors. Something glistened on the floor in the torchlight, and it took Medoc several moments of straining before he realized, with incredulity, that it was water.

As he tried to make sense of this, Medoc caught sight of Tejusi shouldering his way through the crowd toward him. Medoc pulled him out of the entrance, trying to find a place in the tunnel quiet enough to speak without shouting. "Report, Cadet."

"He—His Majesty fought all of the princesses, General. In that pit in there, like the Semija games . . ." He trailed off, and Medoc nodded impatiently. He had heard rumors of the King's time spent in the Semija pits and ordered his men not to speak of it. He did not have the energy to reprimand Tejusi now. "He gave them ice. The last two used theirs to make globomb. They were blown to pieces, and the King was badly injured. His Guards carried him out."

"By the Lava Lake and All . . ." Medoc smoothed his mustache. A globomb in Market. The King injured. He would not be the only one, not in that crowded cavern. "How many citizens were injured, Tejusi?"

"They haven't made a tally of the dead or injured yet, General. But there were shopkeepers in their stalls who reported the shards hitting them. For the spectators close to the pit . . . it was a massacre, Sir. At least one hundred dead, by my estimate."

"Who is in charge here?"

"Serg Linou took charge after the King's Guards got him out."

That was good. Linou was a capable man. Medoc dismissed Tejusi, ordering him to report in an hour on the Serg's progress, then headed for Dynat's quarters. Bolv would need to be notified. "Freeze me," Medoc muttered under his breath as he hurried down the hall. The last thing Chraun needed now was an incapacitated King.

There were no Guards on Dynat's doors, and when he knocked, the Semija who kept His Majesty's parlor informed Medoc there was no one at home. He was on his way to the Throne Room when a Guard approached him with a bow.

"The King requests your presence immediately, General. He awaits you in your quarters."

My quarters? "Is he well?"

"He has been healed to a full recovery, by the grace of the Fire Spirit. Fireblood protected him from the worst of the blast."

Medoc followed the Guard to his own quarters, confused and relieved. When he arrived, Dynat's honor Guard held his door, Medoc's wife sat at the oval soapstone dining table, and across from her sat King Dynat, eating delicacies handed to him by Medoc's own Semija. He felt unreal, and wondered if he had fallen asleep in the baths and drifted into a dream. He almost asked his wife to pinch him, but the look on the King's face stopped him.

Medoc's four daughters sat around the table as well, each staring at the King as if he were a slink in a hunt, a little dangerous but still something they would like to tangle with. Of course. The King was not married, and each of Medoc's little ladies would love to be Queen. They were approaching marriageable age, and what better husband for the daughter of the General than the King himself?

Looking at the angry red flames dancing in his King's eyes, Medoc, in his third traitorous thought of the week, decided that he would die before he saw any one of his precious daughters marry the madman before him.

"Ah, welcome, General," the King said, as if he did not sit at Medoc's own table. "Please join us. Your daughter—Selimne, is it?—she was telling an enchanting story."

"I fear she will need to finish it another time, Majesty. I must have words with you. Wife, daughters, be dismissed."

Wilmina gave him a hard look as she rose and herded their daughters from the room. He was sorry for his curt dismissal, and would be sorrier still the next time they were alone together, but he did not have time now for the chatter of women.

Medoc bowed, and when Dynat did not give him leave to sit, remained standing before him. "I am relieved to find you well, Majesty. Apparently your audience was not so lucky."

"The Fire Spirit saved me, Medoc. When those treacherous Icers pulled their dirty trick, He gave me the power to withstand. None of the shards went deep enough to kill me."

"Yes, Majesty. Thanks be to the Fire Spirit."

"I sought you here to ask you to hasten your efforts against the icevipers. They are dangerous and we must attack them at once."

"Majesty, I believe there is an even greater danger to Chraun. The water from the lake—"

"Medoc, I gave you an order. I am not accustomed to being disobeyed."

"Disobeyed, Majesty?"

"Have you forgotten as well as shirked my orders? Do you not recall being told to begin planning the attack and capture of the icevipers?"

"I told Renault—"

"Renault is not General of Chraun, Medoc. At least, not yet."

Medoc's blood ran cold. Dynat continued speaking. "Next time I give an order of this importance, I expect it to be followed immediately, by you, not delegated. I have covered your slack this time, but it will not happen again."

"Majesty, the baths—"

"I am sure Bolv has them well in hand. They are not your concern. This is what you must focus on now, Medoc." He gestured to a map etched in gold plate on the table before him. "I have drawn up the battle plan. We are tunneling above their little cavern, around their burial ice. They will be expecting us from below, but never above. Your troops will enter through these tunnels, here, here and here. Renault is already at work—twelve tunnels in all. We will tunnel right into the Burial Shaft. You will send the message down, then fire, and the army will enter through the stone tops of the walls. The Iskaloners will be terrified and surrender easily. But if they do not, kill indiscriminately. I will not have them escape to plague me further. The Dreamer is to be taken alive at all costs."

Medoc glanced at the plate with symbols and arrows indicating troops and movements. He could tell from that glance that the plan wouldn't work. The Icers would scatter. His Warriors would take perhaps fifty percent captive and kill a few thousand more, but there was no guarantee that the Princess would be among those taken. A parley would be a much more effective way to root her out. But none of that mattered. "Majesty, Fireblood has contaminated the drinking pools and the fungal caverns. Cababar are drinking the stuff and dying. Corpses are clogging the Solph. Your presence is needed in the baths, Majesty. I believe we must send the captive Icers to cleanse the lake. It is the only way to stop it."

"Medoc, not another word about those confounded baths from you!" Dynat sat up straight in his chair, looking every bit the King. "I will not hear it. You have enough to concern yourself with. These domestic matters are Bolv's province. Send the Icers to the lake? We just fought a war to get them away from it! In any case, they are all dead. I ordered them killed, for what their princesses did to Market. They are too dangerous to keep alive. You would know that if you were doing you duty as General instead of playing in the baths."

Medoc stared at his King for a long moment. All of the Icer prisoners killed? Medoc had known Dynat intended to kill the Princesses, but not the other Icers. He stared into Dynat's fiery eyes, staggered by the sudden uselessness of his plan to save Chraun from the poisons in the lake. Medoc was no stranger to death and killing, but the coldness of the King's action, coupled with the number of corpses he had seen in the last few hours coming down the Solph and the deaths in Market, was overwhelming.

If any harm should come to the King, we will follow you. No. He would not kill the man he had sworn to follow, not even for the good of Chraun. There had to be a better way. He bowed his head lower than he need for the King. "As you command, Majesty."

Dynat stood, and Medoc followed him to the door.

"The tunneling will take a bit longer. Spend a few hours here with your wife, General. I think she misses you."

Medoc bowed again. The King was mad. Again, Medoc had that utterly clear sensation. He knew what he must do. He simply did not know how it would be done.

Stasia

Stasia sat on a simple stool fashioned from ice, on a platform above the Council, Wyfus's nasal voice making her more and more drowsy. Far above, the impenetrable burial ice glowed with its soft purple light, and her copper-clad ancestors watched the proceedings with lazy eyes. Once, it would have been considered sacrilege to live and hold council in a chamber as sacred as this. But hard times called for change, and Stasia did not think the Ancestors would begrudge them this refuge.

Beneath her, a full council of thirty-five sat on simple, back-less stone seats, no more than benches, really. In the front row, Mowat and Cygnet flanked Wyfus's empty space, their eyes glazed and chins drooping. Beyond the Council, a small crowd stood, where in the Council Hall the benches would have been. Beyond them, filling the rest of the widened cavern, recruits were practicing with scavenged weapons, the sound of metal ringing against metal and occasional grunts and curses punctuating Wyfus's speech about re-capturing the lake.

Glace and Larc stood side by side at the front of the "benches." Stasia had so little support there that she had ordered Glace to leave the recruits to another Officer and attend Council, to argue for her position on important matters. He looked restless and impatient where Larc looked fascinated, as if there was nowhere she would rather be than stuck in another Council Meeting.

Slightly behind Stasia's stool, Casser sat close enough that she could hear his quiet breath. Kiner sat beside him, but a little further back. Stasia had realized quickly that although Larc was an excellent advisor, Casser was more seasoned, and Larc's force on the floor could turn the council to favor Stasia. Barely. The whole council, even Guilds which had full heartedly supported her father, seemed to hate Stasia. Even Larc's brilliance could scarcely make up for that.

Stasia was beginning to understand why her father had wanted her in council so often. While the Royal representative could not speak, anyone in the audience could, so it helped to stack the audience with allies; people who understood and supported your position. Stasia would have given all the Ancestors above to the Svardark to have more than two allies in this crowd right now.

Bored by Wyfus' arguments, for she had heard them over and over in the nearly two months since Iskalon in Exile began holding Council meetings, Stasia let her thoughts drift. Things had been going well, lately, though not nearly well enough to consider an all out attack on the lake. But the last raid had resulted not only in a huge cache of food, but in piles upon piles of weapons as well— swords, maces, axes, even knives. Though they'd lost five Icers and several Warriors in the raid, Stasia knew with regret that the find was worth the loss. The weapons were nearly enough to arm their recruits.

The loss. Stasia did not think she would ever become comfortable with ordering people to their deaths. How had Father borne the guilt, the feeling of inevitability every time he saluted a squadron and sent them out to the tunnels? Yet balancing that guilt was the tremendous weight of all the lives depending on her. In the face of the survival of ten thousand, five lives seemed a small price to pay.

The worst was that she did not know if she was being effective as Regent. After the first council of Iskalon in Exile, she had been meek as a baby raihan. Even when it meant giving way on important issues, she had tried to show the Council that she would not be a tyrant, tried to be fair and just, even when the Council's decisions seemed utterly foolish. But did that make her a good leader? Casser seemed to think so, and Larc applauded her efforts. She wasn't sure. Didn't a good leader make the difficult decisions, the ones no one else was willing to make? If only Father were here; he could surely tell her. Stasia realized that he had tried to tell her many times, tried to involve her in the leadership of Iskalon, but she had shut him out. She could only hope that one of her sisters showed up soon, so she would be relieved of her gnawing doubts and the lonely burden of ruling.

On the floor, Mowat was heaving up from her chair, interrupting Wyfus. Stasia snapped alert, curious. "You are taking this discussion in the wrong direction." The molebear-sized woman's cheeks had shrunken so far that it looked as if there were holes on either side of her mouth. "Re-take the lake? We can barely even feed our people. Thirty cababar are not enough to feed ten thousand mouths. The people are dying. True, we have a small army gathered, but they are pitiful compared to what the Fire Kingdom has. And the worst is that they have our people in their hands."

This was a surprise. In all the Council meetings Stasia had ever attended, Mowat had never contradicted Wyfus. Even though their Guilds competed to feed Iskalon, they shared many common interests, and always backed each other. She continued, "What we should be discussing is not more raids, more actions that will antagonize the Fire King. What we should be discussing is surrender."

Both the council and the audience exploded with sound as the people reacted to that audacious statement. Stasia pressed her lips together so tightly that they went numb. Were they testing her, to see if she would hold to her proclamation? Were they baiting her to break her silence and lose the few allies she might have gained? If that were the case, it would not work. She would wait out the Council in silence, then send Glace and a team of

Warriors for Mowat.

Mowat's deep voice rose above the crowd. "I said discussion, not anarchy! What do you all think this is?" It took her several tries, but at last the voices died back. Before she could speak again, however, Cygnet rose from her stool.

"I quite agree with Mowat," Cygnet said, her voice still clear and musical in spite of the sunken, dark circles around her eyes. Her willowy form was thin and haggard under a loose gown of dusty ruby-sewn websilk. "The Fire Kingdom has won. It is time to admit it. They hold our people as slaves and prisoners, if any remain alive. For the good of what remains of Iskalon, we should surrender."

"Perhaps if we surrender, they will give back the lake," Wyfus put in. "After all, what good is it to them? They don't even eat fish."

Stasia had been staring at the Council, pressing her lips together, growing angrier and angrier. When Wyfus spoke his last word, something inside of her snapped. They had planned this. All of Wyfus' talk of taking back the lake was a ruse, to set up the moment for Mowat to mention surrender. Looking back on his talk, she could see how he had painted his discussion to make taking the lake seem hopeless, even as he spoke in favor of it. More and more councilors were speaking, voicing reasons to surrender. Glace and Larc were both looking at Stasia with worried expressions. She was helpless, bound by the constricts of Council Law, to sit and listen while they crafted a proposal for surrender. Oh, she could refuse their proposal when they finally laid it before her. She could even have every last Council member arrested for treason. But to do so, especially if it held the support of nearly every Guild, would be a political disaster. She would be seen as a tyrant, and treated like one.

Very well. They had forced her hand; if they wanted a tyrant, they would have one. But they would have her now, not after hours of discussion. Rising from her stool, she drew T'Jas from the ice until nothing remained but a pool of water at her feet.

"SILENCE!!!" Her voice cracked through the burial chamber and down the tunnels beyond, magnified by cold. She cast a wave of cold air, rippling toward the Council, pulling them off of their stools to hover in midair, just a few feet above the floor of the burial chamber.

The room went so silent that she could hear the water from her stool dripping off the edge of the platform. She spoke into the silence, raising herself slowly above them.

"Do you truly think you could survive surrender? Do you think they will give you a herd to tend, Mowat, or let you contentedly keep fishing the lake, Wyfus? And you, Cygnet. They don't need another human to cut gems. I'm sure the Fire King will find a different use for you. They have a word for humans, in Chraun. They call them Semija. Slaves. That is what you will be, for the rest of your lives. We Icers, who they'll kill, we will be the lucky ones."

She gazed coldly at all of them, full of contempt. Some were struggling, trying to get their feet back on the ground, but most hung limp, mouths wide with shock. They were like children playing a game, and they hadn't realized yet that this was real, that this could only end badly, unless they fought for their lives. True, the resistance was going poorly. But at least they were resisting. If they held out just a little longer, if they could raid enough weapons and train enough new recruits, they *could* take back the lake.

"If you want to live your lives as slaves, you have my leave. But I will not allow you to take the rest of Iskalon with you. If I must disband the Council to stop it, I will."

With that, she released T'Jas, and let them drop. She meant for them all to land on their feet, and some did, but many sprawled on the floor in shock. Wyfus stood stiffly, then sat with dignity. His eyes were sharp as the spikes on Glace's mace. Stasia lowered herself so that she stood on the platform, watching them recover. Glace and Larc both stared straight ahead, avoiding her eyes. Behind her, Casser and Kiner were silent.

Wyfus waited for the rest of the council to pick itself up, then stood again. "I have a proposal to lay before Regent Stasia," he said. Beads of cold sweat on his brow revealed that he was drawing all his courage to speak. Stasia watched him in silence, wary. In spite of his haste, any proposal would have to be approved by three councilors before she could vote on it. They thought her a tyrant, when they put forth a proposal without opening up the floor for debate? "I propose that we lift the restriction on the Regent, and that she be allowed to take part in the raids."

Mowat had fallen all the way to the floor, and councilors on either side were helping her pull her extensive girth upright. "I second that proposal." Her deep voice cut through Stasia like a Flame's fire-whip.

"I give it a third, and carry it to the Regent." Cygnet stepped nimbly forward, and though her words were sure, she hesitated before approaching the platform. Fear glinted in her silver eyes, as if she was unsure of what Stasia might do. She bowed formally, her long hair reaching the ground, and said, "The Council proposes to lift the restriction keeping the Regent from joining in the raids. Will you rule on this proposal, Regent Stasia?"

If she hadn't been so angry Stasia could have laughed at their transparency. They thought she was impetuous and would hurry out in the next raid to get herself killed, allowing them to put Casser on the throne until her sisters were found. As if she were that stupid.

However, it wouldn't hurt to have more freedom. "My rule is to pass this proposal. The Council bears witness. This meeting is adjourned!" She snapped the last, and turned away, hurrying down the platform so she would not have to see the relieved glances pass between all the councilors who wanted her dead.

Glace

Glace shadowed Stasia down the Spiral Tunnel. She had insisted, now that the Council had lifted its restriction, on joining the next raid. Had she been merely the monarch and not his sworn charge, Glace would have approved; a Royal presence could help the morale of the Warriors marching ahead of them down the tunnel. But though she had told Casser she would not take part in the fighting, Glace did not trust her to keep her promise in the heat of the battle.

And after what Stasia had done in Council, her presence might actually be a hindrance. Though only a short time had passed, whispers of her outrageous actions were spreading through Iskalon in exile. Infiltrating the ranks. The men in this raid stepped carefully around the Regent. The whole Kingdom walked as if on ice-shards. Casser had been furious, scolding his niece quietly but thoroughly in the privacy of her little chamber. Larc had voiced her disapproval just as clearly, if somewhat more tactfully. Stasia had not argued, or shouted, or railed against them as Glace had seen her do in the past. Instead, she'd said quietly, "I would not expect you to understand. You were right to insist on the lines of succession, Casser."

Her quiet calm worried Glace more than a tantrum. Anger would have been expected, something he was accustomed to seeing in his little mistress. Stasia was changing. Power was changing her. Was it for the better? Glace saw the scene in the council vividly in his mind. All those bodies rising above the chairs. What if she had raised them to the ceiling, and let them drop from there?

But she hadn't. She wouldn't. She was still Stasia, the lost little Icer wandering about the tunnels. Not a murderer. Not a tyrant. Stasia. She ghosted ahead of him now, a cool presence drifting down the tunnel behind the raiding force. Her hips swayed slightly under her chirsh armor. Her hair shimmered in the dim icelight. Glace cursed her silently for insisting on this raid. He was sure she would join the fighting if she saw an opening.

Musche shadowed Glace, padding along silently on huge paws behind him. He had recovered from his wounds, and was getting sleek and healthy on flats and other rodents in the Spiral spurs. Glace suspected he had found wild female slink in the spurs as well; he disappeared for longer and longer periods.

"We are nearing the cavern, Regent. Best that you stay back, and watch from here." That whispering voice was Serg Kabre, the very young Icer who was leading this mission. Glace could see torchlight in the distance. The scouts had brought word of a cavern full of human prisoners from the war, near the bottom of the Spiral Tunnel. Apparently the Flames were running out of places to keep their prisoners in Chraun. This was a mission not just for weapons or food, but for freedom. If they were successful, what better way for the people to be welcomed than by their own Regent?

"There is an alcove up here, Majesty," Glace said, gesturing to the wall nearby. "It is warm, but we can see down the tunnel clearly, and we can hide if Flames come by."

Stasia hesitated, and Glace had a sinking sensation in his chest, but then she said, "Yes, of course, Glace. Help me up, I want to conserve my vaerce." Glace made a step with his hands and she pulled herself up. He savored the gentle pressure of her boots pushing against the palms of his hands. He jumped up beside her, and soon he felt Musche joining them, crowding them together on the ledge. It was warm, but Stasia's armor remained stiff with ice, and Glace thought she would have enough cold to protect herself if anything went awry.

Glace had led raids during his training, in which he commanded the warriors without engaging at the front of the fighting, but watching a battle from this far away seemed strangely detached, as if he and the Princess were spectators to some grisly entertainment. The cavern entrance and the Flames guarding it were concealed by the steam sublimating off Kabre and the others' chirsh armor in the heat. Here and there, Glace could see a torch shining through and steel glinting as his warrior's swords flashed. He wanted to be in there, fighting with them, and he could feel the same urge in Stasia. He heard shouting, and screams. It was impossible to know what was happening.

Then a figure came toward them out of the mist, and Glace saw Kabre silhouetted against torchlight, his armor gone, his flesh glistening blackly in the yellow light. "The battle has turned," he shouted, not looking at the alcove where Stasia sat next to Glace, trembling with adrenaline. "There are more Flames than we expected. Flee!" A Flame followed him out of the mist, fire shooting from his fingertips.

Before Glace could stop her, Stasia was on the ground, daggers of ice shooting from her hands. They entered the Flame's chest in a spray of blood, and he fell to the tunnel floor without ever seeing what hit him. Kabre looked up at the Regent before he collapsed beside the dead Flame. His chest ceased heaving, and Glace knew he was past healing. Stasia must have known as well, for she made no movement toward the young Icer.

"We have to go now," Glace said. The fog was dissipating, the torchlight growing stronger. This raid had failed. Stasia was gazing down the tunnel past Kabre as if she was considering going toward the light.

"Take his body, Glace."

"Princess?"

"I am not the fool they think I am. Take his body. We must leave the rest, but we will at least give Kabre a decent burial." She turned abruptly and hurried up the tunnel toward Iskalon in Exile.

Glace did not hesitate any longer. The Flames were approaching. He reached for Kabre. The young Icer was heavier than he expected. Icers were generally lighter than humans, but in death the boy bore down on Glace's shoulders.

Stasia

Stasia reached the burial chamber just ahead of Glace. She knew he was behind her without even hearing his footfalls; she could sense his presence. The great chamber was full of activity, people taking advantage of a day without a council meeting to move around in the larger space, out of their tiny caves. Larc stood, strangely idle — her friend seemed always to be healing or singing or organizing or doing something—staring up at the ceiling and the amethyst glow of burial ice. The dark Icer did not notice her presence until Stasia placed a gentle hand on her shoulder. Then she gasped and apologized.

"I was just thinking of them—they almost seem like they are still alive. The burial ice preserves us. All those souls who perished in fire, they will never be buried . . ."

Stasia nodded. "Well, we have one more to bury today, Larc." She did not know if Larc had been close to Kabre, but words weren't enough, so she entered her friend's mind briefly and showed her the image of the Icer coming out of the fog, collapsing on the tunnel floor. Tears came to Larc's eyes and she began to hum softly, a burial rite. Glace approached and laid Kabre out on the Royal platform.

"Save your song," Stasia said to Larc. "Send out a call for all we can fit in this chamber to meet for a public ceremony. Tell them we have a hero to bury. He will be buried in this chamber, as a symbol of what we are fighting for."

So far, all of the dead had been taken to other Burial Shafts. It had seemed too gruesome to have to live and meet under the recently dead. It was one thing to look up and see long past, revered ancestors, but to see the faces of loved ones close enough to touch? On her walk back to the burial chamber, Stasia had thought long and hard on this decision. It was too easy for everyone to forget how cruel the Flames were, what evil monsters Iskalon faced. Kabre's body in the ice above would be a symbol of what Chraun had taken from Iskalon. It was a cold decision, but with luck, it would quell talk of surrender, and gain Stasia's efforts more support in Council.

Normally, only a few people were present for a burial ceremony, close friends and family of the deceased. But for Kabre, she waited while the burial chamber filled with people. Because it was not an official council meeting, the stools of the councilors were given to elderly citizens. Soon, the chamber was crowded as word spread through the alcoves and down the tunnels that the Regent was holding a special ceremony. Only a small portion of the thousands of exiles could fit in the cavern, so Stasia had people stationed at the entrances to relay the ceremony to the rest.

She mounted the platform and sat on her stool, with Glace, Casser, and Larc at her side, while Kiner spoke the Warrior Guild rites for Kabre and laid his glory medals on his chirsh. Then four Icers raised Kabre to the ceiling. They pressed his body to the ice, and the ice, which would not part for the strongest T'Jas, melted slowly around his body, reforming at the edges. It took a long time before he was completely subsumed. The copper-clad woman seemed to welcome him as he entered; her eyes brightened, her arms spread very slightly. Stasia shivered, reminded of the dream she'd had just before the war, of the burial ice parting and swallowing her alive. *I'm not dead yet.* Something tickled at the back of her head, as if there was more to the dream she could not remember. Minutes dripped by, and finally Kabre floated free in the ice, timeless as the ancestors.

Larc drifted toward the ceiling and began to sing. Haunting, echo-y, her voice conjured up the deepest sadness, bringing to the surface all of Stasia's fears and doubts and sorrows. It was a song without words, but there were no words to express what everyone in the chamber was feeling. After Larc's voice resonated through the chamber alone for a time, Stasia joined in, and then Casser, and then Cygnet, who had a lovely soprano, and soon the whole cavern was singing. The four Icers still hovering above placed their palms on the burial ice, a gesture of farewell.

Deeply moved by the music, Stasia grieved, not just for Kabre, but for all that Iskalon had lost. She felt the loss of her family and her Kingdom deep in her heart. Even if they regained the lake, she realized, Iskalon would never be the same. Tears poured from her eyes, and she knew she was showing all her citizens weakness, but she did not care.

Stasia was wiping tears from her eyes when she heard a thud and a gasp from above. She looked up in time to see a large, round, black object bounce off one of the Icers in the air and fall to the ground at her feet. Another fell, this one straight from the ceiling, and then the cavern filled with chaos. Screams and shouts echoed off the walls, and people on the ground began to stampede toward the tunnels. Icers rose and made ice-shields. Before Stasia could react, Kiner and Casser formed a dome of ice around the dais, protecting Stasia from the falling objects.

Within seconds, it was over. The floor of the cavern was empty of people; the citizens who had not fled to the tunnels were pressed against the walls, looking up. Stools lay overturned amidst the smattering of black boulders. Stasia dissolved an opening in the dome, though she kept her cold close, wary of another attack. She was dimly aware of Casser and Glace flanking her, of Kiner hurrying out of the chamber, his whispered orders echoing off the ice ceiling like the calls of ghosts. She walked toward the nearest object and knelt beside it, picking it up and turning it in her hands. When she realized what it was, she was hit by such a multitude of emotions that she dropped it immediately. Shaking her hands convulsively, she rocked back and forth in waves of disgust, sadness, loss, and anger.

It was a head, blackened by fire, but still intact enough that she could recognize her sister Pasten, staring at her with dead, agonized eyes. Stasia managed to reach around herself and clutch her arms with her own hands, holding herself tightly, still rocking. Her head shook as if she could deny what her eyes saw. She closed her eyes, but that could not block out the sight of Pasten's eyes staring back at her, of Lotica's high cheekbones, of the crown of Iskalon on Maudit's head. Twelve heads, twelve sisters. Every member of her family, gone now. Except Casser. She was still rocking when he knelt behind her and took her gently in his arms. She wanted to lean back and soothe herself in his comfort, wanted him to make everything better.

She could not.

"Iskalon stands," she said softly, but in the shocked silence of the cavern, her voice carried all the way to the tunnels. She pushed Casser away and stood. She remounted her platform and sat in her stool. Her whole body was shaking. All she wanted to do was curl into a ball and join her sisters in death, but she had to be strong for Iskalon. People were coming back to the chamber, Kiner's officers trying to organize the chaos; the air hissed with whispered questions.

Stasia looked up. Large holes peppered the surface of the burial ice. They were closing up, smoothing over, but they told Stasia volumes. The Fire King knew where they were. Though no living Icer could penetrate burial ice, fire could melt right through it. At any instant, he could send anything out of that Ice—Flames, Semija warriors, more of her people's corpses. The tunnels below were well guarded, but they had never thought to guard the burial ice itself.

"Yes," Casser said, his voice loud, strong, resonant. "Iskalon stands. And today, we have a new Queen." He stooped and plucked the crown of Iskalon gingerly from Maudit's sooty brow, ran his hands over it, and placed it on Stasia's head. She fought intense revulsion. She could not be ill, not now, in front of all of her people. The crown sealed her fate to Iskalon, and if she faltered now, Iskalon would fall.

She rose slowly to the ceiling, staring at it defiantly. "Hear me! Iskalon stands!" she shouted. "You lake-slime eating sons of molebears! You'll pay for what you've done! The Ancestors bear witness to your crimes!"

The ceiling erupted into fire.

Chapter 10

Iskalon's Sacrifice

Medoc

Medoc listened to the silver-haired Icer ranting below, then sighed and gave the order. "I had a feeling the King's 'message' would only stir the pot," Renault confided after he had passed the command down.

"Just make sure they know not to kill the princess—or should I say Queen, now," Medoc said, shifting in his cramped position. He sat in a tiny alcove of stone adjacent to the burial shaft. In spite of the flaming Fireblood on his armor, the air was cold. He could not get used to feeling the ice through the stone, so close. He could see the immense shaft of burial ice rising above the cavern through the drop hole. T'Jas would not penetrate the purple, glowing ice, but it had parted with surprising ease for the Fireblood-coated torches. It had taken mere seconds to open the holes for the heads to roll through. Another hole in the rock, much smaller, revealed the cavern so that he could watch and direct the battle below. He preferred to lead troops, but under these circumstances, the first few waves would probably perish. So much for ending things without more bloodshed. Dynat's plan was ridiculous. Had it been up to Medoc, he would have sent emissaries with terms for surrender, not the heads of their Royalty.

Renault was speaking. "You should say Semija; I'm sure that's what his Majesty intends. Why he cares so much, I can't imagine. Do you think he's—you know?"

"I'm sure I don't," Medoc replied curtly. "If you've nothing more to do than gossip about your King like a damn woman, I can find another officer who'd like your spot."

Renault grunted, but took the rebuff in stride. Medoc felt a twinge of fear. Dynat was losing respect. If Medoc continued to support him wholeheartedly, would he be overthrown along with the King? The men said they would follow him, but if he refused to lead, they might look to another. Renault would be the next in line. Unsettled, Medoc turned his attention back to the battle.

He could not see much; the cavern was filling with smoke and steam as his Warriors went to work. The air in the tunnels became chokingly close, and Medoc drew T'Jas from his fire and created a shield around his mouth and nose. "Come on, iceworms," he muttered. He wanted this battle ended, as swiftly as possible. He needed the Icers taken alive for his plan to work.

Presently a young Scout came up the tunnel, his lava running in patterns that looked like veins. He bowed low and awkward in the tight, steep tunnel before Medoc. "Scout Gerad reporting, General."

Medoc nodded shortly for him to get on with it.

"We killed several, and took prisoners in the large chamber below. But the bulk of the frozen ones have retreated into their smaller tunnels, and sealed off the entrances so that we cannot see where the tunnels start. We have Flames tunneling, but those who can dig through rock are weary, General."

"The Princess?"

"Seems to have escaped, Sir. According to the first Flames in, her Semija guard rolled her out of the attack, and the other Icers formed a thick shield of ice while she tunneled away into the rock. We broke the shield, but she was gone by then."

Medoc swore. A damn simple operation, and they had botched it. Dynat would be furious. But then, this whole plan was Dynat's. Why by the Lava Lake had he wanted to send in the Princesses' heads? Was he setting Medoc up for failure? The King had been very clear that Medoc's future as General rested on his ability to deliver this Dreamer Princess. Well, he was done with Dynat's plan. He would get her, but he would do it through tact, not force. "Is the chamber secure?"

"Yes, General. All Iskaloners remaining below are dead or under guard. Shall we begin to send them up—"

"No. I'll come down." A chance to stretch his legs would be good. Medoc uncurled himself and followed Gerad's shoulders down the nearly vertical tunnel. After a moment of scrambling through rock and ice, hoping his fire would keep him warm enough to preserve his lava, Medoc popped out of the ceiling, and hovered against it, looking down at the cavern below.

There were more bodies charred and scattered across the whole floor of the place than there were frightened, huddled prisoners against the far wall. The tiara-clad heads lay scattered among bodies of Icers and Flames, presumably where they had first dropped. Medoc headed straight for the prisoners, drifting through the air. He regretted the use of his fire; the cavern was chilly, even with all the torches and Fireblood flaming away.

A mix of Icers and their untrained Semija stood before the wall, while others were led away in groups by Medoc's officers. A quick estimation of their numbers told him he'd taken only about a hundred prisoners—just a hundred out of the thousands of Icers living in exile. They looked terrified, and for a moment Medoc tried to imagine himself in their position, trapped, hopeless, sure that death or worse awaited. It was a good battle strategy, putting yourself in the enemy's mind, but it left a bad taste in his mouth now. He scanned their faces, looking for the face of a leader, an Officer who would be frightened enough to cow but stood high enough that his negotiation would carry weight with the princess-now-Queen.

His eyes passed over one prisoner and jerked back to rest on her. She was tall for an Icer and dark skinned, another rarity. Medoc's heart skipped a beat when he met her eyes, narrow and defiant under dark lashes. She had a regal bearing, was a leader of some sort—if he had not known better Medoc might have mistaken her for the Princess—but she was not likely to be cowed. If she had not been an Icer, he thought absently, if her bones had been a little thicker and her frame a little taller, she might have been beautiful.

"Stand forward, Ice fairy." Medoc beckoned to her. She hesitated, but then her will seemed to crumple, and she lurched forward, less gracefully than he imagined she would move, as if her feet were blocks of stone. "Where is your Queen?"

The spark came back to her eyes. "I would not tell you if I knew, son of a molebear and a bottom-raker!"

Medoc considered her without really seeing her. He needed the Dreamer. His livelihood, perhaps his very life, depended on it. He also needed to clean the Icer's lake. For that, he needed as many Icers as he could find. He could chase them through the tunnels until Chraun dried up completely, but he might still never find the Dreamer, and he might kill all the Icers in the process. Meanwhile, Chraun's water would remain contaminated.

His own Officers and Flames filled the cavern, looking for the escape tunnels, separating out the bodies of the dead, and moving prisoners down toward the Spiral and Chraun. It was too crowded to have a conversation without starting tongues wagging. He reached out and grabbed the Icer's wrist, pulling her after him. "I'm going to question this one myself," he said roughly to the closest Officer. "She's almost pretty enough for a Flame!"

That would start some bad rumors in itself, but nothing like treason. The Icer looked terrified, and she winced at the pain his hot fingers caused her wrist, but she did not scream or cry or struggle. Medoc thought his own daughters would not have been so brave. He took her to a distant wall that had been well cleared of bodies, out of earshot. He pressed her against the wall, standing close over her, intimidating her, smothering her with his heat. He could almost feel the eyes of his Officers boring into his back.

"We can destroy your people completely," he said softly. She stared up at him with dark, hating eyes, reflecting the purple light of the ceiling above. "We can hunt you down and kill every last one of you, man, woman, child, Icer."

"Better dead than slaves." She spat. Medoc felt the spray of moisture. He lifted a hand to cuff her, but let it drop unused. He had not brought her here to beat her senseless.

"It doesn't have to end this way. I want you to go to your Dreamer Queen, ice fairy. Deliver her a message. If she and the Icers surrender, I will stop pursuing your people. The Icers will be free to return to the lake."

She laughed without mirth, and anger surged in Medoc's blood again. "You lie, flaming fish slime. Why would you stop after you have her? Who would stop you? At least with the Queen, we have a chance."

"I hope, for the sake of your people, that your Queen has more sense than you. I have honor, and I keep my word. If they surrender before my Flames break through your tunnels, we will end this war. All Icers will be returned to the lake."

"And the humans?" He could see her battling against

hope. "We are not like you, to treat them as less than cababar. I will not buy my own safety at the expense of my friends' lives."

"That is for your Queen to worry about. I can make no promises about the Semija. Will you deliver the message?"

She stared past him, and he realized that she was gazing at the bodies littering the floor. Most of his Flame losses had been cleaned up, but there were still piles and piles of scorched Icers and their Semija. Beyond them, thirty or forty prisoners remained.

Medoc felt an odd sensation on his chest and looked down to find her pounding her fists against his flaming armor. The fire must have hurt her, and her hands were red and blistered, but she kept pounding. It was like a little flat attacking a slink; he saw how helpless and angry and desperate she was, and instead of pushing her away he let her struggle for a few moments. Her face was scrunched up with hatred, and her thick hair shimmied like a snake. At last she stopped and slumped against the wall, tears leaking out of her eyes.

"Will you deliver my message? I swear on the Fire Spirit—I will even swear it on your Ancestors, if you like—that I will keep my word."

She gazed past him again, and he turned to follow her eyes, which rested this time on the remaining prisoners. When she looked back, her tears were salty streaks on her cheeks and her face was more calm.

"I will carry your message if you free every prisoner you've taken today. I will not leave them behind."

"Out of the question, Icer. You are in no position to bargain."

"You are the one who needs something from me. If you didn't, you would have killed me. You need my help, and so I can make demands."

Medoc almost smiled. He smoothed his mustache instead. He had never actually spoken to an Icer; his contact before had been limited to killing them outright or listening to an Officer's report from an interrogation. They were more clever than he would have expected. She was almost correct.

"I can kill you where you stand, and get another of those to deliver my message." He gestured behind him at the prisoners. "I can also kill one prisoner every hour that your Queen does not come to this cavern. Their deaths will be on your shoulders, Ice Fairy."

She shook her head. "No. They will be on your shoulders, Flame. May the ghosts of the unburied follow you to the end of your days."

In spite of himself, Medoc shivered. He did not believe in ghosts, or Ancestors, or any of their ice dogma, but for some reason, her curse made him nervous. He thought of the bodies flowing down the Solph River, thought of Icer ghosts parading through the tunnels of Chraun. He glanced around the cavern again. His men were still watching him. He almost thought he could see the ghosts of the dead Icers, walking amongst the bodies.

"You could get another," she continued. "But none know the Queen as closely as I, and none can gain her ear as swiftly. If it is truly results you wish to see, and not more bloodshed, you will send all your prisoners with me now. She will pay your message greater heed if I say, 'here are the prisoners this Flame freed in the name of his honor,' than if I say, 'he is slaughtering our people even as we speak.'"

Medoc considered her. How many Icers would it take to clean the lake and the tunnels above Chraun? Most of the prisoners were humans; he had only thirty Icers at most. Surely he'd need more than twice that number. The more he thought about it, the more sense her words made. "What is your name, Icer?"

She bit her bottom lip before answering. Medoc noticed that it was plump; at least some part of her bore enough flesh. "Larc."

"Larc, you and the Icers and Semija are hereby granted safe passage to deliver a message to your Queen. You have the word of General Medoc that you will not be followed, and you will not be harmed while you deliver your message. I will give her ten hours to respond."

She sagged against the wall, and for a moment Medoc wondered if he had said something wrong, but then he realized it was relief. "I will deliver your message, Flame Medoc, and I will advise my Queen accordingly. You are not the only one who wishes to avoid further bloodshed."

Medoc nodded curtly and turned away, shouting orders to Renault. His men's eyes were full of questions, but none were voiced as the prisoners were brought back up from the Spiral and allowed to tunnel away from the burial chamber, led by Larc.

"What now, General?" Renault asked when the rock sealed over, hiding the back of the last Icer from sight. Medoc shivered again, and let his fire flare up over his armor. He pulled a stone bench to the center of the room and sat.

"Now, Luten, we wait."

Larc

Larc walked slowly through dimly lit, narrow rock, following the ten Icers tunneling ahead. Behind her, the scuffling sounds and groans of nearly one hundred people, many wounded, some carried by the Icers who had regained their strength in the cold tunnel, seemed distant to her ears. For the thousandth time since the Flames had parted the walls of the burial chamber and let them leave with nothing more than Larc's word to deliver a message, she wondered if the whole thing had been an elaborate trap, and the walls would close in and crush them all.

She shook her head and nearly bumped into General Kiner, who was resting. When the burial ice had erupted with fire, Kiner had acted as a hero, clearing the chamber and organizing his Warriors to evacuate the people in the alcoves. He had ordered Larc out along with the other citizens, but she had feared for Stasia and turned back. By then, Stasia was gone, but the Flames had overwhelmed the small force of Officers and Warriors guarding the rear, and they were cut off from the escape. Kiner was among them. Larc wondered why the Flame General had not recognized his medals and negotiated with him rather than her.

She had tried to help him and the others tunnel, after the Flames sealed the burial chamber away behind them and the air in the tunnel grew cold enough to draw T'Jas. But she was not strong with stone, and Kiner told her curtly to save her vaerce. She had been embarrassed in front of Kiner and all the other people she had rescued . . . She pushed away chagrin and focused on that; she had freed all these people, by standing up to the Flame General. The scouts she had set to monitoring the rock in the tail end of the tunnel, and closing it behind them, had detected no signs of Flame tunneling. They were not being followed. Strange as it seemed, the Flame had given his word, and was keeping it.

"We must be getting close, Kiner." Larc lowered her icelight so that it did not shine right in his eyes. "Do you feel any openings ahead?"

"I keep feeling them, and then losing them." Kiner hurled a fist against the wall in frustration, then shook it, chagrined. "It is as if . . ."

" . . . They didn't want to be found?" Larc nodded. Of course. Stasia would not take chances at being discovered by the Flames. She imagined her friend—Queen, now—huddled in the dark, in a passage as narrow as this, with the remnants of Iskalon. What was she planning? Medoc's offer almost seemed palatable—perhaps death was not, after all, better than slavery. At least in slavery, there would be a chance to escape later. "We need to get a message through, somehow. To let her know it is us."

Larc threaded the fingers of one hand through the other, toying with her rings. She had lost five of her seven, and the two that remained were dulled by dust and dirt; she hadn't had the time or energy to clean them. Her chirsh armor, too, was ragged and dusty. At least she had clothes—some of the people had lost the very lakehide on their backs to the fires of the war.

At least she had her life! What a time to be vain. She would gladly trade her rings and clothes and all for the lives the Flames had taken. She might as well take the last two rings and throw them down here in the dirt for all the good they would do her now.

She tugged one off and raised her hand to throw it down the tunnel. Kiner gave her an inquisitive look, and she paused. Inspiration struck, and she lowered her hand, held the ring out to Kiner.

"Can you shoot it through the rock, next time you feel an opening nearby?"

His gaze brightened and he took the ring. "Compared to all this tunneling, it would be a dip in the lake."

Larc hung back, watching him approach the head of the tunnel. He paused. "She may think it a ruse, a trap."

"Of course she will consider that," Larc agreed. "But it may be the only chance we have to reach her. At the least, she will send someone to investigate. Do it."

"Yes, Lady Larc."

Kiner placed his hands on the rock, pressing the ring against it. Larc watched, pondering his last statement. *"Yes, Lady Larc."* The General of Iskalon was deferring to her, even though her place in the ranks had been lower than his, when she had served her conscription in the military. Was it because of her status as advisor? Did it give her power over him? She hadn't thought of that—she merely wanted to advise Stasia because she loved politics and she wanted the best for Iskalon. Did she now have the power to command troops? She remembered what Stasia had said in her first address to the full council—that Larc stood in line after her and Casser, to rule if they both died. Kiner's deference made sense, as did his concern about conserving her vaerce. Larc shivered. If Stasia surrendered, only Casser would remain between her and the throne. *If* Casser had survived the attack.

As Kiner pressed T'Jas into the rock, and Larc felt the resulting tremor in the tunnel wall she leaned against as her ring shot through, she thought about how ridiculous her situation was. Just a few chimes past she had been a mere Icer, not a very good one, sitting on the benches, waiting for her turn to argue the proposals, with fifteen lives between her and the Throne. Not that she would ever have been selected as a potential Regent, if Stasia hadn't been the only survivor. Now here she was, giving orders and negotiating treaties with the enemy, and only two lives stood between her and the Crown of Iskalon. The idea scared her. She thought of how she was going to advise Stasia to surrender, and wondered why. Did some part of her desire power, and was that why the Flame General had so easily convinced her to carry his message?

As this treasonous thought took hold, the rock in front of Kiner parted, and a soft blue glow reflected toward Larc from the long tunnel opening in front of them. And suddenly Stasia was passing Kiner, taking Larc into her arms. Glace, behind her, peered at the refugees in suspicion. Larc relaxed into Stasia's embrace, feeling the grief they both held passed between them like secrets between children. At last Stasia backed away, held Larc at arm's length and looked into her eyes. Larc wondered how she could have worried about wanting power for herself? Even with the Crown of Iskalon weighing down her temples, Stasia was still her best friend.

"I knew it was really you! Glace thought it a trap, but I told him the Flames were not so subtle in their cleverness."

As Stasia put the ring back on her finger, Larc said, "Where is Casser, darling? Did he—"

"He survived. We are near the mines, and Casser is gathering everyone in an old storage cavern there. We are missing between two and three thousand bodies, but it would have been much worse without your quick work, Kiner." She saluted him gravely. "And it looks like you are bringing in a few more. How did you escape?"

Kiner was silent. Deferring to her. "We must hold a council, Stasia. No, not a full council, don't look at me like that. I must speak with you and Casser immediately. We haven't much time, and you have a hard decision to make."

Stasia

"But who will protect the people, after all of the Icers are gone? This sounds like a trick, Larc." Stasia sat on a hard rock ledge in a tiny cave. Flats, displaced by their impromptu meeting, clung to the diamond spires of her crown, confused. The walls were dusty with cavewebs and old snakeskins. The cave was an old ore-sorting room near the Outer Tunnels. The rest of the survivors had been convened in a vast cavern opened up centuries ago by the extensive mining of a vein of zirc.

Why was Larc pushing so hard for surrender? Stasia could not turn over the people, especially the humans, to a lifetime of slavery. Better that they die than live like cababar. But could she make that decision for the people? She did not have time, and she was torn with indecision. Death or slavery?

"I don't know how to explain it, Stas. He sounded sincere. And he did let our people go. I think he truly wants to end the bloodshed, but at a price to us. 'If she and the Icers surrender, I will stop pursuing your people.' He called you—" she glanced around the room nervously "—the Dreamer Princess. And he wants the Icers to return to the lake, I believe he does, but there was something odd about that. He was holding something back." Larc sat beside her on the ledge. Across the tiny cave, Casser and Glace were perched on small boulders. Kiner stood by the entrance keeping lookout, listening quietly to the conversation.

"Imagine that—a Flame, lying," Stasia said with a sneer. "I wouldn't have thought." Was she to be a trophy? The Fire King had killed all of her sisters, did he just want to finish the job? Or was it the connection with her Flame mother? Did he think she posed a threat to Chraun?

"We haven't much time, even if the Flame truly plans to give us ten hours," Casser said calmly. "It took you most of that to reach us, Larc. Stasia, you will need to make a decision before they find us."

A flat dropped onto her shoulder and she flicked it onto the wall, annoyed. It clung there and scuttled toward a juicy spider. "Well. You are my advisors, how do you advise?"

Glace spoke up, his tone hurried, as if he feared being interrupted. "Your Majesty, I advise that you do not put yourself into the hands of the Flames. They have killed your sisters and your father; what will stop them from simply killing you? This entire thing must be a ruse, to separate you from your army, and the Icers from the people. The people of Iskalon need the protection of the Icers, and we are sure to be enslaved if we surrender, no matter what this General says. And I for one would rather die in combat, fighting for Iskalon, than live while you walk into a trap."

"What your Captain says makes sense," Casser said, brushing cobwebs out of his hair. "However, we seem to be lost either way. They will rout us from these tunnels in time. We can stand our ground, and die with honor, or we can take our chances on the mercy of the Flames. We may be surprised; having known one kind Flame, I can accept that they are not all monsters."

"Yes," Larc said. "The General did not seem like a monster. Ruthless, focused, determined, but not evil. I advise you to surrender, Stasia. I cannot say why. I will go by your side as you do, if that is your choice. I will take my chances on their mercy, if it will end the killing."

"Flames enjoy hunting," Kiner spoke up, not turning from his vigil. "If all they wanted was our deaths, they would have killed us and continued pursuing you through the tunnels, not offered a chance of peaceful surrender."

An idea crept in. Stasia tried to deny it, but the more she thought about it, the more she was convinced that it was the only way to give the Flames what they wanted and save a remnant of Iskalon. It would be a sacrifice, but it was one that had to be made.

"I have come to a decision," she said out loud. "There is a third option that no one has mentioned. Assemble the people, I will make an announcement."

Larc and Kiner saluted almost in unison and hurried from the room to obey. Casser stared at her with searching eyes, and she stared back defiantly. She had offered him the Crown, after they'd escaped the attack in the Burial Chamber. Once again, he'd refused her. If he had taken it, he could have ordered her to surrender or not and she would have to obey. As it was, he would have to obey her. He gave a little shake of his head that could have meant anything and left without saluting.

Glace stood, but instead of leaving, he drew closer, meeting her in the center of the tiny room. "What are you planning, Stasia?"

He sounded worried. Stasia looked at his strong, scarred face, and realized suddenly what her decision meant. That understanding seemed to bring home all the loss she had suffered in the war. Her whole family was gone, and now she would not even have Glace—Glace, the man who had been by her side as long as she could remember. His absence would be like a missing limb. And for his part—he would have to overcome all of his training and forge a new identity.

She stepped toward him and reached out a hand to touch one of his. "I wish you could protect me from this, as much as you do," she said. "But we both know you can't."

He surprised her by taking her hand in his huge one, lifting it, and kissing it. "I have a right to know if you will live or die."

"Only the Ancestors know that, Glace," she said as gently as she could.

He leaned over, put both hands on her hips, lifted her until her face was level with his, and kissed her full on the mouth. His lips were big and cool and they made hers tingle, a sensation that crept over her whole body until she thought she would explode from the pleasure. She was not aware of time passing—an eternity could have gone by and she would not have noticed—until he set her on the ground again. Her skin was hollow in the absence of his touch.

"I've been wanting to do that for years," he said.

Then he knelt. "I'm sorry, Majesty. That was not proper."

Stasia glared at him. He gave her a kiss that made her float without T'Jas and then called her Majesty? "If you ever call me anything but Stasia again I will—"

She cut off, her throat choking on the words. She was going to say, "send you away and never see you again," but it was too close to what she was about to command, and she would likely never see him again. So instead she leaned over and gently grasped his mop of sandy hair, pulled his head back so that he was looking her in the eyes, and kissed him.

They were still kissing when Casser came to announce that the people had assembled to hear Stasia speak.

Glace

Glace did not put a dutiful pace between himself and Stasia when he emerged with her from the cramped cave. Instead he walked in step with her, not caring what it might look like to Casser or anyone else. His heart was a maelstrom of relief and anxiety, relief at having finally told Stasia the truth, terror that he might lose her now. He was watching her beautiful face, seeing the icelights play in her golden-green eyes, when her expression twisted into a frown. He followed her gaze into the large cavern they were entering, every muscle in his body ready to fight, and saw what displeased her.

The Council of Iskalon had convened, not just the people. A ledge had been shaped at one end of the widened-out tunnel, and before it, the members of the Council stood. There were gaps, councilors killed in the invasion of the burial chamber, but the majority of twenty required to offer proposals was present. Behind them, about a thousand of the remaining citizens of Iskalon filled the vast cavern. Those who could stand stood shoulder to shoulder. The wounded and ill were crowded together in one corner. Icers hovered in the air to leave room for more humans on the ground. Thousands more citizens filled the tunnels and the ore-veins beyond the cavern; nearly ten thousand Icers and humans had been tallied by the scribes. Most were out of earshot, but the words of the Council would be passed along to them. Most of the Warrior Guild was absent; Glace had helped Kiner station them in tunnels further down, where they could give warning if the Flames broke their word and attacked.

Stasia marched stiffly up the steps of the ledge and stood before the Council. Glace followed her, along with Larc and Casser. Instinctively, he knew they would be of more use standing beside her than in the crowd. And he did not intend to leave Stasia's side until she ordered him away.

Wyfus had survived, and he began to speak. For once, he came straight to the point.

"Your Majesty Queen of Iskalon, this Council has received word that the Fire King will let us go if you alone surrender."

"How did they find out, Larc?" Stasia asked the question through her teeth, lips barely moving, inaudible to the assembly.

"I don't know, Majesty," Larc replied just as quietly. "The prisoners released with me—they must have heard it from the other Flames."

Below, Wyfus continued. "The Council has a proposal to lay before her Majesty." He stepped forward and knelt. Stasia's gaze was colder than burial ice. "We ask that you surrender to Chraun for the protection of the people of Iskalon."

Stasia was silent for a long moment, continuing to stare at Wyfus like he was a rockworm under her foot. Glace wanted to jump down and throttle the man. Throttle the whole Council. How dare they? What did they think would become of them, without her?

Without warning, Stasia laughed, an incongruously merry sound in the midst of the solemn moment. Wyfus, still kneeling, gaped like a fish. Stasia's laugh ceased as quickly as it began, but she continued to smile as she spoke.

"I came in here full of pride, ready to sacrifice myself, and here I find I have already been sacrificed by my people," she said. Her face grew somber. "So much for pride."

Stasia used T'Jas from the cold rocks at her back to amplify her voice, and the crowd hushed. "I will accept the proposal set forth by this council. However, I do not intend to ask you to wait with hope and trust the Fire King's mercy. Today our tunnels will branch."

She paused, and the crowded cavern echoed with a susurration of murmurs. Glace barely heard it. Surrender. Even if no one else died, Stasia would. Chraun wouldn't leave her alive to raise trouble later. When she died, there would be nothing for him—he would cease to exist. Would he know the moment of her death, if he wasn't there, or would he hear of it later? Foolish as it was, with all the dangers she'd faced, Glace had never allowed himself to consider the possibility of outliving her.

Stasia was speaking again. Glace forced himself to listen. "I ask for fifty volunteers to sacrifice themselves for the survival of the Kingdom. Do not make this decision lightly. It is very likely that you will die or be enslaved."

There. His last chance. He would go with her, a volunteer. At least he could die by her side, even if he couldn't die to save her. "Casser will rule Iskalon in my absence. He will lead the people of Iskalon who cannot fight into the Outer Tunnels. There, you will seek a new home where the Flames will not find you. I have seen this in a Dream. I promise, you will find it. Casser, you will choose your path long after the volunteers and I have gone. We must not know your path, for our minds will be read."

The noise of the crowd grew louder. Wyfus pounded his gavel and Mowat bellowed for silence. Glace glanced at Casser. The older Icer's lips were compressed in anger. "Lady Larc, General Kiner, and Captain Glace will lead all able Icers and warriors to guard the rear of this escape and misdirect the Flames' army."

An emptiness opened in the pit of Glace's stomach and threatened to swallow him whole. Of course. He was too valuable as a warrior. He would not be allowed to surrender with her. His last chance to do his duty, denied. She would die alone in Chraun, and he would fade from this world. Duty and her were all he had. Once, he had thought he must choose between loving her and doing his duty. Now he was to be denied both.

As if she could sense his thoughts, Stasia turned from the crowd and faced him. "I'm sorry, Glace. I have to do this. Please. This is your duty to me—to protect my people."

Glace stared at her, drinking in every line, every hair, every inch of her. He wanted to sweep her off the ledge and carry her away to safety. But, Ancestors, there was no safety to take her to. When the cavern shook and scouts ran in from all the tunnels, heralding the approach of the Flames, he found his voice.

"Your wish is my command, My Queen."

The pain in her eyes as she turned away was the last he saw of her. Then he was down, off the ledge, wading through the crowd, shouting orders. Doing his duty.

Stasia

Stasia drew herself up, pulling back from Glace. She could not let him weaken her resolve. Casser's eyes bored into hers as she turned to face him. The crowd below them was chaos. Larc's voice rang high above the crowd as she tried to organize the Icers, and Kiner's harsh voice soon joined hers. The human Warriors were already heeling to Glace. But the Council was engaged in a knot of shouting matches, the other non-fighting citizens looked from them to Casser. And Casser stared at her, frozen as though already buried.

The whole cavern shook again. The Flames would be through the walls soon, and the people must be gone. Stasia had to surrender now. "Casser." She had warned him of this day. Why couldn't he accept it? "This is an order from your Queen, Casser. You must save Iskalon."

"Ancestors melt you, Stasia. How can I convince you that V'lturhst is just your wild imagination? There is nothing higher than the Burial Shafts, and they keep going until they reach the Svardark. To say anything else is to blaspheme."

"Nonetheless, to save Iskalon, you will try to find V'lturhst."

"Stas—"

"I would take your place, Casser. But the Fire King seems to want me in particular. I need you to take all of my Dreams and memories and do what I have not been able to do. Look for the tunnel that leads to V'lturhst. I'm sure it exists. I know you do not believe, but you will see."

Casser shook his head. "You will die alone in Chraun, little one."

"I am not alone, Casser. Look, I have my people with me." She gestured to the cavern floor. The Council was still arguing, likely about whether her last commands had held weight after her decision to surrender. But a few Icers were rising above the crowd and approaching the ledge. Her volunteers. Not quite fifty, but they would suffice. The walls shuddered, and a small rockslide started at the far end of the cavern. "We haven't time to argue. Go. Ancestors willing, we will meet again."

The anger in his eyes faded to resignation, and he reached out and pinched her cheek. She glared at him, rubbing at the skin angrily. "What was that for?"

"I used to do that when you were a babe, Stas. I'm sorry. I don't know what came over me. Farewell, my Queen."

"Farewell, Casser." With that she drew T'Jas and drifted off the ledge, over the crowd, nodding to the fifty-odd Icers to follow. When she reached the rockslide, she placed her hands on the wall, drew T'Jas, and pushed open a wide tunnel. Her power met hot rock and rebounded; the result was a thin curtain between her tunnel and that of the Flames. She drew T'Jas again and pushed past the hot rock, opening the curtain wide.

"General Medoc?" She amplified her voice, savoring the coldness of T'Jas as she did so. She might never feel it again. "I am Queen Stasia of Iskalon. I have come to surrender to Chraun."

Part 3 ~ Captive

My friend, blood shaking my heart
The awful daring of a moment's surrender . . .

The Waste Land, T. S. Eliot

Interlude

Khell, Nine Summers Prior

Maia

Maia stood outside her egla, still as the Doaltooth Mountains above, while the two women on either side finished fixing her long black hair into tight braids and knelt, facing the rest of the camp, palms up, hands outstretched.

"We present to you the new Healer of the Liathua Khell," they said in unison. One was fourteen, still a maiden. The other was a Grandmother, soon to Journey over Ice. Which meant Maia stood between them as a woman grown, mother to the whole tribe. She bowed her head as the ritual directed.

"I live to serve," she said. "I am Mother Healer to the Liathua Khell." The women on either side took bone daggers from their parkas and ran the sharp edges down her bare arms, leaving a trickle of blood behind. "My blood is your blood. In birth, in battle, in death, I will Heal you." She let the blood drip onto the ice beneath her feet. "When the Liathua bleed, I bleed." She ran her thumbs, coated with a clotting seaweed, over the thin wounds. They sealed up as if by magic. "When I Heal, the Liathua are Healed." She raised up her arms, high over her head, so the whole camp could see.

A whoop went up from the assembled Khell, and a bonfire

blazed into being at the center of the winter camp. Deep sounds from horns of boareal tusks rumbled from the tops of egla. The period of mourning had ended with Maia's presentation to the tribe, and the celebration had begun. A boareal had been slaughtered; one less beast to get them to the summer camp, but it would be a delightful feast after the lean winter.

Antahua, the healer who had served the Liathua for thirty summers, had not withstood that winter; though she was still younger than many of the Grandmothers, she had taken the Journey over Ice just after Three Days of Night. The winter had been too bleak for the Liathua to emerge from the egla for the presentation ceremony until now, nearly two months later. So the tribe had undergone an exceptionally long period of mourning.

Though Maia had participated in all of the expected rituals, she did not harbor any grief for the old healer. Even after the woman had taken her on as her apprentice, she had been cruel, criticizing Maia's efforts and beating her when she complained or faltered. Maia had not learned as much as she expected to in the past eight winters; she had learned more as a child from her mother. Antahua's methods were often clumsy and inefficient. Far from grief, Maia felt relieved to be out of the woman's shadow.

Eight winters spent with the Liathua. It was the same number of winters she had lived with her birth-tribe. Fitting, that she would be made a woman on this day. Of course, she was not entirely a woman yet.

As if he knew her thoughts, Hakua was at her elbow. "Now that you are Healer, we can mate!"

Maia turned to look him over. At fifteen winters, Hakua was a strong warrior. His muscles were obscured by his thick furs, but Maia could see his strength in the set of his jaw, the thickness of his hands. He would make any woman in the camp an admirable mate. She turned away, closing her eyes briefly. Her braids swung as she moved. She thought about her mother's braids, the little shell beads she had woven into them.

The bones did not always reveal what Maia wanted to see. She never should have asked such a frivolous question, anyway. Always use the bones only for the good of the tribe, Mother had said. But

Maia had been fourteen and shy around the young warriors and desperate to know what her future held. Her answer had been her punishment. And now, looking into his eager face, how could she tell Hakua that he was not for her, nor she for him?

"The Healer mates with the Chief," Maia said in a teasing voice. "Your father is Chief, not you."

He looked startled, then angry. "Fine," he said, and walked away. Maia watched him go with regret. She had only hoped to delay the inevitable, to spare him with humor from the danger she had seen in the bones. She walked on, joining the crowd at the bonfire, accepting a choice cut of roast boareal. She did not chatter with the young girls as she had done just a few nights past. Instead she stood apart. She was still part of the tribe, but now she was more than just another young girl.

Hakua's father approached, and Maia felt an intuitive misgiving. Chief Lubar was a large man. Hakua had inherited some of his mother's gracile build, but there was nothing gracile about Lubar. Maia made a signal of respect, and he made the signal back, chief to healer. He stood close, towering over her.

"Come to my egla," Lubar said. There was nothing of asking in his voice. "Hakua has informed me of your decision."

"My decision?" Maia's mouth went dry.

"There is no reason to delay. It is a good choice. I feared you would be aloof and prudish like Antahua. I am glad to see that you understand the sense in Healer and Chief joining."

Maia cringed away, putting more distance between herself and Lubar, eyes darting toward the people by the fire. Would they help her? After eight years, though she was their healer, she was still an outsider. And Lubar was chief.

"Whatever Hakua told you was false," Maia said. "A mistaken jest. I—Antahua said there is a curse on this joining among the Liathua. That is why she refused you." It was a lie, but Maia felt no compunction. She would say anything to avoid him.

Lubar sneered. "She refused me because her cave was dry and desolate as Pebble Beach," he said with a coarse laugh. "You are different. Young, dripping, tender, like a piece of meat." With each word, he stepped closer, and when he said "meat," he took the half-

eaten roast from her hands. With his face inches from hers, he took a bite and chewed. Juice dribbled down his chin.

Maia shuddered. She stepped backward. "We must not mate," she said. "I have seen it in the bones. If we join, the tribe will perish."

Another lie, but it made him pause. He did not try to follow her. He took another bite and chewed thoughtfully. He had seen the power of the bones, she knew. She had him. She seized her power and made another thrust. "And if you take me by force, I will kill myself. None but myself and my daughters, when I have them, will be able to read the bones. Even if the Liathua survive, they will not have a healer to protect them."

Lubar appeared to consider that, and then he grinned. "I shall have to wait until you have a daughter, then." He stepped close again, reached inside her snowkit-fur parka. She tensed. "It will be worth the wait. The best meat is cooked very slowly over the fire."

He pinched her nipple, sending an involuntary shiver up her spine, before he removed his hand. He tossed the hunk of meat aside on the snow and moved past her, chuckling, to the fire. Standing alone in a daze, Maia heard him greet the other warriors. Tears began to glisten on her cheeks. When she could trust her legs not to shake so much she couldn't walk, she pulled herself in the direction of her egla.

Glancing back toward the fire to be sure that Lubar did not follow, she saw Hakua standing on the outer edge of the ring, watching her go, something between regret and satisfaction in his eyes.

When she reached her egla, Maia placed two doal femur bones across the small entrance of the egla, the signal that the healer did not wish to be disturbed. She let the coals grow dim, huddling under Antahua's thick furs. Cold tears leaked from her eyes and she shook and sobbed as silently as she could. She heard a rustle and tensed— would the bones across her door be enough to stop Lubar? Would her threats be enough?

She was Healer, but she no longer had the protection of maidenhood. Cruel as Antahua had been, the woman had sheltered her from this. The Chief could take what he wanted, and none in the tribe would stop him. Maia did not sleep that night, but lay shivering until daylight brought the sounds of camp being stricken. Then she rose, straightened her Healer's braids, and went to face the day.

Chapter II

Marked by Fire

Dynat

Dynat watched from a ledge high above the prison chamber as the last Icer was pushed into her cage. Her silver hair was piled on her head in intricate designs. The elaborate crown holding it in place gleamed in the yellow light. *That's her . . .* The Fire Spirit's voice was unconfined excitement.

"Is that her?" Dynat did not turn to look at Medoc, but continued staring at the prisoners below. Fewer than fifty Icers sat huddled in separate cages. They looked miserable, ill from the heat. They had pleaded to be sent back to their lake, said something about promises made under the condition of surrender. Dynat had ordered a few killed as an example to put a stop to it. But Dynat did not really care about the other prisoners. He was just relieved that they finally had the Dreamer. Now, perhaps, the Fire Spirit would give him peace.

"That is her, Majesty." Medoc's voice was sullen. "Majesty, I still think—"

"Yes, yes, you have told me what you think. For the

last time, Medoc, they will not be sent to the lake. Whatever you promised them, it worked, but I did not authorize it."

Killllllll, the Fire Spirit drawled, and Dynat felt a sense of relief. At last. *Killll them all. But keep her close.*

Not kill the Dreamer? Dynat almost questioned the Fire Spirit, but stopped himself. Frustrated, he passed on the orders.

"Have a cage shaped beside my throne, and transfer her to it."

They were the Fire Spirit's words, but they came out of Dynat's mouth, and neither Dynat nor Medoc considered disobeying. The next words Dynat spoke were his own. "Question the others. We know there were more than fifty Icers living under that ice shaft. I want to know where the rest of them went. When you are done, kill them all."

"Your Majesty, I promised them—"

"Silence!" Dynat was surprised to find himself shouting. Or was it the Fire Spirit? "The Fire Spirit wishes them to die, so they will die. I will not hear another word on this, Medoc. Go now. Transfer her yourself, and give the orders."

Medoc bowed quickly and turned away before Dynat could see his expression. Dynat took a deep breath, calming his anger. Medoc over-thought things, that was all. What were a few broken promises? No one would be alive to care, after he had routed the rest of the Icers and their untrained Semija. Iskalon would be finished, for once and for all.

He continued to watch the prisoners. After a time, Medoc entered the cavern below and melted away the bars to the Dreamer's cage. They exchanged words that Dynat could not hear, and the Icer stood stiffly, unmoving. Medoc waited far too patiently before he simply reached out with a mass of warm air and scooped her limp body from the cell.

Her Dreamsssss . . . Silent for a few moments, the Fire

Spirit's voice once again whispered through Dynat's mind, an echo coming down a long tunnel. *Plunder her Dreamsssss.*

"Her Dreams?" Dynat spoke the words out loud, but the Fire Spirit fell silent. Dynat squeezed his fist so tightly that a trickle of lava fell from it to the floor and hardened. Dynat was to enter her mind? No. Surely Dynat could learn her Dreams by questioning. He could not enter her mind, for then she would know him completely, and if she did she would know the truth that he had buried long ago. He would question her and kill her, that was all.

Dynat turned away from the ledge and swept down the hallway toward his throne room. The Fire Spirit returned, murmuring about Dreams and visions. Dynat fought an urge to run in the other direction, to seek comfort in Bolv's touch or solace in a slink hunt, something to quiet the endless whisper of flames in his head. The Fire Spirit had never led him astray. He had to continue to trust.

When he entered his throne room, the Icer was there already, cramped in a little cage directly beside his throne. She sagged against the bars, unconscious from the heat. Her long hair shone like burnished silver in the dim red light. He could see her face, and though he had never seen her before, she looked familiar. It was probably her resemblance to her treacherous sisters. She wore the same crown Maudit had worn when he killed her, but she did not look half as impressive as the eldest of the Ice King's daughters. This Queen was a little, weak, cold, pitiful thing. He knew he should wake her and begin to squeeze her Dreams out of her, but for a long time he just stared at her, strangely fascinated by her lithe form and her shallow breath. The Fire Spirit did not prompt him to begin; it was reveling in victory in the back of his mind. Dynat was still staring at her some time later when Medoc brought his report on the search for the remnants of Iskalon.

Stasia

Stasia woke from a dreamless sleep to intense heat and a roaring sound that filled her ears. She did not raise her head or open her eyes; she might learn something useful if her captors thought she was still asleep. The heat made her drowsy and nauseous, but she fought the feeling. She did not know why she had been separated from her people, but she did not like it. She remembered the General demanding she come with him, and refusing, and then nothing until now.

"The answers to the questioning were difficult to decipher, Majesty." That was Medoc's voice. "They don't know how many of their ilk were killed or imprisoned when we first took the lake, and none can agree on how many were killed later, during their raids, or in the last attack. One thing was certain, however. It does seem that most of them did not join the other captives in surrender, but instead struck out for the Outer Tunnels."

"Find them, Medoc." The Fire King's voice was shaky, like one of the guildless who had succumbed to madness. It crawled up Stasia's spine like razor-footed spiders. "Cowards, running away. Destroy every last one of them."

There was a moment of silence, and then Medoc spoke again. "Majesty, I would like you to reconsider and allow me to bring some of the Icers to the lake. The problem with the baths stems from the lake, and I think I can fix it if the Icers—"

"I am not accustomed to repeating my orders," Dynat said. "General, you will see to this personally. Now."

"As you command, Majesty."

"Leave me, Medoc. Tell the Guards to admit no one."

Stasia fought to control the fear that gripped her heart. If the Fire King saw her shaking, he would know that she was awake. She was afraid of being alone with him. She wanted to call out for Medoc not to leave. Why she thought the General would be any better than Dynat, she could not say. She heard his footsteps echo away, and then the heavy thud of a stone portcullis being lowered. The heat seemed to increase by a fraction, making her more ill. In spite of the nausea, she tried to draw the heat inside her.

For a short time all she could hear was the roar that filled the cavern, and then the clink of armor and thud of footfalls approached her cage. He must have been very close, for she could hear him breathing even over the white noise of the roar. "Yes, yes." The Fire King muttered to himself. "I know. The Dreams."

The footsteps came closer, and she sensed a hand on the bars of her small cage. "I know you are awake, little Ice Fairy. You might as well stop pretending."

Stasia slowly pried her eyelids open. The light in the cavern blinded her, a piercing red-orange glow instead of the soft blues she was used to. With an effort, she pushed herself up on her elbows. If she stood, the top of the cage would force her to stoop. Instead, she sat up with her legs folded under at the knee, trying to appear dignified.

She was completely naked, and although it had probably been intended to humiliate her, she was grateful. The chirsh she had worn before would have trapped the warmth of her body in the intense heat of this room. Her skin was slick with sweat, and she had to blink it back where it ran past her eyebrows into the corners of her eyes. Her hair was matted to her back, but the crown of Iskalon still sat heavy upon her head. After a moment, Stasia reached back, divided her hair in two, and swept it forward in an effort to cover some of her nudity. The ends tickled the tops of her thighs.

The Fire King towered above her, clutching the bars of the cage with one hand. His long black hair was tied back, and in a completely different context, she might have thought him handsome. His chin and cheeks were round, but his jaw was hard, and there was a wild look in his eyes, shining gold in the wretched light, like a dangerous male slink. She wondered what he intended. Once, she had thought that no Flame and Icer union was desirable or even possible, but now that she knew her mother had been a Flame, she had to wonder. Had he caged her here beside his throne because he desired her as a woman?

"There she is. The Queen of Iskalon, as you commanded."

Who was he talking to? Not her, certainly. Was there someone else in the room? No one else spoke. The Fire King's face changed, as if he saw her for the first time.

"They didn't tell you, did they, Queen. The Fire Spirit himself speaks to me. I am his chosen one."

He paused, as if expecting something from her about this revelation. When she remained silent, the Fire King continued. "He is quite interested in you, Queen of Iskalon. Particularly your Dreams. I can't imagine what in your Dreams would possibly interest him. Can you?"

The Fire Spirit? Stasia dimly recalled that the Flames worshiped a being called by this name. She almost told him she had no idea, then thought better of it. Perhaps she could glean something by playing along. "My Dreams? But of course. He would want to know all about them. I will tell you of them, if you tell me what will become of my people. Do you intend to let them live?"

Stasia prided herself on not flinching when he laughed. She kept her eyes, sore from the light, glued to his golden ones, letting all of her hatred seep through. She almost felt that she could reach into his mind. His expression did not change.

"You are not in a position to bargain, Ice Fairy. You will tell me your Dreams. You will tell me in vivid detail."

Stasia considered. She saw no harm in his knowing of her Dreams. Lately, they were all about the burial chamber, and that he had already discovered and destroyed. But she did not think he would be satisfied with that. And she did not relish giving him what he wanted after what he had taken from her. She cleared her throat and spat through the bars of the cage.

Stasia did not scream when the lava-hot whip of fire

struck her back. In spite of the agony rolling through her skin and up her spine, she only let out a small gasp. The Fire King stood in front of her, hands at his sides, using T'Jas to create the painful sensation. The whip struck again, and then a third time. She clenched her teeth to keep the scream back on the fourth strike. On the fifth, she reached through the pain to the heat, trying to take draw T'Jas from it. After ten lashes, she abandoned her attempts and succumbed to the pain. She heard herself screaming, but could do nothing to stop her own mouth. She left her own mind, fleeing from the pain. She did not know how many times he had struck her when she begged him to stop. It was not her begging, but a husk of her that she could not control.

"Tell me of your Dreams," he shouted after the final lash. Stasia lay curled in a ball on the bottom of her cage, dignity and defiance abandoned. She had never truly felt pain before this. Tell him her Dreams? She could scarcely think, let alone try to put together a sentence. As the pain receded and she began to come back into herself, shame washed over her, sparking a different kind of pain. Just a few lashes, and she was defeated. What kind of Queen was she?

"The cavern. Burial chamber." Stasia kept her eyes squeezed shut. The torture had not been intended to wound her permanently, only to show her that he could inflict unbearable pain on her at any moment.

"What of it?"

"My Dream. I enter the ice in that Burial chamber. Where you—found us. I drift up, and then there is a yellow light, soft blue ceiling, warm breath."

"And then?"

She forced her eyes open and saw him leaning against the bars, his face close to hers. He was so close, she could have reached out and gotten her hands around his throat. She would have, if she had not known that he would merely fill her with agonizing heat. "That is all. V'lturhst, my people call it. It is forbidden to speak of. But I Dream of it often."

"That is not all!" The words, shouted so close to her face, hurt her ears, but the pain was nothing compared to the lashes that came next. "Tell me where you go then. After the yellow light."

"That is all, I swear it!" Stasia's own pleading voice faded as her vision went black.

The heat ceased, and she was overwhelmed with relief as the Fire King stepped back. "That is enough for today. I will have the truth out of you, lying Ice Fairy."

In spite of his confident words, the lava mesh on his face was clenched in a knot of frustration. Stasia saw madness burning in his eyes. He released the bars and stepped back, turning toward the door. He called out something she did not understand, and the portcullis scraped open. "Where is the Kinyara?" he bellowed.

"She is in the Baths, my King," a guard answered.

"Have her brought to my quarters at once."

Only when the heavy stone door slammed to the floor again, cutting away the sight of the King's broad back, did Stasia take a deep breath. It was not a breath of relief; the air she inhaled was hot and stale. She uncurled herself, reaching through the bars to stretch her tight, sore muscles. The second beating had been intended to last, unlike the first. Her skin screamed in agony, and every slight brush against the bars felt like another strike of the Fire King's whip. Once she had stretched the cramps out of her muscles, she settled into a cross-legged position on the bumpy floor and tried to focus on anything other than the pain, nausea, and despair.

For hours, she dwelt in an amalgam of fear and hopelessness she had never before experienced. For the first time in her life, she was truly alone. Glace's slink was not going to appear here, sit down, and start washing himself. Glace himself would die long before he reached this chamber, even if he disobeyed and came to her rescue.

Casser, Larc, all of Iskalon—she could only hope that her sacrifice had truly bought their escape. She huddled in her cell, wrapped her arms around herself and tried to think of a way out of her situation.

She thought of the time just before the war when she traipsed down the Spiral Tunnel to the burial chamber, alone, fearless, reckless. How easily she could have been captured by Flames, her scorched head sent to her father just as her sisters' had been sent to her. She had thought herself brave, but she merely hadn't known the depth of her cowardice. Before, she had known Glace was just a few tunnels behind her, known that she was protected and sheltered. But now, for the first time in her life, nothing stood between her and death.

"I am a coward," she whispered into the dim red light. And she knew it was true. She was terrified to be caged by this madman, terrified of how he would hurt her when he returned. If she had known what he wanted, she would have given it to him gladly in order to escape another beating. But she did not even have that luxury. She had told him her Dream, but he had not believed her. All she had to look forward to was pain, and eventually, a fiery death. She was a coward, she realized, because she would do anything, no matter how perverse, to escape that death. In spite of all her speeches to the Council, she *would* rather live a slave than die bravely.

Even as the shame of that truth washed through her body, she heard her oldest sister's voice, scolding her. "You'll do no good sitting and sulking," Maudit would have said. If she was going to do anything but die in this cramped cage, she would have to act on her own.

She quieted her mind and focused on the loud roaring sound that filled the empty cavern like a thousand people talking all at once. It came from behind her, the same direction as the intense heat. Stasia recalled Casser's words about the Flame youths and the river of lava. The roaring sounded like the rivers that ran off the lake, though many times louder. It must be their lava river, close by. Instead of cringing away from the heat, she reached out for it, just as she would have quested for cold. Sitting in her tiny cage, she drifted out of her body and felt her way along the heat as she would a tunnel wall in the dark, not taking it inside of herself, merely feeling its presence.

The heat burned her as she drifted through it, but the river nearly destroyed her. When the air ended and she was grasping pure lava, there was no question of drawing it. It was all she could do to keep it from drawing her, sucking her in and burning her to cinders from a distance. She withdrew sharply, receding into her cage, grasping herself with both arms. She stared blankly at the torches by the door for several seconds before she realized that she was alive. Then she closed her eyes and quested out again, more carefully this time.

After several tries, and several close encounters with the all-powerful lava river, she became sensitive to its boundary, aware of a tiny change in the heat gradient at its threshold. She spent a long time sitting in her cage, feeling the heat at the boundary. If only her Flame mother were here, or Casser, or someone to show her what to do next. Even Glace would be a comfort, if not a help. No, she was truly alone. And she had no idea how to proceed.

She did not even know if her people were safe. Had they escaped to the Outer Tunnels? Had Casser found V'lturhst? Or had the Fire King and his General routed them? Were Glace and Larc and Kiner and any of her people even alive? There was no way to know, and nothing Stasia could do for them now. She was at the mercy of the Fire King. The more she thought about it, the more hopeless the situation seemed.

She squeezed her eyes shut and reached for the lava.

The world became fire and pain. Stasia burned harder than she had when she'd taken the Flame's heat on the day of the battle. This pain was liquid, white hot, smothering everything, burning not just her body but her soul, the very center of her being, until there was nothing left of her. She was molten lava, part of the river; Stasia the separate entity was no more. Her consciousness faded away, and she became one with the intense heat. She drifted forever until she flowed into a huge body of molten liquid. It was not a lake like Lentok; it was a giant molten ball. She went to the very center, and the heat and pressure were more than even lava could stand.

Stasia was aware of distant screaming and realized it was her body, screaming in her cage. Her body. She was Stasia, she had a self and a body and a place separate of this vast heat. Her body was burning, and the pain of it dragged her away from the core of the lake, back along the lava river, through the hot air, and back into consciousness.

Just as she opened her eyes, the portcullis scraped open and General Medoc marched into the room, followed by several Flames. "What happened in here?" He approached the cage and stared at her. "Why—"

He cut off, staring in alarm, a foreign emotion on that stoic face. Stasia tried to speak, but her lip was cracked and swollen on one side, so much so that she could not open her mouth. With a wincing effort, she raised her right hand to try to touch her mouth, and saw that her palm was black, with cracks of red showing through. Moving hurt. Pain covered the whole right side of her body like a second skin. She let her right hand drop and raised her left hand, then stared at it dumbly, too shocked to think.

The skin on the back of her left hand was crisscrossed with tiny welts, dark burn marks in the same pattern as a Flame's lava mesh. As she became aware of the marks covering the entire left side of her body, she realized that a spot on her forehead radiated a sharp heat. Without thinking, she drew T'Jas from the heat. She was only able to manage a trickle, and it was tiny compared to what she could have done with a comparable amount of cold, but it was just enough to do the one task that required the least amount of T'Jas. She would have preferred enough power to destroy her cage, fight off the Flames, and free herself, but she would take what she could get.

Ignoring the agony in the right side of her body, she pushed her mind into Medoc's.

The General was too stunned by the idea of an Icer using heat to enter his mind to push her out immediately, and for a moment, their minds intermingled. She knew everything he knew, and he knew all of her. She saw herself staring back at him from the cage, small and pitiful, half of her hair burned off her scalp, a glowing dot of lava on the left side of her forehead, just under the rim of the crown. She knew his doubt about his King's sanity, his reservations from the beginning about invading Iskalon, his frustration over the contamination of the baths. She felt his hatred and contempt for the Icers, but also an underlying disgust at his own King's treatment of them. She saw him giving the order from Dynat that the Icers who surrendered with her would be killed, thrown into the Lava River. They shared a moment of empathy; he sensed her sorrow and shock, and it caused him to regret the waste of lives even more. He bore her kind no love, but neither was he a cruel person by nature.

She pressed past her sorrow and burrowed into his mind like a rockworm, plundering his secrets. She saw his boredom and ambivalence toward his wife, his concern for his daughters' future. She saw his memory of his own testing at the lava river, and his pride in the neat hexagonal patterns on his mesh. As his thoughts rushed into hers, more and more memories flooded through, and she processed them as quickly as she could, storing anything that might be of use later. It was difficult; the Flame had a rich and complex mind, and she was nearly overwhelmed by his thoughts.

At the same time, she observed him taking in her own knowledge and experiences, the loss of her family, the revelation of her Flame mother, Dynat's strange treatment, and then her own hopeless plunge into the lava river, and the mixed result. She saw understanding dawn on his face, mirroring his thoughts, and then fear. He tried to push her out, but she clung to him, playing on what she had read in his doubts about his king. "You needn't bow to his tyranny." She pressed the thought into his mind desperately. "I can help you overthrow him. Together, we can free both of our kingdoms."

Just before he succeeded in pushing her out, she read his parting thought. It was one of contempt and disgust. As if she, half burned to death in a cage, could be of any help to him. And she the product of the perverted relationship between a Flame and an Icer. She might as well be half cababar.

"Heal her," Medoc said to one of the Flames behind him. "Our King has had his fun, but he will want her whole again for the next round. Leave the lava burning, though. It seems he wants her marked."

It was thin as ice clinging to the shores of the lake, but his lie gave her hope. When he left the throne room, he left the portcullis open.

Dynat

Dynat paced his bedroom in time to the chant of the Fire Spirit in his mind. *Dreams, Dreams, Dreams. Lying little Icer. Enter her mind. Take her Dreams.* The hissing voice was louder than the roaring Lava River below.

Dynat knew he must obey, but he could not bring himself to do it. He had been so careful. No one alive knew his secrets, not even Bolv. He had to keep it that way. "I'm not disobeying," he said, marching from bed to balcony, to the door to see if she had arrived yet, then back to the bed. "Only delaying." It was ok to delay, the Fire Spirit had told him that long ago. Only direct disobedience would be punished. Dynat had dim memories of punishment from the last time he had truly tried to defy the Fire Spirit, years past. A shadow of the pain was enough to make him want to obey. The Fire Spirit seemed more urgent and obsessed with this command than ever before. Dynat did not think he would be able to delay very long.

He heard the outer door open, and in a moment Bolv swept into the room, hips swaying and heels clicking. "My King," she said, bowing slightly.

Dynat stared at her in shock. She was covered with soot from head to toe. Her golden plate-cloth was black and dull, her hair in disarray. Dark circles ringed her eyes as if she hadn't slept in days. "By the Lava Lake," Dynat whispered. "Did you come from the Baths, woman, or the Mines?"

"The Baths, my King. You see that they are not in any shape for bathing. Your presence is needed there sorely. The Nobles—"

"There is a pitcher in the other room. Have a Semija get you cleaned up. Quickly."

The last thing Dynat wanted to hear about was the Baths. He needed a distraction, and Bolv had always provided one in the past. In her arms, he could almost forget the Fire Spirit existed.

She frowned, making her plain face even worse. "Majesty, this is no time—"

"NOW, Kinyara!" Dynat roared. Her eyes widened and she scurried from the room. Dynat stared after her, confused. He had never had to order her to this; always before she came willingly. What was wrong with everyone? Medoc all tense, disobeying orders, and now Bolv being difficult? Dynat ground his teeth and began to disrobe.

By the time he was ready, Bolv lay on the soft furs of Dynat's bed, nude and voluptuous, her spread body welcoming the soft torchlight of the room. Her eyes glinted, narrow not with passion but fury. Normally, her anger would spur him to greater depths of passion, but now he remained limp. He climbed onto her anyway, trying to thrust inside of her like a noodlesnake pushing into its burrow. Every other part of him was hard. Bolv turned her head to the side, staring at the wall; her anger cold and distant.

Dynat snarled in frustration as his manhood shriveled completely. He kept pushing against her, trying to relieve his own anger. It was like making love to a doll. Bolv had never been like this before. The Ice Queen's face reared in his mind. Cold and angry. The Fire Spirit continued to whisper. *Enter her mind. Plunder her Dreamsssssss.*

He pushed into Bolv over and over, slapped her cheeks and bit her neck. Finally he rolled off her and towered above the bed. "You call yourself Kinyara?" he asked as she stood and began dressing. "You are worthless. You do not know how to please me. I will find a Lady who can satisfy me!"

"Dynat, the Baths—"

"Fire Spirit take the Baths to the Lava Lake! You are as worthless at that task as you are at this. Your one duty is to keep Chraun running smoothly. You have failed. I will throw you in the river and take a real woman for my Kinyara! Send me a Semija."

She did not look at him again as she slunk from the room. Dynat lay down, panting and angry on the soft furs of the bed. After a moment a Semija entered and knelt.

"Send for Lady Jisthe," Dynat gasped. "And Lady Mavel, and a few of their friends. Send for blissi and powderlux."

The Semija bowed and left, and Dynat noticed how little of her body her furs covered. The Fire Spirit still hissed in his mind. *Enter her mind. Take her Dreams, Dreams, Dreamsssss . . .*

Medoc

Medoc walked away from the throne room in a stiff, formal march, his features perfectly even. He wasn't aware of where his feet were taking him until the air grew slightly humid, and he realized he was halfway to the baths. Well, that made sense. Of course he would go there to calm his nerves, soothe away the shock of the last few moments, to quiet his mind—which still rang with the Ice Queen's thoughts.

I can help you, she said over and over again, as if she was still linked with him. What had happened in there? He understood, but he still couldn't believe it was possible. The very idea repulsed him now, but when he had been a young Flame, pondering such things, he had always assumed that if a Flame mated an Icer, the union would produce no offspring, like the perverse matings with Semija, or a mating between a hippole and a cababar. At the least, the offspring should be deformed, sickly, unable to survive for long. Not hale, like the Ice Queen. Not able to draw T'Jas from both fire and ice. Why had the Fire Spirit willed that something like her would be allowed to exist? And who was her mother? The image in the Icer's mind hadn't been clear enough for Medoc to identify her. But he had heard a tale once of a Lady fleeing to the frozen tunnels. Her family had been executed for plotting against a King—was it Rodev or Ritnu? Medoc could not recall. The Lady had returned and been executed herself, after her mind was plundered for any secrets she might carry from Iskalon.

None of that mattered. The truth was, the Ice Queen *could* use heat T'Jas. Medoc was not staunchly religious, but he kept the rites as he was required by his position, and he often prayed to the Fire Spirit before battle. He believed that when he died, he would be consigned to the lava river and his spirit would flow to the lava lake, as it had during the testing, to rest for eternity. The Ice Queen had gone to the lake, been tested in its center, and survived, even returned with the mark of the Fire Spirit, though the lava mesh had not fully formed on her body—probably because her blood was contaminated. Medoc's stomach churned again. The whole thing was revolting.

And dangerous. Medoc had lied about his King, told the Guards that Dynat had tortured the Ice Queen, marked her, when he had not. Sooner or later, his lie would be revealed. Why had he lied? Did he really think the grotesque half-breed could be of use? She had seen his mind, knew that he had considered treason. If Dynat discovered that, Medoc would be lucky to be thrown into the Lava River. He would have to kill her somehow, without Dynat finding out that he had done so.

The humidity grew, and the stench of black smoke rose into the tunnel, covering a layer of delicious sulfur smell. He stood for a time in the tunnel. He would find no peace in the baths now, no quiet contemplation. But Bolv would be there, and he needed to speak with Bolv.

He found her in the large, communal bathing cavern. He leaned against the arched doorway, watching her address the crowd that gathered there. She stood on a ledge of stone, Semija kneeling at her feet. Fifty or so commoners listened, scratching heads, muttering, and tapping feet. A few nobles, standing out in gemcloth and golden plate, stood alongside them.

" . . . King Dynat is aware of the situation, and grieves with you. He is very busy. I remind you, the war is just now over. The baths will receive their due attention."

The commoners did not seem well pacified by Bolv's promises. One of the Nobles spoke up. "It's not the baths we care about, Kinyara. It's the cursed drinking water. Half the tunnels by the baths are contaminated. These common Flames are coming up to our tunnels to fill their buckets. It has to stop."

"We are working on the problem—"

"That's what you said five days past! What are we paying for, anyhow?"

"My hippole are all coughing blood! Will I have to pay taxes on hippole I can't even milk?"

"Ah, here's the General, maybe he has word from the

King—"

Medoc would have liked to duck away, but instead he marched to Bolv's side. "What the Kinyara said is true. We are working on the problem. The King has been busy with matters of war, but he will turn his attention back to this. He is already speaking with his top advisors."

Medoc's second lie of the day left a bad taste in his mouth. He gestured with his head for Bolv to follow him, and pushed through the crowd, shielded by Bolv's Semija. The shouts continued. He wondered if he would have to put down a riot.

After a few moments, Bolv followed him into the tunnel. There was something different about her. She was cleaner than the last time he saw her, scalecloth and hair perfectly in place, yet Medoc had a sense that she was fraying, coming apart at the edges. When had she last slept? For that matter, when had he last slept?

"Perhaps if you spoke with him yourself, Kinyara—"

"Do you think I haven't tried?" Her voice rose, and she took a deep breath, attempting to calm herself. "He sent me away. He couldn't—I heard that he summoned Lady Jisthe to replace me, and a whole string of Ladies after her. There are rumors that he has lain with Semija. Perhaps he is lying with them even now."

She began to cry. Medoc stood by awkwardly, hoping no one would come up the tunnel. When Wilmina cried, it was always in the privacy of their chambers, but he never knew what to do then, either. He could fight a thousand battles, but a woman weeping made his blood run cold.

"Kinyara," he said softly. "This will not solve anything."

She gave one more heart wrenching wail, then straightened, took another deep breath, and let her tears puff away in steam over her disorderly lava mesh. Medoc gave her a moment to gather herself before he spoke.

"Our King, he is like a different man, Kinyara. Will you think badly of me if I say I do not see him as fit to rule in this state?"

Her eyes widened slowly. Though her anger at Dynat had brought her to tears, she had not yet considered treason. He saw her taste it on her tongue, swirl it around in her mouth, consider whether to swallow it or spit it out. She did neither, and Medoc continued to speak.

"I have no wish to govern, Kinyara. Believe me. I am content with my station, and I have served Dynat faithfully for many years. But I fear for our Kingdom. I fear that Chraun will not withstand Dynat's madness. He will pull us all with him into the Lava lake."

She spat. Anger crept into those dark, tired eyes. "And so what if he does? If the Fire Spirit wills it, so it must be. Perhaps these are the end times for Chraun. Perhaps we are destined to be reunited with the Lava Lake, as we were cast out before. The Fire Spirit will welcome us home with open arms."

Medoc nodded. "And so it must be, if it is willed. But we are talking about the lives of our people, tens of thousands of people. And the Semija? They will never survive the Lava Lake. We have a duty to them. What are we to do, leave them to their own devices in these tunnels? They will surely perish, even as the cababar would without us to feed and tend them. And what of all the untested children who will die? Do they not deserve a chance? Should we not at least try to save our Kingdom? If we try and fail, I will go to the Lava Lake content. If we do not try, there will be no place for me there."

"What is it you propose?"

"I would like for you to confine Dynat to his quarters. Bind him there with ice if you must. We can tell the Kingdom that he is ill, or taking a retreat—it would not be as odd as any of his other actions. Let everyone think our commands come from him. Keep him away until I am done with the Icers in the Outer Tunnels. I intend to make them clean their lake. After that, we can let the Nobles decide our fate. I know the military will back me. I do not know about the Nobles, but once the Baths are clean, they should support me."

She had begun to shake her head at the first sentence, and her movements became more exaggerated as he went, but he could not stop, and by the end of his proposal she was flickering like a flame. "No," she said. "It is too risky."

Medoc's blood froze in his veins. He had revealed everything to her, sure that she was as fed up with Dynat's non-rule as he was. Did she love Dynat? He hadn't proposed harming the King, merely keeping him out of the way while he, Medoc, did the King's duties to the people. If she told Dynat, Medoc could be executed within the gong for treason. His body would be entombed in solid rock, or fed to hippole, never to join the Lava Lake and dwell with the Fire Spirit.

A survival instinct, honed by many years of warfare, sent unpleasant, unbidden thoughts into his mind. She was a strong Flame, but with surprise, he could best her. "Let us walk a bit," he said, keeping his voice light. "I need to stretch my legs."

She nodded, and he relaxed a little. At least she was not ready to run to Dynat at this moment. Perhaps she too clung to the element of surprise. He started walking down the tunnel, and she followed at his elbow. He was very aware of her presence, and tried not to alter his T'Jas in any way that might alert her to his thoughts.

"What is it you fear, Kinyara?" Medoc turned down a tunnel toward the lava river. It would be nice to bask in that heat, as the baths were not available.

"If we bound Dynat and then released him, we would both be executed for certain. The Nobles favor Dynat. No one would take our side, at least no one of consequence. If we are to do this and survive, Dynat must die. But his blood must not be on our hands."

"But if we spoke to the Nobles, made them see—"

"The Nobles are fickle, General. They will support whoever suits them in the moment. They will use you for their own ends, turn their heads while you imprison their King, and then cry foul when Dynat reappears, turning on you—on us. You know well the ways of war, General, but not of politics. You've seen many Kings rise and fall in your time, and you think it is due to your coup, but I tell you it is the Nobles who chose."

"The military—"

"How far would you turn your power on our own people? All the military has is its might. Unless you are prepared to use that might, it is worth absolutely nothing."

Medoc stroked his mustache. The heat from the lava river radiated through the rocks, though they were still several caverns away. She was right. He had to have the support of the nobles, or else his uprising could turn into a bloodbath, him killing the very people he wished to help. Some would have to die no matter what. But he wanted that number to be as small as possible.

"So. What do you advise?"

"In order for you to succeed, Dynat must die. But your hands must be clean. The Nobles will jump at any chance to grab power for themselves. There are several houses already eyeing the throne. If they can prove you have killed Dynat, they will depose you as a murderer. You must have someone else kill him, someone absolutely loyal who will not betray you. Or someone you can force a confession from and then kill. Someone of no consequence."

Medoc thought of Cadet Tejusi, and his heart felt sick. To use someone loyal to him for such a purpose was not in his nature. Even to kill Dynat himself . . . Medoc had sworn to Bretle that he would always protect his son. He had knelt before Dynat and sworn to serve to his own death if necessary; how could he kill him? But if he did not, what would become of Chraun?

Bolv was still speaking, and he forced himself to focus on her words.

" . . . Adopt policies that will gain you support from

the Nobles. You lower taxes, which are already low enough that we can barely maintain the Kingdom, you look the other way while they sport with Semija and common Flames. You let Chraun run itself, and spend your days hunting slink so that you never see the injustices done in your name. Dynat was doing it right. He just let the crisis of the Baths get out of control. Now the Nobles are unhappy."

Her words chilled him to his very core. Had he been so blind to politics all his life? Was it really the Nobles who controlled the Kingdom? Medoc had always thought the Military was the soul of Chraun, holding it together.

They walked for a time in silence, as the roar of the river came into their ears. Soon it drowned out the click of Bolv's heels against the smooth stone floor. They came to a deserted landing, and Medoc went straight to the edge, hoping she would follow, and looked over. Like a giant vein, pulsing life into Chraun, the lava river roared below, glowing red-hot, so bright it nearly hurt his eyes to look at.

Bolv hung back, leaning against the wall of the landing, and Medoc turned at last to confront her. To his surprise, she was smiling. "Do you think I am a fool, General?"

She had to shout, to be heard over the roar of lava, but the smugness in her tone was clear. "You are so easy to read. Could you have done it? Just one little push? You've killed hundreds in battle, but I don't think you have it in you to kill this way, in cold blood."

Medoc stepped back from the river, only to be met by a wall of fire. The Kinyara was drawing power from the lava river, and using it against him. For all her doubts about his ability to kill her, he did not think she would hesitate if she saw an advantage in killing him.

"I will not participate in your treason, General." Medoc wanted to cover her mouth with his hand. She was shouting still to be heard by him, what if someone came by and heard her words? "But I will advise you, and reap its rewards."

So, he was not to die today. But what did the Kinyara want? He had known before he had uttered a word to her that she would drive a hard bargain. He had expected to approach her from a place of power, not backed up against his own death. Though the lava gave him strength, if she wounded him enough, the fall would melt the flesh from his bones.

"You will swear, right here, on the Fire Spirit and your place in the Lava Lake, to make me your Kinyara, should you become King of Chraun. And I shall not be a quiet, meek Kinyara like King Ovid's little Shareema. I will rule by your side, a Queen like the Kinyara of old."

It was a sickening thought. She was not even his cousin! To make her his Kinyara would breach an ancient custom. She was supposed to follow the King into the Lava River, when he died. The common Flames would protest. But the Nobles who supported Dynat's rule were less concerned with tradition, and they would be pleased to see the Kinyara who understood their arrangements stay in power. Wilmina would not be pleased, however—far from it. Nor would his own cousin—he could not remember which of his many sisters' daughters was eldest.

But this was not about Wilmina, or Bolv, or even Medoc himself. This was about saving Chraun from the monster Dynat had become. Bolv's words echoed in his mind. A Queen. Suddenly, Medoc saw a way to bring Dynat down without any blood on his own hands. Like the solution to a complex battle plan, worked at for many gongs, everything fell into place.

First, though, he would need to keep Bolv out of the way, bound in her own complicity. "I swear, by the Fire Spirit, the Lava River, and my own place in the Lava Lake, that when I am King of Chraun, I will make you my Kinyara, Bolv."

The words, shouted, were lost in the roar of the river. Bolv's mouth stretched in a triumphant smile, but Medoc barely saw it. He was already looking past her, planning his next battle, setting his warriors in place.

Chapter 12

A Dangerous Decision

Stasia

The steady red glow in the throne chamber never changed, and Stasia lost track of the time she spent in the tiny cage. At intervals, a great vibration passed through the walls, shaking the whole room slightly, but she was too miserable to try to measure the time between each vibration. After her stomach began to crawl with a hunger so great it overcame her nausea, a human slave brought her water and food. It was a Chraunian Semija, not a captive Iskaloner. Stasia tried to talk to her, but the slave acted as if she were deaf, and Stasia gave up, wondering how many of her own people were being turned into slaves like this one. The water was warm and stale, but she drank it. The food was peculiar, a soft, chewy meat that she told herself must be cababar.

The lava continued to burn a tiny hole in her forehead. It hurt, but the pain was bearable, and it did not seem to be endangering her. The Flame whom Medoc had ordered to heal her had been thorough, and the lava and a thinness in the hair on half of her scalp were the only signs of her injury. Even the ghost-mesh scars on what she had begun to consider her "Flame side" were gone. But Flame healing was rough and hot, and it left her weak and ill, in almost as much pain as she'd suffered from her wounds. When the Flames were gone and she was alone again, she pulled as much heat from the lava on her face as she could bear, then tried doing simple tasks with it. She already knew she could enter another person's mind. She scraped her fingernail against the tender skin on her forearm, breaking it but not drawing blood, then tried to heal it. The small welt smoothed over as if it had never been.

Excited, she continued, but that seemed to be the limit of her small power over the heat within. She could not create an external flame; nor could she shape the bars of her cage and free herself. She could not manipulate hot air, thickening it and dispersing it to create solid air; it slipped through her hands like water when she tried. All of these failures made her glad she had reached out for Medoc's mind instantly, rather than wasting time trying to fight the Flames.

For all the good it had done. He, and the Fire King as well, seemed to have forgotten about her. Time crept immeasurably and maddeningly. With every passing moment she grew more and more worried about her people. What was happening beyond her lonely prison? Had Casser found V'lturhst? Had the Fire King slaughtered all of her Icers? Did Glace live, a slave waiting on some cruel Flame?

Sleep was rare and brief, broken by the pain of cramped muscles and the choking stench of her own defecation. Stasia Dreamed, but they were not useful, informative Dreams. Instead, she dreamed of the burial chamber, of the copper woman beckoning her on, of being trapped in burial ice. She often woke up shouting that she wasn't dead yet. But that dream was utterly useless. Or was it a predictive Dream? Did it mean that she would die, and would be entombed in the Ice? Death seemed likely, but a proper burial was out of the question.

Stasia was tracing her fingers over the surface of the bars of the cage, wondering if she would know the exact moment that she lost her mind, when the portcullis scraped open. The Fire King stood in the doorway, his dark silhouette framed in the brighter, orange light of Flame torches in the hallway outside. A full cloak of dark fur hung from his shoulders all the way to the stone floor. He stared at her a moment, then stepped closer to peer intently through the bars.

"What is that on your face?"

Stasia remembered their last conversation, and the Fire King's belief that the Fire Spirit spoke to him. Perhaps she could use this knowledge to trick him. She attempted a smile, but it felt more like a grimace.

"Your Fire Spirit came to me, from the river yonder. He touched my forehead with his finger and said that I was marked as his, and that I have his protection. He said he would punish you if you killed me."

She had hoped to get a reaction from the Fire King, but she was not prepared for what came next. Flames seemed to leap from his eyes, and his face contorted in rage. "Say you are lying." His voice betrayed an undertone of danger. He was whispering, but she could see he wanted to shout. "Tell me you are lying right now, and I will forget this blasphemy."

Stasia supposed the smart thing would have been to apologize and then make up a new, more convincing lie. But she was intrigued by his overreaction, and curious as to how far she could push him. "I wish I was lying," she said, as if unaware of his anger. "It hurt tremendously, and even now my forehead burns. He was not very gentle, this Fire Spirit of yours."

She braced herself as the fire in his eyes intensified. Veins bulged and pulsed on his forehead. She wondered how great her healing abilities were. If he beat her nearly to death, would she be able to heal herself?

To her surprise, instead of raining fire down on her helpless body, he spun on his heel and stalked out of the room. The portcullis slammed shut behind him.

Alone again in the dim red heat, Stasia ruminated on the Fire King's strange reaction. She had expected to be beaten, to be screamed at, to have the lava wrenched forcibly from her forehead. She was startled to think that she would miss the burning pain; it gave her a strange sense of security. Why was he so certain she was lying? It seemed a plausible conclusion, if one believed in a Fire Spirit that haunted the river of Lava, to think that it could come ashore and mark the Fire King's prisoner. What had she said that made him so angry, and was it something she could exploit when he returned?

Dynat

Dynat left his throne room shaking with rage and fear. As he stalked the tunnels, not sure where his feet were taking him, he listened intently inward. The Fire Spirit still whispered about Dreams and plundering the Ice Queen's mind. It was time. Dynat could put it off no longer. He must kill her as soon as he had taken what she knew. He would make sure she did not reveal his past to anyone.

But what if she was telling the truth? She did have lava on her face, and it hadn't killed her. The Fire Spirit had not commanded Dynat to kill her. What if it commanded him to spare her?

"I will kill her!" he shouted at the walls. Nobles in the tunnel stared at him; Semija prostrated nervously. "Get back to your duties," he said coldly. He had hoped that announcing his intention would prompt the Fire Spirit to agree or deny him, revealing his ultimate intention regarding the Ice Queen, but it did not. The Fire Spirit continued to rant about Dreams. Dynat turned and marched purposefully to his quarters.

The parlor was dim and empty. The whole place

reeked of powderlux and stale blissi. One of Bolv's Semija
cowered in the corner, naked and shaking. Dynat stared at
her without really seeing her. Shameful memories flickered
through his mind, and he looked away from the Semija,
focused on the Roughert painting.

The Ice Queen was lying. She had to be lying. Dynat
was losing control of this situation, losing the will to even
walk into his own throne room. He had to get rid of the
Ice Queen. But how could he, if the Fire Spirit protected
her? She was lying about that. She had to be. But that
smile—

"Tell me what you intend for her," he pleaded,
watching the flat skittering across the walls of his quarters.
"What do you want me to do? Have I not always done
your bidding?"

"Dynat? Is that you? Who are you speaking to?"

Bolv appeared in the entrance to their bedroom. She
looked weary and angry. Why did everyone look so weary?

"What are you doing here? Aren't you working on
something?" He vaguely remembered having ordered her
to do something. What was it?

"The Baths? They are still contaminated, Dynat. We
are making sand, to filter the water before it reaches the
drinking vats. It takes some time, and I thought I should
try to rest while they work on it."

"Ah. Yes." The baths, that had been it.

"Who were you speaking to?" her eyes bored into his,
and he shivered. How much had she heard? All of Chraun
knew the Fire Spirit spoke to him, but no one knew what it
was like, having the deity in his mind always, constantly
whispering . . . Bolv was the only friend he had, and he
wished he could tell her the truth. A dim memory surfaced,
of cold anger, her head turned aside, slapping her. Had he
done that?

"No one, I was just—just—never mind. What
happened to the Semija?"

"Do you really not remember? I tried to order her

away, but she said you commanded her to stay like that. Why, Dynat? She was my favorite, and you ruined her . . ."

Another memory, of what he had done with the Semija. It was disgusting; he might as well have gone down to the stock caverns . . . It was all the Ice Queen's fault. She was driving him mad. He had to take her Dreams, and kill her, so this would all be over.

"Where is Medoc? I have a task for him."

"I don't know. I don't care. What is wrong with you, Dynat?"

Dynat nodded and turned to go. He would plunder the Ice Queen's mind, then order Medoc to kill her. If the Fire Spirit wanted her spared, Dynat could blame her death on Medoc.

"Dynat?"

He paused. He heard Bolv approach him, her heels clicking on the floor.

"Where are you going?"

"To look for Medoc. I have a task for him"

"Very well," she said. "Good-bye, Dynat."

She was overtired. "Stay here," Dynat said, turning. "Let someone else take care of the Baths. Have a bath shaped here. Buy a few new Semija. You need your rest, Kinyara."

She smiled sadly at him. Why was she so sad? "As you command, my King."

"It is a command. I won't have my Kinyara looking like a common Flame, overworked. When I return, you will be refreshed and happy again."

"Yes, Dynat. I will be here. Good-bye."

He traced his fingers over her plump lips, then turned and left. The cloak still weighed on his shoulders, but he kept it on. Perhaps, after he was finished with the Ice Queen, he would go hunting, to savor the quiet solitude of the slink tunnels.

He found Medoc in the Warrior's mess cavern,

surrounded by Officers. They were leaned in together, heads almost touching, talking earnestly, and they went silent when Dynat entered, standing and saluting him with deep bows. He ignored them and beckoned Medoc. "Come," he said. "I have a task for you."

He turned, not questioning whether he would be obeyed. When Medoc caught up to him in the tunnel, he said, "What were you planning in there? Perhaps some of the Warriors should help Bolv with the baths. I think she is overworked."

"You are no doubt correct, my King. We were discussing that very matter—what the military will do next, once we root out the last of the Iskaloners."

"And?"

"Well—we did not reach a conclusion, my King. Of course, our next task is yours to decide. But I like to speak with the men and get a feel for their mood."

"Yes. Well, I have a task for you, Medoc, though it should be a brief one."

"Of course, my King."

"There is a pitviper in my throne room. I want you to get it out."

"My King?"

"The Icer in the cage by my throne. I'm bored with her. I'd like you to exterminate her, like one would destroy vermin in the fungal caverns."

The Fire Spirit remained silent. That was good. She must have been lying. Surely if the Fire Spirit did not want her killed, he would have spoken up.

Dynat turned up the corridor to his throne room. He could hear the clunk of Medoc's stiff steps behind him. "Yes, I want you to exterminate her. General, no matter what I say in there, you are to follow this order. Even if I command you to stop, you must kill her."

Stasia

Stasia did not have to wait long for the Fire King's return. She was trying to stretch her toes out to ease a cramp in her calf when the door scraped open again. The King strode through, followed by Medoc. Stasia's blood curdled when she saw him. Had he told the Fire King of her limited ability to Flame? She was tempted to link with the General immediately, but her instincts cautioned her. If the King was still unaware of her ability and the fact that she had entered Medoc's mind, doing so now might give her away. The Fire King might be able to read the cues that showed their minds were linked.

"Get rid of her cage," he ordered Medoc. "You, get out. We are not to be disturbed under any circumstances." He waved away the guards who had followed them into the throne room and flung down the heavy portcullis behind them.

The General concentrated, and the bars surrounding Stasia receded back into the floor and ceiling, ordinary stalas once more. Stasia scrambled to her feet at once. Or at least, she tried to. She could not be certain how much time had passed since she'd last stood, but it was long enough for her leg muscles to forget how to work. While she was trying a second time, the Fire King lost patience.

"Bring her," he said, and strode past the throne toward the back of the room. Stasia felt queasy. She was sweating with terror. Why had he brought Medoc here? The General must have betrayed her. Which meant that she would very likely die now.

Medoc approached her and wove a rope of fire from the heat in the air. His expression was unreadable, but his hands were gentle as he bound her wrists with the painful blaze and pulled her to her feet. Her muscles cramped as blood reached tired tissue, and her soles burned as if she walked on coals.

"Drag her if you must," the Fire King's voice came over the roar of lava, from the back of the cavern. Medoc put a hand on either of her shoulders.

"March, prisoner." There was no anger or hate in his voice, and he met her eyes with a stern look. Stasia remembered where she had heard that tone before—it was listening to Glace train recruits. It was not sympathetic, but it was encouraging. She placed one foot before the other, and found she could do that again, and again, and she could even move faster when the King shouted for them to hurry. They passed into a wave of heat, and Stasia realized where they were headed.

From her cage, even facing the back of the throne chamber, she'd never seen the lava river, only its telltale glow. Now it spread out before her, deep in a gorge that separated the back wall of the cavern from the floor on which they stood. She wasn't sure if it was the heat or the sheer height that made her dizzy. The Fire King stood staring at its depths as if mesmerized by the glowing heat, but he turned to face her as they approached.

"Chosen of the Fire Spirit," he spat at her, bringing his face close to hers. "Protected! We shall see. Medoc, hold her by the edge. Be ready to throw her in on my command."

Stasia decided it was time to enter Medoc's mind, in spite of the risk. *Last chance, Medoc. I can distract him while you strike. Or you can wait for his insanity to destroy us all.*

Medoc held her arms. She could feel his hesitation and uncertainty as if they were her own. She saw a plan in his mind disrupted by Dynat's command. He had planned to use her, to put her in a position to defeat Dynat and escape, then take control of the throne himself. He was wavering now, uncertain if his plan could be salvaged, or if he should bide his time and find another pawn.

"You are linked," Dynat said. "Why would you enter her mind, Medoc?"

Desperate, Stasia pushed her tortured body into action. She kicked backward, connecting with Medoc's shin and distracting him long enough to pull her arms free.

She dove forward and threw her arms, still bound with fire at the wrists, over Dynat's head, pulling him close.

Startled, the Fire King pushed her away, but her bound wrists caught on his neck. His lava mesh burned into her body. She tried to do what she had done with the Flame Soldier at Grimshore, pulling the heat from his body into hers. She thought she could take it better this time. It was minimal compared to the rushing heat of the lava river.

But unlike the other Flame, he was ready for her trick. Holding her close, he began to pour heat into her, but it was not just the heat in his lava mesh. She screamed when she realized what he was doing. He pulled heat from the lava below and pumped it into her body; he was like a net through which water passes but is not held. As her skin began to crack and burn, he shouted, "Get out of her mind, Medoc! I must take her Dreams before she dies!"

Medoc withdrew. Stasia was alone again with the heat and pain. With all the heat of the lava river pouring into her, Stasia knew that she was going to die, half-Flame or not, lava-tested or not. She had to make the most of her last few moments, or her death would be entirely in vain. She must do something to be sure her people survived. Drawing a trickle of T'Jas from the heat pouring into her body, she reached out for Medoc's mind one last time, to plead with him to stop his insane King.

Before she could reach him, she was falling toward the hard floor of the cavern, and her head slammed against a stalam. Somehow, though her body was tiny compared to his, she had pulled Dynat down with her, and he covered her whole body with a muffled whimper. As his face fell over her shoulder, she saw a look of surprise in his eyes.

Then Medoc was pulling the Fire King's body off her, pulling her up, healing her with rough fire.

"You killed him," Stasia said, amazed. She truly had not thought he would be able to attack his King. *He* had not believed he could.

"No," he said. "He is merely stunned. A dangerous

prisoner, half Icer, half Flame, escaped from her cell and overpowered the King. She had already fled with him when I arrived."

Stasia was too stunned to move. "You're going to free me?"

"I will have an escort take you to the Lake. From there you will send a message to your people. You will be held at the Lake until it is clean."

"The people of Iskalon. Will you spare them?"

"I will pull back my troops to secure Chraun under my rule. After that, the safety of your people depends on how quickly and thoroughly you can clean the Lake."

"What of the guards? Won't they kill you when they see me leave with him?"

Medoc walked to the door and rapped on the portcullis. It opened, and he whispered something she could not hear to the guards. Then the portcullis slid shut again. "The Royal Honor Guard follows the throne, not the man. If they had seen me attack him, I would be dead. But I told them that he is dead; they belong to me now."

"Why not just kill him?"

The General did not have an answer for her this time. He stared at the cloak-shrouded heap as if wondering the same thing, and smoothed his mustache with vigor. Stasia thought of her people desperately trying to survive in the Outer Tunnels, and the Icers who had surrendered with her, now dead. Lava was too good for him. She kicked the Fire King's unconscious form in anger.

Medoc grabbed her arm. "Do not make me change my mind. He is still . . ."

Stasia shook her head. Whatever Medoc thought Dynat was, he had changed that forever with a single blow. There was no going back now. She had seen his plan in his mind, though Dynat's attempt to kill her had altered it. She was to take the blame for Dynat's disappearance, so that Medoc's loyalty would never be questioned. He would even make a pretense of sending Flames to re-capture her.

But if she was found by Flames who were not loyal to him, the truth of his treachery would out. She saw his need to have the Icers clean out the lake, and trusted him for that alone. "You are as close to a good man as a Flame can get," she said. She thought of her mother, and wondered if Medoc had known her.

A rap came at the door, and Medoc opened it. Four Flames in decorated steel armor entered and saluted Medoc sharply. Stasia began to breath again as she realized these men were loyal to Medoc.

"Take her to the Lake, Tejusi. Be sure that no one sees you. Keep them hidden under his cloak until you reach the Spiral. She is to send a message to her people from the Lake."

Stasia looked down. The Fire King was still breathing, his lava still glowing. His face was peaceful, almost like the face of a child. Tejusi picked Dynat up like a dead raihan and slung him over his shoulder. The cloak draped all the way down to the floor along his side, and Stasia stepped close to him, hiding herself in the folds.

"Go quickly," Medoc said. "If any Flames ask you questions, kill them."

Interlude

Khell, Four Summers Prior

Maia

Maia rode her boareal proudly across the ice, soothed by the undulating motion of the beast propelling its giant girth on fat, short limbs. Its tapered body was smooth under her hands, bristling here and there with a few stiff hairs. Its tusks scraped the ice as it cast its head back and forth, sniffing the air. A memory arose, less and less common these days, of Maia's childhood, riding a furry white, sphere-shaped polloon as it drifted over the water from the summer beach to the sheltered winter cove. Her people had not ridden the boareal, only hunted them. But she was no longer a Nuambe child, she was the healer of the Liathua. When Antahua died, all of her belongings, her egla, her clothes, her dishes, even her boareal became Maia's.

Today the Liathua people rode for their summer camp, a long stretch of beach covered by smooth, fist-sized stones in varying shades of grey and black. Maia rode near the head of a long line of Khell, behind Lubar and Hakua, who rode side by side and shouted to each other about the route. Each boareal dragged a sled behind it, covered with the belongings of the people; hides, clothes, bones for the frame of traveling egla, and weapons for hunting. The sleek, wide-tailed doal ran in teams alongside the boareal, dragging sleds with smaller loads, young children, and infirm. Most of the tribe walked in a long line behind the boareal and the sleds. The Liathua had swelled in the five summers since Maia had become healer, in part due to some of the mildest winters the Khell had seen. They numbered two hundred and fourteen, the fourteenth born two days prior in the traveling camp. Maia had slapped the healthy baby boy to life, and now he rode on his mother's back while she walked amongst the others.

Maia smelled the summer camp before she heard it, and she heard it before she saw it. First a waft of dung and brine and rotten fish rolled over her, overwhelming her nostrils. The smell was vile, but also welcome, a smell of life after the cold deadness of winter. Then a furious cacophony of grunts, snorts, groans and huffs assaulted her ears. It drowned out the chief's conversation with his son, and Hakua blew four long, low notes on his boareal tusk horn. Maia shook her head at that; she barely heard the sound beneath the noise from the beach. Lubar and Hakua crested a ridge, then disappeared beyond it. Maia followed, and Pebble Beach came into view, its namesake obscured by thousands of boareal. They writhed in a mass of territorial battles, matings, and desperate scrambles by females to get out of the rampaging males' paths.

Maia stayed her boareal at the top of the ridge, watching the scene below. She could feel her beast's desire to join the fray. Though the creature was gelded, its instincts remained strong. Maia held tightly to the guiding rope, and stroked the boareal's neck to soothe it.

Hakua and Lubar did not restrain their beasts. They dug in with their knees and rode directly into the mob. Maia watched as fifty more warriors and hunters followed on their boareal. The men shouted and threw spears, and soon the beach ran red. The tribe would feast well this summer.

Maia turned and rode along the crest of the ridge. The people followed her to a place where the ice plain rose to meet the ridge, forming a level table overlooking the beach and the crashing waves. The people began cutting blocks of ice for egla and setting up camp. Two pens were made strong with bones and ice for the tame boareal, one for the gelds and one for the cows. A group of women took greased hide bags down to the shore and waded into the surf to gather *seaweed. Fire pits were built with pebbles from the beach.*

There was little for Maia to do. The people built her egla, and once she had moved her belongings in, she looked for some way to make herself useful. She checked the boareal in their pen, looking for injuries. She visited several egla, checked the health of the newborn, and spent time with a grandfather who would be making his Journey over the Ice next winter, if the Dhuciri did not take him in the tithing.

The days were long, though they were not close to the midsummer Day of Light, when the darkness did not come for three full days, and then only for a few hours. The tribe had arrived at Pebble Beach around midday, and it was nearly dusk when the warriors returned. Exhausted and covered in blood, whipping their boareal to steer them away from the endless contests and matings on the beach, the hunters and warriors dragged hundreds of carcasses to the summer camp. The women received them, ready with knives, scrappers, boiling bags, and bonfires. As soon as the loads were unstrapped, the hunters drove their boareal into the pens.

Maia had ordered a small structure built nearby, closed on one side to the wind with ice and hides, but open on the other for easy coming and going. In this little half-egla she built a fire and put down layers of soft, thick furs and hides. After each warrior secured his beast, the ones who were injured came to her for treatment. All of the injuries she saw were serious. The warriors with minor wounds passed her by and went to the bonfires, their blood still hot from the hunt, eager to join the feast and bask in the attention of their wives and the maidens.

As Maia cauterized and sewed up a deep gore in a man's calf from a boareal tusk, she saw Hakua and Lubar arrive, driving a wild boareal between both of their beasts. The giant bull reared and snorted, thrusting his long tusks this way and that. They held him with leather ropes tied to the tusks and surrounding the animal's neck. He reared up, nearly wrenching the lines from their hands. They whipped him with the ropes and shouted, driving him forward into the pen of cows. Once he was in, twenty camp men rushed forward and blocked up the pen with bones wedged upright in the ice, and more blocks of ice stacked around the bones.

The walls of the pen shook, and Maia could hear the cows squealing as the male overcame his fury at being imprisoned and began to do his duty. Lubar bellowed with laughter, and Hakua blew on his horn. They sent their steeds into the other pen and raced off toward the fires, surrounded by brothers and warriors. Maia finished patching the young man on her furs and sent him off with a bowl of broth, warning him not to put weight on his injured leg. Then she beckoned the next hunter forward. This one had a crushed ankle, smashed when his boareal had rolled over during the hunt.

Maia worked until the sun came up over the plain. A few women brought her food partway through the night. In the early morning she sent the last warrior to bed, then doused her fire and walked down to the water's edge. She took off her furs and washed herself in the cold, salty water, listening to the rutting boareal further up the beach, smelling their pungent scent. When she stepped out of the waves, shivering, Hakua stood on the beach, watching her. She dressed slowly in front of him and began to braid her hair, waiting for him to speak.

"Father is planning a raid," he said just before the silence became unbearable. "He asks that you cast the bones."

Maia smiled, wrapping the base of the first braid with a small length of hide. "Asks? I did not think to use that word in the same sentence with Lubar."

Hakua kicked at the stones at his feet, and Maia felt a sudden moment of pity for him. It was not his fault that his father was a brute and cruel to her. Whatever his faults, Hakua was a kinder, gentler man than Lubar.

"I ask it, then. If you will be petty, we will make the raid without your foresight."

"Why this raid, Hakua?" The last three raids had been made without consulting Maia. The two before that, Lubar had ignored her advice and made the raids at inauspicious times, resulting in the deaths and capture of several Liathua. Maia wondered why he had bothered asking her to cast the bones, if he was going to ignore what they said.

"Lubar is getting older, Maia. He is nowhere near his Journey, but he is weakening. His aim is less straight, his reactions slower.

Bahar did most of the work securing the bull. Lubar took the ropes from him before we reached the camp." Bahar was Lubar's youngest brother. Maia began to thread tiny, bright blue shells into her braid.

"So you want to know if you will be chief before the summer is out?"

His silence answered her question. *"Why does it matter? You will be chief eventually. Knowing if it will happen this summer or next will not change that fate."* She had seen that in bones; Hakua would be chief.

Hakua picked up a large smooth stone and rubbed his thumb along the edge. *"You know it is not that simple, Healer. Not easy, like it was for you."*

He hurled the stone into the brine. *"When Lubar dies, the tribes must be gathered and I must have already gained the favor of ten other chiefs."*

Maia secured her braid with a scrap of stretchy sinew and threw it over her shoulder. She understood what Hakua wanted, now. When the chief died, he was not automatically replaced by his eldest son. First, all of his sons, and sometimes their cousins, waged a staged battle fought with blunt spears. Then the winner of this battle must prove himself before the chiefs of ten other tribes, passing whatever trials and tests they decided to impose. Nine times out of ten, the firstborn son won chief-hood. But there was that one in nine who did not. For Hakua, Lubar's death would not mean a simple ascension to power. It would mean a summer spent fighting to prove himself strong enough to lead the Liathua Khell. Though the bones said Hakua would be chief, they could not remove the obstacles that stood in his way.

Hakua wanted to know if he should prepare himself for the struggle this summer. The answer would affect his course of action now, in planning raids. All Khell tribes raided and sparred, but if the Liathua were overly aggressive this summer, other tribes might seek to weaken them by crippling the selection of the new chief, or scheming to support a weak chief. On the other hand, if Lubar had many winters remaining as chief, the Liathua could raid vigorously, expand their territory, and make friends later.

"Will you truly listen to me, even if the bones do not tell what

you wish to hear?" Maia found herself wondering this aloud. She started on her second braid. "For the bones have spoken to me already on this matter."

"What do they say?" Hakua stepped closer, back straight and chest forward, looking every bit the chief already. "Is this Lubar's last hunt?"

Maia watched him impassively, refusing to be intimidated. How could she be afraid of him when she knew his fate, and her own, so intimately? "It is," she acknowledged. "But you will not be chief before summer is out."

Hakua's dark eyes grew angry. "Who?" He demanded. "How? I know I will win the battle. Which chiefs deny me, and why?"

Maia closed her eyes. The bones were not specific, and the effects of the urchin spine, while they clarified the message of the bones, always left her mind cloudy. She did not know the answers to his questions. "You will be chief of the Liathua Khell, Hakua. Never doubt that. But it will not happen this summer. Lubar—I saw only darkness around him after this raid. He will not rise to fight again. Nor will he die. There is something strange afoot that I cannot see."

Hakua still wore an angry expression. "You speak in riddles, healer. Is he to die or not? Am I to be chief or not? We might as well have sent you off in the tithing, for all the good your bones do us."

Maia shuddered. She had heard those same words many times from Lubar's lips. "I can tell only what I see, Hakua. This will be Lubar's last raid. If you will not be chief this summer, I am certain you will be chief the next."

Hakua stared at her. Maia resisted the urge to look away from that searching gaze. "If you are wrong, healer, I will send you away with the next tithing. I will plan my strategy this summer as if you are right."

He turned and walked back up the beach toward the summer camp. Maia watched him go, her heart racing. A memory flickered through her mind, a sweet young boy, his face close to hers. "You are welcome to live among us, if you like."

Maia wondered if that welcome would survive the trials ahead of the Liathua.

Chapter 13

Rockfall

Larc

The Outer Tunnels were cold, but never quite cold enough. That was one reason that Icers normally avoided them. The air was cool, and the water that seeped from the walls would have made a Flame shiver, but actual ice was rare. Still, there was some, and as the commander of the second phase of the retreat, Larc had a small cave lined with ice. She sat in its center, legs crossed, spine straight, trying to relax enough to sleep a little before the next attack.

It was futile. Her mind spun with worry, and not even T'Jas healing would soothe it. She thought about Stasia, wondered if she was still alive. There was little chance of that. Larc had sent her to her death. Larc had thought that somehow, if they all surrendered together, they would be able to make a stand within Chraun and demand that the General make good on his promise. The fierce pursuit of the Flames against their forces, even after Stasia had surrendered, made it clear that would not happen. She worried about Stasia's strange plan, her command to

Casser to find V'lturhst. When Larc and Casser had parted, the old Icer had been furious. He did not understand his niece's blasphemy any more than Larc did. There was no V'lturhst. Stasia had backed them into a corner, and they would be trapped here by the Flames until they all died of starvation.

In the tunnels surrounding the burial chamber, there had at least been small animals, flats and jewelsnake, to eat, but the Outer Tunnels were barren in comparison. The few animals that lived there were large, strange, and often dangerous. Cave howlers, giant moleworms, and stranger things with no names and sharp teeth prowled the narrow, labyrinthine tunnels. Many of them had poison in their flesh from feeding on concentrated metals in the rock of the Outer Tunnels. Entire tunnels were dominated by giant vine-fungi that could trap and engulf a person as they tried to walk through. None of this would have been insurmountable if there had been enough cold. The Icers were taxed enough by the fighting; having them kill and purify the few animals available would take the last of their vaerce and leave the retreat defenseless. Larc would be commanding walking dead, Icers who would drop in the middle of battle from the sheer exhaustion that took all Icers when their vaerce were gone.

I should not be commanding at all, Larc thought. She had never commanded an army, never even considered the possibility. She was a Healer, not a Warrior. An Advisor, not a Commander. Fortunately, she had General Kiner. He was able to make most of the decisions and guide the troops. There was little for Larc to do but worry.

A howler's deep, echoing call sounded in the distance. Larc tensed, then began her deep breathing again. She had been relaxing, but had not realized it until the call gave her something else to worry about. Cave howlers were the most dangerous creature in the Outer Tunnels. Dark, hairy, shy creatures, they crept through the tunnels, clinging to vertical rock faces, moving in large family bands. It was not physical aggression that made them dangerous but the low, loud call of their leaders. Noises like that were bound to trigger cave-ins. The Outer Tunnels were like a child's sculpture built from the loose, wet sand at the lakeshore, porous and fragile. Larc was sure the call she heard had collapsed a tunnel. The howlers seemed almost deliberate about it.

Larc rose and tried to neaten herself. Her chirsh armor was dusty and tattered, her hair a tangled mess. She had not seen standing water since the fall of Iskalon. She thought she might give her life just for a chance to bathe. But there was no use pining over what could not be. She brushed the dust out of her face and left her cave. There would be a messenger with news about the damage caused by the howler. She should listen and try to understand whether it interfered with Kiner's defense plan.

When she entered the narrow tunnel lined with small cave-quarters like hers, Larc discovered that the messenger was neither an Icer nor a Warrior. It was Hali, one of the guildless, small and waif-like even on the tiny raihan she rode. They had found a pocket of guildless in the Outer Tunnels who had been hiding there since the war, surviving on fungi and stock they'd looted in the chaos of the initial attack on Iskalon. At Casser's command they were adopted into the highly depleted Guilds. Hali had joined the scribe Guild, most of whom served as messengers since the destruction of the Palace library. Hali was a go-between for Casser and Larc.

Well, there was a tiny relief. Larc had not heard from Casser's group for several days, and she had worried immensely about them. Hali saluted and Larc returned her salute curtly. It was strange to think of the guildless being able to join society. It made her just a little bit uncomfortable. "Report, Scribe."

"Yes, Lady Larc. Prince Casser sends word that the people have reached a narrowing of tunnels, about one half-day's travel from here by raihan. He believes that there is something larger behind them, wider tunnels or perhaps even caves."

"Why does he believe that?"

"He says there are drafts and water-flows through the rock that indicate a wider space, Lady. He has ordered the people to tunnel a way through the narrow tunnels to the other side."

Larc let a whuff of breath hiss between her teeth. Tunneling by hand was a dangerous business. Icers could manipulate rock so that it remained stable, so that widening a tunnel created a denser, stronger bed of rock. When humans tunneled with tools, they weakened the walls, opening fractures and dislodging loose rocks. Casser had only a few Icers with him, and if Larc recalled correctly, they were not much better suited to work with rock than she. He must truly believe that there was something worth the risk on the other side.

Hali continued. "There have been several small cave-ins, my Lady, and a few casualties. But he is determined. He asks that you send any Icers you have to spare to the people, to assist them."

Larc clenched her teeth. There were no Icers to spare. The ones who were not fighting were resting, conserving vaerce, trying to stave off exhaustion. Still, if Casser continued to tunnel by hand, he could cause a huge rockfall. She would have to send Icers to him.

"Feed and water your animal, then meet me back here," she commanded Hali. "Get yourself a ration, too."

Hali saluted and led her beast away, stroking its long nose. The raihan's glowing white hide was covered with grime and sweat; she must have ridden it hard. Larc would have liked to give her a fresh beast. But there were as few raihan to spare as there were Icers.

Larc poked her head into five different sleeping caves, waking the Icers within. Terean was the highest ranking officer she chose—he had been promoted from Scout to a Luten—and all five were strong in their abilities with rock.

When they were up and crowding the narrow tunnel, she explained their orders. They looked askance, but even Terean did not question her. Hali returned, saluted again, and mounted her raihan. Larc stood in the tunnel, watching them fade out of range of the icelight, until she could see only a faint glow from the raihan, beyond the dark shapes of the Icers. Hopefully the risk was worth it. Perhaps there would be something other than empty caves on the other side of Casser's digging. Something to justify the hole that would be created in her defenses.

Larc went to the storeroom next for her own ration. Two Icers guarded it, and a few human warriors within organized the food and handed out strictly rationed portions. They had slaughtered and purified the few wild molebear they could find in the outer tunnels. Glace and his scouts had found an old fungal cavern above the mines; though it was no longer cultivated, the fungus had continued to spore. She had ordered a scribe to calculate out the rations and how long the food would last, and the results were not encouraging. They had days, rather than weeks, before the army could not feed itself. Casser could not be faring any better. He had taken all of the breeding cababar with him, but the stress of being moved around was preventing them from breeding.

The ration today was a piece of tunnel-fungi the size of her fist and a thin strip of molebear. Larc tried to savor her only meal of the day, but she could not keep her mouth from chewing and swallowing too fast. The food hurt her shrunken stomach.

Oh, Ancestors, please let there be food in the caverns that Casser sought, Larc prayed. She let herself imagine a small lake full of fish, a network of wild molebear tunnels. Without realizing what she was doing, she crafted a grand fantasy of a whole new Iskalon, complete with burial chambers.

She stopped herself angrily. There was no good in fantasizing about what she didn't have. She had work to do here and now. She stalked down the tunnel, headed for the command center, a cave not much larger than her own sleeping quarters, surrounded by a maze of tunnels that had been rigged with all sorts of traps, should the Flames try to navigate them. It was lit by a bright icelight in a glass globe hanging from the ceiling. The globe, along with a tall glass sandclock, had been scavenged from the mines. The walls were lined with weapons, and armor hanging and stacked on shelves, making the small cave feel more like a storeroom than a study. In the center, a waist high, round stone table was etched with maps of the surrounding tunnels. Kiner sat on a small boulder before it, looking at a piece of gold plate. His chirsh was ragged and dusty. Larc could not see a single vaerce on his hands or face, and she wondered how many he still had underneath. He looked up and saluted Larc when she entered.

"At ease, Kiner." This was another thing Larc hated about commanding. Kiner had been a friend, but he treated her differently now. They did not laugh together and speak as equals. Not that there was anything to laugh about, but now he was always stiff and formal around her. "What do you have there?"

"Plate from Captain Glace, Lady Larc. He reports that they are holding position. The Flames have dwindled in number, though the attacks still come. It is almost as if they are pulling back."

That was curious. Larc hardly dared to hope that it might be permanent. More likely, the Flames were trying to lull her into relaxing her defenses. "Is there anything else of interest to report?"

"Did you hear that howler a short time past?"

Larc nodded. "I'd like to be able to say it woke me from my slumber, but there wasn't any slumber going on."

"For once they've done us some good. The tunnel that collapsed was one we meant to seal up in any case."

Another small blessing. "Anything else?"

Kiner glanced at the sandclock near the back entrance.

"Only that Terean and a few others are late reporting for duty."

"They won't be reporting. I've sent them to help Casser."

Kiner locked her gaze in his. He started to speak, then stopped. He was furious at her decision, but adherence to rank kept him from questioning her. Well. He deserved some explanation. She hesitated. Should she ask him to keep it secret? Would her revelation boost morale? Or would it dampen spirits if it were revealed to be nothing more than empty caves?

"Casser thinks he's found something, Kiner. I'm not sure what, but he's tunneling through by hand, so he must be certain. It won't do us any good to protect them from Flames if they collapse the Outer Tunnels."

"I will ask you not to tell my troops of this," Kiner said. He did not appear surprised or heartened by her news. "Best if molecubs are not banded before they are born."

"Agreed," said Larc. Kiner saluted and left the room for his ration and resting period. There was little more for her to do but wait. She sat in the command room and listened to reports as they came from Glace's segment. She tried not to chew at her lips or mess with her hair; tried to look official and leaderly. She had an inkling of what Stasia must have felt in Council. It was a sensation of complete uselessness. But thinking of Stasia made her sad and angry and hopeless, so she tried to think of other things. Long hours trickled through the sandclock before Kiner returned to relieve her.

Her return to her own quarters was not much relief. She extinguished her icelight, but she was too plagued with worry to sleep. She lay with her mind spinning. Once she had completely exhausted every concern she could think of, images of the destruction of Iskalon flooded her mind. Burning buildings, bodies in a cart. Dead men she was supposed to heal so that they could die again. The driver sat before her, and then there was only a pile of soot and bones on the cart-seat. The Palace falling, huge chunks of ice dropping on the burning city. The images rolled through, over and over, until Larc thought she would go mad. She hummed to herself very quietly, not wanting to disturb anyone who might actually be sleeping nearby. The humming soothed her a little, but it could not stop the images from coming.

Sometime in the long dark hours, she heard a distant rumbling sound, and her cavern shook with mighty force. She grasped T'Jas and pressed it against the ceiling, trying to keep the rock stable. Fist sized rocks slid down the walls where she could not focus. "Ancestors save us," Larc whispered.

The shaking lasted only seconds, and when it was over, she left her quarters and hurried to the command center. The tunnel was full of Warriors and Icers, but they made way as soon as they saw her. Command was in chaos. The sandclock was shattered, the floor littered with the weapons and armor that had lined the walls. Warriors and Icers filled the room, picking themselves up from where they had fallen, glancing around at the mess as though unsure what to do.

"I didn't hear a howler," Kiner was saying, looking perplexed. "It must have been a loud one, to cause that."

"I don't think it was a howler," Larc said grimly. "Casser was tunneling by hand—"

"Go," Kiner said, for once dropping his formal deference. "I'll restore order here. Go and see—"

He could not finish the sentence. Larc finished it for him in her mind. *See if anyone still lived.*

Icers were milling in the hall, and a drone of voices created a buzzing white noise. "I need ten volunteers," Larc said in her council voice. "Good with rock." The hall went quiet, and far more than ten hands shot up. Larc chose the ones she knew were strongest, walking through and giving the chosen ones a tap on the shoulder. "We will investigate the damage," she said. "The rest of you, return to your shift. Be vigilant, there may be further shakes."

She said nothing about what she suspected had caused the cave-in. They would learn in time, and if she was wrong, there was no use making everyone else worry. Icers trailing her closely, she flew up the steep, rough tunnels, past the sleeping quarters, in the direction Hali had gone. Tears leaked from her eyes as she flew. "Why couldn't you wait for them, Casser?" she muttered between gulped breaths of air. "What was so important?"

A few hours up the tunnel, she was nearly gored on Hali's raihan. The guildless girl was racing her beast down the tunnel at a breakneck speed, her eyes as tearstained as Larc's and her breath just as labored. Larc held the girl's hands while she caught her breath to report, but she didn't really need to hear the words. Hali's eyes told the story just as well. The Icers who had accompanied Larc waited behind her, frosty and silent.

"They were all going through when we got there," she said. "The last of them were entering the narrow tunnels. All but the few at the very end of the line were drenched in rock, Lady. The noise—" She broke off sobbing.

Larc hugged her close. Casser. All of the people they were supposed to be protecting. Dead. At the very best some had survived, but if so they were trapped beyond the rockfall. "What of Terean and the others?"

"They shielded me. Rock poured down the tunnel . . ." She breathed deeply, trying to collect herself. "They are back there, trying to dig through."

Larc nodded. "You were very brave, Hali. Go now, and tell Kiner just what you've told me. Tell him I will send another messenger down when I reach the cave-in. Do you understand?"

"Yes, Lady Larc."

Hali stood straighter, wiped the tears off her cheeks, and saluted Larc. Larc gave her a full warrior's salute in return. The girl leapt up on her raihan again and faded down the tunnel, leaving Larc and the Icers with hours yet to reach the cave-in.

She stood still for a moment. When she saw the debris of the cave in, she would have to accept what had happened. She wanted to delay that reality. But she could not. The Icers with her were needed. She drew T'Jas and flew through the air again.

Larc was panting and gasping when she reached the rockfall, but the scene there made her forget her own exhaustion in a heartbeat. Fewer than twenty people were huddled in the narrow tunnel. They stared at her silently as she passed, their eyes full of shock and sorrow. Larc did not see Casser among them. At the end of the tunnel, Terean and the other four Icers stood before a pile of dusty stones, their hands upon it, wholly focused on trying to make the rock obey their T'Jas. Terean turned away from them as Larc approached. The Icers with Larc hurried to join their comrades on the rocky debris. Larc hung back, catching her breath, and Terean closed the gap between them. He had stripped off the shirt of his chirsh, and was covered with cold sweat. His thick black hair was matted with it. In spite of her shock and sorrow, Larc found herself noticing how few vaerce glimmered on his torso. Were all of the Icers this depleted? Vaerce were considered the private business of each Icer, and inquiring too closely about them considered impolite, but Larc thought she might need to have a scribe take stock. It would tell her exactly how much fighting power remained in her army.

Terean began to salute, but stopped mid-gesture and knelt instead. Larc stared at him wild-eyed. "Get up," she said finally. He rose stiffly, not meeting her eyes.

"Report."

"We were following the guildless one up here. When we reached the point where the tunnels narrow, we saw only a few people. They were all entering a narrow passage.

We asked what they were doing, and they said Casser had widened the walls and was guiding the people through. Then the whole tunnel shook. It happened fast. We tried to reach into the bedrock with T'Jas to make it stop. We didn't have enough cold. It was all we could do to shield ourselves and the people."

Larc stared at the pile of rocks and debris. Terean's words sounded distant, unreal. He continued. "We have been feeling through the rock, but the cave-in was extensive. Even with full cold, it would take us days to tunnel through."

Larc nodded slowly, looking up at the Icers, straining to brace the weakened walls and move rocks around. Her newcomers were removing their soggy, warming chirsh. They did not have full cold. They did not have days. The Icers did not have enough vaerce to spare for tunneling. They had a choice: dig through in the hopes of finding survivors, or stay in the Outer Tunnels and fight. How many lives could she waste to find corpses? But what was the point in fighting, with nothing to protect?

Out of the corner of her eye, she saw Terean go down on one knee. *He's injured,* she thought, then, *No. He is kneeling. Casser is gone. I'm the last one.*

As she had this thought, Terean said, "We await your orders, Regent Larc."

Chapter 14

A New Crown

Stasia

After the first few steps, Stasia caught the rhythm of Tejusi's stride and stayed hidden in the cloak as they glided over the smooth stone floors of Chraun. The Flame's long legs made it hard to keep up with him, and even more difficult was trusting that he wouldn't run her into a stalam; she was completely blind in the dark folds of slink fur. The Flames with her were silent, so all she could hear was the steady tap of their marching feet.

She could smell Dynat's sweat under the faint odor of slink musk, and the rage it awoke in her was frightening. She had seen in Medoc's mind his intention to give the former Fire King to her once the Lake was clean, payment for Chraun's crimes against Iskalon so that he would not have to take any responsibility for them. Dynat must stand trial and execution; killing him now would be selfish at best. Iskalon would see justice done.

A short time after they left the Throne room Stasia heard shouting and screams in the distance. Medoc's war for the throne had begun. War between brothers and friends. Stasia shuddered to think of it. War with an enemy had been horrible enough; what if she had been forced to fight with her own sisters? Civil war had occurred in Iskalon, but very rarely. It seemed to happen non-stop in Chraun.

A sulfur smell penetrated the cloak and Stasia realized the baths were near. Tejusi's stride changed, and Stasia nearly had to run to keep up. Her body, still recovering from Dynat's treatment in spite of the rough Flame healing Medoc had given her, protested the vigor of her movement. But her discomfort was pale beside fear. Pleas of mercy drifted down the tunnels, strangled by screams of pain, swallowed by loud explosions.

Tejusi halted suddenly and Stasia walked past him, her crown, face and one foot spilling out of the cloak. She froze as three Flames stepped out of an open doorway before her and her escort. They wore sturdy steel plate armor without decoration or medals—Warriors, she guessed, from what she had seen of Chraun's ranks. Two were men with glowing lava mesh and one was a large, mannish woman, her mesh patterned in squares. They were laughing and talking, and stopped short, staring at Stasia. She fought the urge to hide under the cloak again, and instead stepped out. Hiding now would only cast more suspicion on Tejusi.

"What are you gawkers doing standing around?" Tejusi's voice was loud and sharp, very different from how he'd spoken to Medoc. He stepped forward, approaching the Flames and standing between them and her so that she did not see his face, only the gleam of red torchlight on his short, dark hair and the lava on his bare shoulders, nearly-hexagonal circles. The two Warriors with him stood on either side of her. She wondered if she could sneak behind them and get away while they were all distracted. The Spiral must be very near. "This is no time to be roaming the tunnels. The King needs all hands."

"Which King would that be, Cadet? New Kings, old Kings, it's all rather confusing."

"King Medoc. The only King, now. And it's Luten—

I've been promoted. See?" Stasia heard a faint clank as he tapped the medals on his chest.

"That's a fine cloak, Luten Tejusi. Fit for a King, wouldn't you say?"

The muscles on Tejusi's shoulders knotted and Stasia felt a subtle difference in the air, almost a chill. The torches flickered and faltered, replaced by a dim glow of smoldering torch-heads.

The darkness erupted with flashes of white-hot flame and glowing balls of fire. Stasia knew this was her chance to run, but she was paralyzed, rooted to the smooth stone floor. It was as if the fire was hypnotizing her. She could see the battle taking place in slow motion, could see how Tejusi concentrated the heat before he flung it at the other Flames, how the woman wove a rope of fire from the swift, forward motion of sparks, how Tejusi's Warriors fought in tandem, one shielding with a firebreak, the other throwing fireballs. She had never seen Flame T'Jas in this light; before it had been a confusion of fire. She almost thought that she could do it herself, and she tried to make a fire-rope using the woman's techniques, thinking she could help Tejusi . . .

Her attempt fizzled spectacularly, and before she could try again, darkness had fallen in the tunnel. She could hear heavy breathing, saw seven bodies laying on the floor, their lava dimming. Were they all dead? She began to back away, her former paralysis gone, but steel scraped against stone and one of the bodies stirred.

"Please . . . Heal me . . . Ice Fairy . . ." It was Tejusi. Stasia stopped in her tracks. Did he have the strength to chase her down if she ran? He had killed the Flames because they saw Dynat's cloak. He would not hesitate to kill her to protect Medoc's secret.

After a moment of silence, the Flame spoke again. His words were slurred, delirious. "Denu . . . Never liked him. Scum shouldn't . . . Get promotions . . . Because of father's money. But Adkiel . . . Bunkmate . . . First

Training. Rotta, she . . . drink any man under the table . . . wake at first Gong bright-eyed while the rest of us were dragging."

It took a moment for Stasia to realize he was not talking about the Warriors who had accompanied them but the ones he had fought and killed. He was in deep shock. Sympathy tugged at her heart, but she pushed it down. She could fill hours talking about the friends she had lost to his people. What were his two to her?

"They should not have had to die, Ice Fairy. I should not have had to kill them."

His words were more lucid this time. Sympathy tugged again, and Stasia let it in. Chraun had been at war with itself for centuries, as King after King was deposed and replaced. What Tejusi faced was nothing new, but it must be painful to be pitted against your friends. She stepped closer, still uncertain if she should heal him or flee.

She kicked a body with her next step, and when she reached down to feel it, she realized it was Dynat, still wrapped in the slink fur. Hatred seized her, washing away sympathy. Heal Tejusi? What was she thinking? She should kill the Flame, if anything. A thousand deaths would not make up for her loss.

With Tejusi stuck in shock and the rest of the escort dead, she was free. She picked up Dynat's unconscious body and heaved it over her neck. Her spine protested the weight with a sharp, piercing pain. She ignored it. She would not leave the former Fire King where he might be rescued, and she did not have enough cold here to kill him.

Tejusi shouted after her, and Stasia ran awkwardly, hindered by tired, cramping legs and too much weight, toward the Spiral Tunnel and freedom.

Medoc

Medoc stared at Tejusi's retreating back for a moment, ignoring his own admonitions to haste, watching his former King bob away on his shoulder. After he and the two Officers accompanying him had passed out of sight, Medoc glanced one last time at the abyss of lava below him, and then walked calmly to the throne and stood before it, facing Renault and the King's ten honor guards. He had told the Ice Queen that the King's Guard followed the throne, not the man. That was true. If they did not believe the man held the throne, they would not follow him. The fact that they had not acted against him yet gave Medoc confidence.

"Your army stands ready, my King," said Renault, stepping forward and kneeling. "The attack shall commence at your command."

"Try not to think of it as an attack, Renault. We are not to attack our people. We are keeping order while the Nobles come to accept my rule. We are ensuring that none other is raised in Dynat's place."

"Yes, my King."

In spite of his words, Medoc knew he was painting an elegant lava picture over rough, scarred rock. There would be resistance, and he would have to kill some of his own people to secure his power. Bolv had been working tirelessly to shift the favor of the Nobles to his cause, but there were some who simply had deep loyalty to Dynat and would not change. Some were deeply religious, and truly believed Dynat was the Fire Spirit made flesh. Others he had inherited from his father, King Bretle. Medoc was one of those. The Nobles who could not be persuaded or purchased would be executed, their children sent to the orphan's tunnels. That was what happened in shifts of power. Medoc had seen it many times.

"Are the guards in place with the Kinyara?"

Renault sneered, unable to hide his distaste that Medoc would keep the current Kinyara rather than consigning her to share Dynat's fate, but he did not give voice to his opinion. "They are, my King."

"Then pass down the command. Secure Chraun for

my rule."

Renault bowed and left. Medoc watched him go down the tunnel. He itched to join the man, to lead the fight. But he was no longer a General with that privilege.

The King's Honor Guard still stood before him, and Medoc saluted them with a very faint inclination of his shoulders. They stepped forward and knelt. Then, moving as one, they took up their positions in the hall again.

Medoc turned and looked at the great throne in the center of the room, staring at the crown attached to the seat, where Dynat had left it last. He stood without moving, a pillar of certainty among the thin stalam. Though he raged inwardly, wanting to pace and twitch, he resisted the urge. Being a King was much like being a General, he reflected. It was all about waiting. Unless something went horribly wrong in the next few hours, Medoc was now King of Chraun.

He pulled T'Jas from the intense heat in the room and used it to detach the crown. It was a simple, gold circuit studded in the very front with the emblem of Dynat's house, a crouching slink, also in gold. Medoc sat down on the throne and laid the circuit in his hands, running them over the emblem. He poured T'Jas into the very molecules of the metal, shaping and changing it.

Footsteps came up the hall, and Medoc tensed. It had been nearly an hour since Renault left; he would not be reporting so soon unless something had gone awry. His Guard's positions did not change, but Medoc sensed a readiness in their postures. He drew T'Jas and waited.

Tejusi burst in. His armor was melted into misshapen lumps, his hair singed off. He knelt briefly at Medoc's feet and then looked up with wild eyes.

"Forgive me, my King, she has escaped."

"Stand and report, Cad—Luten."

As the Flame obeyed, Medoc saw him wince. The Luten had not wasted time healing himself completely. "We were passing the baths when a soldier recognized his cloak. The little Ice Fairy was foolish enough to show herself. I ordered my men to attack them."

"Did any escape but her?" Medoc asked sharply.

"No, my King. I was the only survivor, and myself barely. I was lying on the tunnel floor, trying to heal myself enough to stand when she slipped past. I tried to stop her—"

"What of the K—Dynat?"

"She took him with her, my King."

Medoc felt a moment of relief that Dynat was not lying outside the baths, perhaps waking even now, but it was only a moment. If Stasia were captured, everything would fall apart. Dynat would wake, and the truth would come out; Medoc would be executed, all of his loyal Flames thrown into the river after him.

Even if she made it through to her people, the little Ice Queen could cause him trouble. What if she refused to clean the Lake? What if she revealed Medoc's hand in Dynat's defeat to the rest of Chraun? She knew everything Medoc knew, intimately. She had plundered his mind. And she hated him intensely, hated all Flames. She could use her knowledge to wreak havoc in Chraun for years to come.

Medoc cursed himself for not throwing them both in the lava river when he had the chance. He had not had the strength. He had still been thinking of his carefully laid plan, perfectly timed and executed.

"Go to the Kinyara," Medoc said slowly.

"My King?" Tejusi looked nervous.

"Have her heal you. She's trustworthy—or as close to it as we'll come. Assemble two patrols of Flames as loyal as you can. Warriors who won't talk. Search the Spiral top to bottom. She can't have gone far, especially not carrying him."

"Yes, my King."

"Kill them both and leave their bodies to feed slink. I'll have to negotiate with someone else about the Lake."

It was too dangerous, having the Ice Queen running around with all his secrets in her head. It had to be done. It was the only way to keep his power, and more importantly, to keep Chraun whole.

Tejusi was bowing and leaving. The time to rescind the order was passing. Medoc refused to feel regret. Two more deaths were small in the face of the sheer numbers of citizens of Chraun dying outside these doors, he told himself. He thought of the tallies from Ritnu's ascension, and Bretle's. Had it been ten thousand, with Ritnu? Or was that the King before him? Would it have been better to let things continue as they had under Dynat? No. The Kingdom had needed change, and if Medoc did not provide it, someone else would, and their overthrow would have been just as brutal, if not more.

He uncovered the emblem on the circuit. It was no longer a slink; he had shaped it into the perfect hexagon of his house. The band and the emblem gleamed in the platinum of Medoc's official color instead of Dynat's gold. He lifted the circuit to his brow, and placed it over his greying hair. It settled heavily around his head, and his brow wrinkled under the pressure. He set aside the doubt plaguing his heart, and became the King of Chraun.

Stasia

The bottom of the Spiral Tunnel was steep, far steeper than further up toward Iskalon. Stasia could hear sounds of war coming up the tunnel from Chraun. She was utterly exhausted. Worse, though she was no longer lost, she had no idea where to go.

She turned into the first spur tunnel she saw and laid down Dynat's unconscious body. She took the crown of Iskalon off her head and turned it in her hands, thinking of how it had rested on her father's head, leaving a red line on his brow that she would rub at, standing on his lap as a child. She thought of Maudit, already an adult by the time she was born, putting the crown on in Father's study, sitting in his chair and imitating his stern voice, she and her sisters dissolving into giggles at the resemblance. She placed the crown on her own head again, and it seemed not to fit. The Ancestors had made her Queen, but she did not feel like a queen. Casser led most of the people now, the rest were in Larc and Kiner's competent hands. Stasia had fully intended to die in Chraun when she surrendered.

But she was alive, and the crown and the former Fire King were both burdens she could not ignore. She would have to find her people and deliver Medoc's message, and bring them back to the lake when it was safe. She had to keep Dynat alive to stand trial and execution for his crimes against Iskalon. Until Medoc's forces were called back from the Outer Tunnels, though, her best chance for survival was to find a place to hide out. Somewhere with enough cold for her to heal herself and keep him under control.

It was too warm here. Stasia hefted Dynat again and started back up the Spiral Tunnel. It was all she could do to put one weary foot before the other. Her entire body ached as if she'd been struck by a rockslide. As the air grew cold, she felt a painful tightening on her forehead. It took a moment to realize what was happening.

Her lava mark from the river was hardening. The colder the tunnel grew, the harder it became. Finally she pulled it off, like pulling a scab, and tucked it up in her hair with her crown. She felt strangely vulnerable without it, as if she was accustomed to having a source of heat T'Jas. She continued up the tunnel, exhausted and sick, starving and half-crazy from her time in the cage. She needed cold and a chance to rest.

Footsteps coming up the Spiral Tunnel behind her meant it would be sometime before she got the latter. She hurried to keep ahead of them. From the sound, it was an entire patrol of Flames. Just as their torchlight appeared around the corner, she slipped into a side tunnel. She recognized this one. It led to the burial chamber where the copper-clad Ancestors rested, where she had taken refuge after the war and built Iskalon in Exile. Where her sisters' heads lay on the floor, scattered at the orders of the very man she carried on her shoulders. She could just barely squeeze him into the narrow tunnel. She paused for a moment, listening, and heard the steady march of footsteps and the jingle of steel plates pass the opening and fade up the Spiral.

She set the Fire King down and grasped the hood of his cloak, dragging him after her. The burial chamber would be a good place to refresh. There might be some wild fungi growing in the patches of spore that the Fungal Guild had been starting, or some dried meat in the alcoves. Perhaps she could even take some time to bury her poor sisters. If the sack of molebear dung she dragged behind her woke, she could freeze his limbs, leaving him alive but immobile. And when she gauged enough time had passed for Medoc to retreat, she could seek the Outer Tunnels, send a few Icers to the lake to test Medoc's word.

She had survived. She had given herself up for dead, but she had survived. Dragging her burden up the steepening tunnel, she felt suddenly unstoppable. She had come out on top, again. Perhaps she was even worthy of the monstrous crown on her head.

But when she reached the entrance to the chamber, pausing to survey it before she entered, a sound from behind stopped her heart cold. The sound of marching, coming up the tunnel behind her. The jingle of plates of armor. Flames. Were they patrolling at random? Using the tunnel as a shortcut? Or pursuing her? Had Medoc's grab for the throne failed, and someone loyal to Dynat sent Warriors after her?

Stasia hurried forward, pulling Dynat into the chamber. Ominous dark lumps littered the floor, glowing ghastly purple in the light of the Burial Shaft above. As she'd thought, the Flames had not bothered to clean up the carnage of their attack. Her previous enthusiasm for this place curdled. She did not want to spend another minute here, even if there weren't Flames advancing.

But she was bone-weary. She had to stop and rest for a moment. She drew T'Jas, healed away her aches, took deep breaths. The footsteps were still far away. There was a tunnel on the far side of the chamber. It led to a fork, one branch heading back to the Spiral and the other toward the mines. She gathered her strength to heft the Fire King again and continue.

A noise from the floor drew her gaze down and at first she thought one of the corpses was stirring. But it was Dynat. He was waking. "Cold," he murmured. "Too cold."

"Melt you," Stasia muttered. Could he have picked a worse time to regain consciousness? She hurried to him. If he made too much noise, he would betray her to the Flames coming up the tunnel.

As if he knew that, he began to shout. "I will take her Dreams. I can still kill her. Just give me heat. I will kill her! I swear it!"

Interlude

Khell, Four Summers Prior

Maia

The party returning from the next raid answered Maia's confusion about the bones she had thrown. They carried Lubar on a stretcher made of boareal bones and hides. He lived, but he had been wounded very badly. Hakua walked beside the stretcher, concern in his eyes.

Lubar's brothers set him down in Maia's egla. "What happened?" she asked.

"He was thrown off his boareal, then trodden by one of the enemy's steeds." Bahar spoke; Hakua's attention was on his father. Lubar's normally hearty face was grey, slick with sweat. He was moaning and muttering incomprehensible words. Hakua held his hand while Maia cut away his furs and inspected his wounds.

His legs and pelvis were crushed. Maia got to work cleaning and stitching. She shouted instructions for the warriors surrounding their chief to bring fermented urchin broth to sedate him, clean hides, snow for cooling his wounds. More warriors held the huge chief while Maia set bones and wrapped shattered limbs tightly.

She worked on through the night by boareal fat lamps. When she was done with Lubar she tended the other warriors' more minor *wounds. Hakua hovered nearby, asking futile questions.*

"I don't know if he will survive," she said for the tenth time.

"What good are the bones, anyway? I will give you up at the next tithing, useless woman!"

Maia knew he would not. That, at least, she had seen in the bones.

Lubar lived. After weeks of being wracked with fever and infection, days and nights where Maia and Hakua sat by his side and held his hands as he thrashed in wild fever dreams, he woke, lucid and aware for the first time since the raid. Lucid and angry. Bitter. Confused when Maia told him his legs would never carry him again. Angry when his repeated attempts to stand proved her words.

Hakua ordered a sled constructed especially for Lubar, drawn by the biggest, fastest doal in the camp, cushioned with hides and furs. It did not salve the chief's anger. When the other tribes began to arrive at the beach to trade shells and hides and stories, the Liathua camp was avoided. Maia heard whispers from other healers about the bad spirits infecting the chief of the Liathua. Rumors drifted on the wind from the enemy tribes, that the Liathua were being called "chiefless." A chiefless tribe was a vulnerable tribe.

A few weeks before the winter winds began to blow, before the tribe left for the shelter of the mountains, Maia cast the bones and saw the darkness of tithing coming soon. She visited Lubar's egla, where Hakua stood by the entrance, looking sullen. She could hear Lubar inside, shouting at his current mate. Maia said nothing, merely looked at Hakua. Hakua looked away.

"This cannot continue, if you wish the tribe to survive," Maia said at last. "I am here in my capacity as Healer, to advise you. You must act."

"You have always hated him. You worked some magic on him, to cause this to happen!"

"You know that I did not, Hakua. If I could have, I would have done it long ago . . . No, I do not have that ability."

"What can I do? He is still alive. He is still chief."

"He is not chief, Hakua. A chief would be raiding. A chief would be making trades, speaking with the other chiefs, leading hunts. He is doing none of that."

"He cannot—"

"He cannot use his wound as an excuse. When I was a child, a warrior in our tribe had a lame foot. He could not run in a raid, he could not drag carcasses back to camp. But he could ride a boareal and throw a spear. He did what he could and did not worry about what he could not. This is what your father would do, if he were still chief. As it is, he will destroy the tribe."

"What can I do?" Hakua's face had turned pleading and he looked lost. Maia felt sad for him; though she did not pity Lubar, she knew Hakua faced a difficult choice.

"I do not know but I must tell you that the tithing is nearly upon us. If Lubar appears at the tithing as chief he will bring the Dhuciri down upon the whole tribe."

"You foresaw this?"

"It is common sense, Hakua. You know what the Dhuciri expect. Will Lubar be able to hide the fact that there are more than fifty Khell in the tribe? Will he be able to grit his teeth and smile at the Dhuciri, bow to them? Listen to him! He is screaming at his own mate in there."

"I know," Hakua said miserably. *"That is why I'm out here."*

"You must do something, Hakua. Think of it as your first trial as chief."

She left him alone. Lubar was his father, and the decision was his to make.

Chapter 15

Into the Ice

Dynat

Dynat was surrounded by the misty forms of ghosts. Hundreds of transparent faces hovered over his body. Some he recognized, some he did not. Bretle was there with his ever-accusing eyes. Nameless Warriors killed in raids he'd ordered. Children. So many children. Had so many children truly died during his reign? And Icers. Thousands of Icers, crowding the cavern and the surrounding tunnels, chilling the air. He shivered.

"Too cold," he murmured. Where was the Fire Spirit to warm him, to keep the ghosts at bay? To Dynat's relief, flames sprang forth in his mind as they always had. But the Fire Spirit's words were cold.

"You have failed me," it roared. Its flames lapped angrily at Dynat's mind, threatening to burn him away. "A simple task. Find the princess and steal her Dreams. But you could not do it, could you? Worthless piece of meat. You do not know what you could have had. I would have given you an honored place. You would have ruled by my side." The Fire Spirit had never spoken to him so clearly.

It burned in his mind a moment longer, then left, taking all heat with it, leaving Dynat cold and alone. The ghosts crowded in again. "No," Dynat said. "I will take her Dreams. I can still kill her. Just give me heat. I will kill her! I swear it!"

A cold breath of air wafted toward him. A ghost's face hovered near, framed in blue icelight. It was the little Ice Queen, her crown high on her head. The rest of the ghosts faded away. "You, a ghost?" Dynat said. "But I didn't kill you." He had tried to, he remembered that. He recalled grappling with her, pouring heat from the lava river into her, ordering Medoc out of her mind so he could plunder it, and then—

"No, you didn't." The Icer's face wavered and then receded, but the soft blue glow and the cold presence remained. "But I will kill you if you don't get to your feet right now, fishslime."

Dynat closed his eyes against her light and tried to imagine the Fire Spirit. Always before, he had given Dynat a source of heat and T'Jas when there was none. A memory rose, of a frightened, lonely time, Father taken away by his own Warriors, Dynat alone in his quarters, locked in, all the Semija gone, the food running out. Warriors coming for him, ignoring his questions. Seeing Mother's face again, her beautiful, soothing face, but it was wreathed in flames, and then she was just ashes on the floor, and he tried to run to her but they wouldn't let him. The Orphan Tunnels loomed ahead, dark, close, no one to trust, food fought for in bloody little battles, and his winnings never quite enough. His skin growing pale and pasty in the cool dark, his mind slowly slipping away, as the pain of losing his parents, his home, his life faded. A face of flames bursting in his mind, testing him with fire, bringing the Lava River to him, since Dynat could not go to the Lava River.

"I said, get up!" Dynat found himself wrenched into a sitting position by a hard blast of cold air. He struggled against it for a moment, but he was weaker than a newborn hippole. His lava was hardened and cracking, sloughing away in bloody chunks. The cold made him sick to his stomach, and his head ached as if from a blow. The Icer grasped his shoulders with her hands, and suddenly he came awake. She was no ghost. Her hands were real, cold and smooth.

Unless they were both ghosts. His body grew colder and colder. Why had he stopped killing her in the Throne Room? Medoc was there. Medoc should have protected him from her. What happened? "Are you taking me to the Lava River?"

"You will never see lava again." Her tone was harsh, full of hatred. In spite of the cold, which hurt so much that Dynat ground his teeth, his body began to feel stronger. The last of his hardened lava fell to the ground, leaving a ghost mesh behind on his skin. His nausea eased slightly, and the pain in his head receded. She was healing him. When she withdrew her hands and the cold faded away, he began to notice his surroundings. He sat on the floor of a large chamber. The ceiling was burial ice, with its ghastly purple glow. The floor was littered with bodies, weapons, and here and there a scorched head. He was in the burial chamber where he had sent the heads of the princesses of Iskalon. His memory of that seemed hazy, as if he was looking down on it through murky bathwater. Why had he sent the heads down through the burial ice?

The Ice Queen stood before him, her yellow-green eyes locked on his, carefully not looking at the carnage surrounding her. She wore the crown of Iskalon and nothing else. In her hands she held something large and dark. It took him a moment to realize it was his cloak. Why did she have his cloak?

"Warmth," he whispered. "Warm cloak—"

"Keep silent," she hissed. "If you speak again, unless I ask you a question, I will gag you with a chunk of ice, and freeze your eyes shut."

Dynat was quiet, but he eyed the cloak with wholehearted longing. Nestling in that, even in this cold air, would bring his body temperature up to normal, perhaps even make him hot enough to draw T'Jas. The Icer smiled grimly. She knew exactly what she was keeping from him.

"Get up." To Dynat's surprise, he found that he could, and even more importantly, that he wanted to. All he had to do to get back in the Fire Spirit's graces was to enter her mind. He merely needed to bide his time. He was unsteady on his feet, but he was able to place one foot before the other without falling. The Icer pointed at a tunnel to the far end of the cavern, but she was glancing nervously over her shoulder. Dynat remembered from the battle-plans that the passage they were heading away from led directly to the Spiral Tunnel. Why could he remember some things so clearly, but not others? What had happened? Where were his Guards? Where was Medoc?

"Walk."

He obeyed, and she followed close on his heels. His body shielded the icelight she held, so he could not see where he was walking. He tried to turn to let the light through, but she extinguished it altogether. "If you do anything other than what I tell you to do, I will kill you without hesitation. You know I will. I may kill you even if you obey. But your best chance for life is to do exactly as I say."

Dynat did not reply. He believed her. After a moment, he heard a rustle in the dark, and then she said, "Walk straight up the tunnel. I will tell you when to turn."

Dynat obeyed, urged on by the cold presence of her behind him. He continued to follow her instructions as she led him further up the tunnels, and the air grew colder and colder. His stomach churned with illness, and he felt as if his blood would freeze right in his veins. At last, he could bear it no longer, and he wilted against the side of the tunnel. "Too cold," he murmured. "Please—" He gagged on his words, and began taking deep breaths, controlling the urge to retch.

Then cold air entered his mouth and expanded, solidified into ice that froze his tongue to the roof of his mouth. He could breath through his nose and move his lips, but speech was impossible. At the same time, she froze his feet in place. His whole body was immobile. She stood silently behind him, barely breathing. Then he heard a sound ahead in the dark. Footsteps. Loud, marching footsteps. He saw a soft glow spring to life. Flames. If only he could get around her gag, Dynat could shout for help.

She swore softly. Dynat was towed harshly backward down the tunnel, away from the approaching Flames. Why were Flames patrolling here? Dynat remembered giving no such orders. Medoc—

Dynat did not believe it was possible to grow any colder, but his blood ran cold when the pieces came together. Medoc had betrayed him. Medoc had struck him down and given him over to the enemy. Dynat had been deposed. It was the only possibility. The Ice Queen alone could not have defeated him on the banks of the Lava River. If Medoc did not sit on the throne, a Noble from some other house surely did.

The urge to shout for help withered. If these Flames found him, they were likely to execute him. Whoever sat on his throne, they would not suffer him to live to retake it. The Ice Queen was dangerous, but she had not killed him yet, and if the Fire Spirit was good he might still escape her. He would not escape a patrol of Flames armed with Fireblood.

They stumbled into the burial chamber again. Dynat watched, helplessly encapsulated in cold air, while the Icer ducked down the tunnel leading to the Spiral. When she came back a few moments later, her face was even more pale. Fear shone in her eyes. She examined a wall full of pockets in the back of the cave, then came back, stood before Dynat, and began to mutter.

Her voice was low, but he caught the words "foolish" and "dangerous." Then, to his surprise, all the cold but the gag eased away. He could move his arms and legs again. She thrust the cloak toward him.

He stood still for a moment, unsure. "Take it," she snapped. "Take it before I change my mind. And remember. Even if you can Flame, I have infinite cold here to draw from. I will freeze you where you stand the second you make a wrong move."

Dynat hesitated no longer. He took the cloak and wrapped it around his body. The hood fit snugly over his head, cutting off his view of most of the ghosts in the shadows on the cavern. The relief it brought from the cold was instantaneous. As the cloak filled with his own warmth, Dynat drew the warmth back in as T'Jas. Soon, he would have enough to create a flame. The heat was comforting, though he didn't know what he would do with it. She was right—the cloak alone would not give him enough heat to battle a fully endowed Icer. Or to evade the two marches of potentially traitorous Flames who seemed to be converging on this cavern. What did the little Icer have in mind?

She was kneeling on the ground beside him, a stick of firestone in her hand. She was dipping it into something dark on the floor. After a moment he realized it was a patch of the Fireblood; like the firestone, presumably left from the attack. Once she had a torch constructed, she held it out to him. He could see fear shining in her eyes.

"Light it," she said.

He stared blankly. She was letting him create a flame? He would not let her handle ice, if she were still his prisoner. He had learned that lesson from her sisters. He pulled the cloak tighter, drawing as much T'Jas from the heat as he could. He wasn't entirely sure he could light the torch if he tried. What did she intend? He could not speak, but he could move his face. He raised one eyebrow in question.

She gritted her teeth, as though speaking with him made her nauseous. "Take it. They will be here any moment." She gestured with the unlit torch at the ceiling. Dynat could see several dark figures suspended in the glowing ice. "We can enter the burial ice with this fire. It is the only place to hide."

Dynat reached for the torch. She flinched, but then held it out to him. He grasped the firestone and let some of his warmth seep into it. When it reached the Fireblood, the top exploded into a small flame. It would burn for hours, as long as he kept feeding it heat.

Dynat did not bother to suppress his smile. The small flame made the ghosts scatter, though they gathered again in the shadows, watching him from a distance. The heat he was feeding into the torch was magnified by the Fireblood, and he could draw back more than he put in. Once he had enough T'Jas to kill her, he would enter her mind and take what the Fire Spirit wanted. Then the Fire Spirit would return and help him win back his crown. He had not failed, not at all. Medoc had merely delayed the inevitable.

Chapter 16

A Slow Death

Glace

"Ancestors shelter you, friend. May you find peace in the Ice." Glace stared into Glint's glassy grey eyes for so long that the messenger behind him cleared his throat. Glace startled, then reached out and gently pressed his former comrade's eyelids closed before rising from his crouch by the body and turning to face the small, dim cave that served as his headquarters.

"Not soon, likely," the messenger said matter-of-factly. A fat neithild rode on his shoulder, her legs clutching the tears in his tunic. Glace wondered why the Weavers allowed him to keep it. "Burial ice is rare as zirc in the Tog, these days. I imagine this one'll rest in stone."

Glace suppressed an urge to strike the man, aware that his anger came from Glint's death and the messenger's news, not his lack of tact. Tog was what the guildless called their former home, and this former guildless man had never considered burial ice an option himself; why should he care if Glint were deprived of the privilege?

"How long did she say?" Glace knew every single

word of the message, could hear it echoing in his ears in both Larc's sweet, strong voice and the messenger's greasy tone. He just wanted to change the subject.

"Five days to tunnel. If they don't find anything by then, she'll call you back in a retreat and mix up Icers and Warriors again. But you're to hold out five days without Icers."

Five days. Glace would send the Icers back with the messenger, leaving his own defenses slashed. He had never fought Flames without Icers by his side. Traditionally, the Flames fought the Icers while the human Warriors took on the Semija Warriors. Without Icers, his men would face an inferno with nothing more to protect them than leather and steel.

"Cataya's tits," he muttered, glancing at Glint's silent form again. Musche nuzzled the dead Warrior's hand, sniffing it as though trying to understand. How many men would he lose to this decision? He knew the answer, though he did not want to think it.

"Captain . . ." The messenger trailed off, and Glace returned his gaze sharply to him.

"Yes? Was that all? You can tell her I will obey. It is our purpose, after all, protecting the people of Iskalon." Larc would not have given that order without knowing that it would mean.

The man cleared his throat, and his next words were smoother. "I'm an able hand, Captain. I wasn't born guildless, and in my youth I served conscription. I know how to hold a weapon. Put me with your men, Sir. I'll fight for Iskalon, flawed though she may be."

Glace considered the man's request, looking him over like he would eyeball a recruit. He was missing teeth, smelly, and his clothes looked even worse than those of the rest of the refugees, but there was a broadness of shoulder, a muscle tone that most guildless, half-starving all their lives, never gained. If the man could swing a sword . . .

"No," Glace heard himself say. "I'm sorry. I can't put a weapon in guildless hands. And count yourself lucky for that. One more body won't stop what's to come."

He turned away from the disappointment in the man's eyes, turned away from Glint's still form, and went down the tunnel to relay Larc's orders and get the Icers moving away from the front. By the time he'd reached the third battalion, he'd already planned his tactics.

He was forced to wait two days to use them. In the span of two days, not one single Flame was seen in the Outer Tunnels. The second day, Glace sent scouts to the Mines, looking for sign of them. There was none to be seen.

The third day, the scouts he'd sent to check the Lake came back, reporting Flames hot on their heels at the first battalion. After that brief respite, Chraun was redoubling its efforts, and Glace began to count time in bodies. Five, ten, fifty corpses interred quickly in stone with little ritual.

The only way for humans to fight Flames was to take them by surprise. Glace used his knowledge of the Outer Tunnels to his advantage, setting up pitfalls and ambushes in the maze that must have been maddening for the Flames to navigate. He had his men build dead ends from stone, funneling the enemy force toward trap fungi and howler territory.

All of this took bodies, and on the fourth day the balance tipped. A recruit rushed into the cave where Glace sat futile, giving orders and waiting for reports, unable as commander to engage in fighting on the front. "They are coming, Captain! They are coming!"

"Slow down, Warrior. Report."

The Warrior was young. He had been in the Gem Guild, learning to be a miner, before the war had demanded that all able Guildsmen join the military. He brushed blonde bangs out of his eyes and said, "The Flames are coming this way, Captain Sir. They overran the first battalion. I don't know about the second—they sent me to report."

Worry and guilt shone in his eyes, and Glace understood. Whoever had sent him was dead, now. Well. Perhaps Glace could at least spare his life. "Report to Icer Larc. Tell her we are overrun. Tell her—" Glace choked. He had failed. Stasia had given him a task. Protect the people of Iskalon so they can escape. One more day, and the Icers would have returned. He had failed.

"Tell her I'm sorry. We couldn't stop them. Go swiftly, boy."

After the Warrior had left, Glace stood and began removing his weapons and armor. He sent Musche after the boy, giving him a sniff at a gold plate with Larc's scent on it. He knew the second battalion, and the third, had not been able to hold the Flames back. They would have fought bravely, their resistance buying a little more time for the Icers, time for the boy to carry the message to Larc. Glace could charge the tunnels and buy a few more seconds with his own death. But just like one more body, a few more seconds would not make enough difference. He pulled off his long-swords, hefting them before setting them on the stone table where his maps of the tunnels were engraved. He stood in his tunic with his arms crossed, waiting.

When the Flames came, he was stoic as they bound him in firerope. He did not struggle as their Semija looted his weapons and dragged him down the tunnels. His time to fight was over. Alive, living as a slave in Chraun, he might at least learn of Stasia's fate, if not join her in it.

Larc

Larc sat huddled in a crevice of stone, overlooking the site of the latest breach. Below, Icers scrambled to repair the wall. Smoke and heat poured through a fist-sized, growing hole. Kiner and five others held their hands to the rock, keeping it from growing any faster. Soon, though, Larc knew the Flames would be through and she would have to move. There were countless other hidey-holes, but she had thought this one secure. It had kept her and a few Icers safe for nearly a day.

Since Glace's warriors had been overrun six days earlier, Larc and the other Icers who were not working on the cave-in had been playing hideme with the Flames, trying to keep them away from the cave-in and the few survivors. This scattered battle was taking an even greater toll on the Icers than the destruction of Iskalon or the battle of the burial chamber. Larc had her troops working in rounds, taking extended rests when they could, but keeping the Flames on the run took almost every body she had.

Nearly once a day, another Icer dropped dead from exhaustion, their vaerce depleted prematurely. Larc had ordered the vaerce of the remaining Icers tallied and tried to stop making use of those who had too few. But sometimes there was no other way to fill her defenses. The death of one Icer could save the lives of a few others. That was just one of many difficult decisions.

Decisions that Larc was forced to make completely alone. With the cave-in cutting off any chance of getting messages to Casser, and Stasia most likely dead at the Fire King's hands, Larc had become something she never would have believed possible: Regent. Regent in a time of war, when the councilors were dead, captive, or gone with Casser. The remaining citizens gave her blank stares when she asked for input. They were all in deep shock, and no healing could seem to cure it. So Larc could not even debate her decisions. She realized now how much the debate focused her mind and clarified her position. Without opposing views, her own thoughts became muddy.

She had tried discussing matters with Kiner and other Icer warriors, but they did not really have the time or energy to help. Kiner was extremely useful for planning military maneuvers, but Larc soon learned that he did not have much capacity for the full picture. He thought of only the next moment of battle, not the war as a whole. So Larc was, indeed, alone making decisions.

Decisions like how to ration the last of the dried molebear. There was not much left. Icers could heal away the effects of their own starvation for a time, but eventually, the lack of food would wear down their ability to take in T'Jas. And that healing also cost vaerce. The last of the living cababar had gone with Casser and the others. She had a few Icers scavenging what they could, flats and pitvipers and even rockworm, but decontaminating them of metals was a long process, and wasted yet more vaerce. The fungus in the old fungal cavern was depleted. Before long, her army would be destroyed by starvation and vaerce depletion. Who to keep strong until the end? Or should she distribute all the food equally, keeping them all equally weak? There was scarcely enough for one more meal. Larc had begun to see Icers as stockpiles of vaerce, rather than individuals. When one died, it was fewer vaerce for the war effort, not a precious life. She hated herself for thinking in those terms. Had Krevas faced that, when the attack of Chraun began, what seemed like a lifetime ago?

Below her alcove, darkness fell over the Icers as the hole sealed completely. She heard a soft clanking sound; then an icelight sprang to life. Had Kiner and the others managed to repel the Flames completely? That ought to buy them enough time to get further into the tunnels. She stayed where she was, in case this was some trick. Kiner and his Icers were talking softly. The hole did not reopen.

"A message for you, Regent." Kiner's icelight blinded her dark-adjusted eyes for a moment. He hovered in front of her crevice, gripping an outcropping above it to preserve some of his T'Jas. "From the Fire King." He held a gold plate in his fingers, dangling it like a pitviper. Larc snatched it out of his hands and made her own icelight.

The other Icers in the tunnel below continued to monitor the wall. Kiner crawled into the crevice beside her and waited while she read.

Icer L,

It has come to pass in Chraun that power has shifted. The former Fire King, who made war on your people, has come to an unfortunate end. With his end has come the end of our military policy in regards to the people of Iskalon.

I ask that you attend me in Chraun to discuss Treaty and terms of peace between our people. You may bring an honor guard of no more than twenty Icers. You will be greeted with all the honor and safety accorded to your position as Regent.

Please attend promptly. We have much to discuss. I will withdraw my troops for forty-eight hours as a sign of good faith.

Sincerely,
King of Chraun
Prince of Flames
Exalted Commander
Medoc

"A pretty websilk to dress a demand for surrender, isn't it?" Kiner sneered. "Well, forty-eight hours will be welcome, if they mean it. We can work on clearing the rubble, try to find a way through to Casser."

Surrender? Yes, Kiner was right. That was what the letter demanded, although Medoc's sweet language dressed it up in finery. Twenty Icers? Why should she give him even one more Icer? He had lied at every turn. His promise that the Icers who surrendered with Stasia would be returned to the lake had been a sham. Her scouts had seen the lake, and it was still covered in ash and what the Flames called Fireblood, still patrolled by Flames. There were no Icers there. And Stasia—why would he be writing Larc if Stasia still lived? He had claimed the other Fire King, the one he now said was dead, had wanted her, but how could she know that was true? She remembered his intense eyes, the way he had looked at her in the burial chamber, right before she had gone to Stasia with his message and convinced her Queen of his sincerity. Because of him, Stasia was gone, and Larc was forced into a position of rule she had never desired.

While Larc fumed, Kiner waited calmly for her orders. She needed to tell him to send a scout deeper into the tunnels, to find another hole to hide in, and another scout to spread word among the other Icers that she had moved again and that they might have a reprieve. She looked at her friend. His shoulders sagged, his movements were slow and lethargic, his cheeks sunken and hollow. He had been malnourished for a long time, since they had convened in the burial chamber. And today she would ration out the last of the molebear meat, and then there would be nothing. It was not his appearance but the look in his eyes she dreaded. Only she and the scribe had seen his vaerce tally, and it was grim.

Once, in the fungal tunnels, Larc had found a slink dying of a deep wound. The animal was already half gone, and not even her healing could save it. But it had a look in its eyes of determination, even through the pain and suffering. It would keep trying to live, even though life was futile. Larc had reached out and gently frozen the beast solid, ending its suffering. She believed she had done the right thing; the Heritage acolyte she'd spoken to afterward agreed. But she had never forgotten the look in its eyes, the struggle to live against the odds. Had she allowed it, the beast would have gone on suffering.

Kiner's eyes bore that look. Even in his deepest suffering, on the brink of death, he was determined to keep fighting. All of the Icers were.

Only Larc could choose to end it.

She tucked the gold plate neatly into her ragged chirsh. "Kiner, you must take a message to the rest of the troops. They must be ready and willing to obey this message. It is a thing I scarcely have the right to command. However, I believe it is our only salvation."

Kiner stared at her. His brow was etched with deep lines of concern.

"I will be going in alone to negotiate this Treaty. If I do not return after two days, you must attack Chraun en mass and fight to the death."

"But we will all die! You will die, for certain, and to attack en mass, with these troops—"

"Kiner, we are already dying." Her quiet tone cut him off. "Even a pretty surrender will be better than this slow death."

He shook his head. "You have too much faith in them, Regent. The Flames are monsters. They will simply kill you."

"I have made up my mind. You are in charge while I am gone, Kiner." Larc let go of his hand and started to squeeze her cramped body out of the crevice. "It may be that you are right. But it is the only chance we have."

She drifted down and walked alone through the tunnel. She heard Kiner bellowing orders out behind her. *Oh, Stasia*, Larc thought. *You would never give up like this. But don't you see it is the only decision I can make? We are dying, and I must end it.*

Part 4 ~ Burial

What are the roots that clutch, what branches grow
Out of this stony rubbish?
. . . You cannot say, or guess, for you know only
A heap of broken images, where the sun beats . . .

The Waste Land, T. S. Eliot

Interlude

Khell, Four Summers Prior

Maia

The Dhuciri came as Maia had predicted, three days after the Liathua Khell had left the summer camp and begun the long trek back to the mountains for the winter camp. They came at sunrise, and the grandfather on watch spread the word quickly and quietly. Maia doused her fire and left her egla of bones and draped boareal hides. She stood at the edge of the camp and watched tiny dark specs in the pale sky turn to giant flapping birds. Five of them; they circled the camp twice before landing on the ice a short distance away. The birds preened themselves like gwenwing after a dive.

As always during the tithing, Maia saw flashes of memories from long ago. Dust everywhere. Black figures surrounding the egla. Screams and moans. Her feet running over ice.

"A fine day for tithe." Hakua spoke behind her. She turned and saw that the tithing party had arrived. Lubar lay on his doal-drawn sled, his face pinched and drawn with bitter rage. Around him stood the tithe, ten people, one fifth of the number the Liathua claimed to have. In the camp, about forty people wandered between the egla. The rest huddled within their dwellings in silence.

Four warriors surrounded the tithe as they moved out over the ice toward the dark birds. There were three grandfathers in this group, who would never take their Journey over the Ice. A woman nursing a babe; they were Liathua, a volunteer sacrifice; her mate had died in a raid and she would have killed herself. The rest were captives from the summer raids. Two children, about the age Maia had been when her tribe was taken. Two warriors, their tongues cut out, the tendons in their wrists slit so that their hands dangled limp and useless. And a maiden a little younger than Maia, with a look of terror on her face. The Dhuciri demanded a cross-section of the people in the camp, rather than all the old or all the young. Maia wondered why they would care. The people would all be dust soon. Why did it matter if they were young or old, male or female?

As she walked, a wave of stench hit Maia, worse than a months-old boareal carcass. She tried to breathe only through her mouth, but that didn't help; she could taste rancid meat. The Dhuciri stood a few paces away now, gathered in front of their birds. There were five of them, one rider for each bird. They were tall and wiry, draped in black garments made from the feathers of their steeds. Their faces were pale and gaunt, void of emotion.

The warriors herded the tithe toward the Dhuciri. Lubar stopped his sled just short of them. He began the ritual greeting, bowing his head. Maia and Hakua bowed low and then rose, smiles plastered over their faces, both watching Lubar anxiously. He did not wear a smile. He opened his mouth and began to say the words of the ritual, offering the tithe in the tongue of the Dhuciri, but the words were spoken with heavy anger, not the soft monotone that was expected. He still was not smiling. Maia was aware of the Dhuciri watching him intently, their eyes sharp like the eyes of their birds.

"Boareal-dung doal-rapers. Take the whole tribe! Take my worthless sons and my good-for-nothing mate!" Lubar spoke Khell now, but even if the Dhuciri did not understand his words, his tone was unmistakable. "Take everything and give me back my legs!"

Hakua spoke quickly, interrupting Lubar. "Many apologies, Dhuciri Masters," he said in their tongue. "His mind has gone. He thinks he is still Chief. I ask that you take him as an addition to the tithe, a gift to you for your mercy these many winters."

Lubar spat and cursed and began to yell at Hakua. Hakua

smiled through his teeth and bowed again to the Dhuciri. Then he began the words of the ritual, nearly obscured by Lubar's shouts, in a gentle monotone, offering up ten Khell to appease the Dhuciri this winter. As he spoke, Maia watched one of the Dhuciri step over to the sled to inspect Lubar.

She was close enough to see something strange. The Dhuciri was shaking slightly, trembling and sweating. His face seemed even paler than the others. Maia realized where she had seen such a thing before. It was hard to imagine any similarity between the Khell and these dark creatures, but she had seen warriors who drank too much fermented urchin broth during the summer, then be unable to drink it when supplies ran low in winter, shake like this. The Healer in her realized she was looking at a creature suffering from the urchin-shivers, or something very similar.

The Dhuciri stepped closer and reached out to touch Lubar's forehead. The former chief went silent; even in his madness, he was aware of the danger. In the same moment, Hakua's ritual ended in silence, and the only noise was a soft breeze whistling through the feathers of the giant birds. The Dhuciri touching Lubar breathed deeply; the shaking ceased, a little color returned to the Dhuciri's face, and he seemed strong, a warrior at high summer.

Maia saw the light go out of Lubar's eyes. His face went ashen, and froze in time. The wind gusted and it melted Lubar's features, carried them away in a stream of black dust. Maia stepped away so the dust would not fall on her.

She was sick to her stomach. She saw again the patches of black dust covering the ice where the camp of her tribe had stood. It took all her strength not to cry out or retch. Even Lubar had not deserved to end like this.

A tongueless groan broke the silence and Maia realized that the raid-taken warriors had begun to struggle. Hakua straightened from his bowing posture to help his own warriors restrain them, but black chains had closed around all the necks of the tithe. The Dhuciri began to walk away, towing the offering of the Liathua Khell to their birds.

Maia and Hakua stood together beside the dirty ice that had been the chief of the Liathua, watching the black birds circling higher and higher. Hakua sent the warriors back with sled and doal, ordering that camp be stricken. Then he knelt by the line of black dust, uttering the words of ritual that sent the dead safe on their journey over ice. He cut off his long black hair, a sign of mourning, and cast it onto the patch of dust. The strands blew across the ice as he stood.

Maia left her braids intact. Everyone knew that the tithe must not be mourned. Hakua could not accept the manner of his father's death, she realized. He wanted a nobler end for the former chief of the Liathua Khell. Maia stepped closer to him, took his hand in hers. It hung limp in her grip.

"What?" he asked her. "Do you wish to mate, now that I am chief?" His words sounded as lifeless as his hand felt.

"We can never mate, Hakua. I saw this in the bones. There is a man coming who will take me as his. If we are mated when he comes, you will die."

His lip twisted in scorn. "Let him try. I will prove the better warrior."

"I wish only to offer you comfort, Hakua. Remember when we were children, and we comforted each other? Can we not have that now?"

He pushed her hand away. "We are no longer children, Maia. I am Chief, or will be next summer, and you are Healer. I think—" his voice caught for a moment "—I think there can be no comfort for us."

Maia took his hand again. He did not pull away this time.

"I begged him to stay in egla. I told him I would handle the tithing. What could I do, Maia? It was as you said. His madness would have brought them down on the tribe."

Maia said nothing, just squeezed his palm. After a time they walked back over the ice to the camp, mounted their boareal, and rode into winter, leaving the dark patch of dust and hair behind to be blown away by the coming storms.

Chapter 17

In the Heart of Chraun

Glace

Glace stood in a vast, sweltering cavern, clothed more fully than he had ever been before, draped in all kinds of hides, most of them cababar or Chraun's svelte hippole, but some he suspected were slink. He felt more naked than he'd ever felt before. His weapons were gone; Chraun's Semija warriors carried them now. He had never been more than a few feet from his mace and axe; even when he was swimming, they were waiting for him at the shore. It was a frightening sensation, and coupled with his parting from Stasia and the only purpose his life had ever known, it made him feel both helpless and useless at the same time.

Still, he stood straight and proud. The other people in the vast cavern were even more frightened and helpless than he, and even if he was a slave like the rest, he could still lead them by example.

It did not assuage his feeling of vulnerability that the woman standing before him was undressing him with her eyes. She had a plain face, and was of a height with him, full bodied and larger boned than he was accustomed to. Her lava mesh glowed brightly in swirling patterns, and she wore a sort of dainty, fake-looking scale armor that sparkled with diamonds. Her hair was straight and black and as stern as her dark eyes. After staring at him for several moments, she gestured sharply to the woman kneeling at Glace's feet.

"Take away the brown hides," she said. "I think the white hippole and black is more becoming, with those blue eyes."

Before she stood, the girl by Glace's feet touched her forehead to the floor. Then she hastily began pulling all the brown hides from his shoulders and waist, leaving only dark slink furs and pale hippole. Glace allowed his gaze to drop to the girl while she rearranged the remaining hides in a semblance of clothing, an arrangement designed to display his muscles to any who cared to look. To his horror, he recognized her. Her pale skin and fine dark hair marked her as a citizen of Iskalon. He had seen her often on Market Ave, hawking fungal pastries for the Cooking Guild, though he had never spoken to her and did not know her name. She did not raise her eyes to meet his.

He stood stoically, refusing to let his reaction show. The Flame could have used one of her own humans for this task, but she wanted him and the others to see one of their people as a slave, to see how beaten down their people had become. To see what they would be, when she was through with them. A cool, slow rage built in his chest, and he shoved it down quickly. He could imagine all too easily the satisfaction on the Flame's face at seeing him lose control.

To distract himself from anger, he searched the Flame's features, looking for a weakness. *The first task, facing an opponent, is to find their weakness. Then, look for ways to attack that weakness directly.* The words of his father rang in his ears as if the man were standing at his shoulder. Perhaps he was there – Father had not received a proper burial;

perhaps he was wandering around these warm tunnels with the other ghosts of Iskalon.

There. In her eyes, impatience, frustration, intense fury, hiding just beyond that lazy, lidded gaze that pretended not to care. The Flame did not like this task, and would just as soon leave it to someone else and be gone. There was some other matter she needed to attend to, and she wasn't able to because Glace and his fellow captives had been dumped in her lap. It was like seeing Stasia impatient in council. The thought of comparing his lovely Queen to this over-sized molebear fem struck him suddenly as funny, and he smiled briefly before he could stop himself.

The Flame's eyes, which had been wandering down his body, returned sharply to his face, piercing him. "When you are with other Semija, you may express yourself freely. However, you will learn never to do so in the presence of the Flames you serve. I will be lenient because you are new to our ways. The next breach will earn a beating."

She drew herself up to a full stance, and her heels clicked loudly as she stepped closer. She spoke loudly, so that her voice reached everyone else in the cavern. The Semija—no, he told himself sternly, the person, what was her name? The Cook, he would think of her as that— finished arranging his garments so that they hung neatly, and knelt again at his feet. "That is only one of the many things you have to learn as Semija. Another is to never meet any Flame's eyes." A blow struck the back of his head, forcing his face forward and his gaze down. A strong breath of hot air held him with his head bowed. "Yet another is to always prostrate yourself before your owner." His flesh heated, and his legs turned to bone-jelly and gave way beneath him. He crumpled to the ground, unable to control his own body. "You will learn to anticipate your owner's needs, and respond immediately. Your owner comes before you in all things. You must be a useful tool, or you will be discarded."

The heat around him dissolved, and Glace raised his head and stared into the Flame's eyes defiantly. She smiled at him knowingly. "This sort of behavior will only earn punishment."

Glace waited for the blows to fall, but they never came. Instead, the Cook screamed in agony and began to writhe, her neat prostration abandoned in a helpless flailing roll. The Flame continued to smile at Glace. "Shall your punishment continue, Semija? Only you can decide that."

He stared back at her, testing that weakness. Could he make her angry enough to kill him? The thought of dying here in this cavern, purposeless, brought Stasia's face to mind. Stasia, his purpose in life, her cool, smooth lips, warmer than expected. To die now was to abandon her, abandon any possibility of discovering her fate. If there was any chance she still lived here, he could bide his time, figure out a way to rescue her. His need for her went beyond duty—it always had, he could see that now. He would not fail her by taking the easy path of death.

Glace dropped his gaze and let his forehead press against the hot stone floor. He felt his betrayal of Iskalon and his own humanity as he did so. The girl's cries faded into muffled whimpers and he heard her rearranging herself into prostration. He heard a multitude of shuffling and scraping sounds behind him. If he stood and turned, he would see the rest of the captives following his lead.

He cringed when the gentle pat fell against his matted hair. "Good Semija," the Flame woman whispered. "You are a fast learner. Some of your kind took many lessons to reach this point. You will be a very good Semija. Perhaps, someday, you will even be chosen to serve the General, or the King."

The Semija quarters sprawled in the cooler outskirts of Chraun, far from the baths and the Lava River. Glace was led to his new home by a troop of stout humans who had been born, or as the Flames put it, bred, in Chraun. They looked similar to the Flames, tall, full-boned, and dark skinned, just as Iskalon humans resembled Icers in their supple, pale grace. They wore the same sparse hides as all the other Semija, but a black brand ringing both upper arms marked them as a special class—crew masters, the Flames called them. Glace thought of them stubbornly as slave masters.

Glace's cave could hardly be called quarters. A dark, long, low-ceilinged room, it was crammed elbow to elbow with at least one hundred other slaves, a mix of Chraun humans and Iskalon captives like himself. There were no furs, no bunks, no possessions. The floor was rough rock, with just enough room for each of them to lie supine. Glace began to take his fur vest off to make a pillow, but one of the Chraun slaves stopped him. "If called to duty, you must be ready," the man said. He did not meet Glace's eyes.

Glace considered ignoring the man's words, but he decided to leave his clothes on. He already felt naked enough. Instead of lying down, he sat with his back against the wall as if on watch. He had sometimes dozed lightly thus in front of Stasia's quarters. But here, jagged rock pushed into his sore muscles. The heat made him sweat even when he wasn't moving. The long burning, steady flames of the firestone torches never ceased. There was no gentle dimming of Palace icelights to lull him to sleep.

Even without the blazing lights, Glace thought sleep would have been impossible. Stasia drifted into his thoughts, but he tried to banish her. Wakeful slave-masters lined the corridors outside, ready to alert the Flames of the slightest transgression. Even if he got past them and somehow found her, he would be killed long before he got her out of Chraun. No, he had to be patient, bide his time, learn the weaknesses of this place, and hope that she still lived.

I will find her, said the desperate part of him that needed her, loved her, thirsted for the taste of her. I will find her and save her.

He thought about Musche instead. Had the slink survived the rout and escaped further into the Outer Tunnels? He hoped the beast had not tried to follow the captured warriors into Chraun. If he had, he would be dead now, his hide being tanned to decorate a Semija. Glace shuddered again, thinking that the fur loincloth was most likely from a slink. It felt filthy against his thighs.

He exhaled noisily and tried to get comfortable. The man lying next to him opened his eyes and looked up. He was from Iskalon, with pale skin and a bushy blonde beard. Glace thought he had seen him before the war, in the Palace. The man glared at him, then struggled to sit up, his expression softening.

"It's hard to sleep at first, isn't it?"

He spoke very quietly. A few other Semija stirred, but did not wake. The man leaned against the wall next to him and began to speak of his life in Iskalon. He had been a scribe, one of the King's best, he said. He spoke of the Scribe Guild, of his love of gold plate and his affinity for the little marks and dashes of the written language. He had been taken in the first attack on Iskalon, had been a slave all this time. Glace let him ramble. It was soothing to hear the man speak of the home they had left behind, destroyed now, sunk beneath the lake and scattered in the Outer Tunnels.

When the former scribe paused, Glace asked, "How do you bear it? You will probably never touch gold plate again. How can you stand being a slave?"

The scribe glanced around the cave, as if checking to see that everyone else slept and they were not overheard. "We have always been slaves," he whispered.

"What do you mean by that?"

"Oh, in Iskalon they have fancy names for it, dress it up in a structure of Guilds and families. But have you ever really thought about that structure? Who does all the work to keep Iskalon running? The Guilds. Who does all the work in Chraun? The Semija. It is all one and the same."

"But we work by choice," Glace said. He did not like the turn the conversation had taken. "We are not beaten or starved or forced to mate."

"True, the Icers aren't cruel like these masters. They don't have to be—the structure of the Guilds keeps us all in line. Have you ever considered the guildless? They are unable to work, cast out of the Guilds, and look how they are treated. Relegated to the tunnels, given a pittance. I did charity work in the tunnel of guildless. I've seen how some Icers treat them."

"Not all Icers," Glace insisted, thinking of Stasia and her compassion for the guildless. "Anyhow, most of the Guild members treat them just as bad."

"Yes, just like the Semija here treat each other. Consider our slave masters, waiting out there with whips to keep us in line. The Flames don't have to raise a finger, any more than the Icers did. Think about it. You were the bodyguard of one of the princesses, right?"

Glace was silent, but the man continued as if he had agreed. "What would have happened if you had asked to be relieved of duty? Say you wanted to join another Guild. Say you wanted to join my Guild and be a scribe. Would they have let you go? If you ever get a chance, if we somehow are miraculously freed and Iskalon resumes its daily business, ask her, Warrior. Ask her to let you go. Just to see what she says."

"She is royalty. They can command us, that is natural. But no ordinary Icer can command a Guildsman."

"Can't they? Have you ever tried refusing one?"

"Have you?" Glace countered, more anger in his voice than he'd intended to reveal. He wanted the scribe to be quiet. How dare he compare Stasia to a Flame?

"More than once," the scribe said proudly. "They set a great store by duty, our Icers. Always they say: it is your duty as a Guildsman. If you refuse, you inevitably get in trouble with the Guild. It has happened to me many times.

I worked for the King, but other Icers would command me to do their work all the time. Take diction from this Lord, send a message to that Lady. Didn't matter if I was already busy with another task. Surely you have time to do your duty, they would say. I'm working up a very important plate for the King, I would reply. Well, then you can do it after. Once, a Lady came back and her work wasn't done. The work for the King took longer than I thought. The Lady was upset, and I got angry. I gave my anger voice. The next day, I was demoted to being a runner again. After fifteen years of inscription work."

"That's absurd," Glace said, his anger boiling over at last. "The King would never allow that. He would have protected you. You are lying."

The scribe looked him in the eye and smiled. It was a tolerant, patient smile, the kind Glace might give to a small child who wanted to spar. "Believe what you like. But ask your mistress, if you ever get out of here. Ask her if you can walk away. The structure may be different, but the chains are just as tight. Ask the Fungal Guildsmen. Or the stock handlers, or the miners. They work just as long and hard as the Semija here, and they are quartered just as poorly—while your Icers are lording it up in the Palace. Just ask her, Warrior."

The scribe fell silent, and finally laid down and settled into sleep again. Glace tried to forget the man's words, but they writhed in the back of his brain like an itch between his shoulder blades. He dozed lightly, but he was not really sleeping when a Semija wearing the scorched black brands of a slave master entered the cave and began to bellow out orders.

Glace stood and tried to make sense of the man's rapid, sparse speech. "You!" the slave master yelled out, pointing at Glace. "Wipe sleep out of eyes and put on pretty face. Kinyara is engaging Nobles for morning feast. You will attend her."

Glace followed him out of the cave, rubbing at his

eyes. The Kinyara was the plain-faced woman who had conducted the first training. The idea of being in her presence again repulsed him even more than the slink fur around his waist.

But a meeting with Nobles sounded informative. Perhaps he would learn of Stasia's fate, and that of the Icers in the Outer Tunnels he had failed to protect. He remembered the conversation with the scribe, and brushed it out of his mind. There was no comparison between Iskalon and this brutal slavery. The man was paranoid, driven crazy by his imprisonment in Chraun. He was to be pitied, not taken seriously.

Glace slowed to brush the dust off his furs, and reeled forward as a hot whip of fire danced on his bare shoulders. "Faster," was all his master said, but Glace obeyed, and though his back was in fiery agony, a quiet hope was alive in his heart. He would be waiting on the Kinyara, but he would be serving his Queen.

Larc

Larc could not disguise her terror as she walked down the increasingly warm Spiral Tunnel, flanked by Flame Officers. They could kill her at any moment, simply reach out and end her life. She had not even been so afraid during the attack on Iskalon, or the later attack on the burial chamber. Then, she had been surrounded by other Icers, by Warriors. Now, she was utterly alone and her life was completely at the mercy of Flames who had murdered countless Icers. And the heat was growing, making her stomach churn, her head ache, and her heart weak.

The Spiral ended and the tunnels leveled out. They widened into brightly lit halls with tiled floors and lime-washed walls. Common Flames, dressed in drab furs and skins, bustled past, leading their slaves, eyeing Larc and her escort nervously. Larc kept her gaze straight ahead as the Officers guided her through the maze. Further in, the costumes changed, and Noble Flames clad in gaudy clothes of precious metals and gems stopped and watched her with curiosity, as if she were a strange animal they had never seen before. But curiosity turned to recognition on some faces, followed quickly by anger and hatred. Though Chraun had initiated the war, some of these Flames had clearly lost loved ones to it, and their blame would rest on the only Icer at hand—her.

Larc tried to reassure herself. Medoc had not killed her emissaries; he had sent them back with an agreement to meet, so perhaps he would not kill her, either. But he had lied before. He had implied at their last meeting that Stasia's surrender would purchase reprieve for the rest of Iskalon. It had not. Then again, Stasia's idea of sending the people into the Outer Tunnels had not been what Medoc expected or desired.

The Flames led her through a crowded tunnel, full of color and noise and bright light. The smell of food, even the Flame's scorched stuff, made Larc's mouth water. She kept her eyes straight ahead, hoping her sudden desire not only for food but for this kind of normalcy did not show on her face. People in alcoves along the tunnel were selling goods, just like an ordinary day in the Market of Iskalon. Most of their customers were common Flames. Ordinary people, going about their business. Here and there a Noble shopped with a large entourage of scantily clad slaves. Larc saw pale skin on a few of them, and knew they were Iskaloners, perhaps captured in the fall of the lake, perhaps taken since.

"Ice Fairy!"

Larc turned to see a common Flame in a leather scale dress, hands on her hips, glaring at her. "You killed my son. I hope the King gives you what you deserve!"

It took Larc a moment to realize the woman was speaking generally; her son had died in the war, and Larc was the only available Icer to blame. Anger choked her as she thought of her father, and her brother, still missing—

perhaps dead at the bottom of the lake. She had lost so much, these Flames had destroyed her whole world, and they dared blame her for the war? Before she could open her mouth to speak, however, the cavern began to echo with the shouts of other Flames.

"Murderer!"

"Lava is too good for you!"

Larc did not understand half of the epithets that followed, but she understood their tone. Her guards slowed as if they relished giving the people a chance to abuse her. Sweat dripped from her brow, filled with the grime of weeks without a bath. She tried to quiet the thud of her heart, to channel the anger and hatred that the Flames aroused into energy for the debate ahead. She thought of the meeting as a council, where Medoc was the assembly and her job was to convince him that her side was the correct one. What did she know, what could she use to tempt him to her cause?

It came down to the lake. For some reason, it was crucial to Medoc that the Icers be returned to the lake, under guard or free. He had indicated as much to her at their meeting in the burial chamber. The lake was the key, somehow. What did he want from it? Was there something the Flames had lost there, something that he needed returned but did not know how to find? Larc could not imagine what would possibly be so important. But for some reason, Medoc needed Icers. Whatever he wanted, it was something Flames and humans could not do.

By the time they had crossed the wide Market Tunnel, Larc was shaking. She was not sure she could trust her legs. The Guard led her along without sympathy, briskly now, through quieter tunnels. More Officers, in sturdy steel plate armor, ignored Larc completely and saluted her escort. The air here was scorching, and sweat ran in rivulets over her skin. A thick metal portcullis loomed in the tunnel. Squaring her shoulders, Larc took a deep breath, stilled her nausea, and prepared for what might well be her final debate.

Medoc

Medoc sat on the throne, enjoying the heat from the Lava River behind him. Bolv sat on a cushioned stool to the right of the throne, surrounded by members of the ten most powerful Noble houses in Chraun and an entourage of Semija from the recent captives. They were almost comical in their attempts to act like true Semija. There were certain concepts they simply couldn't grasp, like anticipating a Flame's needs before they were spoken. They were practically useless, but Bolv had suggested that their presence might assist Chraun's position in the negotiation with the Icers. Medoc didn't think they'd have much effect, but he was learning to give way on small matters.

That, and occupying the Kinyara with small tasks, kept her mostly out of Medoc's way. Mostly. As soon as Medoc had secured Chraun, she'd had the audacity to order his troops back to the Outer Tunnels, sweeping up hundreds of Semija and killing thousands more. Too late, Medoc had pulled them back and sent his message to the Regent. If he hadn't, they would have killed what remained of the Icers, and the waters of Chraun would never be cleaned.

A knock sounded on the portcullis, and Medoc nodded at the guards by the door. They peeked out the spy slot, then raised the portcullis with a raspy scrape. Medoc sat up straighter, the Nobles quieted, and Bolv stopped fussing with her Semija. The Icer stood in the doorway, silhouetted by the brighter lights in the hall. All he could see of her was dark curves, the roundness of her cheeks and hips. She did not enter, but stood staring into the throne room.

Medoc grew impatient. How dare she make him wait? Was she making a point? He would not be meeting with her at all, except that the baths were still full of Fireblood;

the Solph river was still clogged with bodies. Other things were coming through as well, a kind of sediment that made the people sick when they drank it. Flames could heal it away, but many of the Semija were ill.

The pretty, dark Icer took a few steps into the room and stopped, staring at Medoc with unreadable eyes. Her Icer armor was soggy and stained with rust and dirt. Her hair was combed and neat, bangs nearly obscuring her dark eyes. Her skin glistened moistly in the torchlight. Her eyes flickered to Bolv and the Nobles and then back to Medoc. She should be frightened and vulnerable, a lone Icer in a den of Flames, but she looked confident, like a young warrior hot for battle. Medoc suddenly felt foolish, surrounded by all these guards, as if he needed protection from her. Then he felt angry for being made to look a fool.

"I told you to bring an honor guard," he said, knowing he was starting on a weak foot. Bolv's disapproval bored into his back. "Why have you come alone?"

"We haven't any honor guard to spare, I am afraid."

Her voice was musical. It sent a strange sensation up Medoc's spine. He thought of Stasia, and her Flame mother and Icer father. He cursed himself. He should have let Bolv speak for him. Now he would have to continue to negotiate.

"Since the last parley was broken by Chraun, we decided to risk only one life on your word."

An honest answer, and logical. It irritated Medoc even more. He was tempted to tell off a few of his guards, but it was too late for that. He saw that the Icer's eyes had strayed beyond him, turned and saw her looking at a large male Semija with dusty hair. He pounced on that weakness.

"Would you like your Semija back? If you agree to my terms, I may let a few go with you."

"I'm afraid that just won't do." The roar of the Lava River made all petitioners project their voices, and often the result was an uncomfortable, desperate-sounding shout. The Icer did not sound desperate at all but strong, as if she was accustomed to speaking with authority. "Why take a few of our people back when we have no assurance that we won't all simply be killed or enslaved? I know you want something from us, Fire King. I will give you what you want, but only if you agree to our terms. A peace treaty that ensures our safety. The return of all of our people, including our Queen. Complete independence from Chraun. Cababar for eating and breeding, and enough fungal spore to repopulate our fields. Otherwise, we might as well just keep fighting till we die. In fact, I have instructed my people to do just that if I do not return with this treaty. I am sure they will not be much use to you dead."

Just like that, she had laid it all out. Medoc had expected more subtlety, more back and forth. This for that. "You do not even know what we want."

"They need Fireblood cleaned from the lake! It has cont—"

Medoc turned, furious. One of Bolv's Semija had spoken. He lay on the floor now, writhing and screaming, deep red burns appearing all over his huge body. Bolv would kill him in another instant.

"Make her stop!" The Icer's voice, raised in a shout, drew Medoc's attention back. Her pretty lips were trembling, her eyes bulging in sympathetic pain. "Don't let her kill him! If you kill him, I will kill myself here and now! You will never get what you need from us."

"Bolv, stop." Medoc did not turn to see if his command was followed. The heat dissipated and he heard the screams cut off. The Icer rushed past Medoc, startling the guards, and managed to get all the way to the side of the large Semija. Medoc's guards hurried after her, but he waved them away. He stood and turned, watching the Icer cradle the burned Semija's head to her chest, sobbing.

"Heal him," Medoc commanded Bolv.

She was not happy to do it, but she could not disobey

his orders in public. The human looked to be in as much pain from the healing as from the punishment, but when it was done he could sit up. The Icer helped him, glaring at Medoc. "You are horrible people. You are all horrible. We should refuse to clean the lake and let you all die of your own poison. You should all die for what you have done." She started sobbing again. The Semija was comforting her now.

Medoc wished he could tell her that he was not horrible. He wished he could tell her that he never wanted to destroy her home, that it was Dynat, not he who had ordered the surrendered Icers killed. That in the end, he had tried to redeem himself by freeing the Icer Queen. That this too had gone awry, because he had to protect his position for the stability of Chraun. He could not say what he wanted to say in front of Bolv and the Nobles.

He could draw this out, play from a position of power, try to bully them into taking less for more. But he hadn't the heart for it. He thought of the bodies in the Solph. A vision swept through his mind, of the restless ghosts of all the Icers killed in the war, wandering among the baths, reaching long, ghostly fingers down the tunnel to where he slept in Dynat's old quarters.

"Yes," Medoc said. Bolv stared at him as if he was a pitviper. "We agree to your terms. You will take all of your Semija, you will get five hundred pair of breeding cababar, and fifty sacks of spore. Not the Queen. I don't have her; she escaped, and if she has not found her way back to you that is her problem, not mine. But hear me. If the lake is not clean by the time the slinks come down to breed, you will pay dearly. I will take what Dynat began and finish it. No Icer or Semija of ice will remain alive in Sholaen. This I swear, by the Fire Spirit."

The pretty Icer's sobs began to calm and she wiped away tears. "As you say, Fire King. By the Ancestors, speaking as Regent of Iskalon, I so agree."

Larc

Larc gripped the gold plate as she marched up the Spiral Tunnel, running her fingers over the sinuous marks Medoc's scribe had impressed in the metal. She should have tucked it into her armor, but she wanted to hold it in her hand, wanted to believe that it would really protect her people and that the nightmare of war was over at last.

Glace hovered at her elbow, and weary as he was, she sensed his impetus to pass her and run up the tunnel. He had regained his strength enough to help her to organize the freed prisoners, but she could sense a change in him. His stance no longer as straight as it once had been, his eyes downcast when once he had gazed intently into her eyes—were these things wrought by the war, or the loss of Stasia, or his time as a slave to the Flames? He had not mentioned Stasia's absence. Larc believed Medoc when he said she still lived. If she was dead, why try to hide it? But she did not think Stasia had escaped. How could a lone Icer have escaped from that place? More likely, Medoc still had her, and was holding her back to use later if the Icers refused to clean the lake. Larc could only hope that he would free Stasia once he was satisfied that Larc would follow the Treaty.

Behind Glace, over forty thousand humans made their way up the Spiral Tunnel toward home. The long line of freed prisoners, now refugees, stretched all the way back to Chraun. Until she could find scribes to count the people, Larc had only the assurance of the gold plate in her hand that all of her people would be released. There was no one down there watching the tail of the Spiral except Flames. She wondered if she had made the right demands; how was she to feed so many with a thousand cababar and fifty sacks of spore?

Larc had sent a few of the stronger survivors to the Outer Tunnels to fetch Kiner, and he met her at the head of the Spiral with the remaining Icer army, less than two thousand strong. From there, Larc ordered the least exhausted Icers to scout ahead. She did not know what to expect of the city, but she imagined the ruins being a dangerous place, still coated in Fireblood and full of pitfalls and loose buildings. Until they were stabilized, she would need a space large enough to house all of the people.

The vast Fungal Caverns were cramped, but just big enough. A few patches of spore had sprouted here and there, but the giant sheets of fungus were gone, destroyed in fire. Soot covered the columns, poison to the spores. Bodies sprawled among the columns, covered with pale fungus, glowing blue under her icelight. Larc ordered them stacked against the walls, the fruiting fungi carefully harvested and rationed, and the columns washed. It was a wearying, disheartening homecoming, and she could see it on the people's faces. Those who had tasks took to them mechanically, as if they were still slaves. The people with nothing to, when they realized the march was over, sat or laid where they were and did not move, talk to each other, or look around. The children were the saddest. Larc's heart ached to see them wandering around the cavern like ghosts, looking for parents they would never find.

Before she could begin to think of doing something for them, Glace and Kiner were at her side, returning with scouts from the lake, urging her to see it with her own eyes. The swath of bodies continued through the livestock caverns. A few chirat gone feral hissed in the dark. There was barely space to step in the cavern of the guildless; the bodies were piled high. Larc thought of Hali, wondered if she had family lying here. Then she saw that the bodies wore chirsh and leather armor; they were Warriors, not guildless, and she remembered that some of the guildless had been taken into the city during the war. Others had fled to the Outer Tunnels.

Larc thought the deaths of the royal family, and the

surrender of Iskalon, had broken her heart as deeply as it was possible to break it, shattering it into millions of tiny pieces. When she left the cavern of the guildless and saw the unrecognizable lump of melted ice that had once been the Palace, saw the dark slick of Fireblood coating the lake, still burning in places, saw the bodies, half decomposed, floating in the water, her heart broke completely, turning to dust as fine as powder ice.

She wanted to fall to her knees at the foot of the sunken Fire Bridge, and weep for all that was lost. The vast cavern, once a lively bustle, was silent, save for the lapping of the water at the shore and the soft gasps of the scouts behind her. She walked out past the bridge, hovered above the lake, and drew T'Jas deeply from the cold air. The familiar act was soothing, but it did not fill the hollow where her heart had been.

She was overwhelmed, thinking of how much work there was to do. Just clearing the caverns around Iskalon would be a task, let alone fixing the bridges, sorting the rubble, and rebuilding the Palace. Larc would have to oversee it all. She could not grieve yet. The war was over, but her battle was just beginning. She shifted from sorrow to thinking of what they did have to be thankful for. There did not seem to be any Flames here; Medoc *had* called them back. And it was cold—deliciously, blessedly cold.

She left Kiner and Glace and the scouts trying to mend the raising-gears of the Fire Bridge and headed back alone through the grisly tunnels to the Fungal Caverns. She stood in the entrance to the cavern, looking in. A few slow groups were still trickling up from the Spiral. The caverns were overfull; she would need to order new arrivals diverted to the mines, to be housed there. It struck Larc how quiet the cave was. A similar sized crowd in Market Ave would susurrate with conversation. No one was speaking who did not have to, here. The people did not look at each other in sympathy or curiosity. Demoralized by their long imprisonment, they were a people in profound shock. It was up to Larc to give them hope, to make them understand that they were home.

"People of Iskalon," she called out, using T'Jas to amplify her voice so it resonated around the cavern. A few people looked toward her, but far more kept their eyes on the ground. "Do not be disheartened by what you see here. Iskalon has been struck a great blow. We have lost much. All of us have lost family, friends, homes, innocence. But we have our lives and our freedom, and that is more than we had yesterday. Together, we will rebuild Iskalon to be stronger, more beautiful, than ever!"

More heads rose. A few people stood, and they began looking at each other, really seeing that they were alive and free from Chraun. Larc watched a woman reach out and pick up a child who was wandering alone and cradle it to her breast. The cavern was coming alive as the people began to think of themselves as a Kingdom again, not just a bunch of slaves.

"When the Ancestors gave us Lake Lentok, there was nothing here but a lake, a rock, and a few wild animals in the Outer Tunnels," she continued. "Our forefathers took that and built the mighty kingdom of Iskalon. We have more than they had. We have spore, we have stock, we have all the pieces of our Kingdom, and we have each other. Together, we can put them back together."

A small cheer rose and grew, louder and louder until it filled the cavern like the rumble of a rockslide. A small part of Larc's anxiety quieted for the first time in many days. There were many strong Guild members among these forty thousand freed, who would not hesitate to put their backs into rebuilding Iskalon. She remembered Stasia's first words as Queen, and felt compelled to repeat them.

"Iskalon stands!" She shouted into the roar, and it echoed back to her ears as forty thousand voices rose together.

"ISKALON STANDS!"

Chapter 18

A Vast Blue Cavern

Stasia

The flame on the torch flickered dangerously, guttering on the edge of extinction. Stasia tried to will it to stay lit. She had never thought she would be praying to the Ancestors for fire. Another drop of water fell and it hissed madly. Stasia used a bit of her precious T'Jas to push the dripping water to the sides of the small cavity in the ice where she stood with Dynat. The water hardened back to ice beneath her feet as she traveled up the shaft, creating a floor that sealed her in completely. Surrounded by burial ice, Stasia could not simply tunnel her way out; she could not manipulate it, could not even draw T'Jas from it. Tiny veins of air running up and down the ice kept the cavity filled with oxygen, feeding their lungs and the flame. She would not suffocate, but if the flame went out, she would starve at the very least, if not be crushed by the resealing ice.

Dynat held the torch aloft, and she thought it was sheer willpower that kept his arm up. He had not tried to fight her command; she thought he was uncertain of his own Warriors' loyalty, as afraid of them as she was. Hours surrounded by ice had taken a toll, and her cold Icer's healing had not provided enough strength for him to combat the seeping cold. Even wrapped in his cloak, he looked worn and haggard. His lids drooped as if they might fall shut at any moment, and he winced every time the cold water splattered on his face or scalp. The outside of the cloak was soaked, and the hood was thrown back, frozen nearly stiff.

Stasia felt no pity. Walking through the burial chamber past the heads of her sisters had torn her heart open again and left it raw. It had been all she could do not to claw his eyes out, back in the burial chamber, not to freeze the blood in his veins and watch him suffer a millionth of the pain he'd caused her. No, there was no pity in her for him. But she did worry—if he went too cold and lost his power, then the torch would go out. She and the former Fire King would be drifting corpses for eternity.

How long should she wait up here? Were the Flames patrolling the floor of the burial chamber even now? Stasia had pushed Dynat hard to get them high in the shaft, far above the copper-clad Ancestors. The red haired Lady had seemed to beckon Stasia onward. Beyond her, the garments of the corpses grew more and more ancient, accented with metals and gems that were only legends to the people of Iskalon. Their expressions and features were strange as well, and Stasia thought that these people had been in the ice for a longer period of time than she could comprehend. The bodies surrounding her now wore soft, light robes like the finest websilk. There was little chance that the Flames would look up and glimpse her and Dynat; unless they had an iceospectacle, they would think them only two more bodies. Stasia had left the crown of Iskalon further down, near the copper-clad Lady. The Flames might see that, but with luck it would appear just another relic to them.

In retrospect, the Burial Shaft seemed a foolish place

to hide. There was no way of knowing if it was safe to leave, and sooner or later she would have to take the risk. She should have merely tunneled into the rock wall of the cavern. The Flames would have felt that, though, and it would have taken longer than entering the ice. For something that Icers couldn't budge, burial ice was surprisingly responsive to fire. Why had the Ancestors made it thus?

Frustrated, Stasia stared at the wall in front of her. She could see her reflection in the glowing ice. She looked pale and weary. Fear shone in her yellow-green eyes, and dark circles ringed them. A deep scar marred her once perfect forehead, and her long, silvery hair was shortened and patchy on one half of her head, where the lava river had burned it away. She wondered if Glace would still want to kiss her if he could see her now. Most likely he would be horrified. She thought of Larc's gentle Icer healing soothing away all of her hurts, and almost broke into tears. Did they live? Medoc had promised to withdraw—but had he even won the throne, or did some other Flame hold the fate of her people in his hands?

Through her own image, Stasia could see the nearest corpse, suspended upright in the ice, nearly parallel with her. The woman's face looked familiar, and her features appeared as an echo of Stasia's reflection, the same high cheekbones and thin lips and narrow eyes. Her eyes and hair were dark, though, and she was taller than Stasia. She wore a dress more purely white than a pearl, and it looked luxuriantly soft. Stasia would have liked to reach out and touch it, but at least five feet of solid ice separated them. The woman's expression was grim, tight, almost a snarl. She did not look serenely pleased to be guarding Iskalon from the Svardark. And she appeared to be Iskalon's first defense. Above her, there were no more bodies, only the infinite shaft of burial ice.

A burst of color was silhouetted against the woman's bodice. Stasia gazed closer and saw that it was a red stain, seeping through the white fabric of the woman's dress from her stomach. Blood, perfectly preserved in the ice. Stasia looked at her face again, and saw the snarl was a rictus of pain.

"Ancestors," Stasia whispered. "What happened to her?"

The Heritage would never bury a body in that state. Corpses were always carefully washed and bandaged before they were placed against the ceiling of the burial chamber. Had this woman, like Stasia, entered the ice alive with fire? She bore no firesticks. She did not have visible vaerce, but Stasia was certain she was an Icer. Why hadn't she healed herself? Stasia was still trying to figure it out when Dynat fell.

He fell so quickly that Stasia did not see him drop, only saw the torch teeter in the air for a second after it left his hand. Her physical reflexes overrode her Icer's instincts and she reached out with her hands and caught the torch. The warm stone burned her skin, and the flame shrank as Dynat's warmth left it.

Stasia pressed the firestick into his hands and held her hands over his so it would not fall. There was not enough room in their tiny ice cave for him to have fallen prone; he slumped unconscious against the walls. Stasia remembered to breathe as his little warmth went into the torch and the flame sprang up again. If she had reached out with cold to grab the falling torch, the cold air would have chilled the firestone, and they would have been trapped.

She leaned against the wall opposite Dynat, pondering her options. She could help him hold the torch to the ground and try to tunnel back down. Going down should be easier, because he would not have to hold the firestick up, and they could crouch down. Surely the patrolling Flames would be gone by now.

But what if they weren't? Stasia looked back to the woman in white as if she held the answer, and noticed something strange. Just above her head, a single dark spot, red like the stain on her dress, hovered in the ice. Stasia's eyes travelled upward, and she saw a dark mote in the ice another ten feet or so above the woman, and above that, another tiny, dark spec.

Stasia looked at the woman's face again, and suddenly she understood. This woman had not died in Iskalon and been pressed up into the ice like the rest. She had come down through the ice, leaving a trail of blood behind her. Stasia was looking at one of the Ancestors, those who had come out of the Svardark and found Lake Lentok and given it to the Icers.

Or had she come from the Svardark? Nearly all of Stasia's dreams of V'lturhst led her up, to the Outer Tunnels or Burial Shafts—toward the Svardark. "V'lturhst and the Svardark are one and the same," she said aloud, and saying it, knew it to be true. This was what her Dream of the Burial Shaft was trying to tell her. V'lturhst had always been just a Burial Shaft away.

Stasia looked back at Dynat. He was still unconscious. The flame was sputtering again, imperiled by constant drips of water. Stasia reached down and transferred the torch so it sat in one hand, and took his free hand in hers. She pulled heat from his body into her own, and felt him shudder as she did so. She shuddered as well, fighting the nausea and weakness that always came with the heat.

With his heat coursing through her body, Stasia took the torch and held it aloft again. She let all the heat she could bear to feel run through the firestone and feed the flame. The ceiling began to melt again, and she could not split her focus between using heat T'Jas to keep the torch alive and using cold T'Jas to keep the melt water away from the flame. Instead she moved the torch back and forth, trying to predict where the next drop would fall. The burial ice continued to re-seal beneath her feet, pushing her and Dynat further up the shaft.

They travelled like this for longer than Stasia could imagine. It might have been hours; it might have been days. All around them, the burial ice shone with its constant, unique glow, independent of Icer T'Jas or Flame torch. Every ten feet or so, Stasia would see another drop of blood, and it would give her hope, just as her arm grew too weary, and her strength nearly faltered.

A time came when she had not seen a single drop of blood for many hours. She looked far up the shaft, wishing for an iceospectacle. Short, dark rods like spent firesticks rested in the ice, at least twenty feet above her head. Had the woman in white carried them, and had they extinguished and left her trapped, as Stasia's might?

But what she saw above renewed her strength. Far above, past the firesticks, past a layer of bright burial ice glow, lay a huge, dark shadow. It was like looking at the underside of one of the bridges from below the surface of the lake. If they kept going just a bit further, they would reach that darkness. Stasia renewed her efforts, though terror and doubt gnawed at her. What would she find? Would there be a world of legend up there, as her dreams had implied? Would she be able to find more firestone on V'lturhst, to return to Iskalon and help her people survive? Or would she run afoul of whatever had wounded the Ancestor, to fall back into the Burial Shaft, a corpse at last? She should not be doing this at all. She should have gone straight back out of the Burial Shaft, gone to find Glace and Larc and Casser and deliver Medoc's message about the Lake. But if she could find V'lturhst here, if the Outer Tunnels were not the way, and she had sent Casser in the wrong direction—she could find a new home for Iskalon, in V'lturhst. She was so close already. So she continued.

Finally, the torch penetrated the last of the burial ice and melted through something different. It was still ice, but it did not glow. Stasia shimmied her way up and rubbed her cheek against it, drawing the cold, testing it. The jolt of T'Jas felt good, but the torch weakened, so she pulled away. It was normal ice, though its composition was strange. It was as if someone had made a mound of powder ice and then pressed it down hard, until it was so compressed that it was nearly ice again. Stasia wondered why anyone would do such a thing. Why not just make ice in the first place?

She could tunnel through this with T'Jas. But they might need the torch, and the heat, to return through the burial ice. So she pressed the torch carefully into Dynat's hands. She released all of her heat back into him. He stirred a little. "Bolv?" he murmured. "Is it time to rise?"

Stasia shivered. She forced herself to picture her sisters again, charred and anguished. "Hold tightly to this, Flame. Keep it lit. Our lives depend on it." He slumped again, but when she released his hand, he held the torch steady. She drew cold from the compressed powder ice and tunneled through it at an angle, slanting gently upward so that she would not have to bear Dynat's full weight. The glow of burial ice shone through the normal ice beneath them for a time, then faded until they were surrounded by darkness lit only by the meager torch. Stasia did not see any more evidence of the woman in white, neither blood nor firesticks.

Sometime after the burial ice faded below them, perhaps an hour, perhaps longer, Stasia heard a rushing noise, like the roar of a river, only not so constant. It was faint at first, and she thought she was imagining it. But it grew louder, and Dynat's head lolled from shoulder to shoulder as if he heard it too. "Shush, Bolv," he muttered. "I'm trying to sleep." Then he was still once more.

It no longer sounded anything like a river to Stasia. It was unlike any noise she had ever heard, varying in tone and volume; the closest she could come to describe it was someone whistling and breathing loudly, yet magnified a hundred times over what a person's mouth could do. The sound grew louder and louder the further up they went. Soon it roared in Stasia's ears. The cold was growing more intense. It was easier to levitate Dynat and herself, and her tunneling went faster. She almost felt that she couldn't control it, that the cold was using her rather than the other way around. When the sound grew unbearable, they were rushing headlong straight up the powder ice. The ice grew softer and softer, until suddenly, it ended altogether, and Stasia and Dynat tumbled out of the narrow tunnel into a pitch-dark cavern.

The torch went out. A massive force struck against Stasia, knocking her to her knees on a floor of gritty powder ice. Everything was utter blackness. Powder ice swirled around them, pressed against them by that strange force. The sound roared in her ears, deafening, pushing against her skin like a giant, cold breath of air. Stasia felt tiny against it, as if it could blow her away like a pile of spore.

The cold was so incredibly intense that Stasia could not control it. It went to her like steel goes to magnet ore, froze her skin, entered her body, and overwhelmed her with power. If she could control the massive amount of cold flowing through her, Stasia could have brought the dead to life, could have destroyed the entire realm of Sholaen, could have frozen a thousand Lake Lentoks. She could have rendered the Lava River to cold stone in seconds. If she could control it.

She could not. The corners of her vision went dark as she began to pass out, a strange perception when the entire world around her was dark already. Her mind was compressed like the powder ice beneath her. She could sense Dynat beside her, huddled against the ground, nearly dead from the intense cold. He would die, leaving her alone in this strange place with no way to return home. Then she would die, overwhelmed and frozen to death by this force.

Propelled by terror, she fought through the pressing darkness and edged backward down the tunnel, out of direct contact with the blowing breath, pushing Dynat behind her. Shielded from the overwhelming power, she drew T'Jas from the surrounding powder ice and sealed off the entrance, blocking out the breath completely. Pressed against her enemy, she felt a moment of revulsion and panic. She widened the tunnel, raising a solid ice dome over their heads. When she was finished, there was room for both her and the Flame to lay flat without touching, with a hole at one end of the little ice cave that was the tunnel back to the Burial Shaft. The breath howled against the dome, furious at being shut out.

Stasia lay still for a long moment, staring into the darkness, breathing deep, even breaths. She had never felt so powerful and so helpless at the same time. It was terrifying and exhilarating. Part of her wanted more, wanted to shatter the dome and give herself completely to the power.

She reached out in the darkness and felt Dynat. The skin of his hand was cool, and he was breathing, but barely. Let him die, Stasia thought. It is more than he deserves. A merciful death, asleep in the powder ice.

She could let him slip away into the cold, but she would be alone in this strange, dark world without anyone, even an enemy, by her side. Only fire could penetrate the burial ice, and she did not have enough strength with heat T'Jas to return through the shaft alone. Without him, she would be trapped in this place forever. So much for finding a new home for Iskalon. If it was V'lturhst, it was not anything like her Dreams. Perhaps the Heritage was right; there was no V'lturhst, only Svardark, and the howling beast without must be the latter. Did Svardark lurk beyond the Outer Tunnels as well? Had she sent Casser and the refugees to face this unstoppable power? She had to get back to Sholaen, to call him back, if it was not already too late. For that she needed Dynat, healthy and warm.

She sat up and brushed the ice off her skin, then made an icelight, casting a soft blue glow over the ice cave. Dynat lay on his side. The powerful breath had blown the cloak part way off, leaving his legs exposed. His toes looked stiff and dark. Stasia drew cold and touched his feet, healing the freezing flesh. "I should let them freeze right off," she muttered. She hated the thought of wasting vaerce on his comfort.

The normal color returned and he stirred. "Cold," he gasped through clenched teeth.

Stasia pulled the cloak all the way off and laid it flat on the lumpy surface of powder ice. She rolled Dynat back onto it, lay next to him, and then rolled them both over, twice, until they were completely wrapped in the huge cloak. Then she released all her cold into the surrounding ice. Her icelights went out, and they lay in darkness once more.

The ice cave protected them from the raging monster that howled outside. It was relatively warm inside. Wrapped up in the cloak, the warmth of their bodies growing, Stasia's disgust at touching the Flame hastened her nausea. She tried to imagine it was Glace she held in her arms, or Casser, or Larc, or anyone except for this hideous person who had killed her family and destroyed her life. As the heat increased, darkness pressed down on her mind. She felt dull, and thinking became hard, as if she was looking at her thoughts through a thick layer of ice. She fought the lethargy. If she lost consciousness, the Fire King would surely wake, invigorated with heat, and kill her. She needed him, to return through the burial ice, but he would not need her, once he had gained enough heat to re-light the torch.

Perhaps he was warm enough now. Stasia wriggled an arm free and struggled with the cloak, clawing at it, trying to free her other arm to push her way out. Panic gripped her. Her limbs were like water, weak from the heat. She felt Dynat move against her. He was waking.

She renewed her struggles. Her body grew cold as he pulled the heat from her, and she started to draw T'Jas, but he pressed a palm against her forehead. "Stop moving," he said. "I can kill you in an instant."

She could not draw enough cold to stop him. Gripped by panic, Stasia fell back on the only trick she had: she drew T'Jas from the heat of Dynat's body and entered his mind.

Stasia and Dynat

The Fire Spirit exploded through his head as Stasia entered, flaming face burning relentlessly, dragging Dynat's mind into hers, joining them as one. In an instant, Dynat knew Stasia, and she knew him. Information poured forth, filling them so they thought they would burst.

The Fire Spirit heated him, bringing fire and light into the ice cave. Dynat held Stasia's forehead in his hands, trying to incinerate her brain, but the Fire Spirit stopped him. *Don't kill,* it said. *Find her Dreams.*

It forced him to look within her mind. He saw the charred heads of her sisters floating before his eyes, felt anguish at their deaths. Krevas buried under rubble, burned away to ashes, never to rest with the Ancestors in burial ice. Iskalon in ruins, destroyed by his insanity.

Stasia screamed as the Fire Spirit burned through her mind, a high-pitched wail that echoed off the ice and penetrated the howl of the giant breath battering her shelter. She tried to pull away from the burning deity, but its power held her fast. Unwillingly, she *knew* Dynat, knew intimately the adrenaline of the slink hunt, the pleasure of fighting and killing her sisters, the boiling hiss of the Fire Spirit's endless whispers.

Dynat tried to retreat. He did not want to know the Ice Queen any more than he wanted her to find his secrets. The Fire Spirit was too powerful. It pulled him further in, plundering her memories. He saw a large Semija male holding her hand, making her feel safe. He felt the loss of her family and too many friends to count. Underneath her cool exterior was a dervish of grief, anxiety, and anguish, explosive as Fireblood. In the depths of the Icer's mind, through the growing fury of the Fire Spirit's flames, Dynat saw a woman's face peering out from a heavy veil of fish scales. She had a pretty smile, scarred skin and golden eyes. *His* eyes. Why did she have *his* eyes?

Stasia struggled out of the blankets and crawled away from Dynat, huddling on the far side of the cave against bare ice. Dynat let her go, his limbs limp with shock. Her body convulsed with nausea and pain. She lit an icelight so she could see if he came after her. She tried to disengage, but the Fire Spirit held her mind in his teeth and would not let go. Helpless, Stasia dove back into Dynat's memories.

She saw Lianda's face as it looked in Casser's mind, but crisscrossed with glowing lava. Dark, dimpled cheeks loomed close, and lips brushed her forehead. "I'm so sorry, Son. I have to leave you, for a time. Be a good boy while I'm gone."

Then she was sitting on her mother's lap, looking into loving golden eyes. *How can that be? I was a babe when she left.*

"Mother?" Dynat whispered into the cave. The word echoed off ice and was lost in the howling fury. Together, deep in Dynat's memories, they saw Lianda's face in agony, flames wreathing her golden eyes, ashes drifting upward. Ashes strewn over Dynat's home. More and worse memories dislodged from the depths of his consciousness and drifted to the surface. Walking through Market, holding his father's hand; his father's head staring at him under the axe, eyes blank and empty.

Her mind full of fire and traumatic memories, Stasia struggled know the present. Dynat was weak, distracted; if she could gather enough T'Jas she could—what? Kill him?

Mother! He was screaming in his mind, lost in memory. *Don't leave me, Mother! Father! Where are you?*

Stasia tried to exorcise compassion. Another memory burst up, of the Fire Spirit: *Put aside the pain and live, Dynat. Take what you need, and forget the rest.* Flames exploding in his head when he tried to delay or disobey orders. Years of never being alone in his own mind. Darker and darker commands, until he was told to take the princesses and destroy Iskalon.

To take Stasia, the Dreamer. To destroy her home. Pity warred with hate. All the deaths of her family, brought about because a neglected, orphaned boy went mad from pain and loneliness and created a deity to keep himself safe. Or had he created it? Burning through her memories, the Fire Spirit seemed real as T'Jas.

Lianda's face surfaced again, golden eyes glowing with pain, and they both cried, "Mother!"

Confusion tore through their minds. In the ice cave, Dynat stood and stepped toward Stasia. Stasia drew cold from the ice, preparing to defend herself.

The Fire Spirit flared, and suddenly they were all Dreaming.

The ice cave grew vast, swallowed the howling monster, burst into color. A bright, yellow light shone from a vast blue ceiling. The cavern went on and on. Dynat thought that he could walk for days before touching a wall.

V'lturhst, Stasia thought.

Yesssss, the Fire Spirit hissed. And then?

The floor of the cavern was bare and dusty, the air hot. Stasia and Dynat were marched across it in high speed, racing over the dust without stirring it, the light on the ceiling running up and down the cavern walls, traveling across the apex of the ceiling. The dust under their feet turned green, with a texture like coarse fur. The fur grew tall like hair, and huge piles of rock and ice loomed on all sides. The Fire Spirit glowed with anticipation. Where? Where is it?

They stepped onto the rocks, and they were looking down over the green ground, searching. They became giants, and walked over the huge rocks, small to them as chunks of ore. They came to a river running over the floor, cutting a deep chasm.

The Dream faded like a slink slipping into shadow, and Stasia and Dynat stood facing each other in the dim cave, still linked, he wreathed in flames, she clutching the cold wall.

The Fire Spirit became an inferno, exploded in rage. *I know you have it, Dreamer! Show me! Show me your Dream!*

Stasia pushed at the flames, trying to banish them from her head. Her ears popped and her eyes bulged. The Fire Spirit clung to her, burning her core, probing every memory of every Dream she'd ever had. Dynat burned like a torch, his hardened, peeling lava starting to glow with heat. He raised a hand, and flames danced on his fingertips.

"I have to kill you," he said. "Fire Spirit, forgive me." *Mother,* he thought, *if I kill her, you'll be buried again in my mind and the pain will stop.*

Stasia sent an ice rope snaking out of her hands, but he melted it away. Ice daggers hurled at him fell in little sprays of water to the icy floor. Still bound to her mind, he anticipated her every move. She could anticipate him too, but his strategy was simply to push a wall of fire closer and closer until it swallowed her. Stasia considered making a globomb, but that would kill her too, in this cramped cave. Dynat's heat pressed into her, weakening her, draining her of cold T'Jas. She drew T'Jas from the heat, but couldn't conceive a clever way to use her meager abilities with it.

Dynat advanced, the thrill of the fight taking over his senses. The Fire Spirit didn't seem to care, it was buried in her memories like a worm burrowing blindly into rock. "You will die in fire, Sister," he said. "If your heart is pure, you will be with Mother in the Lava Lake."

Fury blinded Stasia. He dared call her Sister? He had killed her sisters one by one, he was about to destroy her, and he dared to be sanctimonious? It was too much. She would see his death if it killed her too. She abandoned her cold T'Jas and drew heat from his wall of fire. She reached for the ceiling with heat T'Jas. The ice dome began to crack and buckle, blowing away in a fine powder. The walls shattered, and the roaring force crashed into them both, blowing away Dynat's fire and all the warmth of the Fire Spirit.

Stasia screamed as burning cold seared her skin. Her icelight flickered and grew, until everything was blue instead of black, blindingly bright. Stasia tried to release T'Jas, but the power of immense cold dug into her bones, poured into her core, filled her completely, took away her control. Powder ice blew across her field of vision, blinding her.

Within Dynat's mind, the Fire Spirit shrieked. The sound made blood trickle out of Dynat's ears. Tiny shards of ice burned into his skin. Iceropes beyond Stasia's control snaked across his body, pulling away the cloak, strangling him.

Stasia could have escaped from his mind in the Fire Spirit's moment of weakness, but instead she began to terrorize Dynat from within, drawing up the most painful of his memories, forcing him to see them. A distant voice told her *stop, he's your only hope of returning home, you need him alive*, but she could not listen to reason through the volume of T'Jas pouring through her veins. Hatred overwhelmed her. She would hurt him as he had hurt her. Not just kill his body. She would destroy his soul first.

The Fire Spirit flared in his mind, burning white hot, trying to regain control of the battle, to give Dynat enough heat to combat her. *You!* Stasia raged at the deity. *You caused all of this, you took everything from me, it was your command.*

Within her mind, she blasted the flaming face with cold. The flames fled before her T'Jas, revealing a handsome, middle-aged man with dark hair, a mouth gaping in astonishment, startled brown eyes. A mole on one cheek. A tuft sticking out of one dark eyebrow. She knew with certainty she'd seen that face before, but couldn't think where. He made her think of ashes. She tried to enter his mind, but the face disappeared, leaving Dynat cold and alone and helpless before her.

Dynat was overwhelmed by a vast emptiness filled immediately with numb fear. Without the Fire Spirit, he would die in this cold waste. In the same instant, Stasia was startled out of her power-madness by her victory over the Fire Spirit, and knew that if Dynat died she would never return home.

She climbed on top of Dynat and struggled to cover him with the cloak. She fought to control the writhing iceropes. A thousand spikes of ice were driving into her brain. The cloak flapped across her body, as if it too had come to life, and was trying to get free. Desperate, Stasia tried to use T'Jas to form a cave around them. She imagined a smooth dome of ice rising from the ground.

T'Jas surged through her blood and the remnants of the original dome surrounding them exploded. The sound of cracking ice was even louder than the sound of the breath howling. Ice rose around them in jagged columns. Shards of ice pulled loose and whipped toward Stasia's head, and she crouched down, holding the cloak over her and Dynat, pushing it under his legs and arms.

Ice shards bruised Dynat through the hide. The rampant icelight was so bright it shone through layers of fur. Dynat saw his face in Stasia's mind, slick with blood, eyes wide in shock. Her heart thudded against his chest.

Then the cloak was wrenched from her hands once more, still wedged under his legs, flapping in the wild air, exposing her back. Colder than cold air rushed into the gap. Her icelight flickered, a bright chunk of ice sped toward her face. She ducked, but pain blossomed on her scalp, spreading into her skull, and darkness crept into the corners of her vision. She slumped over Dynat's body and awareness faded.

Maia

Maia sat in her egla, listening to the storm rage around the traveling camp. Four winters had passed since Hakua had become chief of the Liathua Khell, and they had been mild, almost not worthy of the long trek to the mountains. This winter had seemed until now as if it would be as gentle as the others. Maia had not seen this harsh spring storm in the bones, and she had supported Hakua's decision to start for Pebble Beach early. Two days out, they were surprised by a fiercer storm than Maia had ever known. A traveling camp was erected hastily, but even so five hunters and two boareal were lost to the ice, separated from the tribe by blinding, howling snows.

Hakua and the warriors had blown the horns nearly nonstop, hoping to guide the hunters back in, but to no avail. Maia overheard whispers about her abilities fading. She was only twenty-five winters old, young for a healer, and she had been Healer for nearly ten winters. Over-use of the bones, gossiping mothers said, as if they knew anything about it. Maia ignored them. The bones did not always predict the weather, even storms that killed five members of the tribe, she told Hakua. She did not tell him that she too had been lulled by the mild winters, and hadn't cast the bones since they left Pebble Beach in autumn. She took her pouch out now, stoking the embers of the fire. With luck, she would learn if any more people would be lost in these storms before they reached the coast. Or if the tribe should turn back, and huddle longer at the base of the mountains.

Ten grandfathers and grandmothers shared her egla, and they all leaned in when she spread the little grass mat and flung the urchin spine powder into the flames. The tribe had been pressed to set up the egla quickly and were not able to build a full camp, so all the dwellings were as crowded as hers. She had ordered that the elderly be placed with her so they would be near, if they needed tending, and because they seemed to be immune to the effects of urchin.

Maia breathed in the pungent smoke, then flung the bones out over the mat as she had done many times. They scattered in a pattern she had never seen. All bones but two fell off the edge of the mat, scattering on the icy floor. Two bones, one brown with age, the other nearly white, stood on end on the center of the mat, like two people standing on the ice. They were close, but did not touch.

"Time flying closer like a Dhuciri bird. Come, they come, to rescue us all from the coming darkness. The hide is torn and they come. Cold, cold coming to rescue us. He burns like fire. He burns me. He burns—" Maia shrieked. *Dhuciri were coming toward her from the walls of the egla. Dark figures, draped in feathers, turning the grandfathers and grandmothers to dust.* "Crossbones," *she whimpered.* "Rescue us."

The figures stopped mid-motion. She squeezed her eyes shut, but could not shut them out. They hovered on her eyelids, dark red. "Come, rescue me." *She heard Hakua's horn in the distance, saw the storm swirling around the egla. She crawled out of the entrance. The storm tore at her furs but did not touch her skin. Her eyes were still closed, and the Dhuciri followed her through the walls of the egla, into the storm.*

She walked toward the beaches, away from the mountains. The broad white peaks faded behind her until she stood in the middle of the icy plain. The storm continued to rage around her, driving shards of ice into her skin, sending her to her knees on the snow again and again. Again she struggled to her feet and trekked on. At last she saw a great dome, a giant egla, its edges smooth, no seams where blocks of ice come together. A fire burned within. It let off neither smoke nor flame. She reached inside the walls and took the fire inside her.

"The fire will rescue us," Maia whispered. *The child of ice sat inside the dome, full of power, drunk on it. She swelled bigger than the dome itself. The dome shattered and the fire went out.* "No. They must survive. They must rescue us."

When Maia awoke, the storm had abated and Hakua was striking camp. A grandmother fed her a replenishing broth while her egla was deconstructed around her. She rose shakily and went immediately to Hakua. He was strapping his mate's heavy boxes of shells onto their pack boareal. "We must make for the beach," Maia said without greeting. "There will be another storm, greater than this one. But we must travel swiftly over the ice, blowing the horns all the way. There are survivors between us and the beach."

"Some of the five?" Hope glistened in Hakua's wind-watery eyes. His hood was pushed back and he struggled with the ropes as the boareal shifted. Maia went to the beast's neck and stroked it soothingly.

"I don't think so. Someone from another tribe, perhaps. But we must rescue them. I have seen this in the bones."

"But the storm that is coming. Will we lose even more people? It's no good finding survivors to take for the tithing if we lose our people in the process." He grunted as he yanked on the ropes, testing the load. Maia stepped closer.

"I know it sounds odd. But you must trust me. Trust the bones." She did not tell him that they must not give these survivors in the tithe. There would be time enough for that argument later.

"Hakua . . !" His mate was calling. Maia grinned. He had stolen her from another tribe last summer, and she kept him on his toes. She was an expensive trophy, beautiful but demanding.

"Very well. Kaliri has been at me to get down to the beach early. She wants to get the best shells before the other tribes arrive. We will head beach-ward, not turn tail like frightened doal and run for the mountains."

Maia breathed a sigh of relief, and wasted no time mounting her own boareal and urging it forward. As the camp pulled out, spreading into a long line of doal sleds, boareal and walkers moving across the ice, Hakua's horn began to blow long, clear notes into the deceptively mild spring day.

Dynat

Dynat woke in a vast blue cavern, in agony and shivering cold. His back, lying unprotected against the ice, was completely numb. Stasia lay over him, emanating a tiny bit of body heat. His cloak trapped her heat against his chest. She was unconscious, barely breathing. Her breath and his own were the only sounds.

The ceiling was not the dark blue of an icelight, or the black blue of the Icer's lake, or even the mysterious purple blue of a Burial Shaft, but a light, soft blue that Dynat had never seen before. Toward the apex, a single feature marred the blueness, a perfectly round white sphere that looked like the ghost of a ball. Toward the floor of the great dome, blue faded to hazy white, almost pink. A few feet away, a circle of twisted columns of ice, like a sculpture made by an insane Icer, towered all around.

Help me, he called to the Fire Spirit, but there was no answer. For the first time in memory, he was completely alone in his own mind, cold and empty and desolate as the huge cavern he lay in. *Please come back. I can still kill her.*

Only silence followed the plea, accompanied by loneliness so deep Dynat thought he would drown in it. He remembered Stasia's cold power blowing the flames off the Fire Spirit's face, revealing an ordinary man, darkly handsome, with startled eyes. How could a deity feel surprise? Had Stasia defeated the Fire Spirit?

It was inconceivable, but the evidence was in the absence. Whether the Fire Spirit was destroyed or merely fled, Dynat was utterly alone, in a wild cold cave with no source of heat. He could kill her when the opportunity arose, but right now Stasia was his only hope for survival.

He willed his legs to move, but they did not. His arms were too weak to lift. He nudged the little Icer with his chin. "Wake up, Stasia." Perhaps she could make a shelter. At the least, she could heal his back. He thought the skin must be dead from the cold. Dead. He would be dead soon. He could feel his strength to resist the cold ebbing away.

Stasia did not stir. Dynat tried again, digging his chin into the top of her head, with no success. He yelled in her ear, convulsed so that her body shook, but nothing woke her. Frustrated by a feeling of helplessness, he lay back and stared up at the vast blue ceiling.

Far in the distance, a sound rose and grew. It was a low, vibrating sound; it swelled loudly and faded slowly away. It rose and fell, rose and fell, over and over again. Dynat listened, entranced. It sounded like music, a sound made with a purpose, not something natural like the dripping of water or the roar of the lava river.

The sound meant there were people in this huge cavern. He was going to die if he lay on the ice much longer, and Stasia was still unconscious. People might have heat, might be able to rescue him. Then he would not need Stasia in order to survive. Dynat took a deep breath and screamed at the top of his lungs.

Stasia did not stir at the sound. Dynat kept shouting and screaming until his throat grew hoarse and his lungs hurt from breathing cold air. When he stopped, he heard the vibrating sound again. Rising, falling, rising, falling. He kept shouting.

The noise grew perceptibly louder and nearer. Dynat began to hear other noises—loud barking, a scraping sound like hides being dragged over ice, and the high, chattering voices of people. He could not make out any words, even when he heard a shout right above his head. He looked up and saw a hideous creature staring down at him. A long nose like a fat arm protruded from its face. Its forehead bulged over beady black eyes, and long white tusks jutted over its lips, slicing the air above Dynat's nose. He gulped a deep breath to keep from screaming. Then, the face was passing, and Dynat saw its bulky body shuffle close by. It was twice the size of an Icer's molebear, and its hide bristled with brittle, sparse hairs. It wallowed over the ice with a humping motion on fat, stubby legs that seemed ill-designed to carry its massive weight. On its back, nestled in the crook just behind its head, sat a stout human with a dark face, covered head to toe in tan-colored, shaggy hides. He looked warm.

"Thank the Fire Spirit," Dynat gasped. "I'm saved."

The man reached down and grasped Dynat's cloak. He yanked it free and examined it, then draped it over his own shoulders. "Hey!" Dynat yelled. "Stop! Too cold!"

The man ignored him and lifted Stasia into the air. He settled her across his knees on the back of the beast and raised a hollow tusk to his mouth. The vibrating sound rang out so loud it hurt Dynat's ears. The creature swung its head back and forth and brayed like a cababar fem in heat. It shuffled on its way, leaving Dynat alone on the ice, exposed to the cold air. He shivered convulsively, shouting at the man, rewarded only by a spray of powder ice from the creature's broad, flat tail.

Then another ugly nose was snuffling at his face, tusks nearly skewering his eyes. The rider who leaned toward Dynat had softer features and long braids glinting with green gems. Her hides were white as the ice and soft as steam from the baths. And warm. He wanted to bury himself in them. "Please," he said, shamed to his core to have to beg a human. "Please. I need warmth."

She made nonsensical sounds at him, braced herself against her steed with her thighs, and grasped his arm. She pulled him off the ground, huffing from the effort. He let her lay him across the creature's back without struggle. He knew from their clothing that her people needed warmth. They must have a fire somewhere.

It did not occur to him to wonder if they were friendly.

Epilogue

Resignation

Glace

Glace stood on the shore of Lake Lentok by the training grounds, staring out over still waters, when First chime sounded, ringing clearly across the city. He did not move during the whole sounding. His armor and weapons lay in a heap at his feet, and cold water beaded over his skin and dripped down his legs, tickling him where it ran. Several months had passed since he had returned to Iskalon, and the lake was finally clean enough for swimming, after the remaining Icers had worked every chime of the waterclock to dredge out the bodies and skim off the Fireblood. The city behind him was still in ruins, but he could hear the sounds of building as it was reconstructed stone by stone, house by house.

Glace did not feel refreshed or renewed by his dive. He had not eaten breakfast, but he felt ill, as if something wasn't sitting well in his stomach. He watched the first boats of the Fisher Guild drift out from the shore, their long poles casting ripples on the still surface, ripples that bumped into each other in a chaotic motion. It looked so ordinary that he could hardly believe there had been a war, that he had been a slave. That Stasia was gone. The normalcy made his heart ache. In a moment, he would have to move. He would have to gather his weapons and don his armor and walk onto the training square and pretend as if nothing had changed.

Everything had changed. The words of the scribe ran through his head over and over again, as they had every day since the return to Iskalon. *You are all Semija. You think you are free? If you ever return to your life, ask your mistress to let you go. See what she says. See if she treats you any different from one of her pets. They are all the same, Flame, Icer.*

Stasia is not the same as a Flame, he told himself, stooping and pulling his heavy leather armor over his head. A Flame does not even recognize me as human. A Flame sees me as an animal, a pet, nothing more than a cababar to be bred and trained and beaten.

Those thoughts did not make his heart any lighter. If Stasia were here to ask, he would not have bothered; he would never have asked to leave her side. But now the Warrior Guild held no purpose for him. He thought of the scribes and their monumental tasks of sorting and repairing the plates found in the rubble. Glace could be useful there, with his knowledge of the plates from the Palace Library.

Larc had not removed him as Captain, though he no longer had a Royal to watch over or a Guard to command. Glace wondered how long that would last. Would he be assigned to whoever was chosen as the new Royal Family? Larc was convinced that Stasia lived, that Medoc still held her prisoner, but Larc had not lived in Chraun and heard the rumors that the Fire King had been killed by the dangerous Icer prisoner. Stasia would not have been suffered to live under those accusations. If she had escaped, she would have returned to Iskalon by now. No, Stasia was dead and gone, and it was time for Glace to move on.

Resolved, he picked up his spiked mace and tucked it into the loop on his belt. He left grief and a puddle of lake water on the shore, and went to speak with the Regent. Musche, who had showed up after Glace's third day back at the lake, shadowed him through the city. That, at least, had not changed.

It was early yet, before Council, and Larc could be found at this time in the room she had ordered built off the throne room in the new Palace, a replica of Krevas' old study. Glace walked through heavy ice doors and past the empty throne of Iskalon, saluting the Icer guards who stood at the entrance. They saluted back. Glace's muscles tensed as he walked past them, and he imagined the sting of a firewhip across his back. They are not Flames, he reminded himself. Icers don't hurt us. That Sem—that scribe was wrong.

Larc was shifting through a stack of gold plate and muttering to herself when he entered. She looked up distractedly and Glace bowed low, a bow worthy of a Queen. He hoped they left her as Regent, or at least kept her on as an advisor. She did not have the same flair for drama as royalty, but in his opinion that was only another asset to accompany her wisdom and leadership.

"What is it, Glace?" She suppressed a yawn that garbled her first words. "I thought we already had a Gendarme meeting yesterday. Do you have something new to report?"

Glace watched her for a moment. She clenched a gold plate in her hand. Her thick hair was messy, as if she'd just risen, but her eyes bore the deep circles of one who hadn't slept in days. They flickered from him to the inscriptions before her.

Glace reached across his back and unstrapped both of his long-swords. The room warmed slightly; she was looking at him attentively now, a frown marring her pretty face. Was her reaction merely reflex for an Icer, or did she truly think he would harm her?

Glace laid both swords on the floor and unbuckled the heavy belt that held his axe, mace, and several of his larger knives. The belt and weapons joined the swords. He stooped and took the knives out of his boots, the little daggers hidden in his armor, until every weapon he owned sat on the floor. Or had he really owned them? They were property of the Royal Family, like everything else, his room in the Palace, his armor, perhaps even himself.

"What is this, Glace?" Larc brushed back her bangs and set the plate down with a little *clack*. Glace removed the top portion of his armor and set it on the weapons, but stopped there. It would not be appropriate to disrobe to his small clothes before the Regent. He could turn in his leather skirt-of-armor later.

"I hereby resign my post as Captain of Guard to the Royal Family. I hereby withdraw from the Warrior Guild. I will draft a formal notice of withdrawal for Kiner."

Larc's face fell and she looked lonely and terrified. Then the emotions washed from her face as if they had never been, replaced by the same firm set of jaw she showed in Council. "Glace, don't be absurd. Resign? You can't resign. I need you. I wasn't planning on replacing you. I will appoint you as Captain of my Guard until Stas—until we have a Royalty again. You will continue to lead the human Warriors. I need you to gain and train new recruits. You must make our army strong again."

"Is that a command?" Glace pressed quietly. "If I insist, will you command that I stay?"

She was silent for a time, staring at the wall behind him, eyes unfocused. Then she said, "If I must, I will. Iskalon needs you, Glace. As a Warrior, not as a guildless has-been. If we are to stand any chance against Chraun, we must put all of our assets to best use."

There was regret in her eyes. He felt foolish, standing half-naked beside a pile of weapons. Of course she would not let him go. Of course he must keep fighting for Iskalon. The war was over, but the threat had not passed.

Glace stared at her for another moment, then picked up his armor and donned it again, started tucking away his weapons. Larc's shoulders sagged with relief and she picked up her plate again as if he wasn't there.

It felt so much like the Flame woman's treatment of him, as if he were a piece of furniture, that he shuddered. He was shaking so hard he could barely do the straps on his swords. He left without bowing and took deep breaths that barely filled his chest when he reached the hall. He felt like he was drowning in the lake. When he had calmed himself, he headed for the training square. His mind squirmed with questions. He would continue to fight for Iskalon. But what was he fighting for? A nation of slaves, worse off than Semija? At least the Semija knew they were slaves. In Iskalon, the slavery of humans *was* disguised under a structure of Guilds and a pretense of Council. Yes, amenities were better, they weren't beaten or sold or bred against their will. But they were not truly free.

Glace had his answer. In the training square, Icer and human warriors alike saluted him as a Captain, but he knew what he really was.

The End

The tale continues in Dreams of QaiMaj: Book II

Glossary

Ancestors: In the theology of Iskalon, the Ancestors are worshiped as deities. Iskaloners believe the Ancestors came from the Svardark and made Lake Lentok their home. They fashioned the burial shafts to protect them from the mysterious dangers of the Svardark. The Ancestors are considered to be at once the physical predecessors of the current Icers of Iskalon, as well as god-like beings with unimaginable powers. For example, Queen Cataya's blood is said to run in the royal family, but Cataya herself is worshiped as an Ancestor.

Antahua: Healer of the Liathua Khell.

Blissi: A fermented beverage made from the saccharine fruit of the bliss fungi.

Boareal: A large mammal in Khell, with a long, bulbous snout, and a thick, bristling hide. They have sharp tusks and four sturdy feet with vestigial flippers for toes.

Burial Shafts: Long veins of ice rising from Sholaen. According to Iskalon theology, the Ancestors used T'Jas in a way now forgotten to make them impenetrable by T'Jas. Only the dead can enter. Iskaloners bury their dead in the shafts to protect the living from the Svardark.

Cababar: Cababar are giant, meaty rodents bred for meat in Iskalon and Chraun. They are nearly hairless in Chraun, but the Iskalon variety is covered with velvety, pale fur. They also give milk.

Cadet Tejusi: A young Flame who carries messages for Medoc.

Captain Glace: A human Warrior of great renown, the Captain of Stasia's Guard.

Chief Lubar: Chief of the Liathua Khell and father of Hakua.

Chime: A unit of time in Iskalon; when the first hour in a twelve hour cycle passes through the water clock a chime sounds over the city; each consecutive hour adds a chime. For example at Fifth Chime, five chimes sound.

Chirat: A hoofed animal of Iskalon with a thick, soft fur, the fibers are spun and woven into fabric. It requires a cold environment for their fleece to develop, therefor they are not found in Chraun. Chirat are very valuable, highly prized animals, kept with utmost care. They are fed on bluecap mushrooms, which may contribute to the blue-violet color of their fur.

Chirsh: The wool gathered from the chirat; it is thin-spun into garments for humans, as well as felted, soaked and frozen into thick armor for Icers.

Chraun: The Kingdom of fire in the bowels of Sholaen.

Colonel Kiner: An Icer Colonel in the Iskalon army.

Councilor Cygnet: The representative of the Gem Guild on the Council of Iskalon.

Councilor Mowat: Council representative of the Livestock Guild.

Councilor Wyfus: Representative of the Fishing Guild and also the Speaker for the Council, undoubtedly the most politically powerful human in Iskalon.

Dhuciri: A mysterious pale race; they ride giant black birds and take a tithe from the tribes of the Khell.

Doal: Doal are a land animal of Khell. They have small, muscular canine bodies, with sleek, thick, waterproof fur. They have long, flat feet that keep them above soft snow. The people of Khell keep them as pets and use them to draw sleds, though they will also eat doal if they must. Doal have a large double flap of skin as a tail, thought to be a vestigial tailfin from when they were swimming animals.

Doaltooth Mountains: A mountain range that cuts across the continent of Khell and provides shelter for animals and tribes in the winter storms.

Dream: Also Dreamer, Dreaming; a talent of T'Jas that is very rare; it is the ability to have prophetic Dreams. The last recorded Icer with the talent was Queen Cataya; Princess Stasia is the only one since her to be born with it. The Flames have no record of any Dreamers, although there are allusions to Khanten being a Dreamer.

Egla: The Khell term for dwelling; it can be a winter egla, built from thick blocks of ice, or a traveling egla built from boareal hides and bones, or a summer egla which is a combination of ice and hides.

Fire Spirit: The sole deity in the theology of Chraun, the Fire Spirit dwells in the Lava Lake. According to Chraunian legends, he cast the Flames out of the Lava Lake long ago, sending them up the Lava River to make a new home.

Fireblood: A thick, black, flammable liquid used by Chraun in battle.

Firerope: A construction of T'Jas used by Flames, it burns but is also hard at its core, so that it can bind things. It adheres to itself, so that tying is not necessary.

Firesticks: Sticks made from coal that burn easily but slowly; Chraun uses them for torches and other utilities where a long burning, steady flame is needed.

Firewhip: Similar to firerope, but a firewhip has less substance and more fire. It is intended to inflict pain, as when used on Semija, or to kill, as when used in battle against Icers.

Flames: A race that can draw T'Jas from heat and use it to accomplish feats beyond ordinary human capability.

Flats: Small, flightless rodents with vestigial wings; they crawl across tunnel walls eating bugs. Their guano is important in fungal culture.

General Medoc: The current General of Chraun.

General Zental: The current General of Iskalon.

Globomb: A weapon used rarely by Icers. It is a ball of ice fashioned to explode when it comes into contact with heat. Its T'Jas construction traps a huge amount of energy in a small space, and when the energy is released it explodes, sending shards of ice shooting at very high speeds through the vicinity.

Glowmold: A fungus that grows in the fungal caverns of Chraun. It radiates UV light, which causes the fungi growing under it to produce vitamins essential to the survival of the animals of Chraun. In Iskalon, burial ice serves a similar function.

Grimshore: The shore on Lake Lentok where the Fishing Guild processes their catch.

Guildless: Those not included in any Guild of Iskalon, whether by birth, by choice, or rejection from a Guild. They live in a tunnel on the outskirts of Lake Lentok and beg for food and clothing.

Hakua: Son of the chief of the Liathua Khell.

Hali: A guildless refugee appointed as a messenger after the war.

Heritage: The religious sect in Iskalon. They are responsible for keeping the traditions of Cataya alive as well as maintaining the Burial Shafts.

Hippole: Hippole are an animal found exclusively in Chraun. They are kept for meat, milk, and their large, extremely soft hides.

Icelight: A cold, blue light produced by Icers using T'Jas. Icelight is the only source of light in Iskalon, since no fire is allowed. Icelights can be "set" with T'Jas to last days or even weeks, so that the Icer does not have to be present in order for the icelight to function. They can be small or large, bright or dim. They can be different colors, but Icers tend to prefer blue because of its cool feeling. An icelight has no substance, but preserved ones are placed in glass spheres to give humans something to hold onto, or anchored onto something like a wall or ceiling.

Iceospectacle: A long tube with glass lenses used to view objects high up in Burial Shafts.

Icerope: A freezing cold, hard but flexible substance made from T'Jas and used by Icers in battle. It can be used in the same way that firerope and firewhips are used.

Icers: A race able to draw T'Jas from cold and use it to accomplish feats beyond ordinary human capability.

Iskalon: The kingdom of ice between Chraun and the wild Outer Tunnels.

Jewelsnake: A small but bright snake, deadly poisonous but covered with beautiful markings that glimmer like gems. They are especially dangerous to children who reach for them thinking they are picking up a pretty jewel. They are carefully raised by the people of Chraun, and their skins are used for baskets, rugs, and even Semija clothing.

Khell: Refers both to the icy continent of Khell and the people who inhabit it, the Khell.

King Bretle Antah: King of Chaun, deceased; Dynat inherited the throne from him through peaceful family succession.

King Dynat Sikur Antah: Defender of Chraun, Prince of Flames, Keeper of the Lava River, True Ruler of all Sholaen, Chosen of the Fire Spirit. The current King of Chraun.

King Khanten: The first King of Chraun, deceased, founder of the nation.

King Krevas: King of Iskalon, father to Stasia and the other princesses of Iskalon, brother to Casser.

King Ritnu: King of Chraun before Bretle, deceased, overthrown.

King Rodev: King of Chraun before Ticol, deceased,

overthrown.

King Ticol: King of Chraun before Ritnu, deceased, overthrown.

Kinyara: A royal and sacred relation to the King of Chraun. The role is always filled by a female cousin; if there is no female cousin the man cannot be King. She is his lover and advisor, and if they have children, the children are sent across the Lava River to the Acolyte caverns to become Acolytes of the Fire Spirit. She also sees to the politics of the kingdom, making sure that it runs smoothly, while the King attends to the larger matters, like war.

Kinyara Bolv: Current Kinyara of Chraun.

Kinyara Zedya: First Kinyara of Chraun, cousin to King Khanten. It is said that she created the role when she came to Chraun with Khanten and his wife, not wanting to be shunted aside politically.

Lady Larc Chan: An Icer; prominent debater in the Iskalon Council, also best friend to Princess Stasia.

Lady Lianda: A Flame who sought refuge from persecution by King Ritnu in Chraun by coming to Iskalon and throwing herself on the mercy of King Krevas.

Lake Lentok: The enormous lake on which the island city of Iskalon is located. The total distance across, including the island, is two miles. The lake teems with fish and other water-dwelling creatures like mollusks, squid, and crabs. It is crossed by four long suspension bridges. The cavern in which the lake sits slopes slightly upward toward the Outer Tunnels, and a network of streams and rivers pour off the top of it, running down pipe-tunnels toward Chraun. Its basin is sustained by melt-springs from the burial chambers above the city.

Lakehide: A kind of soft, shiny leather made from fishskins pounded and treated with fat.

Lava mesh: All Flames carry a second set of veins in the outer layer of their skin; this is patterned according to the Flame's individual preference and filled with lava which keeps them hot at all times and gives them a source of T'Jas. When Flames venture into regions so cold that they know their lava will harden, they drain the lava, leaving a ghost mesh behind, then refill it later.

Lava River: A river of pure, molten lava that runs through Chraun in a deep crevasse. On the far side lies the mysterious caverns of the Acolytes of the Fire Spirit. The rest of Chraun sits across the river from these caves, connected only by one bridge, which is guarded by the Acolytes. Royalty and Nobles own the caves closest to the Lava River, many of them with balconies and rooms overlooking it, while the common Flames and Semija live in cooler caves further away.

Liathua Khell: A tribe of Khell who summer on Pebble Beach and winter in the middle range of the Doaltooth Mountains.

Lord Barrett: Lord of the baths, he is a wealthy Chraunian Noble who owns much of the property the baths are situated on and collects fees from the other Nobles who use them.

Lord Bralon: Lady Larc's older brother.

Lord Garn: Another Chraunian Noble, owner of a large gaming pit where Flames watch and gamble on Semija fights.

Luten Renault: The Luten General of Chraun, second in command to General Medoc.

Maia: A girl born of the Nuambe Khell and taken in by the Liathua Khell.

Molebear: Shaggy and strong, molebear are the largest mammal in Sholaen. They are slow and lumbering but there are none better for hauling heavy loads. The wild molebear of the Outer Tunnels are smaller and more fierce than their domesticated cousins. They are used only in Iskalon; Chraun is too warm for them. Domestic molebear are gentle with a sweet disposition and small, blunt horns. They have very strong claws and can tunnel short distances through solid rock. They use their long noses to reach into crevices after insects, fungi, and even snakes.

Musche: Glace's slink companion.

Neithild: A large spider domesticated in Iskalon, trained to weave silk garments on plaster forms. They are property of the Weaver Guild and they produce all the websilk for Iskalon. They are very smart creatures and highly trainable. It is said that they form lifelong relationships with their owners and cannot be transferred. Neithild are also kept by a small subset of the Fishing Guild, the Net-weaving Guild, who use them to weave fishing nets.

Nuambe Khell: A Khell tribe of the north coast, Maia's birth-tribe.

Outer Tunnels: A wilderness adjacent to Iskalon, in the upper reaches of Sholaen. The Outer Tunnels are geologically unstable and full of dangerous animals; for this reason, they are not typically inhabited by humans. They are too cold for Flames and too warm for Icers. In spite of all this, the Iskaloners, humans and Icers alike, have scouted and mapped them to the farthest reaches. Several miles past the mines, the Outer Tunnels grow steep, narrow, and dangerously unstable, so no one has scouted past this point.

Pitvipers: A small, deadly snake in Sholaen that lurks in cracks in the rock and strikes rapidly.

Powderlux: The blue, powdery spores of the luxignor fungus, which, needing heat, grows exclusively in Chraun. The fungus itself is a mild narcotic, a delicacy that leaves the diner feeling warm and stimulated, but the chemical is concentrated in the spores which, when smoked, dulls the senses and brings on a heady euphoria. The smoking of powderlux is frowned on in Chraun society, but many Nobles and commoners alike indulge in the privacy of their caves.

Prince Casser: Prince of Iskalon, brother to King Krevas, Stasia's Uncle.

Princess Jelina: A princess of Iskalon, second in line to the throne.

Princess Lotica: A princess of Iskalon, third youngest.

Princess Maudit: Eldest princess of Iskalon.

Princess Pasten: Second youngest princess in Iskalon, Stasia's twin sister.

Princess Roila: A princess of Iskalon, third oldest after Jelina; elder twin of Senlei.

Princess Senlei: A Princess of Iskalon, fourth oldest after

Roila, younger twin of Roila.

Princess Seraph: Princess of Iskalon, fourth youngest.

Princess Stasia: Youngest princess of Iskalon, twin of Pasten.

Queen Cataya: The first Queen of Iskalon, thought to be an Ancestor, founder of the city.

Queen Rashesh: Latest Queen of Iskalon, Krevas's bride, mother to the princesses. Deceased.

Raihan: Pale and softly glowing, raihan are small cave ungulates that can navigate very fast through pitch-dark tunnels. Humans, mainly the messenger branch of the Scribe Guild, ride them when they need to move swiftly over long distances.

Rockfall: A heavy rockslide that causes an extensive cave-in.

Semija: The humans who live in Chraun and serve the Flames.

Serg Glint: A human Warrior serving on Stasia's Guard under Glace.

Serg Kabre: An Icer leading raids after the war.

Sholaen: The term for the entire region including Chraun, the Spiral Tunnel, Iskalon, the Outer Tunnels, and their surroundings.

Slink: A large feline inhabitant of Sholaen with sleek dark hair and huge eyes. They live wild in the Outer Tunnels, preying on rootingshrew and flats. Females are kept as pets by people of Iskalon. Wild slink descend to the Spiral Tunnel to breed, where they are hunted by Flames. Wild males are fiercely territorial and have a strong musk smell about them.

Solph River: A fresh-water river in Chraun that feeds the baths and their drinking water supply.

Stalam: Columns of rock deposits descending from the ceiling.

Stalas: Columns of rock deposits growing from the floor.

Stormbirth Waters: The oceans surrounding Khell.

Svardark: The dangerous dark place or creature from which Iskalon, according to its theology, must be protected. Lake Lentok is a refuge from the Svardark, and the Ancestors buried in the Burial Shafts, along with the recently dead, protect Iskalon from the Svardark. No Iskaloner is certain exactly what it is, just that it is horribly dangerous. See also V'lturhst.

T'Jas: The power or force that enables Icers and Flames to accomplish feats not possible for ordinary humans. Icers draw T'Jas from cold, Flames from heat. T'Jas use is directly proportional to the lifespan of Icers and Flames alike; the more you use, the shorter your life. For this reason, it tends not to be used frivolously.

The Spiral Tunnel: A long, winding tunnel that connects Iskalon to Chraun. It is about five miles from the border of Chraun to the top of the Spiral.

Tog: A slang term use by the guildless for the tunnel they live in; acronym of "tunnel of guildless."

V'lturhst: A place referred to in ancient Iskalon legends. Roughly translated from an older tongue, the word itself means "land of dangerous beauty." According to the legends it is a bright, vast cavern. Some Heritage theologians believe that Svardark and V'lturhst were actually two sides of one deity, Svardark being the dark, destructive side, and V'lturhst being the light, beautiful side.

Vaerce: When Icers are born, they are unable to draw T'Jas. When they begin to exhibit their powers, their skin becomes covered in a soft blue glow. As they grow physically, the uniform glow cracks and spreads over the skin, becoming tiny blue glowing dots. These dots are called vaerce, and Icers gauge their lifespan in terms of their vaerce; as they age, the vaerce fade.

Websilk: The silk produced by neithild spiders for garments in Iskalon.

Zirc: A soft, readily available metal used by both Iskalon and Chraun as coin. Zirc also refers to the minted coin; for example: this necklace cost me thirty zirc.

The Armies of Iskalon & Chraun

Iskalon's Warrior Guild: Is comprised of Icers and humans and contains a large standing army. This is the only Guild open for other Guildsmen to join. Every Icer is required to serve a year of conscription in the Warrior Guild. Humans are not required but encouraged. The Guild is structured like this:

Gendarme: The Gendarme is a branch of the Army that serves as the civil police force. They enforce the rulings of the Council and keep the peace. A branch within the Gendarme comprises the Royal Guard. In times of need, the Gendarme is folded into the fighting force to protect Iskalon.

Officers: Both Icers and humans hold these titles unless noted otherwise.

> **Marshal:** Honorary Warrior title given to the King or Queen.
> **General:** The Warrior commander of highest rank, after the Marshal
> **Brigad:** Commands segments of the Warrior Guild under the direction of the General. Royalty often serves in this capacity.
> **Colonel:** Commands smaller segments of Warriors, directs group maneuvers.
> **Luten Colonel:** Commands Cubes under the Colonel.
> **Captain:** Commands Gendarme segments.
> **Luten:** Commands platoons and small strike forces.
> **Cadet:** Officer in training.

Warriors:

> **Serg:** Oversees other Warriors. Reports to Luten.
> **Scout:** Does tunnel reconnaissance. Some scouts are highly specialized and even spy as Semija. Though they are not Officers, a good scout is respected by officers.

Corp: An experienced and specialized Warrior who has not been promoted to an officer or Serg.

Warrior: The lowest denominator, the basic fighting unit. They comprise the largest segment of the army, and are mostly humans. Icers start as Warriors but they are quickly promoted as Officers if they continue past the year of conscription.

Structure of the Warrior Guild:

Warrior Guild: Commanded by the General.

Brigade: Roughly four different segments of the Guild, each is commanded by the Brigad.

Regiment: About a quarter of a Brigade, each is commanded by a Colonel.

Cube: About a quarter of a Regiment, commanded by the Luten Colonel. Cubes rarely maneuver alone, they usually work together as a regiment.

Platoons: Smaller strike forces, commanded by Lutens.

Raid: The smallest strike force; it works under a Serg or Corp who has been instructed by a Luten. It does not necessarily mean that a raid's function is to raid; it is a colloquial term.

The Army of Chraun: Chraun has a huge standing army. Most of the Officers are Noble, although a clever common Flame can work his way up through the ranks. All Officers and Warriors are Flames except for Semija Warriors.

Officers:

Defender of the Realm: This is always the King of Chraun.

Kinyara in Command: An honorary designation for the Kinyara. She rarely directs troops.

General: Commands the whole army

Luten General: second in command, commands the army in General's absence

Brigadier: Commands the Brigades
Colonel: Commands the Battalions
Major: Commands a Company
Captain: Commands the King's honor guard
Cadet: Serg in training to be an officer.

Warriors:

Serg: Commands platoons of Flames and Semija
Scout: Somewhere between a Serg and a basic Warrior. The scouts of Chraun are not as highly trained or respected as those of Iskalon.
Flame Warrior: basic fighting body
Semija Warrior: secondary fighting body, highly trained, important tactically against Iskalon's human warriors.

Structure of the Army of Chraun:

Army: Commanded by the General, or the Luten General when the General is away.
Brigade: About an eighth of the army, commanded by the Brigadier.
Battalion: About an eighth of that, commanded by the Colonel
Company: About an eighth of a battalion, commanded by the Major
Platoon: Commanded by a Serg, consists of warriors.
Patrol: A smaller platoon.
Fireteam: Two Flame warriors.

About the Author

Selah J Tay-Song was born and lives in Washington State. She graduated from The Evergreen State College with a BAS major in biological sciences and a minor in creative writing. Selah wrote her first fantasy story, about a unicorn, when she was six years old. *Dream of a Vast Blue Cavern*, her debut novel, came out of a real dream where she was crawling through narrow, dark stone tunnels, looking for something. Selah loves writing, and plans to keep doing it for the rest of her life.

Follow her blog about the crazy life of a writer at selahjtaysong.com, and discover her vision of Qaimaj at dreamsofqaimaj.com.

About the Illustrator

Benjamin P. Roque is an illustrator by night, an advertising designer by day, and a gardener on weekends. He currently lives in Manila, the Philippines where he braves the hottest summers and strongest typhoons. View his art and follow his blog at jieroque.blogspot.com.

79632592R00238

Made in the USA
Columbia, SC
05 November 2017